THE FRONTIERS SAGA
EPISODE 14

THE WEAK AND THE INNOCENT

Ryk Brown

The Frontiers Saga Episode #14: The Weak and the Innocent
Copyright © 2015 by Ryk Brown All rights reserved.

First Print Edition

Cover and Formatting by Streetlight Graphics

No part of this book may be reproduced, scanned, or distributed in any printed or electronic form without permission. Please do not participate in or encourage piracy of copyrighted materials in violation of the author's rights. Thank you for respecting the hard work of this author.

This is a work of fiction. Names, characters, places, and incidents either are the product of the author's imagination or are used fictitiously, and any resemblance to locales, events, business establishments, or actual persons—living or dead—is entirely coincidental.

CHAPTER ONE

"Roselle is probably going ape over this," Commander Jento said.

Captain Poc barely glanced at his first officer from his seat at the helm of Scout One. "Perhaps, at first," the captain agreed. "However, Roselle knows that Scott had little choice. He had to give those men as much time as possible to escape. I would have done the same, just as you would have, and just as Roselle would have. Besides, Scott had no way of knowing the Jung battleship could extend their shields."

"Don't get me wrong, Captain, I agree with you. I don't think it's Captain Scott's fault, either. It was just a series of unlucky events. I just doubt Roselle will see it that way." Commander Jento checked his display. "Next jump point coming up in one minute."

"Either way, it was a hard call to make," Captain Poc said. "Scott will have to live with his decision for the rest of his life."

"Let's just hope that decision doesn't turn out to be a bad one," the commander replied. "Thirty seconds to jump point."

"Todson?" Captain Poc called over his comm-set.

"*No sign of them, sir,*" the ensign replied from the scout ship's sensor station.

"Drop a sensor buoy," the captain ordered.

"Dropping sensor buoy," his XO replied. "Buoy away. Fifteen seconds to jump."

"*Good read on the buoy,*" Ensign Todson remarked over the captain's comm-set. "*Third time's the charm, right sir?*"

"Let's hope."

"Five seconds," Commander Jento announced. "Three......two......one......jumping." Commander Jento studied his jump status display. "Jump complete."

"*Starting scans,*" Ensign Todson reported.

Captain Poc breathed a sigh of relief as Scout One started their third grid-search pattern. It had been half an hour since the Jung battleship had escaped into faster-than-light travel with Scout Three in tow. While they had been performing thorough sweeps of each sector along the target's last known course, Scout Two had been conducting shorter searches further out along the same path, in case the battleship had somehow managed to increase their FTL speed without their knowing. If the Jung battleship was still on the same course, they would find it, regardless of its speed. Even if the target had come out of FTL and accelerated, or possibly even changed course, they would pick up old light from their maneuver. It was just a matter of time. Captain Poc only hoped the fleeing battleship wasn't on their way to a rendezvous with additional Jung forces. Although he had no idea how command intended to deny the Jung Scout Three's jump drive, he was quite sure Jung reinforcements would only complicate their plans.

* * *

The door opened, revealing a middle-aged man

in a Takaran officer's uniform. "You must be Mister Hiller," the man said.

"Yes, I am," Yanni answered from just inside their quarters. He immediately noticed the two security guards flanking the officer. "And you are?"

Suvan Navarro's head pulled back, somewhat surprised. "I am Suvan Navarro, leader of House Navarro, and captain of the Avendahl."

"My apologies, Captain," Yanni replied, bowing his head in respect. "I'm afraid I am not yet familiar with Takaran rank insignias."

"No apologies necessary," the captain insisted. "May I?"

"Of course," Yanni said, stepping aside.

Captain Navarro nodded to one of the guards and entered the room. The guard reached in and pulled the door closed behind him.

"If I may ask, Captain, are we prisoners?"

Captain Navarro offered a sympathetic smile. "Not at all, Mister Hiller. However, given the circumstances, it would be best if you and the princess were to remain here, where my men can see to your safety."

"Are we not safe anywhere aboard the Avendahl?" Deliza asked as she entered the main living area from a side room.

"You are safer on board the Avendahl than anyplace else in the Pentaurus cluster," the captain began, "but until I can fully ensure the loyalties of everyone aboard this ship, additional precautions are necessary."

"You do not trust your own men?" Yanni wondered.

"My *crew*, yes. However, many people, including the two of you, have come aboard in recent days.

Considering all that has transpired in the last forty-eight hours... Let's just say that we must *redress* the issue, just to be sure."

"The families of your crew are safe?" Deliza asked.

"The families of my officers were evacuated two days ago. Most of them to either the Darvano or Savoy systems."

"And your enlisted?" Deliza inquired.

"Those who have chosen to continue their service on board the Avendahl were given similar consideration. Those who favored returning to their families were paid accordingly and provided commercial transport back to Takara."

"Then you are not at full staffing levels," Deliza surmised, as she moved to the sofa.

The business mindset of the princess caught the captain off guard, his head tilting to one side. "You are correct. Rest assured, however, the crew that remains will more than suffice." He looked quizzically at the princess, having expected a more grief-stricken young woman. "May I ask what your plans are, Princess?"

"I am not a princess," Deliza firmly corrected. "Not any more. And as to my plans, I expect they depend heavily on what you came here to say, Captain Navarro."

"I see." Captain Navarro gestured toward one of the chairs facing the sofa. "May I?"

Deliza nodded politely.

"First, let me express my deepest condolences on the loss of your father," the captain began as he sat. "Casimir Ta'Akar was an honorable man who gave his life for his people. While I may not have agreed with his methods, I respect his efforts nonetheless."

"Thank you, Captain," Deliza replied without emotion. "And second?"

"As I said, I did not agree with your father's methods, but I did agree that support of the Alliance was in the best interest of the entire Pentaurus cluster, including Takara. That is why I pledged my allegiance to him. That is why my crew and I risked our lives in support of his cause. That is why I am here now, pledging to you, that same allegiance, as the heir to House Ta'Akar."

Deliza eyed him suspiciously. "You would pledge your allegiance to a child?"

"I would pledge my allegiance to the daughter of a man who gave his life in defense of an ideal we shared. A man who made me swear to protect the only thing he had left to die for."

Deliza closed her eyes, taking a deep breath as she gathered her resolve. "You realize I am not worthy of such a pledge," she said in a near whisper.

"Your father thought otherwise," Captain Navarro assured her in similar tone.

"He may have been mistaken," Deliza admitted. "I fear I have no plans at the moment, other than to seek your counsel."

Captain Navarro leaned back in his chair, deep in thought. After a long pause and heartfelt sigh, he spoke. "The situation is grim, but not without hope. Your father was prepared for such events. Just before he was captured, he made one last transmission to me. It seems he invested the last of your family's holdings into a Corinairan company, one of considerable size. He used his connections within the Alliance to secure a lucrative arrangement, one that would ensure your financial stability for the rest of your life, and perhaps for the lives of your heirs as well."

"Will not the new Takaran government move to seize those assets?" Deliza asked.

"Wise of you to consider the possibility," Captain Navarro agreed. "However, it is highly unlikely. First, they would have to realize that such an investment existed to begin with. Second, there is no law that gives the nobles such right of seizure, at least not of assets outside of the Takaran economic system."

"I see," Deliza said. "And I can spend this wealth however I see fit?"

"Of course."

"Even if I choose to spend it in support of the Alliance?"

"Correct," Captain Navarro replied. "However, I must warn you that doing so may place you at greater risk. Some of the nobles will want to be rid of you, to ensure that house Ta'Akar is indeed dead and gone. Then, there are the Ybaran Legions as well. They have never forgiven your uncle for the atrocities he committed upon their people."

"Then we shall set course for Sol," Deliza decided.

"A logical course of action," the captain agreed. "Indeed, the Avendahl would provide a considerable advantage in the Sol sector. However, abandoning the Pentaurus cluster now, before the dust settles in the Takaran system, would put the other members of the Alliance, particularly the Savoy and Darvano systems, at considerable risk. Neither system is capable of defending themselves, should the nobles decide to retake control of the cluster. Such a move would not be out of character, given their current dependence on Ancot for food, and now, thanks to your father, Corinair for propellant. However, if the Avendahl was tasked to protect those systems, not only would it guarantee a continuous stream of basic resources to the Alliance forces and the people of Earth, but also the peaceful cooperation of the nobles." Captain Navarro studied Deliza Ta'Akar for a moment as she pondered his words. His expression softened and he continued speaking in a kinder tone. "Your father believed, as do I, that the best way to protect the Pentaurus sector from the Jung was to help defeat them before they could expand beyond the Sol sector. We may no longer be able to offer military aid to the Terrans, but we can still protect the flow of what resources we *can* supply."

"You are correct, of course," Deliza admitted. "Until things have stabilized here, the Avendahl must remain in the Pentaurus cluster."

"And what of us?" Yanni asked.

"After we have seen to my father's financial affairs on Corinair, we shall go to Sol," Deliza stated with conviction. She looked at Captain Navarro. "I trust you can provide transportation?"

"One of our jump shuttles can have you there in three days' time," the captain promised.

"Good. Admiral Dumar must be notified as soon as possible," Deliza insisted. "Once we arrive in the Sol system, we will be beyond the reach of both the nobles and the Ybarans. I know of only four men whom my father trusted. Now, only three of them remain. Admiral Dumar, Captain Scott, and yourself."

"I am honored to be among such men," Captain Navarro replied as he rose from his seat.

"May I inquire as to our present position?" Deliza asked.

"Halfway between Rama and Devi," the captain

replied. "I only wished a moment to speak with you before choosing our next destination. With your permission, we shall jump to Corinair."

"Thank you, Captain."

Captain Navarro offered a respectful nod before turning and exiting the room.

Yanni looked at Deliza in wonder. "You never cease to amaze me, Deliza."

Deliza looked down at the table, and humbly replied, "I did nothing amazing, Yanni. I merely accepted the captain's offer to help. What else was I to do?"

"It looked more to me like you took command of all Alliance forces in the Pentaurus cluster."

"The Avendahl *is* the only Alliance force in the Pentaurus cluster, Yanni, and I did not take command of her. I simply agreed with her captain's assessment of the situation."

"He just pledged his ship to the service of your house, Deliza."

"House Ta'Akar no longer exists. It fell with my father, and I am not the one to resurrect it."

"I'm not so sure," Yanni replied.

* * *

Admiral Dumar studied the course projections of the fleeing Jung battleship on the tactical display before him. "Their course hints at no destinations, not even distant ones," he mumbled.

"There are some possibilities, with minor course corrections," Mister Bryant said. "However, I agree with your original assessment, Admiral. The battleship went to FTL without concern for their heading. They merely wished to escape with their prize. If that assumption is accurate, then they will have to drop out of FTL at some point. Either to board and take full control of Scout Three or, at the very least, to alter course for a Jung-held system. In any case, they must come out of FTL."

The admiral sighed. "We must find that battleship."

"We will, Admiral. We will."

"Of course." Dumar regained his focus. "What are the latest reports from the surface of the Cetian worlds?"

"Our forces on Sorenson report the planet has been secured."

"Losses?"

"They were light, just as they were on Stennis. Kohara, however, is another matter." Mister Bryant called up several tactical maps showing the engagement zones on Kohara. "The last update from Commander Telles was more encouraging. The Aurora's precision orbital strikes have kept the Jung forces from moving about freely, and the aerial strikes by our few remaining Falcons and combat jump shuttles have helped as well. However, Commander Telles still insists that the Ghatazhak forces on Sorenson and Stennis should be moved to Kohara while they still can."

"He does not believe he can hold Kohara without them?"

"No, sir, he is *quite* sure he can hold. After all, it is Telles we're talking about. The problem is that he expects heavy losses without additional ground forces, or more air power... Preferably both."

Dumar let out another long sigh. "Would that we had such..."

"Comm-drone just jumped in, Admiral," the

Karuzara's chief communications officer reported. "Message incoming."

"Another update from Tau Ceti?" the admiral assumed.

"No, sir," the communications officer replied. "The comm-drone is from the Pentaurus cluster." His expression changed to one of concern as he read the message. "It was dispatched by the Avendahl." The communications officer looked at his data pad as the message appeared on his screen. His skin turned pale, disbelief written across his face.

"What is it, Lieutenant?" Mister Bryant asked.

The communications officer handed the data pad over to Admiral Dumar standing at the rail. The admiral looked at the message, his facial expression unchanged as he lowered the pad to his side. He addressed Mister Bryant. "Casimir Ta'Akar is dead."

"What?" Mister Bryant exclaimed in shock. "How?"

"There was a rebellion on Takara. House Ta'Akar was overrun by the Ybaran Legions. He was captured and executed on the spot."

"I don't believe it."

"Takara is now in a state of civil war. The Avendahl has moved to the Darvano system, under the direction of Deliza Ta'Akar."

"If the nobles should decide to..." Mister Bryant began.

"The Avendahl can protect Corinair, but as long as she does so, she cannot help us." Dumar looked at Mister Bryant. "I'm afraid we are on our own."

"But, the Ghatazhak deployment pods, the Tontakeen, the Juda, the Crippin..."

"Destroyed, or under the control of the nobles," Admiral Dumar said. He turned to the communications officer. "Lieutenant, I have new orders for our forces in the Tau Ceti system."

* * *

Commander Telles stood in the center of the command bunker, studying his data pad. For the first time in his career, he felt as if he had failed.

"What is it?" Master Sergeant Jahal asked, noticing the look on his old friend's face.

"Casimir is dead. House Ta'Akar has fallen, and Takara is in the midst of a civil war. Support from the Pentaurus cluster can no longer be counted upon." Telles looked at his Master Sergeant. "We have been ordered to withdraw, and to do so with minimal casualties."

"What?"

Telles studied the tactical displays as he spoke, their prospects getting worse with each new update. "The Jung forces on Sorenson and Stennis have already been defeated. We shall withdraw those forces back to Porto Santo, then we can use their air-support and jump shuttles to facilitate our withdrawal from Kohara." He pointed to several points on the tactical display. "Have the Aurora target the garrisons here, and here, first. As they come around to the far side, they can then hit the garrisons on the other continents as well."

"Collateral losses will be high," Master Sergeant Jahal warned.

"It cannot be helped," the commander noted. "The admiral wishes to preserve what's left of our ground forces. Once the enemy realizes we are retreating, they will attack with all their forces. We must not allow them such an option. Pounding those targets is the only way to deny them that opportunity."

"Captain Scott will not like it," Master Sergeant Jahal replied.

"He doesn't have to." Commander Telles looked at the tactical display once again, letting out a long sigh as he shook his head. "I was sure we could take Kohara."

"We could have," the master sergeant replied, "if allowed."

"No, this cannot be blamed on events a thousand light years away," Telles insisted. "We knew that we had limited forces coming in. I should have submitted a more aggressive plan."

Master Sergeant Jahal raised his brow at the commander's regrets. "Then why didn't you?"

"I let my association with these Terrans cloud my judgment, weaken my resolve. I should have insisted that we destroy all military targets prior to landing, regardless of their concerns for the civilian population. *That* is how you win wars. This failure was mine." The commander looked at his friend. "It shall not happen again."

"That which other men..." the master sergeant muttered.

"Precisely."

* * *

"How come you're not going ape over this?" Commander Ellison asked, finally breaking the relative silence that had enveloped Scout Two's flight deck for the past forty minutes.

"Believe me, I want to," Captain Roselle replied,

"but as much as I hate to admit it, the kid didn't do anything wrong... at least not technically."

"Not the response I was expecting."

"Maybe I would have taken the shot earlier," Roselle said. "Maybe as soon as I realized those bastards were targeting the escape pods... I don't know. Let's just call it a fucked up situation, and leave it at that."

"I think you're mellowing in your old age," the commander said.

"Fuck you."

"*Contact,*" the sensor officer called over the captain's comm-set. "*Just dropped out of FTL. About twenty light minutes behind us. Bearing one seven four, twenty-seven up relative. Same course and speed as before. It's them, Captain. I'm sure of it.*"

"Is Scout Three still alongside them?" Captain Roselle asked.

"*One moment.*"

"We jumped into this area about five ago," Commander Ellison said.

"They'll see our jump flash in about fifteen minutes," the captain replied. "Tell me you're passive, Ensign."

"Aye, sir," the sensor officer affirmed. "Ever since we started the hunt."

"Let's go cold," Roselle ordered. "Maybe we'll get lucky and they won't notice the flash."

"Want to make a quick course change?" the commander offered. "Low and slow, so we won't be detected?"

"Don't bother. Once they see our jump flash, they'll go full active and light up the area with every sensor they've got. That's what I'd do if I had that much fire power."

"*I'm picking up Scout Three as well, Captain,*" the sensor officer reported. "*Starboard side, facing the battleship's aft, maybe one meter away, at the target's midship.*"

Captain Roselle looked at his XO. "What are they doing, Ensign?"

"Nothing, sir, least not that I can... Wait... Range is changing slightly..."

"To the target?"

"No, sir. To Scout Three. I think they're pulling her in closer."

"They had grappling lines on her before they went to FTL," the commander said.

"They're trying to secure her, pull her in against their hull," Captain Roselle realized.

"Why?"

"Would you want to be in FTL while towing another ship alongside by a few cables?" Captain Roselle asked.

"You think they are trying to secure her alongside, so they can accelerate and go back into FTL?"

"Either that, or board her."

"Or both," the commander added.

"Comms, send a message to the Aurora. Position and situation. Use a comm-drone."

"*We've only got one left,*" the communications officer warned.

"Then let the Aurora know it's our last drone."

"*Aye, sir.*"

"They'll see the comm-drone's jump flash," the commander warned.

"Not for fourteen minutes, they won't."

* * *

"About time," Jessica said as Kata and her porta-cam operator, Karahl, came out of the emergency department at the medical center on Porto Santo.

"That was the most complete physical I've ever had," Kata groaned. "Some of the equipment they used I have never even seen before."

"Neither had I," Jessica admitted. "The Corinairans are far more advanced than us." She looked at the red light on the porta-cam slung under Karahl's arm.

Karahl caught Jessica's notice of his porta-cam. "Is it all right?"

"Sure, as long as we get to review your footage before you broadcast," Jessica replied. "For security reasons."

"Of course."

"These Corinairans, they're from the Pentaurus cluster?"

"Yes. Corinair is a world in the Darvano system."

"And the Takarans? They're also from the Pentaurus cluster?"

"Yup, but from the Takar system."

"And this cluster is a thousand light years away?"

"Nine hundred and something," Jessica replied.

Kata shook her head in awe. "Hard to believe. It was amazing to just jump from Kohara to here, but a thousand light years?"

"You get used to it," Jessica told her. "To be honest, the jump drive sort of redefines how you see the galaxy. Before, nearly everything was too far away to be of concern. Now, everything is reachable. It's just a matter of logistics."

"Where I come from, only the wealthy can travel between planets. Only the Jung travel between the stars."

"Yeah, well, all of that is about to change. Once we defeat the Jung, we'll be able to reconnect all the core worlds in a way like never before."

"Because of the jump drive?"

"Exactly."

Kata glanced out the windows that looked out over the spaceport, with the ocean behind it in the distance. "Why is your base here, on this island? Does Earth have any large continents, or is it all islands?"

"Most of the main continents were targeted by the Jung during their initial invasion, and on their way out when we liberated our world," Jessica explained. "At the time, there were fallout concerns. Besides, the major nations of Earth are still in a state of semi-controlled chaos. It's only been six months since the last time the Jung attacked Earth. Porto Santo was conveniently located and had not been touched by the initial attacks. In the middle of the ocean, it is separated from the chaos taking place throughout the rest of our world."

"The Jung led us to believe that your people were violating the quarantine they placed on you to protect everyone else in the core... That they had no choice but to engage your ships as they attempted escape. They said that your new faster-than-light propulsion system made you an even bigger threat, and because of that, they had no choice but to attempt to eradicate all Terrans."

"What, like a bunch of insects, or something?" Jessica asked.

"Pretty much, yes."

Jessica laughed. "I have to admit, that's some pretty creative propaganda they've got going." She looked at Kata. "Is it working? Do your people believe that?"

"To be honest, yes. As much as I hate to admit it, even I believed it. I don't know if people really do believe it, or if they just choose to believe it because if it turned out to be true..." She took a deep breath and let it out in a long sigh. "The bio-digital plague wiped us out, Jessica. I mean, literally. Everything fell apart. We lived like animals for centuries."

"We all did," Jessica said.

"So, there is no bio-digital plague here?"

"Not in over nine hundred years. Not since the original outbreaks."

Several thunderous claps shook the windows of the medical center. Jessica moved toward the windows and peered outside, just in time to see four more jump flashes, each followed by more sonic booms a second after appearing.

"What is it?" Kata asked as she and her porta-cam operator followed Jessica to the window.

"More jump ships," Jessica replied, a look of concern on her face. "Boxcars." She turned to head toward the exit.

"What are boxcars?"

"Big-ass cargo ships," she said as she quickly exited the building, Kata and Karahl close behind. Four more flashes filled the sky over the spaceport a kilometer away. "They shouldn't be coming back, not fully loaded, at least. Something is wrong." Jessica grabbed one of the med-techs as he exited the building. "Give me your comm-set, Sergeant."

"Yes, sir," the young sergeant replied without hesitation, pulling off his comm-set and handing it over to Jessica.

Jessica placed the comm-set on her ear and

activated it. "Porto Santo Command, this is Lieutenant Commander Nash. I'm at the medical center. What's going on? Why are there boxcars returning fully loaded?"

"*Nash, Porto Santo Command. Lieutenant Fila. Admiral Dumar has ordered the immediate withdrawal of all ground forces from the Tau Ceti system. The boxcars arriving now are from Sorenson and Stennis.*"

Jessica squinted her eyes in suspicion, puzzled by the events. "Withdrawal? What the hell for?"

"*No idea, sir.*"

"What about Kohara?"

"*They're next,*" the lieutenant replied, "*just as soon as we can move the air support from Sorenson and Stennis over to Kohara to cover their withdrawal as well. Things have gotten pretty dicey there.*"

Jessica sighed. "Copy that. Nash out."

"What is it?"

"We're withdrawing all ground forces from Tau Ceti," she replied as she handed the comm-set back to the sergeant.

"From which world?" Kata wondered.

"All of them."

"Why?"

"I don't know," Jessica admitted. "Something must have happened. Something big."

* * *

"The main forces from Stennis and Sorenson have already returned to Porto Santo," Ensign Souza reported from the Aurora's communications center at the back of the bridge. "Their combat jumpers and troop shuttles are moving to Kohara to assist in their withdrawal."

"Why is this the first we're hearing of this?" Nathan wondered.

"We just came out of radio blackout, Captain," Ensign Souza reminded him. "The comm-drone jumped into the middle of the system. We happened to be on the far side of Kohara when it first arrived. We just picked up its rebroadcast a minute ago."

"Why are we withdrawing?" Luis wondered.

"More traffic, Captain," Ensign Souza interrupted. "The message is for you, directly from Admiral Dumar."

"What is it?" Nathan asked.

Ensign Souza looked at his captain.

Nathan felt the hesitation in the ensign's reply, and rotated in his command chair to face aft. "Ensign?"

"It's Prince Casimir," the ensign said. "He's dead, sir."

"Tug's dead?" Nathan replied in disbelief.

"Yes, sir. Assassinated. There's a civil war on Takara."

Nathan closed his eyes for a moment, as he fought to maintain his composure. He felt as if everything was coming apart, spinning out of control.

Luis watched with concern as his captain, *his friend*, struggled to keep his emotions in check.

Nathan opened his eyes as he slowly rotated to face forward again. "I guess that explains the withdrawal orders," he muttered. In a stronger tone he ordered, "Contact Commander Telles. Ask him how we can help."

"New contact!" Mister Navashee reported from

the Aurora's sensor station. "Jump flash. Another comm-drone."

"Incoming message," Ensign Souza announced. "It's from Scout Two, Captain." The ensign's voice became excited. "They've found them! The battleship *and* Scout Three!"

"Status?" Nathan asked in a calm voice, refusing to get excited.

"Scout Two reports the Jung battleship is on the same course and speed as before. Current position is the far side of the Tau Ceti system. They suspect the Jung are attempting to pull Scout Three all the way in, possibly to secure her to their hull before returning to FTL."

"Is the Jung ship accelerating?" Nathan asked.

"No mention of it, sir," Ensign Souza replied.

"Relay the message to both Commander Telles and Alliance Command," Nathan ordered. "Return message to Scout Two; monitor and report changes."

"I've got the data stream from the comm-drone, sir," Luis informed him. "Putting it up on tactical now."

Nathan watched as the tactical display on the Aurora's main semi-spherical view screen changed to show the position and tracks of Scout Two, as well as the Jung battleship and their prisoner, Scout Three.

"They're only twenty light minutes out, Captain," Luis noted. "If they jumped in ten minutes ago... If we don't act quickly..."

Nathan nodded, completing Luis's thought, "... we may lose them again."

* * *

Commander Eckert let go of his data pad, allowing it to float in the air in front of him. "I can't get anything from it," he sighed, "this thing just doesn't have enough power."

"That's what I was afraid of," Captain Nash replied.

"Maybe if we could find a way to jack into the emergency power?"

"No way. The entire detonation system is on a separate circuit from the rest of the ship," Captain Nash explained. "Dedicated batteries, dedicated cabling... It was a bitch to route all the way forward. I'm afraid the connection to Donny's station was the only one."

"If I had access to the jump drive, I could rig up a detonator. It would be manually operated, but..."

"There's no way to get to it from inside, you know that. And the Jung probably have every sensor they've got trained on this ship right now. The minute your head popped out of the airlock, they'd blow it off."

Commander Eckert thought for a moment, looking around the dimly lit, weightless interior of Scout Three. "What's the closest accessible point along that control cable?" he wondered. "I mean, the closest accessible point to the jump drive itself."

"Probably in engineering," Nash replied. "Why?"

"Maybe the circuit isn't fried all the way back? Maybe it's just fried at this end?"

"Doubtful. Donny wasn't stupid."

"Assuming he was still Donny," Eckert replied.

Captain Nash looked at his executive officer. He had only known the commander for a few months, whereas he had known Donald Scalotti for more than a decade. More than that, Donny and he had become good friends. However, the commander was right, the man who had put them in this situation was not the man he had known and served with all those years. "Good point," the captain conceded. "The circuit splits just forward of lateral bulkhead four, just above the central hatchway. It runs along the top edge to either side, then goes through the bulkheads. The compartments on the other side of those bulkheads are unpressurized spaces. That's as close as we're going to get without going outside."

The dull, distant sound of metal striking metal reverberated throughout the ship, shaking the entire compartment. Nash and Eckert both found themselves lurching to starboard, drifting into the dead systems console in the main cabin.

"What the hell was that?" Commander Eckert wondered as he grabbed hold of the overhead rail to keep from bouncing off the wall.

"We hit something," Captain Nash replied as his body spun slowly in the weightless environment. He grabbed the edge of one of the overhead monitors to steady himself. "Something metal."

Eckert looked at Nash. "You thinking what I'm thinking?" the commander asked. "Those sounds we heard earlier?"

"Grappling lines. They've pulled us in close," the captain realized. "Right up against their hull."

"Why?"

"Either they want to secure us, so that we don't drift out of their FTL fields during transit, or they want to board us." Captain Nash pulled himself along the overhead rail, slipping forward through the hatch into the EVA compartment that separated the main cabin from the operations compartment. He opened the weapons locker and pulled out two close-quarters automatic weapons, and two ammunition pouches. "I sure as fuck hope I'm wrong," he said as he passed a weapon to Commander Eckert.

Commander Eckert quickly inserted a clip into his weapon and checked that it was ready, before slinging it over his shoulder.

"Just remember to brace yourself against something before firing," Nash warned. "These things may not have much kick, but it's enough to push you around in zero-G."

"How the hell did you know they had us to begin with?" Eckert wondered as he pulled the extra clips out of the pouch and stuffed them in his utility pockets.

"The pods should have ejected us right after they were activated," Nash explained. "The only way they wouldn't is if there was something in the way outside. Something big."

"Like a ship."

"Exactly."

"But how did you know they had taken us to FTL?"

"I didn't," Nash admitted. "At least not until we came out of FTL. I felt the transition."

"I was under the impression that the inertial dampening systems masked the sensation."

"For the most part, but I've spent a lot of time on this ship. Most of it slipping in and out of FTL. You can tell."

Eckert nodded. "And if we were still in the engagement area, we'd be in comms range with the Aurora."

Captain Nash finished readying his own weapon. "Actually, if we were still in the engagement area, Scott would have nailed the bastards with a KKV, and we'd be dead already." He rotated to face forward. "You head aft and find where the control line splits and see if you can get a signal from the detonators from there."

"What are you going to do?" Commander Eckert wondered.

"We can't defend both ends of the ship. I'm going forward to pull the control cards from all the consoles so they can't take over the ship from ops. Then I'll take up a defensive position just inside the aft hatch into the engineering section. If they do board, I can probably hold them back from there for a while."

"And if you can't?"

"I'll close the hatch and vent the cabin," the captain replied without hesitation.

"If you do that, we won't be able to go forward again," the commander reminded his captain. "How will we get out?"

Captain Nash turned and looked at the commander. "We're not getting out of this one, Skeech, but we're not giving them the jump drive, either. Not without one hell of a fight."

Commander Eckert took a deep breath. "Damn right, sir."

* * *

Jessica ran out across the tarmac toward the flight of three combat jump shuttles that had just appeared overhead and were descending to land. Kata Mun and her porta-cam operator, Karahl, ran behind her, recording every moment. Flashes of light appeared low over the base every few seconds, casting brief, eerie shadows as jump ships continued to arrive from the Tau Ceti system. Ghatazhak soldiers climbed out of the combat jump shuttles as they touched down, immediately moving away from the ships in order to get clear of their lift thrusters that were already spinning up to return to Kohara.

Jessica ran toward one of the combat jumpers just as the disembarking soldiers were moving off, waving for the pilot to hold. The pilot noticed her, but appeared unsure of her intent. He noticed she had an energy weapon holstered on her hip, and appeared quite comfortable in the middle of an active airfield. However, she was also dressed in Koharan civilian attire and was being followed by a reporter and a porta-cam operator who were also dressed in Koharan clothing.

"I need a lift!" Jessica yelled at the sergeant in the side doorway, struggling to be heard over the sound of the shuttle's idling lift turbines.

"Beg your pardon, ma'am, but who the hell are you?" the sergeant asked.

"Lieutenant Commander Nash, Chief of Security for the Aurora! I need to get back to my ship!"

The sergeant looked her up and down briefly, one eye raised in doubt. "Uh... We're going back to Kohara, sir, not the Aurora!"

"I wasn't asking, Sergeant!" Jessica shouted as she climbed into the shuttle. "Besides, you can spare five minutes to drop me on the Aurora!"

"What about us?" Kata yelled from outside the shuttle.

"You can't go!" Jessica replied. "Not until you've been checked for Jung nanites! I'd hate to have to kill you if your eyes rolled back in your head and you went all catatonic on me!"

"What?" Kata yelled back, confused.

"We've gotta go, sir!" the sergeant insisted.

"Stay here!" Jessica instructed. "I'll be back soon!"

"Where are you going?"

"Back to Tau Ceti!" Jessica yelled as she gestured for them to move clear of the shuttle.

Kata and her porta-cam operator moved back as the sergeant slid the side door closed. They both turned around and ran as the whine of the shuttle's engines rose in both pitch and intensity. A wave of hot exhaust slammed into their backs as they fled, nearly knocking them over as the shuttle climbed up into the air. A few seconds later, the wave subsided, and Karahl spun back around and pointed his porta-cam upward just in time to see the climbing shuttle disappear in a flash of blue-white light.

Karahl stopped recording and lowered his porta-cam. "Where did she say she was going?"

"Back to Tau Ceti," Kata replied, shaking her head in disbelief.

"Why aren't we going with her?"

"I'm not sure," Kata admitted. "Something about Jung nanites, and having to kill me."

"What?"

Kata shook her head again. "This is going to take some getting used to."

* * *

"Jumpers and Falcons are arriving in orbit now, Commander," the communications officer announced. "They are requesting assignments."

Commander Telles studied the tactical display of Kohara hovering above the planning table. At least a dozen red and orange icons decorated the semi-opaque globe before him, marking the locations of ongoing combat actions of his troops on the surface. "Start with Alliot, on the far side," he instructed. "It has the least resistance at the moment. Have the Falcons pound the Jung positions prior to the extraction. Then move up to Paront and Marqvia. Contact the Aurora, and have them target the strongholds at Dodson, Monte Corel, and Askva, as they come around. After Marqvia, they will be next."

"Combat jumpers only?" the communications officer inquired.

"Affirmative," the commander replied. "Save the troop jumpers for everything on our side of Kohara. Troops only. Destroy all other equipment in place before leaving."

"Yes, sir."

Master Sergeant Jahal leaned in closer to the commander. "The admiral will not be happy."

"The admiral has many replicators at his disposal," Commander Telles said. "He can replicate replacements. These men are all we have left, and he knows it. That is why he ordered our withdrawal."

"It will not take long for word of our retreat to reach the Jung forces in Cetia."

Commander Telles sighed. "Precisely. That is why I am holding the troop jumpers and boxcars in reserve. When it is our turn to leave, I suspect the Jung will throw everything they have left at us." He looked at the master sergeant. "We may only get one chance at our escape."

"Could the Aurora not pound their headquarters into submission as well?" the master sergeant wondered.

"The facility is heavily fortified. In addition, I suspect it goes deep underground. There have been too many reports of Jung squads suddenly appearing as if from thin air."

"The subway system is inoperable," the master sergeant reminded the commander, "we made sure of that from the start. We even collapsed many of the main tunnels, just to be sure."

"I know. That's what worries me." Commander Telles touched the semi-opaque image in front of him, causing it to zoom in on their present location. "As soon as we withdraw from Alliot, we shall move our forces from the waterfront and western hills districts in closer to cover our backs, in case any more of those *surprise* attacks should occur."

* * *

"We'll be in firing position over Dodson in one minute," Luis reported from the Aurora's tactical station.

"You may fire when ready, Lieutenant," Nathan confirmed.

"Aye, sir."

"Message from the hangar deck," Ensign Souza reported. "Lieutenant Commander Nash just arrived."

Nathan spun around in his command chair in surprise, breathing a sigh of relief. "How?"

"Unknown, sir," the ensign replied. "Master Chief Taggart reports a combat jumper just dropped her off. She's headed up here now."

"Range in thirty seconds," Luis updated.

Nathan turned back forward and scanned the main view screen for a moment, wondering how Jessica would react once she learned about the plight of Scout Three, and her brother. "Any word from Scout Two?"

"No, sir," Ensign Souza replied.

Nathan looked at the time display. It had only been ten minutes since they had learned that Captain Roselle had located the fleeing Jung battleship and Scout Three.

"Range in fifteen seconds," Luis reported. "Charging up both quads."

"New contact," Mister Navashee reported, "it's Scout One."

"Incoming message from Scout One," Ensign Souza announced. "They've received our update and are moving to retrieve the last KKV for repositioning. Transferring position and targeting information to them now."

"Very well," Nathan replied. "At least when we get the order, we'll be ready to fire."

"Target sierra two five now in range," Luis reported. "Locking quads on target. Firing in ten seconds."

"Any update from Telles on how long the withdrawal from Kohara will take?" Nathan wondered.

"No change, Captain," Ensign Souza replied.

"Firing on sierra two five," Luis reported.

"Switch the main view screen to one of our topside cameras," Nathan ordered.

The image of the planet Kohara covering the upper portion of the main view screen from side-to-side disappeared, replaced by a view of the target from orbit. The image faded out and back in several times in succession as the camera zoomed in, finally settling on a magnification factor that provided a view from only a thousand meters above the target.

Streaks of red dove from either side of the screen toward the Jung installation below, superheated as they plunged through the Koharan atmosphere. The rail gun rounds slammed into the building from above, sending debris in all directions. Within seconds, a rising cloud of dust and smoke obscured the view of the target. Several secondary explosions, some of them quite large, pierced through the haze as munitions within the building were ignited by the incredible amount of kinetic energy being poured onto the target. The firing lasted only seconds, but for Nathan, it felt as if he were seeing it in slow motion.

"Firing sequence complete," Luis finally reported.

The glowing, red, rail gun fire streaming toward the surface ceased, leaving only a cloud of dust, secondary explosions still flashing periodically from beneath the haze.

"Range on target sierra two six in three minutes," Luis added solemnly.

"Damage assessment?" Nathan asked his sensor operator.

"Initial scans indicate massive damage," Mister Navashee replied. "The structure *is* destroyed. I'm also picking up considerable collateral damage."

"From our weapons fire?" Nathan wondered.

"Not directly," Mister Navashee reported. "All our rounds were on target. The damage is from debris and shock waves. A lot of it is also from secondary explosions, many of which were quite large, Captain."

"You're firing on ground targets?" Jessica demanded as she walked onto the bridge.

Luis turned to look at the lieutenant commander as she stepped up alongside his tactical console and began studying his displays.

"Why?" she added.

"It's good to see you, Lieutenant Commander," Nathan replied, ignoring her question.

"I thought the Ghatazhak had things under control on the surface?"

"The situation has changed," Nathan replied.

Jessica looked at the main view screen as the cloud of dust over the target began to clear. It was obvious that the initial target had been destroyed, but so had nearly every building around it. "So much so that we're blowing up entire city blocks?" she demanded. "How the hell do you expect to get the Koharans on our side if..."

"Stand down, Lieutenant Commander," Nathan ordered, cutting her off mid-sentence.

"What the..."

"We've been ordered to withdraw all ground forces from the surface of all Cetian worlds," Nathan continued.

"We're retreating?" Jessica couldn't believe what she was hearing. She paused for a moment, trying to find the right words, but ended up with only, "Why?"

Nathan turned slowly in his chair to look Jessica in the eyes. "Tug is dead, Jess." It was only the second time that the words had crossed his lips, and it hurt even more this time than it had before.

Jessica looked as if all hope had been stolen from her. "What?" she replied, barely a whisper. "How?"

"I don't know," Nathan replied, his own voice barely audible. "We're on our own, Jess. Those men on the surface... they're all we've got left."

Jessica's eyes darted around the bridge, as if looking for answers to her millions of questions. "How do you know? I mean, maybe there..."

"I don't know," Nathan admitted. "But why else would Dumar order a withdrawal?"

"Fifteen seconds to sierra two six, Captain," Luis reported.

Nathan noticed Jessica scanning the tactical display for herself, frantically trying to understand the current situation. "We've lost more than half our airborne assets," he explained. "We have to cover the Ghatazhak retreat by pounding Jung assets, even if it means killing thousands of Koharans in the process, I'm afraid."

Jessica looked even more confused as she glanced at the threat board. "Is the system clear?" she wondered.

"For the most part, yes."

"Then why the hurry?"

"There's no time..."

"Contact, jump flash," Mister Navashee reported. "Comm-jumper."

"Message from Scout Two," Ensign Souza announced. "The Jung have launched a shuttle of some kind. Roselle reports that it has attached itself to the topside of Scout Three, directly over their boarding hatch, sir. He thinks they're going to board her."

Jessica's eyes grew even wider as she looked at Nathan.

"Yes, I'm afraid there's more, Jess."

* * *

Josh scanned his displays one last time. "I'm good up here," he reported over his helmet comms.

"Good back here," Loki replied. He keyed comm

to transmit. "Porto Santo Control, Falcon Four, ready for takeoff."

"*Falcon Four, Porto Santo Control. Cleared for takeoff. Fly heading one seven five to outer perimeter. Cleared to jump after fifteen hundred meters.*"

"Falcon Four, cleared for takeoff. One seven five to perimeter. Jump past fifteen." Loki activated the Falcon's jump navigation computer, calling up a standard jump to high orbit plot.

"Time to get back in the fight," Josh said. He pushed the throttle for the Falcon's lift fans forward, just enough to take most of their interceptor's weight off her landing gear. He turned to the master sergeant on the tarmac to his right, who gave him 'thumbs up' gestures with both hands, bouncing them toward the sky. Josh increased his thrust a bit more and the Falcon's landing gear lifted off the ground.

"Off the deck," Loki said. "Gear coming up."

Josh glanced at the master sergeant outside again, as the man braced himself against the blast of air from the Falcon's four thrust fans.

"I've got four greens," Loki announced, relief clear in his voice.

The master sergeant scanned the underside of the hovering interceptor, then looked at Josh and saluted. Josh returned the salute and advanced their throttle further, causing the Falcon to rise upward as the master sergeant turned away and retreated.

Josh watched the ground outside fall away from them. "Guess we didn't take as bad a hit as we thought."

"These ships may be antiques, but they're tough ones," Loki added.

Josh throttled up their main atmospheric engines, causing the Falcon to surge forward. Within seconds, they were rocketing away from Porto Santo and climbing into the twilight over the surrounding ocean.

"Passing fifteen hundred meters," Josh reported. "Jumping."

The canopy turned opaque for a moment, quickly becoming transparent again a second later. The evening sky had been replaced by the blackness of space, the Earth now several thousand kilometers behind them and falling away rapidly.

"Jump complete," Loki reported. "Come to one three eight, sixteen up relative. Accelerate to three five zero."

"One three eight, sixteen up, three five zero." Josh adjusted his flight harness. "Was that three or four reloads?" he wondered. "I lost count."

"Five," Loki replied as he programmed the jump series back to the Tau Ceti system.

"Really? Gotta be a record for us, right?"

"I believe it is."

"On course and speed," Josh reported.

"Jump series in five seconds."

"Did you find out how many ships made it back from Sorenson and Stennis?" Josh asked.

"Jumping." The canopy turned opaque again, as they started their series of twelve jumps. "I asked control on one of the alternate channels," Loki explained. "All they could tell me was that we were down to eight ships now."

"Damn. I don't suppose they told you who bought it?"

"Nope," Loki replied solemnly. "Thirty seconds to Tau Ceti."

"Did you ask?" Josh wondered.

"Why would I ask?"

"I would've asked."

"That's because you're weird," Loki stated. "Ten seconds."

Josh put his hands back on the flight controls in preparation for coming out of their jump series.

"Three……two……one……jump complete," Loki reported as the opaque canopy turned clear again.

Josh looked out the forward canopy, immediately spotting the blue-green dot that was the planet Kohara.

"Aurora Flight Ops, Falcon Four, in system, fully loaded," Loki called over the comms.

Twenty seconds later, he got a response. *"Falcon Four, Aurora Flight Ops. Jump to Kohara. One five seven by three seven, ten thousand kilometers. Execute at zero three two five, mission time. Contact Koharan Command on four five zero point five."*

"Falcon Four, jumping to Kohara at zero three two five mission," Loki confirmed. "Coordinates one five seven by three seven. Altitude ten thousand kilometers. Will contact Koharan Command on four five zero point five." Loki entered the parameters for the jump into the navigation computer as he waited for the confirmation reply from the controller on board the Aurora.

"Falcon Four, Aurora Flight, read back correct. Good hunting."

"Give me ten to starboard and eighteen down," Loki instructed. "Maintain current speed."

"Ten to starboard and eighteen down," Josh replied as he entered the course change and pressed the execute button. "Coming to new course now."

"Jumping to medium orbit over Kohara in five seconds."

"On course and speed," Josh confirmed.

Again, the Falcon's canopy briefly turned opaque as the ship jumped the remaining distance to the Tau Ceti system's most heavily populated world.

"Jump complete," Loki reported as he changed the comms to the new frequency. "Koharan Command, Falcon Four in medium orbit over Kohara at one five seven by three seven. Fully loaded and awaiting orders."

"*Falcon Four, Koharan Command,*" the communications tech replied urgently. "*Join action over Cetia. Locate and destroy any ground targets attempting to converge on our location. Last two elements to the north are being evacuated now. Other Falcons are covering their withdrawal. Flight comms now on three two five point two.*"

"He does *not* sound happy," Josh said as he pitched their nose down toward the planet below.

"Koharan Command, Falcon Four, jumping down to cover you. Copy new flight comms on three two five point two."

"*Just keep them off our ass for five more minutes, Falcon Four!*"

"Copy that," Loki replied. "Twenty-seven to port, eleven down, and drop your speed to two five zero."

"Twenty-seven to port and eleven down. Decelerating to two five zero," Josh confirmed.

"Jumping down to five hundred meters in three..."

"On course."

"Two..."

"On speed."

"One......Jumping."

Josh kept his eyes straight ahead out the forward

canopy as it turned opaque gray, then clear again. The surface of Kohara, which had been ten thousand kilometers below them only seconds ago, was now less than five hundred meters directly ahead and rushing to meet them at the leisurely rate of two hundred and fifty kilometers per hour.

"Jump complete," Loki announced. "Deploying nose turret. Charging wing cannons."

Josh pulled back slowly on the flight control stick to his right and throttled up their atmospheric engines, bringing the ship out of its forty-degree dive toward the city of Cetia.

"Falcon Four, on station, sector one, looking for targets," Loki announced over the comms as the Falcon leveled off just above the buildings of downtown Cetia. He watched as his targeting systems began to identify enemy targets on the streets below. Within seconds, there were more than a dozen red dots to choose from. "I've got at least a dozen targets on the ground, and more popping up."

"Just tell me where to fly, Lok."

"I'm linking them to your heads-up. Just line them up and I'll take them out."

"You got it." Josh reached forward with his left hand, touched the window on his display console and swiped it upward from the console to the air above. Red dots suddenly appeared, with range and type information displayed next to each of them. "Damn, I love this new display system," he said as he rolled the ship to port toward the nearest red dot. All the red target dots circled around him from left to right as he continued his turn, rolling out as the furthest dot to the left moved to center. "How about we take them from left to right to start with?"

"Sounds good to me," Loki replied. "Let's make a

wide arc around the backside of them. Keep all the lead elements on our starboard side so I don't have to swing the turret around as much."

"What's the fun in that?" Josh complained. "Flying a lazy circle and all?"

"You can have your fun when we come back for the ones that got away," Loki promised.

"Just don't let any get away."

"Command, Falcon Four. Confirm our rules of engagement?"

"*Falcon Four! Weapons free! Maximum force! Collateral damage is not a concern!*"

"Falcon Four copies, maximum force authorized."

"Uh, Loki?" Josh said, as the number of red dots floating in the air around him suddenly doubled. "Please tell me this is a glitch in the new display system?"

"Oh, shit," Loki exclaimed. "Command, Falcon Four! My targets have just doubled! Correction! They've tripled! What the hell is going on down there?"

"*Command to all Falcons!*" The controller's voice sounded more stressed than before. "*Multiple ground targets converging on our location! We need air support, now!*"

CHAPTER TWO

"Brakar Two Four is reporting heavy fire from the northwest corner!" one of the communications technicians reported with urgency.

Commander Telles glanced to the right, quickly assessing the position of all his withdrawing units on the main tactical display in the command bunker. "Have One Seven move in from the southeast, and move Two Zero around to the Two Four's north flank to distract."

Dozens of red icons moved about the tactical display in a bizarre, chaotic dance, as Jung fast-attack squads continued to appear out of nowhere. Just as soon as he moved his men into position to take the enemy squads out, they would disappear again.

"Two Four is taking casualties," the comm-tech added. "Brakars One Seven and Two Zero, report your ETAs."

Telles turned to the flight control officer. "How long until the rest of the Falcons arrive?"

"Three minutes," the flight controller answered. "Three of them are on the other side of the planet, and the other two have damaged jump drives."

Commander Telles watched as Falcon Four's icon moved over the icon representing Brakar Two Four. The two red symbols for the Jung fast-attack squads northeast of Brakar Two Four disappeared, after which Falcon Four's icon turned to the left to circle back. Falcon Four blinked out of view a second later. Telles watched for a moment and noticed that Falcon Four reappeared on one of the other displays, six kilometers to the west. It turned around and vanished again, only to join in the same area of battle as before, on the main tactical display.

"Falcon Four reports shoulder launched chasers, Commander."

"That explains their jump," Master Sergeant Jahal muttered.

A series of muffled explosions shook the command center.

"Perimeter breach!" another comm-tech shouted. "Three squads! Two to the north, one to the east! They're firing rockets!"

"Bunker busters, no doubt."

"How many men do we still have out there?" Commander Telles asked, maintaining his composure with ease.

"Twelve squads still on the ground," the master sergeant replied. "One-fifty, give or take."

"Flight, how many jumpers can we expect in the next five minutes?"

"Five troop jumpers, seven combat, and two boxcars, sir."

"Everyone east of us goes to rally point Jojo Seven," the commander ordered. "Everyone west goes to Tongo Four. Two troop, two combat, and one Falcon to each rally point. The rest come here. Have the boxcars return. We're burning all assets on our way out."

"Yes, sir," the comm-tech acknowledged.

Commander Telles noticed Falcon Four's icon as it flew over one of the retreating Ghatazhak squads, causing more red icons to disappear. "Tell Falcon

Four to concentrate their efforts on our location. Let them know we've got unfriendlies in our own perimeter."

"Yes, sir," the flight controller replied.

Master Sergeant leaned in closer to his commander, lowering his tone to a harsh whisper. "You do realize there is not enough space in those ships to carry one hundred and fifty men."

Commander Telles picked up his energy rifle from the side of the tactical display table and activated its charging circuit. "I doubt there will be a hundred and fifty of us left to evacuate," he replied as the command center rocked from another series of explosions. "Shall we join the fun?"

"I was wondering when you were going to ask."

"Gentlemen," the commander called out, addressing everyone in the command center, "stay at your stations until the evac shuttle arrives, then haul ass outta here." He looked at the young men working the consoles. Terrans, Corinairans, and even a few Tannans. Where they were from didn't matter; they all understood the situation.

Telles turned and headed toward the hatch, pausing by the sergeant guarding the exit. "You're the last one out of here, Sergeant. Light the fires on your way out."

"No problem, Commander," the Corinairan sergeant promised with confidence.

* * *

Captain Nash sent the control cards he had collected from the forward end of the ship tumbling aft ahead of him as he drifted through the hatch that led from Scout Three's main cabin into the forward engineering space. The cards drifted into the aft bulkhead, careening off in different directions, tumbling as they floated about the compartment.

Nash grabbed the overhead rail, his feet swinging under him as his forward motion continued to carry his body aft. He twisted around and then pulled himself forward along the rail to the edge of the hatch. "How are you doing back there?" he called to Commander Eckert over his comm-set.

"*I've found where the line splits. I've spliced into the port run. If I can get a signal back from the port detonator, then I'll try the starboard detonator.*"

"What are you going to use for a power source?" Nash asked as he swung the hatch partially closed.

"*I took the battery from one of the portable lights in the maintenance locker back here. That should give me more than enough power to set up a connection between my data pad and the detonators. Did you get the control cards?*"

"Yeah, I got them."

"*Maybe we should destroy them, just to be safe?*"

"Not yet," Nash replied. He grabbed the rail that ran vertically alongside the hatchway, checking to make sure he could brace himself properly while firing. "We might still need them."

"*I thought you said we weren't getting out of this one?*"

"Allow a guy a little hope, will ya, Skeech?"

"*Yes, sir.*"

Captain Nash heard an odd sound coming from the forward end of the ship, like metal scraping on metal. "Something's going on forward." Sparks rained down from the overhead hatch in the middle of the EVA room on the other side of the main cabin. "They're cutting through the hatch," he said, lowering his voice in case the enemy was within earshot. Nash pulled the hatch nearly closed, leaving himself just enough room through which to fire on anyone who might enter the main cabin. He wrapped his left arm around the vertical rail alongside the hatchway to brace himself, then grabbed the close-quarters automatic weapon that was dangling from his chest harness and pulled it up into firing position. "I'm going to wait until as many of them as possible are inside before I open up." He checked that his safety was off and that his weapon was ready.

"*How much ammunition do we have?*" Commander Eckert asked over the comms.

"Four mags, so about two hundred rounds. Plus two mags for my side arm."

"*Make them count.*"

"You just worry about getting those detonators working."

"*Yes, sir.*"

The sparks stopped spraying into the EVA compartment and the overhead hatch swung down and aft. Captain Nash cursed the designers of the old FTL scout ships for inadvertently giving the intruders additional cover during their entry into his ship.

Something moved on the other side of the hatch. A shadowy silhouette descending from above. A helmet, followed by a body and a weapon. Captain Nash leaned back, barely peering around the edge of the hatchway's collar as he watched the first Jung soldier rotate once around, checking both fore and aft for any signs of life. The soldier's helmet lamp cast an eerie set of distorted, moving shadows as it pierced the dimly lit interior of the ship.

The intruder descended further, flipping over

upright as his feet cleared the overhead hatch. His boots touched the deck and affixed themselves with two dull clanking noises.

"Damn it," Nash cursed under his breath. "They're in full pressure suits, and they've got some kind of magnetic boots or something."

"*You can still vent the cabin,*" the commander replied. "*Just punch holes in their suits first.*"

"Yeah, that's the idea, Skeech," Nash replied as he watched two more soldiers drift down through the hatch. Three more soldiers, for a total of six, moved to either side of the EVA compartment, hugging the walls for safety. One of the men, presumably the leader, made gestures to the others. Two of the soldiers turned and proceeded carefully through the forward hatch into the operations compartment. The other four turned aft, in the direction of the main cabin, and Nash's hiding place.

"Two going forward, four coming aft. I'm going to wait for them to reach the main cabin."

"*I've got the emergency purge command ready to activate for everything forward of you,*" Commander Eckert assured him.

Nash watched as the first two men stepped through the hatchway from the EVA compartment into the main cabin. They moved with practiced precision, one going left while the other went right, weapons held high and ready, sweeping them from side to side. They moved along the edges of the cabin, taking note that two of the pods had not ejected.

The next two soldiers stepped through the hatch with equal expertise, again splitting left and right to follow the others.

Nash leaned in just enough to train his weapon on the leftmost Jung soldier and squeezed the trigger.

His weapon burst forth short, staccato flashes of bright yellow fire, sending its deadly projectiles into the compartment. He held the trigger down, sweeping his weapon from left to right, then back again, emptying his clip. The soldier on the far right managed to get a shot off, but his aim was interrupted as projectiles tore through his suit and flesh. Blood sprayed out from all four suited bodies as they shook in morbidly comical fashion, their magnetic boots still clinging to the deck beneath them. They did not fall; instead their arms dangled slightly outward from their bodies at odd, unnatural angles like gruesome marionettes. Globules of blood, varying in size, spread about the main cabin, staining the surface of everything they touched. The scene was surreal, unlike anything Nash had ever seen or heard of. Men, mangled and disfigured with expressions of horror and pain frozen on their faces.

Bolts of red streaked across the cabin, passing between the standing dead to strike the hatch and bulkhead around it. Nash leaned back and quickly changed clips. *Damn!* he thought, *I forgot about the two that went forward!* He returned fire, but again had to retreat as two more sets of energy bolts joined the ones previously fired. "They've got more outside!" he yelled over his comm-set as he changed magazines on his weapon. "They've probably got some sort of boarding ship attached to our hull!" Nash tried to push the hatch closed, but the amount of absorbed energy from enemy fire made it too hot to touch. "Fuck!" he cursed in frustration. He stuck the nose of his weapon back through the hatch and opened fire again, holding the trigger down and spraying back and forth until he emptied his next clip. "Purge!" he yelled over his comm-set.

"*The hatch isn't...*"

"That's an order, damn it!"

"*Purging!*" the commander replied.

The main cabin filled with the sound of rushing air as the emergency purge system, used to combat shipboard fires, vented the atmosphere from the ship's interior out into space. Although the four soldiers still inside the main cabin were wearing pressure suits, they began to carefully withdraw.

Captain Nash quickly pulled out his sidearm and opened fire, aiming in all directions as he discharged his weapon again and again. The air leaving the forward areas of the ship created a suction that pulled the hatch next to him closed. He yanked his weapon out of the way just before the hatch slammed shut.

The compartment went silent. Captain Nash switched his grip on the rail and twisted himself around in order to kick the overheated locking lever into the latched position. He quickly moved to the maintenance locker on the port side of the small compartment and pulled out a large wrench.

"*Captain!*" the commander called over the comm-set. "*Are you all right?*"

"I'm good!" he replied as he drifted back over to the hatch. He braced himself and began to hammer away at the metal latching arm. Although it was no longer glowing, it was still too hot to touch with his bare hands. He continued to pound the latch, bending it inward, making it impossible to unlock from the other side.

"*What are you doing, sir?*" the commander inquired.

Captain Nash stopped hammering, letting go of the wrench and letting it drift away from him. "Just locking the door," he responded, wiping the sweat from his brow.

* * *

Commander Telles donned his combat helmet as he and Master Sergeant Jahal strode confidently down the corridor. He tapped the activation point on the side of his helmet, and it immediately formed to his head, snugly gripping the back and sides of his skull. At the same time, its umbilical automatically protruded out the back and found its connection in the top-center of his utility pack. The comm-set built into his helmet came to life. The voices of the command center's various controllers filled his ears, as they continued to coordinate the evacuation of the last twelve Ghatazhak squads on the surface of Kohara.

The sound of weapons fire grew louder as they neared the north-facing exit of the bunker. Nearby explosions rocked the armored building, making it roll from side to side. The sensation reminded the commander of the days he spent as a child, sailing on Lake Arlatahn back on Takara. For a brief moment, he wondered how the civil war on his home world had affected his parents.

But only for a moment.

Commander Telles and Master Sergeant Jahal stepped out of the north-facing exit from the command center. A massive armored wall covered the exit, protecting them from direct incoming fire. The commander turned to his left as energy weapons fire reverberated off the protective barrier to his immediate right. He could see four of his men pinned down behind one of the many protective emplacements they had deployed around the command center's defensive perimeter upon arrival. They were taking fire from three sides, and were barely able to return the barrage. Telles looked up to his left at the gun turret on the top corner of the command bunker. The protective barrier around it was torn open from the inside, and neither the gun nor the gunner could be seen.

"On the far side, maybe fifty meters past them. Three floors up," the master sergeant said.

Commander Telles dropped his visor, causing its tactical display to come to life. He focused his vision on the spot the master sergeant had spoken of, and zoomed in on the image. "Sniper team."

"Yup, and from the angle of some of the shots from the other two sides, I'd say there are more of them."

"Falcon Four, Telles," the commander called over his comm-set.

"*Go for Falcon Four,*" Loki replied over the commander's helmet comms.

"Floors one through ten, all corners around command. Light them up, maximum force. Danger close."

"*Understood.*"

The commander raised his weapon and sent four bursts of triple-shots streaking toward the sniper on the far side of his pinned down men. The structure around the window blew apart and caught fire, sending debris crashing to the streets below, smoke billowing up into the air. Several shots slammed into the barrier wall next to him and the wall of the command bunker, as the other Jung snipers attempted to suppress the commander's fire. One of the Ghatazhak soldiers spotted his commander, and immediately stood up enough to allow his shoulder-mounted energy weapon to find a target and fire while shooting with his handheld weapon as well. Two more of his men rose and returned fire, as Commander Telles and Master Sergeant Jahal dashed out from behind the barrier toward the men.

Two shots glanced off of Telles' right shoulder and abdomen, his body armor deflecting the energy away from him at an oblique angle. His shoulder-mounted weapon rotated right and found its target, opening up with a sequence of rapidly fired, needle-like beams, each striking an enemy target. As they ran, the commander and the master sergeant strafed the doors and windows at street level.

"Move southwest!" he ordered the trapped men while running toward them, continuing to fire. "We need to get under the protection of the southwest turret!"

Enemy fire slammed into the ground around the commander as he ran and fired his weapon. As instructed, two of the pinned down men began to run. One of them was cut down by a sniper to the north. The second man took several direct hits to his chest and arm, but continued to both run and fire. The last two men rose and fled, letting loose with both weapons. The trailing man took a hit in his right thigh, knocking his leg out from under him and sending him tumbling to the rubble-strewn street.

Commander Telles dropped to one knee beside the fallen man, pouring weapons fire into the third-floor window from where the shot had originated. The window burst apart in a shower of glass.

Master Sergeant Jahal moved in behind the commander, helping the fallen soldier. More enemy weapons fired from several windows, slamming into the pavement all around them and sending chunks of pavement flying in all directions. Two more rounds found their marks. The first glancing off the top of the commander's helmet and the second taking out his shoulder-mounted, automated energy weapon.

The commander's tactical display on the inside of his visor flickered, appeared scrambled for a moment, then came back to life. The building where the shots had come from suddenly exploded in a hail of heavy energy weapons fire. A second later, Falcon Four swooped low over their heads, its nose turret swinging left and right as it peppered the sides of the buildings on either side of the street.

Commander Telles turned and grabbed the fallen man's other arm and helped him up. "You injured, Corporal?"

"No, sir!" the Ghatazhak soldier replied with enthusiasm. "But I'm pretty sure the hydros on my right leg are shit!"

"Stop making excuses!" Master Sergeant Jahal rebuked. "Move it!" he added as he turned back and opened fire on a group of Jung soldiers on the opposite corner.

Commander Telles watched Falcon Four as he ran for cover. The ship streaked away just above the tops of the buildings, then began to arc upward. Several flashes of light appeared down the street, and trails of rocket exhaust traced lines upward in pursuit of the fleeing interceptor. The ship rolled left, dropping bright, glowing countermeasures from its tail just before it was engulfed in a flash of blue-white light and disappeared.

* * *

Captain Nash drifted aft, pulling himself along around the port side of the number two reactor column. "How's it going?" he asked Commander Eckert as he joined him in the space between the second and third reactors.

"I'm querying the port detonator now," the commander replied. "How many of them were there?"

"At least eight. I took out four, maybe five. The incoming fire got so intense I could barely see anything. Damn hatch was so hot I couldn't touch it."

"Do you think the purge killed the rest?"

Captain Nash steadied himself against the bulkhead, grabbing overhead conduits to hold his position. "No way to know. No internal sensors while on battery power. It would have been nice if they had designed a porthole in that hatch, though. The only thing I *do* know is that everything forward of that hatch is unpressurized."

"I doubt that will slow them down much."

"Maybe," the captain agreed, "but they're not getting through that hatch unless they cut or blast their way in. That should buy us a few extra minutes."

"Damn it!" Commander Eckert exclaimed.

"What is it?"

"I'm getting nothing but error codes from the port detonator's control chip. Scalotti must have sent enough of a charge back through to fry it."

"That's not possible," Captain Nash said. "It was an isolated system without enough power running through it to fry anything."

"He must've rigged up an additional power source or something," the commander reasoned. "Or maybe he wired in a relay some place where no one would find it, then triggered it remotely. You said he wasn't stupid." Commander Eckert looked around, desperately trying to think of something. "Maybe the starboard detonator is all right?"

"No, he would have killed them both," Captain Nash insisted. "Just setting off one of them would likely cause enough damage to make it impossible for the Jung to reverse engineer the jump drive. Donny was always thorough." Nash took a deep breath, looking around the cramped compartment for inspiration as he tried to think of a resolution. He looked at Eckert, his eyes squinting as an idea formed. "Was the jump drive down when we lost power?"

"Yes."

"Was it damaged?"

"I'm not sure," Eckert admitted. "The control system for the jump drive gets power from the system's energy banks."

"I thought our jump drives were fed energy directly from our reactors?"

"Not exactly," the commander replied. "The Aurora's original jump drive was designed to work from energy banks. When they came up with the mini-jump drive, it was faster to just use a scaled-down version of the existing design rather than reengineer both the hardware and software. Our system is just a slightly scaled-up version of the mini-jump drives used by the Falcons and shuttles."

"But we can keep jumping over and over again..."

"The Aurora has to take time to recharge her buffers because it takes a lot more energy to jump a ship her size. Her reactors weren't designed for her jump drive; they were just adapted to power it. They aren't powerful enough. We're a lot smaller.

Our reactors can replace energy in the buffers faster than we can possibly use it up, even jumping in rapid succession."

"So there might still be power in those buffers?" the captain concluded.

"If they weren't damaged, yes."

"Can you tap into them with your data pad," Nash wondered, "to see if the system is still functional?"

"Yeah, but why?"

"The only way we can detonate those drives is by accessing the detonators from the outside, and we can't do that while there's a Jung ship parked nearby." Nash paused for a moment, waiting for Eckert to come to the same conclusion.

The commander's eyes widened upon realization of Nash's plan. "You want to try and jump the ship? From a fucking data pad? Are you insane...sir?"

"You got a better idea, Skeech?"

"Just because I don't have a better idea doesn't mean *your* idea is a good one. You know as well as anyone how precise the calculations for a jump have to be..."

"What about a standard emergency escape jump?" Captain Nash said, interrupting the commander. "Those are fixed distance, pre-calculated jumps. They're already stored in each field generator's database, right?"

Commander Eckert's eyes lit up. "To protect against command latency between the port and starboard generators during a snap jump."

"So maybe it's *not* such a crazy idea?"

"No, it's *still* crazy," the commander insisted. "Just not impossible, assuming the jump drive is still working, *and* there is still enough energy in the buffers, *and* all the emitters are still..."

"None of which we'll know until you tap into the systems with that thing," the captain said.

"Yes, sir," Commander Eckert agreed.

* * *

Commander Telles sprinted the last few meters to cover. As he ran, he jumped up and spun around, falling back first against the wall of the building on the far corner, directly below the window he had shot up a moment earlier. There was a deafening sound in the distance, like a steady series of sonic booms and the screech of burning atmosphere. It was followed by a roaring thunder that shook the streets and knocked already loosened pieces off the walls of the buildings. Telles leaned his head out just enough to peek down the street to the west. A torrent of rail gun slugs, superheated to a brilliant yellow-orange by the thick atmosphere of Kohara, pounded the Jung headquarters three kilometers away. He saw a series of flashes, then a cloud of smoke and dust that quickly rose from the target as the Aurora's massive quad-barreled rail guns pounded it out of existence. Two more surface targets in the distance were also lit up, this time by the Aurora's two plasma cannons that had replaced her other two quad rail guns donated to the Celestia. Red-orange bolts of plasma streaked down from above, slamming into target after target as the Aurora's tactical officer fired at every Jung position fed to him by the men inside the command bunker.

Commander Telles dashed back out into the street, this time heading south toward the distant thunder of the Aurora's rail guns. He fired as he ran, each shot striking an enemy soldier. Twisting and ducking incoming fire, he zigzagged his way to his next point of cover on the far side of the street, twenty meters south of the command bunker. He leaned out from his new cover and opened up, sweeping his weapon from side to side in a fashion unlike a Ghatazhak, as Master Sergeant Jahal and the other three soldiers ran across the street to join him.

"We have to get to the far corner and secure this street!" the commander yelled. "This will be our evac LZ!"

"Copy that!" the master sergeant replied. "Brakar One Seven, Jahal!" he called over his comm-set. "Move to intersection Micker Four and hold! We will hold intersection Kato Two!"

"*Brakar One Seven, moving to Micker Four! On station in two!*"

"Make it one," Master Sergeant Jahal ordered as he spun around and fired at Jung troops displayed in his visor. "Brakar One One, Jahal. Move to intersection Micker Three and hold!"

"*One One moving to Micker Three! What about the south corridor! I lost Brakar Niner five minutes ago!*"

"Brakar Niner is with us!" Master Sergeant Jahal replied. "The south corridor is closed for now! How many men do you have?"

"*One One has five from Brakar Two Six! Fifteen total! We'll be on Micker Three in one!*"

"Copy that! Hold the north and west corridors. Everyone be ready to fall back to the east corridor when the evac shuttles arrive!"

Telles and his men ducked into the building, tucking themselves away tightly, as sniper fire from the far northwest corner on the other side of the command bunker slammed into the building above them.

"One One!" Jahal yelled over the comms. "Check the fire from the northwest corner of Micker Three! We've got no shot!"

"*Thirty seconds!*"

More debris rained down around them, striking the ground with a crash. A blue-white flash lit up the street to the south, followed immediately by an ear-splitting crack of thunder and a shockwave of displaced air, as a combat jump shuttle appeared nearly one hundred meters down the street. It flew past them, spinning to starboard as it opened up with all guns on the northeast corner in the direction of the sniper fire. The building erupted in an explosion of glass, stone, and fire, after which several burning bodies fell from the now gaping hole in the side of the building.

"*Holy shit!*" Brakar One One's squad leader called out over the comms. "*Maybe those bastards could warn us before they jump out right over our fucking heads!*"

The combat jumper turned and headed up the northern corridor. Flying not more than twenty meters above the ground, it tried to avoid the Jung chasers that Falcon Four had reported were being fired from the rooftops. Seconds later, it too disappeared in a flash of blue-white light.

"*Telles, Falcon Four,*" Loki called over the commander's helmet comms. "*Four squads moving toward intersection Micker Four from the south and the east. We can target the ones to the east, but we've got no shot to the south.*"

Master Sergeant Jahal glanced at his tactical display, noticing that the icon for Brakar One Seven was missing. "Brakar One Seven, Jahal! Do you copy?"

"Falcon Four, Telles, light them up. Then come back around from the north as quickly as you can and put your guns on the targets coming in from the south."

"Command, ETA to our evacs?" Jahal inquired over the comms.

"Telles, Falcon Four, engaging the targets to the east..."

"Troop and two combat jumpers in three!"

"...We'll come around from the north and hit the ones to the south as your evacs are setting down."

"Copy that," the commander replied. "Let's move!" he yelled as he charged out into the street and ran toward intersection Micker Four at the far end.

"Telles, Command. Brakar Two Niner is dead comms, telemetry only. Coming in from the south, behind the southern targets. Six men, two out!"

Charging Jung soldiers appeared from the swirls of dust at the next intersection. Still charging ahead, Telles opened fire. Red energy weapons fire answered his attack, streaking past him left and right as he dodged the incoming bolts of energy. "Tell them to haul ass, and try not to shoot any of us in the crossfire!"

"Fuck! One One is taking heavy fire from the rooftops to the west!"

Commander Telles, Master Sergeant Jahal, and the last three members of Brakar Nine dropped to the ground as the incoming assault intensified. The ground shook as they returned fire. Directly ahead, Falcon Four's nose turret tore into the targets to the east of intersection Micker Four. As he and his men continued to fire, Telles could hear the sound of the

Falcon's engines going to full power. He could hear the snap and sizzle of at least six chasers launched from the rooftops a block or two away, as the Jung fired at the climbing interceptor just before she jumped to safety.

As he returned fire, Telles heard three distinct claps of thunder to the east. He rolled to his right and fired, then leapt back up to his feet and ran to the edge of the building a few meters further down the street in the direction of the incoming enemy attack.

"*Bulldog Three, inbound to Jojo Seven from the east. Touchdown in two.*"

"*Bulldog Six,*" a second pilot called in. "*Inbound to Jojo Seven from the southeast. One out.*"

"*Bulldog Five,*" the third pilot followed. "*Inbound to Jo... We're taking fire! We're hit! Bulldog Five is going down! We're going...*"

The building shook after another combat jump shuttle appeared in a blue-white flash directly over Commander Telles, its shockwave kicking up dust and debris around him. The combat shuttle immediately opened fire on the Jung squads at the far end of the street as they sped over the tops of the buildings, then banked hard left and climbed away.

"*Combat Seven! I've got a downed troop shuttle to the east!*"

"*Combat Seven, Command. Bulldog Five just went down. Vector to the crash site and check for survivors. Provide cover if possible,*" the flight controller in the command bunker ordered.

Telles continued charging down the street, the master sergeant and the rest of his men following. They all opened fire, taking advantage of the chaos that had just been caused by the sudden attack by Combat Seven.

Two chasers launched from the rooftop to the commander's left. The climbing combat shuttle dropped countermeasures and increased their bank rate, dropping down between the buildings to try and evade the pursuing missiles.

"*Combat Seven's got two chasers, taking evasive,*" the pilot announced calmly.

Telles and his men arrived at the next intersection, finding only the mangled bodies of what had been at least a dozen Jung soldiers. "Intersection Kato Two is secure," he announced over the comms. "We'll take up defensive positions on either side," he told his men. "We must hold this intersection, or none of us are getting off this rock alive!"

"*Combat Seven is hit!*"

"*Bulldog Six is setting down at Jojo Seven!*" the pilot of the troop shuttle announced, as the sound of energy weapons fire echoed in the background. "*Haul ass, boys! This LZ is hot!*"

"*Combat Seven is good! We took a hit, but we're still flying. We're not jumping anywhere anytime soon, though!*"

"Combat Seven, Telles," the commander called over his helmet comms. "You're a sitting duck without a jump drive. Climb to orbit and land on the Aurora."

"*Bulldog Three is setting down at Jojo Seven!*" the pilot of the second troop shuttle announced. "*You're right, Six, this LZ sucks!*"

"*Telles, Combat Seven, negative. We don't have the fuel, sir. We can stay on station, circle high and maybe provide some cover fire.*"

"You'll get tagged by another chaser sooner or

later, Lieutenant," the commander said. "Get clear, set down, and hole up. We'll send someone to get you as soon as we can. And don't forget to burn your ship!"

"Aye, sir."

Two more claps of thunder were heard, this time from the west of their position, then another explosion erupted in the distance.

"Seven! You still there?" the commander asked.

"*Affirmative! Combat Seven is still flying! That was Bulldog Five! They must have set off their jump drive's self-destruct!*"

"Can you see any survivors?"

"*Bulldog Two, inbound for Tongo Four from the west, two out.*"

"*Negative, sir! That explosion took out half the fucking block!*"

"Get clear, Seven. Hole up good. It may be a while."

"*Understood. Good luck, Commander.*"

"*Bulldog Four, inbound to Tongo Four from the northwest, three out.*"

An energy bolt struck the commander's chest, knocking him backward. He stumbled, raised his weapon and returned fire in an instant, letting go three shots, two of which found their target. "Incoming fire!" he alerted his men so they could open fire as well.

The commander heard three more claps of thunder, announcing the arrival of another troop shuttle and two more combat shuttles.

Commander Telles glanced at the tactical display inside of his helmet visor. He noticed two groups of four red dots about thirty meters down the street. Although they were the ones firing at them, that wasn't what concerned him. Four blocks away to the south, and five blocks to the east, ten times as many men were headed their way. He looked at Master Sergeant Jahal.

"The odds are finally evening up!" the master sergeant joked, seeing the same thing on his visor display.

"*Bulldog Six is airborne!*" the troop shuttle's pilot announced over the comms. "*Climbing out!*"

"*Six! Chasers to the north! Chasers to the north! Jump, jump, jump!*"

"*Way ahead of you!*"

"*Everyone at Jojo Seven, keep your heads down!*" another pilot called. "*Combats Thirteen and Fourteen are about to light up the rooftops!*"

"Take out the buildings over them!" Telles ordered his men. "The more shit we put in the street, the more difficult it is for them to advance on us!"

"It also gives them more cover!" Master Sergeant Jahal reminded him as he began firing on the walls above the attackers.

"We just need to put down a lot of it! Like maybe the entire building!"

"*Combat Thirteen, starting our run!*"

"*Combat Fourteen, coming in hot!*"

They heard more explosions in the distance, along with the screeching blasts of plasma cannons as the two combat jumpers strafed the rooftops on either side of the Jojo Seven intersection.

"*Bulldog Three, lifting off!*"

"*Three! Suggest you stay low and jump from between the buildings to avoid chasers!*"

"*That was the plan. Three is accelerating and pitching up.*"

"Thirteen! Three chasers to the west! Coming up fast! Bank right and jump!"

"Thirteen is jumping!"

"Bulldog Three is jumping."

Telles and his men continued to fire on the walls above the Jung soldiers at the opposite end of the street. A large section of the wall came crashing down, sending the enemy troops scrambling in all directions to avoid the falling debris. Another thunderous boom shook the streets, followed by the roar of plasma cannons and jet engines.

"*Keep your heads down,*" Loki called over the comms as Falcon Four streaked over their heads and down the center of the street.

The Falcon's plasma turret swept from side to side with rapid and precise movements, as the interceptor's targeting system attempted to detect and hit every enemy target within its field of fire. Seconds later, the ship pitched up, going to full power and rolling several times as it climbed. With each rotation, its spiral increased in diameter, spitting brilliant countermeasures out of its tail and flinging them in all directions as it rocketed skyward.

Four chaser missiles, launched from Jung soldiers on nearby rooftops, raced upward in pursuit of the spiraling interceptor. Two of them immediately locked onto countermeasures and exploded seconds later. The other two continued into the sky above Cetia, doomed to run out of propellant long before they could catch the fleeing interceptor.

"Falcon Four, Telles. You have anything on board that can take out a building or two?"

"Telles, Falcon Four. Bunker busters. They can take out a whole block. We're carrying four of them, sir."

"I need you to make the corridors to the east, south, and west of intersection Kato Two impassable."

"*It'll be messy,*" Loki warned.

"Messy is what I'm looking for. Give us a minute to get clear of the intersection, then have at it."

"*That's going to be dangerously close, Commander.*"

"You have your orders, Ensign."

"*Understood. Dropping three B7Bs in the corridors to the east, south, and west of Kato Two...in one.*"

Telles turned to face his men. "Everyone, haul ass back toward the command bunker!" he ordered as he started running.

"*Telles, Command. Everyone to the east and west has been evac'd. We've got two more troop jumpers and three combat jumpers that should be inbound from Porto Santo now. ETA five.*"

"Copy that!" Telles replied over the comms as he continued running. "Brakar One One, fall back and hold the east side of the command bunker! Brakar One Seven, fall back and hold the west side! The south approach is about to be closed for good! We've just gotta hold this LZ for five minutes and then we're outta here!"

"*Brakar Seven, Falcon Four! Three away! Impact in twenty seconds!*"

"*Brakar One One, falling back to command east!*"

"*Brakar One Seven, falling back to command west!*"

"*Ten seconds to impact,*" Loki warned.

Commander Telles and his men continued down the rubble-strewn boulevard, jumping over larger pieces of collapsed buildings as they raced to get around the corner before the incoming missiles found their targets a few hundred meters behind them. The initial chaos of Falcon Four's strafing run on the enemy position had begun to wear off and the incoming energy weapons fire had resumed. Bolts of red energy slammed into the ground on all sides. Telles could see at least six red dots moving toward them from behind. The Jung were giving chase.

Commander Telles ran around the corner to his right, followed by Master Sergeant Jahal and the others. Brakar One One was running toward them from the east, seven men in total. "Get behind the barriers!" Telles ordered, as he ran behind the armored barrier protecting the command bunker's south entrance.

Falcon Four may have launched three bunker busters, but there was only one, massive explosion. The entire command bunker seemed to lift up off the ground, hover in mid-air for a split second, then slam back down. Dust and fire shot over their heads, bouncing off the walls of the bunker and deflecting upward. There was a tremendous rumble, mild at first, then quickly growing in intensity until it was deafening.

Telles peeked out around the edge of the barrier just in time to see buildings on either side of the street beyond intersection Kato Two fall over. A wave of dust and misplaced air billowed down the street toward them. Telles ducked back behind the barrier again. "Shockwave!" he warned the others. The barrier reverberated as the wave of displaced air, and the tons of debris that came with it, slammed into the barrier and the bunker walls on either side of it. He and his men remained hunkered down, waiting out the seemingly endless shockwave while curled up as small as they could make themselves behind the massive armored wall. They waited, and waited, and eventually the rumble died down. As the cacophony subsided, the weapons fire resumed... only this time, it wasn't coming from the south.

"East, west, and south corridors to intersection Kato Two are closed," Loki announced.

"Nicely done, Four," Telles congratulated them as he got back to his feet. "Now, if you'd be so kind as to sterilize the rooftops around the command center, especially those along the corridor to the south, it would be greatly appreciated."

"*We'll see what we can do,*" Loki replied.

* * *

"Jump flash," Mister Navashee reported from the Aurora's sensor station. "New contact. A comm-drone."

"Incoming comm traffic," Ensign Souza announced. "From command. New orders from Admiral Dumar. We are to remain on station until the last of our forces have safely withdrawn from Kohara. Meanwhile, use all available assets to destroy Scout Three, and if possible, the Jung battleship holding her... Without delay, sir."

"Ensign, contact Scout Two and verify the target's last known position, then relay to Scout One with orders to launch the KKV when ready."

"What the hell?" Jessica exclaimed.

"Aye, sir," Ensign Souza acknowledged.

"What if he's still on board?" Jessica protested.

"Mister Navashee, how many pods ejected before they went FTL?" Nathan inquired.

"Five pods, sir. All of them were destroyed by the Jung before they could get clear."

"That means three people are still on board," Jessica reminded Nathan.

"I have my orders," Nathan replied, his tone cold and determined.

"Those three men could still be alive!" Jessica exclaimed desperately as she moved forward toward Nathan. "*Robert* could still be alive!"

"Don't you think I know that?" Nathan replied, casting a menacing gaze her direction as she approached.

"Then hold the launch order," she insisted. "Give them a chance to..."

"No!" Nathan replied sternly. "I'm not going to make the same mistake twice!"

"What mistake? Just give them a chance, damn it!"

"Stand down, Lieutenant Commander!" Nathan ordered.

Jessica looked at him with wide eyes pleading for him to change his mind.

"Jess, please," Nathan begged, his voice barely audible as his eyes met hers. "I don't have any choice...and you know it."

Jessica said nothing, matching his gaze without backing down. Nathan knew she understood, despite the fact that her pleading look turned to anger and frustration, most of which was undoubtedly focused on him at the moment.

"Comm-drone has jumped away," Mister Navashee reported.

"Estimated time to KKV launch?"

"All things considered, three to five minutes," Luis replied from the tactical console behind Nathan.

Nathan looked down, unable to bear the look in Jessica's eyes any longer. "Very well."

* * *

"Both field generators are intact," Commander Eckert reported.

"And their energy buffers?"

Commander Eckert tapped buttons on his data pad as he searched for the answer. "Maybe ten percent, but they're falling... Something is draining them. It just dropped to nine percent."

"Why?"

"I don't know. I'm kind of limited with what I can do here."

"How long until they're dead?"

"Hard to say," the commander replied. "Five minutes, ten minutes. I'm just guessing, really."

"Why did they go offline to begin with?" Captain Nash wondered.

"Maybe a bad connection? We were taking damage at the time."

"Or too many failed emitters," Nash said, concerned. He looked at Eckert. "I don't suppose you can check the emitters with that thing?"

"No way."

"*Attention to the Earth vessel,*" a heavily accented voice called over both their comm-sets. "*I am Major Goya of the Jar-Benakh. Those alive must respond.*"

"The Jar what?" Captain Nash said.

"*Jar* means battleship in Jung," Commander Eckert clarified.

"How the hell did they tap into our internal comms?" the captain wondered.

"*We are aware of you...*"

"Damn right he is," Nash muttered as he listened.

"*...and we offer you to surrender to us now.*"

"I'm pretty sure this clown didn't score too high in his English classes," Captain Nash said as he tapped his comm-set. "This is Captain Robert Nash, of the gunship...uh...Pequod. I can't understand what you are saying."

"Pequod?" Commander Eckert wondered.

Nash turned in surprise. "You never read Moby Dick?"

"Moby what?"

"*You to sur-rend-dur to me, on now, to here... Or to you is death of pain.*"

"Not to be rude, Major, but your English sucks," Nash replied over his comm-set. "If you want to discuss the terms of your surrender, you're going to have to find someone who can speak English a whole lot better than you. No disrespect intended, of course." Nash addressed Eckert. "How long until we can jump?"

Eckert stared blankly, unable to respond.

"How long?" Nash repeated, smacking the commander on the shoulder so he'd snap back into focus.

"I don't know, a few minutes, I guess. I just have to find the commands in the database, load them, and then send an execute command, but..."

"*Sur-rend-doer on this moment, or pain will be coming to you into the best... Ack! Worst of places... Ja! Pain to the worst!*"

"Please, get someone who can speak English properly, or I'm gonna open fire and blow your dumb ass to pieces just to shut you up! You're getting on my nerves!"

Commander Eckert stared at his captain. "Sir, is it really necessary to antagonize them like that? I mean..."

"Fuck'em," Nash scoffed. "Get that thing ready to jump us out of here."

"Sir, if even one emitter fails to fire..."

"I know, we'll tear the ship apart and we'll be dead. We're pretty much dead no matter what we do here, Skeech. With any luck, the breakup will ignite our propellant tanks and blow us to hell, maybe even set off the charges on the field generators."

Commander Eckert turned his attention back to his data pad as he began preparing the starboard jump field generator for the jump. "And if by some miracle, we happen to survive the jump, then what? All the EVA gear is forward, in the unpressurized areas."

"There's a maintenance crawler aft, remember?" Nash reminded him. "We can use that."

"What's to stop the Jung from following us?" Eckert wondered. "We're likely only going to jump a few light minutes, an hour at the most."

"We're hull-to-hull right now," Nash said. "We'll probably take a hunk out of their hull when we jump. That might slow them down a bit."

Eckert continued punching in commands on his data pad. "I think I'd like to change my vote back to *insane* again, sir."

* * *

Commander Telles crouched down low as Falcon Four streaked overhead, blasting the rooftops to their left with their nose-mounted turret. Streaks of rapidly fired bolts of plasma energy struck the rooftop, sending debris in all directions as both man and building were torn apart. Telles kept his head low, barely peeking over the edge of the large section of fallen building that was providing his cover. Falcon Four pitched up and banked slightly right, disappearing in a flash of blue-white light as two shoulder-launched chaser missiles streaked upward toward them from the rooftops on their right.

Two more thunderous claps announced the arrival of more jump ships from the north.

"*Combat Eight coming in from the north,*" the pilot of the first combat jump shuttle reported.

"*Combat Three coming in behind Eight,*" the second pilot added.

"*Combats Eight and Three, maintain one hundred meters until Falcon Four finishes their next pass, then descend to Kato Two for evac,*" the controller in the command bunker instructed. "*Watch for chasers.*"

"*Eight staying above one hundred for Falcon Four, watching for chasers.*"

"*I hate chasers,*" the pilot for Combat Three grumbled.

More energy weapons fire began to rain down on the commander and his men from the rooftop to their right, forcing them to duck down tight. Several men tried to return fire, taking hits that their body armor could barely absorb.

"Where the fuck are all these guys coming from?" Master Sergeant Jahal barked.

"*Bulldog One, ten kilometers, southeast at one four thousand, ready to jump in for evac.*"

"I've been wondering the same thing," Commander Telles replied as he raised his weapon just enough to get a string of shots off at the roofline to their right.

"*Bulldog One, Control, got you on the scope,*" the controller's voice called over the commander's helmet comms. "*Maintain approach, I'll call your jump into Kato Two.*"

"*Bulldog One, on approach. Copy you'll call my jump into Kato Two.*"

Several bolts of energy slammed into the large section of building debris that Commander Telles was hiding behind, striking on either side of his head. The third one ricocheted off the top of his helmet, causing the tactical display on the inside of his visor to disappear. "My TDS is down!" he called to his master sergeant. *These fuckers can shoot*, he grudgingly admitted as he returned fire.

One of the Ghatazhak soldiers on the other side of Jahal took several shots in the chest and neck, tossing him onto his back. The master sergeant scrambled over to him, reaching for his neck to check for a pulse.

"Teichert's dead!" he called out.

Another jump flash occurred directly behind Commander Telles, announced by a deafening thunder followed by a powerful wave of displaced air. Falcon Four streaked over their heads again, firing their nose turret at the Jung troops on the rooftops to their right.

"Give me his helmet!" the commander replied as debris from Falcon Four's attack rained down on them.

As Falcon Four disappeared in another jump flash, the master sergeant removed the dead man's helmet, checked it over quickly, then turned to the commander. "Heads up!" he shouted as he tossed the helmet toward his leader.

Commander Telles caught the helmet with ease. He waited several seconds for the debris to finish falling around them, then removed his helmet and quickly put on the one the master sergeant had thrown to him. The helmet automatically extended its umbilical into the top of the commander's backpack and came to life, painting the tactical data onto the inside of the commander's helmet visor. "I'm good!" he yelled, giving his master sergeant a thumbs-up.

"Telles, Control. Jojo and Tongo are both clear. We're all that's left on the ground."

"What about Combat Seven?" Telles demanded.

"They put down on the other side of the lake, far from any unfriendlies. They've already detonated. I've got two Falcons flying cover until someone comes back from Porto Santo to pick them up."

The energy weapons fire had ceased after Falcon Four's last pass, and Telles and his men were able to stand again. The commander signaled Master Sergeant Jahal to position the men to keep an eye on the roof lines on either side, just in case. "Very well," he replied over his helmet comms. "Shut down and double-time it to Kato Two."

"Copy that. Control to all units. We are shutting down and bugging out. Everyone rally at Kato Two. Good luck."

Commander Telles scanned the skies above. He could still hear the exchange of weapons fire from the far side of the command bunker. "Brakar One Seven, Telles. Sit-rep?"

"Telles, One Seven. Holding off about a dozen of the fuckers to our north and west. TDS shows another twenty or so two clicks north, moving toward us."

"Copy. Hold until command bunker is clear, then move to Kato Two for evac."

"One Seven copies."

"New movement!" Master Sergeant Jahal barked as he swung his energy rifle up to fire at the distant roofline. "Check your TDS! Check your TDS!" he yelled urgently as he opened fire.

"One One, Telles. Sit-rep!" the commander called over the din of weapons fire.

"*Telles, One One, taking fire from the rooftops to the south. We've got no shot! Pinned down!*"

"Combat Eight, Telles. Take out targets on the rooftops south of Micker Three! Then circle west and take out the targets in the street west of Micker Four!"

"*Combat Eight, engaging targets on rooftops south of Micker Three and in street west of Micker Four,*" the pilot responded. "*On first targets in thirty seconds.*"

"Combat Three, Telles. Targets in the street, north of Micker Four are yours. Then clear the rooftops around Kato Two again!"

"*Combat Three, inbound for targets north of Micker Four, in the street, then on the roofs around Kato Two. Weapons live in twenty seconds.*"

"All jumpers, your targets are dangerously close! Call your shots. Call your shots!"

"*Combat Eight copies.*"

"*Combat Three copies.*"

Commander Telles noticed a dozen green dots moving up behind him on his tactical display. He glanced behind him to confirm that they were the technicians from the command bunker. Each of them had donned torso armor and helmets, and carried energy rifles of Corinari design. "Bulldog One, Telles. Start your approach. I'll call your inbound jump."

"*Combat Eight! Danger close! Micker Three! Heads down!*"

Commander Telles turned to his right, looking southwest as Combat Jumper Eight swooped in low over the top of the now-abandoned command bunker, firing all of their weapons at the rooftops on either side. It was an impressive array of firepower with eight separate barrels spewing forth bolts of red plasma energy.

"Bulldog One is starting final. Understand you'll call our inbound jump."

"Combat Three! Danger close! Micker Three! Heads down!"

"Stay here!" Telles ordered the fleeing controllers from the command bunker, gesturing for them to get down. "Hunker down and cover your ears!" he ordered as his men continued to fire at the distant roof lines to the east.

"Combat Eight! Targeting the streets west of Micker Four!"

"Combat Three! Clearing the roofs south of Kato Two!"

"Brakars One One and One Seven, Telles!" the commander called as Combat Jumper Three streaked overhead and opened fire on the rooftops south of the commander's position. "Move to Kato Two. Now, now, now!"

"One One moving to Kato Two!"

"One Seven moving to Kato Two!"

"Bulldog One!" the commander yelled over his comms. "Jump, jump, jump!" He turned to his men. "Heads down!" he yelled as he took cover.

"Bulldog One, jumping to Kato Two. Heads down, gentlemen," the pilot announced calmly.

The entire landing zone lit up with brilliant blue-white light, then disappeared as all other sounds were drowned out by the roar of another wave of air. The effect was disorienting to most, even to the Ghatazhak. When a heavy cargo shuttle jumped in that low, the shockwave could knock the air out of a man's lungs.

Four screaming engine pods of the cargo jumper

instantly replaced the sudden clap of thunder as it hovered only twenty meters above them, descending at an alarming rate.

"*Combat Jumpers, Falcon Four!*" Loki's voice called out over the comms. "*Bandits on the rooftops, two blocks to the north and south of the LZ! They've got chasers!*"

"*Three, circling south to engage!*"

"*Eight is taking the ones to the north!*"

"*Bulldog One, setting down,*" the pilot announced as the cargo jump shuttle neared the surface. Its gear doors slid open, and four double-wheeled gears dropped down into position. The shuttle bounced slightly on its gear struts, its engines rapidly spinning down to idle as the shuttle's aft loading ramp swung down into position.

"*Combat Eight! Four chasers on your six!*" Loki cried out. "*Jump, jump, jump!*"

"Go, go, go!" Commander Telles ordered, gesturing for everyone to board the shuttle. He turned to his left, spotting Combat Eight as it banked hard. One of the four chaser missiles pursuing the combat jump shuttle slammed into its aft starboard engine just as its jump field started to form. The shuttle rolled to the right, yawing in the same direction due to a sudden loss of thrust, the forward section of the shuttle disappeared in a blue-white flash, leaving the aft section behind to tumble aimlessly to the ground.

"*Combat Eight is down!*" Loki reported. "*Eight is down, hard!*"

There was an explosion a few blocks away as the tail of Combat Eight struck a building. Telles turned and saw his last two squads running around the corner of the command bunker, on their way to the cargo shuttle. Seconds later, there was another explosion a few kilometers to the northeast.

"*Oh, my God!*" Loki exclaimed over the comms from their vantage point above the action. "*The front half of Eight is down four clicks to the northeast.*"

"Any survivors?" Telles asked, already knowing the answer.

"*No way, sir,*" Loki replied, confirming his suspicion.

"Four, Telles. Did you spot where those chasers came from?"

"*Yes, sir,*" Loki replied.

"Four, Telles. Waste the entire fucking block."

* * *

"I've got the starboard field generator set up and ready to go," Commander Eckert reported.

"They've got to be getting ready for something," Captain Nash said.

"Like what?" the commander asked as he continued to work on his data pad. "You think they're going to blast their way in?"

"And run the risk of accidentally blowing us up? Not likely. They must know about our jump drive, otherwise they wouldn't be wasting their time with us. More likely they'll find a way to tap into our environmental system and pump in gas or something."

"Or they could just wait for us to run out of oxygen," Eckert commented. "Not like it will take very long."

"They can't take the chance," Nash argued. "Too many things can go wrong. We find a way to detonate, the Aurora catches up with us, a KKV strike... They can't afford to waste time here, but they can't afford to take unnecessary risks either. The captain of the Jar-Ba-something out there is probably drooling over the prospect of handing a jump drive to his leaders. Probably get himself a fat promotion."

"*Attention, Captain Nash of the gunship Pequod. Can you hear me?*" The voice was female, with a slight yet different accent than the major who had previously called.

"That's a surprise," Nash commented.

"I didn't think the Jung had any women on their crews?" Eckert said.

"Neither did I," Nash replied as he tapped his comm-set. "This is Captain Nash. To whom am I speaking?"

"*My name is Kaya Allemahn. I have been authorized to speak with you on behalf of the Jung.*"

"Authorized by who?" Nash asked.

"*By the commander of the Jar-Benakh, Captain Tahn.*"

"What do you want to speak to me about? Are you offering to surrender? Because that would probably be a really smart move on your captain's part. Save us all a whole lot of trouble."

"*I expect Captain Tahn would disagree with you, Captain. You are aware that the Jar-Benahk has many times your firepower, and could destroy you in an instant, are you not?*"

"I am," Captain Nash replied, "and *you* are aware that doing so will cause *our* self-destruct system, which is currently armed, to destroy this ship, as well as your own...are you not?"

There was a pause.

"That got them thinking," Nash muttered. "How much longer?"

"A minute or two, tops," Eckert replied. "You realize that even if we *are* able to jump away clean, without tearing ourselves apart, we have no way of knowing if we damaged the Jung ship on the way out. They could catch up to us in minutes."

"I know."

"*It seems, Captain, that we are at an impasse,*" Kaya finally replied. "*You have something we want, and we have something you want.*"

"I know what *you* want," Nash replied. "What is it that *you* think *I* want?"

"*To live.*"

"Good guess, but in all honesty, life back on Earth kind of sucks right now. Your people made sure of that."

"*They are not my people, Captain. However, perhaps had your people not ignored the blockade, had you not attempted to infect other worlds...*"

"What the hell are you talking about, lady?"

"*It is well known throughout the Cetian worlds, as well as the rest of the core, that the Earth is the source of the great plague, and that it is still infected. Your people have been trying to escape your dying world for some time, with no regard to the health and safety of the billions...*"

Nash looked at Eckert. "Lady, I don't know where your people are getting their intel, but the bio-digital plague on *Earth* died out more than nine hundred years ago."

"*If what you say is true, then why are you attacking my worlds?*"

"What worlds?"

"*The Cetian worlds.*"

"She's not Jung," Nash realized.

"A local collaborator, maybe?"

"Maybe." Nash tapped his comm-set again. "We are not attacking your *worlds*. We were attacking the Jung forces *around*, and *on* your worlds."

"*And why are you attacking the Jung?*"

"Because they invaded our world," Captain Nash explained. "It took us months to drive them off. They nearly destroyed our entire planet. They killed billions. And it's not just on Earth, it's all over the damn sector! They took out an entire moon in the Alpha Centauri system. Killed millions there as well. Apparently, it's what they do. We're just trying to stop them. But hey, if you're happy living under their boot heel, then by all means, continue to do so. We'll just take our fleet and go about our merry way."

Commander Eckert shook his head in disbelief as he continued to work on his data pad. "I'm seeing a whole other side of you today, Captain."

"Just hurry up and jump us."

"You know, you and your sister are a lot alike."

"Attitude runs in our family," Captain Nash replied. "Mine tends to come out when I'm about to die."

"*Captain Tahn does not believe you,*" Kaya finally said. "*And...and neither do I. However, Captain Tahn admires your bravery. He would like to offer you your freedom.*"

"To go back and live on an irradiated world? As a traitor?" Captain Nash chuckled. "You're going to have to do better than that."

"*You can live on any world you wish. The Jung can provide you with wealth, power, women... Anything you desire.*"

"How much longer?" Captain Nash asked the commander.

"I'm syncing the field generators now. Just a few more seconds..."

"Interesting proposition," Nash replied over his comm-set. "Mind if I think about it for a few minutes?"

"You will decide now," Kaya demanded, her tone indicating it was not up for debate.

"How much wealth are we talking about?" Nash asked, stalling for time.

"Decide now!"

"I don't like pushy women, Kaya," Captain Nash chided.

"Captain Tahn tires of your games! He has decided that you will die!"

"We're ready," Commander Eckert said.

"No matter," Captain Nash replied over his comm-set. "I was going to tell you to fuck off anyway." He looked at the commander and nodded his head. "Do it."

"Initiating emergency snap jump," the commander replied, pressing the screen on his data pad with his forefinger.

A low rumble quickly turned into an intense, high-pitched shriek as the jump field generators on either side of them quickly pulled the last bit of power from the system's energy banks and distributed it to the emitter arrays on the exterior of the scout ship's hull. A split second later, it went silent.

The ship jerked hard to port, rolling slightly. There was a terrible sound of metal beams and bulkheads under tremendous strain, followed immediately by a series of muffled explosions and the frightening sound of structures being torn apart.

Captain Nash found himself bouncing off the starboard bulkhead, his head slamming into one of streaked out from under their nose, speeding ahead of them toward the buildings below.

"Swinging nose turret onto... Combat Three! Chasers to your four o'clock! Bank left! Full burn, and jump!"

"*Three taking evasive!*" the pilot replied. "*Deploying countermeasures!*"

Loki glanced out to port as Combat Three turned left and pitched up, her four engine pods at full thrust. A string of bright, glowing decoys shot out in all directions as she disappeared in a blue-white flash. With nothing left in front of them, all three chaser missiles that were following Combat Three locked onto the decoys and exploded on impact seconds later. "Three made it!" Loki announced as he turned to his threat display. His eyes widened. "What the... Telles! Falcon Four! Multiple targets! Airborne! Coming in fast!"

"*What?*" the commander replied, genuine surprise in his voice. "*From where?*"

"From everywhere!" Loki cried. "They're coming at you from all directions!"

"*What the hell are they?*"

"I don't know, but they're going to be on you in thirty seconds!"

"*How many?*"

"At least a hundred of them! Twenty seconds!"

"*I thought we owned the goddamned skies?*" the commander cursed.

"They're not fighters, sir, they're too small... They've gotta be drones!"

Commander Telles looked up, scanning the skies beyond the nearby rooftops. Swarms of small black objects came over the tops of the buildings in the distance, headed straight for them. "Incoming drones!" he yelled, raising his energy rifle. "Bulldog One! Lift off now and jump the hell out of here!" he added as he opened fire on the incoming swarm.

The shuttle's engines roared to life as the last of the men on the ground jumped onto the shuttle's rear loading ramp.

"We gotta go!" Master Sergeant Jahal yelled to his commander.

Telles continued to fire at the incoming drones. The nearest drones opened fire, sending needle-like bolts of blue slamming into the ground all around them. The bolts slammed into the commander's body armor, striking him in the chest, arms, and abdomen. He could feel the warmth of the beams getting through to his skin, as well as the kinetic force of the impacts, but he continued firing. He felt someone grab his shoulder and pull him forward.

"Let's go!" the master sergeant yelled at the top of his lungs as he pulled at his commander.

They ran toward the shuttle as it slowly rose from the ground. Several drones dove straight down toward the rising cargo shuttle, firing all the way in, until they slammed into the top of the shuttle. First one, then two, then three, and finally a fourth one slammed into the shuttle's forward engine pod. The pod exploded, and the shuttle's nose dipped as the ship rolled to starboard and struck the ground. Its forward right landing gear buckled and snapped as three more drones slammed into the crashing shuttle.

Commander Telles felt a wave of heat and air pressure hit him head on. It lifted him off the ground, sending him flying backwards a good fifteen meters.

He slammed into the side of the command bunker, the thousands of tiny tubules in his assistive undergarment stiffening to protect him from the impact.

His ears rang and his vision was blurred. He could feel pain in every part of his body. He realized he was sitting on the ground, his back against the wall of the command bunker, his legs spread out on the ground. Something slammed into the ground next to him. Something bright blue. Then something moved in front of him. A familiar figure, bending down to grab him, pulling him to his feet as the figure yelled at him in muffled, barely audible tones.

He stumbled to his feet, by instinct and the help of his friend. His ears were still ringing, but his vision was clearing and his hearing was returning. There were explosions, dozens of them. Tiny ones, from all directions, along with the humming of small propulsion systems and the repetitive zinging of small energy weapons.

A larger explosion nearby grabbed his attention as it lit up everything around him. He could feel the heat from it, seeing the fireball not thirty meters away, rising skyward.

"Move!" the master sergeant ordered.

Commander Telles raised his weapon as he began to stumble away from the explosion.

"Can you make it?" the master sergeant asked as they headed out.

"Yes!" the commander replied. He took several unbalanced steps, the tubules in his suit helping him move, providing him additional strength and balance, without which he might still be sitting on his ass...or worse.

He opened fire on the black, wedge-shaped drones

that were flitting about overhead, firing at anything that moved. Within seconds, the drones had locked in on them and were firing away. He could feel their hot, needle-like beams slamming into his backpack as he ran. His tactical display flickered as he ran while the needle-like beams slammed into his pack and caused it to fail.

They made it to the nearest building, falling through the broken door into the lobby. Four drones crashed through the windows, chasing them inside. The commander and the master sergeant opened fire, quickly taking out all four of the black, meter-wide, wedge-shaped killing machines.

"We gotta get into the corridors where they can't follow us!" Master Sergeant Jahal insisted, as two more drones entered through the front door and pressed the attack. Jahal returned fire, dropping one drone as he backpedaled to cover his friend's escape. They ran down the corridor, more bolts of energy slamming into both their packs as they ran. They rounded the corner and Telles stopped, turning back around. He opened fire, spraying the ceiling and walls, causing them to collapse behind them. "That should slow them down," he said, his voice shaky.

"Your back's on fire," the master sergeant said, panting.

Commander Telles looked over his shoulder and noticed smoke drifting up from his pack. He pressed the release button, allowing the pack to drop away. Without his pack, his tactical display vanished, and his comms went dead. He reached down and opened the compartment on his left thigh armor and pulled out the small comm-set that he normally used while at Porto Santo or on board the Aurora. "Your pack isn't looking so good either, my friend," he said as he pulled off his helmet and tossed it aside.

Master Sergeant dropped his smoldering pack, following his commander's lead and reaching for his comm-set as well.

"Any Alliance unit, this is Commander Telles. Do you copy?"

"*Telles, Falcon Four,*" Loki replied. "*You're broken and weak, but I can hear you.*"

"Four, Telles. What's the situation?"

"*Telles, Four. Bulldog One is down hard. No survivors. Combat Three is holding up high, out of range of chasers for now, just like us. Where are you?*"

"Someplace those fucking drones can't reach us, for now," the commander replied. "What are they doing?"

"*They're just hovering around the building to the northeast of the command bunker, between Micker Four and Kato Two,*" Loki replied.

"They're not coming after you or Three?"

"*No, sir. They may have limited ceilings.*"

"Or they know they'd be wasting their time chasing jump ships in the air," Jahal commented.

"What about Combat Seven's crew?" the commander asked. "Anyone pick them up yet?"

"*Bulldog Six dropped their passengers on the Aurora in order to get back quickly,*" Loki explained. "*They're picking up Seven's crew now, then they'll be returning to the Aurora.*"

"What about ground troops?" Telles asked.

"*Moving toward you from all sides. You've got a few minutes, at most.*"

"Any bright ideas?" Jahal wondered.

Commander Telles shot a withering look at him.

"Well, you *are* the commander."

"Three, Telles. Your jump drive still operational?"

"*Telles, Three. Affirmative,*" the pilot replied. "*What do you have in mind, sir?*"

Telles opened the compartment on his right thigh and pulled out a remote detonator. He punched in a few numbers and waited for a response. A second later, a green light appeared. "Get ready to jump in. Your LZ will be between the command bunker and Bulldog One's crash site. Jump in no more than five meters above the deck, as little forward momentum as possible."

"*Sir, that will put us right in the middle of those drones. They'll be on us before you can get aboard.*"

"I'm going to blow the bunker. The shockwave should knock them down. We should have at least twenty seconds before nearby drones can move in to replace them."

"*Copy that,*" Combat Three's pilot replied. "*Give us a few seconds to get into position.*"

"We'll go in thirty seconds," Commander Telles said. He moved to the nearest door on the street side of the corridor. He opened it up and looked inside. He was immediately met with the sound of broken glass and the zing of needle-like beams of energy from drones hovering outside the windows on the far side of the room. "Well, we've found our exit point." He moved to the door on the opposite side and went into the next room, the master sergeant following him. He crouched down against the wall, then looked at the detonator, arming it. "Three, Telles. You ready?"

"*Telles, Three. Ready.*"

"Detonation in three......two......one......" Telles pressed the button on the detonator. A split second later, the command bunker outside exploded, shaking the entire building. The ceiling above them collapsed, coming down in large sections. Furniture from above them followed, crashing down all around them. The wall they were leaning against caved inward, falling down on top of them.

Telles pushed his way up through the debris. The corridor was gone, as was most of the outside wall in the next room. "Jahal!" he called out.

"Here!"

"Let's go!"

"Right behind you, Commander!"

Telles and Jahal quickly made their way across the rubble and furniture. The room was full of smoke and dust; they could barely see anything outside. Within seconds, they were on the street again. The lingering haze from the explosion lit up a brilliant blue, immediately followed by a clap of thunder and another shockwave that nearly knocked them over again. As he regained his balance, the commander looked up. There, not more than four meters above the debris-strewn street, was Combat Jumper Three, coming to a dead hover a few meters away. More importantly, there wasn't a drone in sight.

Commander Telles looked at his friend, gesturing for him to go first. He watched as the master sergeant took several running steps, then leapt upward with the assistance of his suit, sailing up into the wide-open side door of the combat jumper. Telles followed his friend, taking several running steps as well before leaping upward into the hovering shuttle.

"Chasers!" the pilot called out as the commander landed just inside the door. The shuttle rolled right, turning hard in order to avoid the incoming missiles. Telles felt the deck of the shuttle dropping out from under his feet as it took evasive maneuvers. The chaser missile passed directly beneath him as he felt himself falling back toward the surface.

Then, abruptly, his fall stopped.

Two different hands had grabbed him. One hand belonging to his friend, Master Sergeant Jahal, and the other to one of the combat jump shuttle's door gunners. As the shuttle continued its right turn, they pulled the commander inside, just as several blue, needle-like beams from newly arriving drones slammed into the side of the climbing shuttle.

"We're hit! We're hit!" the copilot reported.

"Flight controls are still good," the pilot reported.

"We've lost both starboard emitters!" the copilot added.

"Can we still fly?" Commander Telles asked as he struggled to get safely into his seat in the rear of the shuttle.

"Yes, sir," the pilot replied, "we can still fly, we just can't jump."

"Can we make it to the Aurora?"

"Yes, sir. It will just take us a few extra minutes, that's all."

"Fine. As long as I get the fuck off this rock."

Master Sergeant Jahal patted his commander on the shoulder, grinning from ear to ear. "That was some bright fucking idea you had there, Lucius!"

A small grin formed in the corner of the commander's mouth. "Well, I am the commander, after all."

* * *

"Flight ops reports Commander Telles's shuttle

and Bulldog Six are both safely aboard," Luis reported from the Aurora's tactical station.

"Red deck," Nathan ordered.

"Red deck, aye."

"Comms, ask the commander to report to the bridge."

"Yes, sir."

"Jump flash," Mister Navashee reported. "Comm-drone."

"Incoming message from Scout One," Ensign Souza announced. "They are on station at the KKV launch point. KKV will launch in...one minute."

Nathan glanced at the mission time on the tactical display on the main view screen. "Helm, break orbit and head for the Jung battleship's last reported position."

"Breaking orbit," Mister Chiles acknowledged.

"Ready a jump, safe distance from the target and Scout Two."

"Plotting jump," Mister Riley replied.

Although Jessica said nothing, Nathan could feel her fear even more so than his own as she stood beside him. He wanted to reach out and take her hand, offer her comfort, but it was neither the time nor place for such gestures.

"Another jump flash," Mister Navashee reported. "Comm-drone."

Nathan spun his command chair slowly to the right, exchanging glances with Jessica momentarily before turning to look aft.

"Flash traffic from Scout Two!" Ensign Souza called out as Commander Telles walked past him on his way to the tactical station. "Putting up audio."

"*Aurora, Scout Two!*" Captain Roselle called urgently over the loudspeaker. "*Three has jumped! I repeat, Scout Three has jumped away! There's a big fucking hole in the side of the Jung battleship, and her port shields are down! She's lost main power and appears adrift! She's wide open for attack! Take the shot now!*"

Nathan glanced at the mission clock. "Comms! Flash traffic for Scout One! Abort launch!"

"Flash traffic for One, abort, aye!"

"Twenty-five seconds," Luis noted, "it may not be enough time."

"Captain?" Commander Telles began.

"How many men do you have with you?" Nathan asked.

"About two dozen." The commander's expression changed as he realized Nathan's intent.

"Are you thinking what I'm thinking?"

Commander Telles did not reply. Instead, he turned and headed toward the exit, tapping his comm-set on his way. "Flight Ops, Telles, ready both shuttles for immediate departure."

CHAPTER THREE

"*One minute to jump!*" the shuttle's crew chief announced over their helmet comms. "*Starting depress!*"

"*Ghatazhak!*" Master Sergeant Jahal barked. "*Stand ready!*"

All twenty-four men stood along either side of the cargo shuttle. The space was already a tight fit for its standard load of twenty soldiers in full space battle gear, let alone for the twenty-six who were currently on board.

"*Thirty seconds!*" the crew chief shouted as he reached for the door controls. "*Ramp, coming down!*"

There was a gust of air as the last of the cargo jump shuttle's cabin pressure was sucked out the back of the ship. The rear loading ramp pivoted outward and downward on its hinges, quickly turning into an extension of the cargo shuttle's deck that protruded a good three meters aft.

"*Five seconds! Eyes tight!*" the copilot called over the comms.

Commander Telles closed his eyes tightly as he waited for the jump, the flash burning through his eyelids as a brief yet intense orange glow.

"*Jump complete!*"

Commander Telles opened his eyes, looking down the narrow corridor between the two rows of men into the black void beyond.

"*Go, go, go!*" came the call from the cockpit.

The two Ghatazhak soldiers closest to the rear of the shuttle walked briskly out toward the end of the ramp, with the eleven other pairs following close behind. Two by two, the soldiers stepped off the end of the ramp, firing tiny thrusters and spreading out in all directions as they floated freely behind the shuttle. Within seconds, all twenty-six men were drifting a few meters behind the cargo shuttle, their distance from the ship increasing by only a few meters per minute.

Commander Telles and Master Sergeant Jahal followed the last men off the shuttle's ramp. The commander looked down at the control stick sitting on a small arm protruding from the left side of the maneuvering pack encircling his waist just below his backpack. "*Rotate,*" he ordered calmly. He grasped the stick and gave it a tiny twist to the right, causing his rotation thrusters to briefly fire. His body rotated around quickly, bringing into view the back of the cargo jump shuttle they had just left. Behind it was the massive Jung battleship, without power and adrift on the outer edges of the Tau Ceti system. Another tiny twist of his control stick in the opposite direction stopped his rotation as easily as it had started.

The rest of his men also fired their thrusters, bringing them around to face their direction of flight. The cargo shuttle in front of them fired its own thrusters, translating quickly upward, revealing the gaping hole in the side of the massive enemy ship only a few hundred meters ahead of them. Several of its guns were still pointed directly at them, as if daring them to drift closer. But they did not move.

"*Eyes tight again, gentlemen,*" the copilot called over the comms. "*Good luck.*"

The shuttle disappeared in a flash of light from behind them, leaving the twenty-six soldiers gliding rapidly toward the crippled Jung battleship.

"*Damn, you sure those guns are dead, sir?*" one of his men inquired.

"*If they weren't, you wouldn't be able to ask that question,*" the master sergeant replied.

Commander Telles examined the nearby hull with his tactical scanners, searching for any threats. His display showed that his men had properly spaced themselves out to ensure that everyone would make contact with the hull of the target at a different point. "*Two hundred meters,*" he announced as they continued coasting toward the battleship. Even at this distance, the enemy ship was all they could see in their visors without turning their heads, and it was getting bigger with each passing second. "*Picking up some activity aft of the target area,*" the commander added. "*Low level energy systems, exterior, mostly.*"

"*Static charges left on the hull, maybe?*" Master Sergeant Jahal guessed. "*Left over from Scout Three's jump, perhaps?*"

"*We'll execute a fifteen second decel burn at fifty meters,*" the commander ordered. "*At twenty-five meters, we power down, then power back up after we've made contact.*"

"Jump complete," Mister Riley reported as the jump flash faded and the interior of the Aurora's bridge returned to its customary, red-tinged alert lighting.

"Bring us along her starboard side, in line with her breach," Nathan directed. "Nose in to keep our forward tubes on her aft propulsion section."

"Aye, sir," Mister Chiles acknowledged.

"Lock all weapons on her starboard guns, Lieutenant," Nathan continued. "One for one. If she so much as flinches, I want those guns taken out."

"She's got more guns than we do, Captain. I suggest we target her biggest ones first."

"Agreed, Mister Navashee. If that ship shows any signs of powering up her engines, don't hesitate to let us know."

"Yes, sir."

"If she tries to run, blow her fucking tail off."

"Locking forward tubes on target's propulsion section," Luis replied. "Helm, give me a forty-five degree roll to starboard for a better firing angle."

"Rolling forty-five to starboard, aye."

"I've got Commander Telles and his forces on opticals," Mister Navashee reported. "They're one hundred meters from the breach, closing at five meters per second."

"Put them on the screen," Nathan ordered.

"Switching to midship topside cameras."

The image of the aft end of the Jung battleship disappeared, replaced a moment later by a close-up view of the enemy ship's starboard midship area. He could barely make out the black figures of the twenty-six Ghatazhak soldiers as they coasted toward the breach on the side of the target.

"Seventy-five meters," Mister Navashee updated. "Still only minimal internal power, batteries I'd say. Not enough to run anything other than emergency lighting, maybe some internal comms. Fifty meters. The Ghatazhak are firing their deceleration thrusters now."

"Any chance the Jung know they're coming?" Nathan asked.

"Not unless they're looking out the window at them, sir. I'm barely picking up anything from them on sensors. Just a tiny amount of electrical energy. They're stealthy as hell."

"How's it looking, Lieutenant?" Nathan asked. He couldn't help but feel nervous sitting less than a kilometer away from an enemy ship that was three times their size and had twice as many guns.

"Nothing's moving, Captain."

"Jump flash," Mister Navashee reported. "Five kilometers astern of the target. It's Scout Two."

"Comms, tell Roselle to keep his tubes on the target's main drive. Fire if they light up."

"Aye, sir."

"Another jump flash, Captain," Mister Navashee added. "One hundred kilometers off our port side. Falcon Four."

"Incoming message from Falcon Four," Ensign Souza announced. "They're just back from Porto Santo, refueled and reloaded. Porto Santo control received your message, they'll have a couple hundred Ghatazhak and a few more Falcons here shortly."

"Decel burn is complete," Mister Navashee stated. "Captain, they're powering down."

"Why would they power down?" Luis wondered.

"I'm sure the commander knows what he's doing," Nathan replied.

Despite what his tactical display had told him prior to powering down, Commander Telles wished he had burned his deceleration thrusters a few seconds longer. The jagged, torn-up decks of the damaged battleship were still coming toward them quite rapidly.

Without comms and tactical display, the commander felt very much alone. No comm chatter and no radio static. No beeps, tones, or alarms from his tactical display as data readouts changed. No whirring of fans blowing fresh air into his suit and sucking out the bad. Just the sound of his own breathing, and the occasional rustling of the inner liner of his suit as he moved his arms. He knew that there were twenty-five of his men spread out behind him, but at the moment, it was just him... and the damaged deck of the enemy ship coming toward him.

Much of the damage line was clean, almost surgical, while other sections, some deeper into the breach, appeared more irregular, with torn, jagged edges. Cabling dangled everywhere like spider webs. Bulkheads were bent and twisted, after their supporting structures were suddenly taken away by Scout Two's jump fields. Pressurized gasses vented from severed pipes and ducts, and various fluids drifted about in groups of odd-shaped globules.

Drops of red and green fluids splattered across his visor as he coasted across the breach threshold. He was a little low, and the twisted deck was coming toward his knees. The commander swung his legs up, bringing his feet up and forward just in time to push up slightly on the deck as he coasted across its edge. Without gravity, he careened upward clumsily, bouncing off the overhead and slamming into a section of ventilation ducting that hung askew from its moorings. The impact caused his body to spin laterally as he tumbled. He felt something drag across his backpack as he continued deeper into the open compartment. Cabling. Lots of it, dragging across him, catching on his equipment and slowing him down. He only hoped it hadn't damaged his life-support or combat systems.

Finally, he came to a stop, floating above the deck, tangled in the mass of cables. He could see Master Sergeant Jahal coming toward him, a grin on his face. The master sergeant reached out and turned on the commander's power for him, then pulled out his combat knife and started cutting away at the cabling. Once he had freed his commander, he turned his own power back on as well.

"That was the most ungainly landing I've ever had the pleasure of witnessing," he mused over the comms.

"Glad you enjoyed it," the commander replied dryly as he pulled on the remaining wires to right himself. He looked around at his men. *"Count off,"* he ordered as he waited for his tactical display to boot up.

The commander activated his mag-boots and made his way toward the nearest hatch as his men reported in.

"Missing one," Master Sergeant Jahal said after the count was complete.

"Korlan didn't make it," one of the men explained. *"Hit a torn piece of sheeting, nearly cut him in two. Bled out in seconds."*

"You know the drill," the master sergeant reminded his men. *"One, three, and five head for command and control. Two, four, and six for propulsion and main power. Three separate levels each way. No prisoners. If it breathes, it dies."*

"Three, set."

"Five, set."

One of the men slapped charges onto the upper

and lower halves of the hatch and activated their detonators. He turned to the commander. *"One, set."*

Telles, Jahal, and the other four members of their team moved off to either side of the forward hatch, as the remaining teams reported their charges were set.

"Ready charges," the commander ordered. He pointed toward the soldier who had the detonator in his hand. *"Execute."*

"Fire in the hole."

The deck shook beneath their feet for a moment as the charges flashed in silence, tearing the hatch apart and sending debris across the damaged compartment. The air in the next compartment, along with anything that wasn't secured, was sucked out into the vacuum. Two crewman, arms and legs thrashing about, were sucked out along with the wreckage, horrified expressions on their faces at the reality that death would be upon them in seconds.

The flow of debris stopped a few seconds later, and the first four men charged into the next compartment, followed by Commander Telles and the master sergeant.

Commander Telles could feel the Jung ship's artificial gravity take hold of him as he stepped through the hatch into the next compartment.

"Clear left," the first soldier reported.

"Clear right," the other followed.

"Setting charges," the third man announced.

"Are we gonna blow our way through the entire ship?" the fourth soldier wondered.

"We'll find an airlock sooner or later," Master Sergeant Jahal remarked. *"Besides, I don't think we have enough charges."*

"I've got the deck plans from the Jar-Keurog. If

these two ships are at all similar, there should be an airlock three compartments forward, as we pass through one of the major structural bulkheads."

"Charges set," the third man reported as he waited for the others to move to the sides of the compartment. "*Fire in the hole.*"

There was another silent flash of light as the charges detonated. Debris shot across the compartment, careening off the far wall. The men charged forward into the next compartment. Flashes of energy weapons fire filled the compartment as the commander followed his men through the hatch.

The weapons fire lasted only a few seconds.

"*Clear left.*"

"*Clear right.*"

On the far side of the compartment, his demolitions tech, Sergeant Arana, was pushing aside the body of a man in an emergency pressure suit that was blocking his access to the next hatch. Two more bodies, also in emergency pressure suits, were lying to the right, blood pouring from open wounds. On the other side were three more men without suits, their hands and faces bloated, with horrified, suffocated expressions.

"*Setting charges,*" Sergeant Arana reported.

"*I'm picking up four energy weapons in the next compartment,*" one of the soldiers reported, "*with about a dozen more in the corridor on the far side.*"

"*Breach charges on both sides,*" the commander ordered. "*There and there,*" he instructed, pointing to the far ends of the compartment on either side of the hatch.

The men shifted to the indicated corners, turning toward Sergeant Arana at the hatch as they got into position. The sergeant tossed a pair of charges to each of the two men, who quickly affixed them to the wall as the sergeant had done on the hatch.

Commander Telles moved to the wall to the right of the hatch, while Master Sergeant Jahal went left.

"*Colmeany and Takore take the right, Jahal and Willette left,*" the commander instructed. "*Arana and I will take center.*"

"*Set left,*" Private Willette reported.

"*Set right,*" Private Colmeany announced.

"*Blow the center first, wait ten, then the sides.*"

Sergeant Arana nodded, armed his detonator, then looked both ways to make sure that the rest of his squad was ready. "*Fire in the hole,*" he muttered as he pushed the detonator button.

The charges flashed, making no sound in the vacuum of the depressurized compartment. Chunks of the hatch flew across the room, slamming into the far wall and falling to the deck.

Commander Telles leaned in and sprayed the interior of the next compartment with energy weapons fire, sending red bolts of energy in all directions. He ducked back as the enemy on the other side of the hatch returned fire. He nodded at the sergeant.

Flashes on both sides of the compartment detonated, opening gaping holes in the wall at either end of the room. Master Sergeant Jahal jumped through the opening, his weapon firing before he entered. There were two mangled bodies on the deck in front of him, torn apart by the secondary blasts. He concentrated his fire on the opposite back corner of the room, spraying toward the center and back, taking care not to fire into the other corner where Colmeany and Takore would be. The enemy attempted to return fire, but only got a few more shots off before they too fell to the Ghatazhak energy weapons.

"*Clear left!*" Master Sergeant Jahal announced.

"*Clear right!*" Private Colmeany replied.

"*Forces in the next corridor are backing off,*" Telles reported as he entered the compartment.

"*Why the fuck would they do that?*" Willette wondered. "*That's the airlock, right,*" he said, pointing at the next hatch. "*They'd have us boxed in.*"

"*I'm guessing they don't know how many of us there are,*" Master Sergeant Jahal said. "*You can only fit so many of us in that airlock at a time. They probably want to let us in a few at a time and pick us off on the other side.*"

"*Or one of our other teams is giving them hell right now,*" Private Colmeany suggested.

"*More likely they're afraid that we'll just open up every compartment to space and suffocate everyone without a pressure suit,*" Commander Telles said. "*Either way it doesn't matter. We try the airlock. Once we're inside the inner hull, we can move a lot more quickly.*"

"*All right, boys. You heard the man. Into the airlock we go,*" Master Sergeant Jahal said, gesturing toward the airlock hatch.

"Captain! New contacts!" Mister Navashee reported from the Aurora's sensor station. "From the battleship. They're launching shuttles!"

"Escape shuttles?" Nathan asked.

"Correction, fast-attack shuttles, sir. Four of them."

"Targeting new contacts with forward point defenses," Luis announced from the tactical station.

"Targets are moving away, accelerating rapidly," Mister Navashee added.

"Captain, Scout Two reports they are targeting the enemy shuttles," Ensign Souza added.

"Targets acquired, ready to fire," Luis reported.

"Open fire..."

"Contacts are going to FTL," Mister Navashee warned. "Contacts are gone."

"What the hell?" Nathan exclaimed.

"Captain, that debris field, the one around the breach in the battleship's hull. I'm picking up familiar alloys and composites. They've got to be from Scout Three."

"Did she break up?" Nathan asked. "Maybe it wasn't a jump. Maybe they managed to detonate their field generators?"

"Doubtful," Mister Navashee disagreed. "Not enough debris, and not enough blast damage to the battleship. I'm thinking she jumped away pretty much intact, Captain."

"Then those shuttles are going after her," Nathan surmised. "Comms, tell Scout Two to track and pursue. Warn him they may be going after Scout Three."

"Aye, sir."

"Captain, if Scout Three jumped, that means someone is still on board," Jessica reminded him.

"Our priority here is to keep Scout Three's jump drive out of Jung hands," Nathan said. He looked at Jessica. "You know that as well as anyone, Jess. Besides, Roselle will try and make contact before pulling the trigger. He's not going to waste any friendly lives unless he doesn't have a choice."

"Are you sure about that?" Jessica asked, her eyebrows raised.

Nathan looked at her again. "Actually? No."

"*Holy shit,*" Sergeant Arana muttered as he stepped out of the airlock and peered down the empty corridor. "*This is too good to be true.*"

Telles stepped out of the airlock after checking his tactical display. "*Anyone picking up any movement nearby?*"

"*Nothing on this deck,*" Master Sergeant Jahal replied.

"*Same here,*" Private Colmeany added.

"*Three, One. Sit-rep,*" the commander called over his helmet comms.

"*One, Three. Light resistance. We just got past the airlock. We've got full pressure here. Going off suit air to conserve.*"

"*Negative,*" Telles ordered. "*Everyone stay on suit air as long as you can. There's got to be a reason they're falling back.*"

"*Three, copy.*"

"*Gas?*" Master Sergeant Jahal asked as the other team leaders confirmed the order over the comms.

"*Like I said, there's got to be a reason they all fell back,*" the commander replied.

"*Let's move out,*" Telles ordered. He continued ahead, his weapon held high and tight against his shoulder, sweeping back and forth as he sidestepped his way down the corridor. His men followed close behind in similar fashion, ready to engage the enemy in the blink of an eye.

"*I'm not liking this,*" Master Sergeant Jahal muttered. "*I'm thinking we should have kept venting compartments, sir.*"

"*Objection noted,*" Telles replied as he continued

forward at a brisk but cautious pace. He turned the corner, coming face-to-face with three armed men. He fired three shots, ducking a single return shot fired by the last man just before the enemy was taken out by the commander's third shot. The commander continued forward, stepping over the fallen without so much as a glance downward. He had no doubt that his shots had been fatal.

Another corner saw eight more men, some properly outfitted for combat, others simply technicians with guns. The commander and two of his men dealt with them without difficulty, their advance barely slowing during the brief confrontation.

"I'm getting a lot of movement above and below us," Jahal warned. "You seeing this, Commander?"

"Yeah, I see it." He held up a closed fist, signaling his team to pause. "Three, One. Sit-rep?"

"One, Three. We've got lots of movement, coming our way..."

"Five! Heavy contact! Maybe fifty! Taking fire!"

"Three is taking fire! At least thirty targets!"

"Sir, movement on our deck, forward of the next structural bulkhead, about fifty meters ahead," Private Willette reported.

"Five, One. Fall back, double-time. Get them to chase you aft," Telles instructed. "Three, drop down to our deck and move starboard. We'll move port and catch the advancing forces on our deck in a cross fire. Then we'll both drop down to Five's deck and pinch those fuckers fore to aft."

"Three copies! Dropping down to your deck and moving starboard!"

"Five is hauling ass back the way we came!"

Telles gestured to his men to follow him as he turned to his left and headed for the ship's port side. "*Two, One, copy?*" he called over his comms as he moved quickly down the corridor. "*Two, One?*"

"*Static charges might be fucking with comms between us and Two, Four, and Six,*" Master Sergeant Jahal commented as they followed the commander.

"*Aurora, Telles, any contact with Two, Four, and Six?*"

"*Telles, Aurora. Negative. You're the only ones we've heard from. Message from Porto Santo. They're regrouping and sending you a few hundred men as quickly as possible.*"

Commander Telles turned the corner, opening fire as the targets on his tactical display came into view. He moved across the intersection, taking cover on the far side. He ducked back for a moment and let at least a dozen shots streak past him, several of which ricocheted off the wall next to his head. Several shots bounced back off the wall opposite him, nearly hitting him as they deflected back across the corridor. "*Fuck!*" He glanced across the intersection at his men, as Private Willette took two ricochets, one in the thigh and the other in his chest armor.

"*You okay, Willette?*" the commander asked as the enemy fire continued to bounce around the corridors.

"*Fucking stings, but I'm still good!*"

"*Stunners?*" Colmeany asked.

"*No good!*" the commander replied. "*Not if they're wearing pressure suits.*"

"*How about a few charges?*" Sergeant Arana suggested.

A shot rebounded off the opposing wall and grazed the commander's helmet, causing him to flinch to the left. "*Fuck! Worth a try!*" He glanced across the intersection as the sergeant started slapping charges together, forming a big ball of explosive material. *"Don't be afraid to be generous, Sergeant!"* Telles yelled.

The sergeant handed the mass of explosives to Master Sergeant Jahal. *"Just roll it down the corridor at them."*

"Would you mind?" the master sergeant asked, looking across the intersection back at the commander.

Telles leaned back out just enough to return fire with a barrage of his own, taking two more glancing blows to his helmet in the process. *"Why the fuck is everyone shooting at my head today?"* he grumbled.

Master Sergeant Jahal reached out and rolled the makeshift ball of explosives down the corridor toward the Jung soldiers. It rolled past the first few men tucked into a doorway, coming to rest in the middle of the spread of enemy troops.

"Fire in the hole," Sergeant Arana announced, a menacing lilt in his voice.

This time, the detonation was not silent. The corridor lit up as brightly as a jump flash, and shook violently as the force of the explosion tore apart the deck, the walls, the ceiling, and the bodies of the Jung soldiers. Smoke and flame shot past the intersection, licking around the corners, threatening to burn everything in its path, including the Ghatazhak. The commander stepped back and turned away, feeling the heat of the blast through both his body armor and his assistive undergarment. He held his position for several seconds, face turned away and back to the blast, waiting until the fireball receded. He peeked cautiously back around the corner. The enemy weapons fire had ceased.

The Frontiers Saga Episode #14: THE WEAK AND THE INNOCENT

"Think you used enough explosives, Arana?"
"You told me to be generous, sir."

* * *

"Jump complete," Commander Ellison reported.

"Whattaya got, Weedge?" Captain Roselle asked.

"Nothing fore or aft," the ensign answered.

"Jump us again," Roselle ordered.

"One light minute, jumping," the commander replied.

"We gotta be ahead of them, Cap," Ensign Marka insisted.

"Jump complete."

"Otherwise we'd pick up their old light," the ensign continued. "If we're ahead of them..."

"I know, they'd be traveling faster than their own light," the captain interrupted. "I had relativistic physics too, Weedge. It ain't the Jung ships I want to find. I want to find what they're looking for."

"Wait," Ensign Marka said. "I'm picking up something. Five hundred kilometers ahead, two to port and four down. It looks like a debris field. Yup, definitely man-made. Something broke up here, sir."

"Take us in closer," Captain Roselle told Commander Ellison, his copilot. "Weedge, send the nav-com the coordinates and feed me your opticals."

"Roger that."

Captain Roselle looked at the screen on his overhead monitor. The image was distant and poorly lit. "I can't tell what the hell that is."

"It's gotta be Scout Three," Ensign Marka insisted. "Same alloys, same composites, there's even a plasma cannon, or at least part of one."

"What about her field generators?" the captain asked. "Are they intact?"

"Wait one," the ensign replied. "There are several larger sections of the hull still intact, but I can't tell what they are yet. We need to move closer. Give me a couple minutes."

Captain Nash groaned, opening his eyes slowly. It was dark, very dark, and it was cold. He could see stars...distant stars, and nearby glimmers of gray. He was inside something... He was floating.

The maintenance crawler. His mind raced, his eyes opening wider in an effort to see what was around him. He tried to see the controls on the panel directly below the forward window, but it was too dark. He looked at the overhead console, finding the main power switch. He flipped it on, but nothing happened. He flipped again and again, but still nothing.

He stopped and thought for a moment. *These things have backup batteries, emergency kits...* He thought back to his training in the cramped little things more than a decade ago. He reached down between his legs, opening the top of the partition and pulling out a small box. He pulled it up and held it in front of his face as he opened it, squinting to see through the darkness. He fumbled around in the small box until he felt something familiar, a small plastic tubule. He pulled it out of its holder and bent it between his thumb and first two fingers until it snapped and began to glow. He shook it for several seconds, intensifying the glow.

Ah, light. Glorious light. He looked inside the case, pulling out several more glow sticks and stuffing them in his pocket for later use. The little sticks would give him about thirty minutes of light each. He used the light to search his control console, looking for something, anything that might help him restore power. He needed electrical power. Without it, he had no heat, no comms, and no idea of how much oxygen he had to breathe. The maintenance crawler had CO_2 scrubbers, but they required power, as did the heaters.

The debris outside suddenly lit up, reflecting a far-off light source. It wasn't from any natural light source, Nash was sure of that. They were too far out from Tau Ceti's sun. It was coming from a ship... *But from whose ship?* He twisted his torso, struggling to look behind him to see where the light was coming from, but he couldn't catch a clear view.

Suddenly, the source of light flew right past him, not more than fifty meters away.

"Hahaaaa!" he cried out triumphantly as he saw Scout Two coast by. He pounded on the window and waved his glow stick, but something was wrong. Their engines were burning at considerable power. They were accelerating, and turning hard, and their laser turrets were rotating to point aft.

Then they began to fire.

Something streaked past him, striking a nearby piece of debris and sending it spinning toward him. "Oh shit! Oh shit! Oh shit!" He braced himself as the wreckage slammed into the maintenance crawler, causing it to tumble and spin at a slow rate. Then he saw them. Four shuttles... Black hulls with broad red bands along prominent edges... And guns, lots of them, all firing at Scout Two as it turned hard to starboard and pitched up, returning fire.

A sick feeling hit Nash in the pit of his stomach as

the maintenance pod continued to rotate and spin. He spotted a large section of the hull, the starboard side, the portion forward of the propulsion section... right where the starboard jump field generator was located. *Oh, God, at least one of them is still intact.*

"Four of them to starboard!" Ensign Marka reported. "They're firing rail guns!" he added as the ship shook from the impacts.

"I kinda figured that much out, Weedge," Captain Roselle said as he brought the ship around. "Garza! Shugart! Target every piece of debris large enough to hold even part of a jump field generator!"

"What about those attack shuttles?" Sergeant Garza replied.

"You let me worry about those fucking shuttles, Flash. You just make sure there's nothing left for them to recover!"

"Plasma cannons are charged and ready!" Lieutenant Oliver reported.

The ship shook violently as more rail gun slugs tore into their outer hull.

"We're venting propellant!" the lieutenant reported. "Starboard side! No fires!"

"I'll have tubes on the first one in five seconds," Captain Roselle assured them. "Be ready with that escape jump, Commander."

"I've got a firing line!" the lieutenant announced.

"Let them have it, Ollie!" the captain ordered.

"Firing forward tubes!" the lieutenant replied.

"Direct hit!" Ensign Marka reported from Scout Two's sensor station. "Target destroyed!"

The ship shook even more violently as rail gun slugs peppered the outside of the scout ship, walking across the hull in multiple directions and creating a deafening rumble.

"Fuck! The other three have got us locked!" Ensign Marka warned.

"Escape jump!" the captain ordered.

"Jumping!" the commander replied. "Jump complete."

"Coming back around," the captain announced. "Gunners, when we jump back in, target the enemy ships first, get them to turn off of us to avoid your fire. When they do, switch to debris and keep blasting away until there's nothing bigger than your fist out there!"

"New jump line is one four seven by two one, by four one," Commander Ellison advised. "Maintain your rate of turn and add four degrees down relative."

"Mas!" the captain barked as he pushed their nose down four degrees and continued turning. "Send word to the Aurora!"

"Our last two jump comm-drones are down, Captain!" the communications tech replied. "They took a beating on that last barrage."

"What about point-to-point?" the captain asked.

"At this distance, it will take at least five minutes for the signal to reach them, sir."

"That'll have to do."

"Jump line in five seconds," the commander said. "Think we can last five minutes?"

"Fuck yeah," Roselle replied confidently.

Captain Nash watched in frustration as three Jung attack shuttles moved into position around his ship's debris field. He twisted and turned, straining to keep his eye on the events around him within the cramped confines of the tumbling maintenance crawler.

A blue-white flash of light appeared in the distance to his right. A few seconds later, two bolts of red-orange plasma energy streaked toward the debris field from the distant speck that was Scout Two. One of the bolts flew past, missing everything, but the second bolt found one of the Jung attack shuttles, landing a direct hit.

"Yes!" Nash cheered in excitement, as secondary explosions from the damaged enemy shuttle finished the job. "Give'm hell, Roselle!" Captain Nash's eyes squinted as brilliant red lights flashed repeatedly from four evenly spaced points on Scout Two's enlarging hull. Pieces of debris exploded into smaller bits. "Oh, fuck," he gasped in horror as he realized Roselle's plan. "No, no, no!"

The remaining two attack shuttles turned and accelerated, firing their rail gun turrets at Scout Two as it turned and jumped away.

"Jesus, I gotta get this thing working!" Nash shouted urgently to himself as he started searching frantically for the cause of the maintenance crawler's lack of electrical power. He continued to glance out the window every now and then, noticing the two shuttles had moved back into the debris field and were approaching one of the larger pieces of rubble. *They're trying to recover a jump field generator,* he realized. *How much did you tell them, Donny?*

Another jump flash, this time from his left. *They're making another attack run,* he realized. Both shuttles began to accelerate and maneuver erratically, as a pair of red-orange bolts of plasma energy streaked by, barely missing them. One of the shuttles opened fire on the approaching scout ship, the other shuttle disappeared as it transitioned into FTL flight. More flashes of bright red light appeared on the hull of the approaching scout ship, and more debris started exploding around him. "No!" he cried out in desperation, fearing that the next bolt of laser energy from Scout Two's turrets would find his crawler and end his struggle to survive. The larger piece of debris, the one containing the starboard jump field generator, exploded into hundreds of smaller pieces. "Yes!" he cried out. *One down, one to go,* he thought as he continued to try and determine the cause of his crawler's electrical failure. He caught a glimpse of the other shuttle coming out of FTL in the distance, entering in from Scout Two's port side. It opened fire as Scout Two turned away. Blue-white light quickly enveloped the scout ship, but it did not jump. Instead, its jump fields flickered sporadically in several places, then faded away without ever flashing.

"NO!"

"Negative on the jump!" Commander Ellison reported.

"Hull breaches! Aft of bulkhead four, topside!" Lieutenant Oliver declared. "Reactors three and four are offline! Reactor two is at half power!"

"Port jump field generator is down!" the commander added.

"Son of a bitch!" Captain Roselle exclaimed as he struggled to control the ship. "I've got no lateral controls!"

"Accelerators on the port drive are fluctuating! I've got to shut her down or the whole damn thing will fry!" Lieutenant Oliver continued.

"They're closing in on us!" Ensign Marka warned. "They're firing!"

The ship lurched to one side, shaking with the impact of the rail gun rounds slamming into their hull.

"They're coming at us from both sides!" Ensign Marka exclaimed. "They're targeting our forward section!"

"I've lost all weapons!" Sergeant Shugart reported.

"Mine are dead, too!" Sergeant Garza added in frustration.

More rail gun rounds smashed into them, reverberating through the hull.

"Breaches, topside!" Lieutenant Oliver reported. "Right above us! Christ! They've taken out our boarding hatch! All pressure in the topside airlock is gone! I'm losing number two reactor!"

"Everyone in ops, head for your tubes and punch out!" Captain Roselle ordered.

"We can still hold her..."

"They're not trying to take us out," Roselle interrupted, "they're trying to *take* us. That's why they're only targeting the forward section now. Kill us and take the prize." Roselle fired his last remaining operational thrusters. "Well, fuck that!"

"What are you doing?" the commander wondered.

"Putting us into a tumbling spin," Roselle replied. "Mas! Send a mayday and then get aft and punch out. That goes for everyone. We're abandoning ship."

"I'll set up the self-destruct on the jump field generators on a one minute delay!" Lieutenant Oliver exclaimed. "Just punch the button on your way aft, Captain!"

"Got it!" Roselle looked over at Commander

Ellison and said in an urgent voice. "Go, Marty, make sure they get out."

The commander looked back at his captain with worry. "You *are* coming, right Gil?"

"Hell yes!" Roselle replied emphatically. "Don't worry, I'm not the *go down with the ship* type."

"Mayday is broadcasting," Ensign Jullen reported. "All channels, omnidirectional. I'm headed aft!"

"*Garza, ejecting!*" the sergeant announced over the comms from his pod.

"*Shugart, ejecting!*"

"*Tucker, punching out!*"

"Self-destruct is set!" Lieutenant Oliver reported. "Head aft!"

Captain Roselle continued adding thrust in an attempt to make his ship's tumbling rotation as wild as possible. More rail gun rounds slammed into them, zigzagging their way across the forward section and midship. *They're targeting midship*, he realized. He added more thrust to make them tumble more end-over-end, making the middle of the ship more difficult to target.

"*Marka, ejecting!*"

More rounds blasted against the ship, nearly knocking Roselle out of his seat. A shrill tearing sound filled his ears, followed by a rush of escaping air. He felt a terrible sucking force, pulling him deeper into his seat. There was an explosion, followed by more shredding noises. He looked down at the self-destruct interface on the center pedestal. He punched the override, canceling the delay timer. "Sorry, guys," he muttered as he pressed the detonation button.

Another explosion. The captain felt himself tossed to one side, his restraints tearing away from the seat. He felt an excruciating pain in his left shoulder. The air continued to be sucked out of the cockpit. There was a loud clang of metal striking metal as the hatch at the back of the cockpit automatically closed and the whoosh of escaping air suddenly stopped. Another explosion caused the cockpit to spin wildly. The artificial gravity ceased to function, and Roselle found himself free-floating, bouncing off the consoles and bulkheads within the wildly spinning cabin. More explosions...rail gun rounds slamming into the hull...his head striking something hard as one last thought echoed in his mind...

At least they won't get my jump drive.

* * *

"I'm barely getting anything from teams Two, Four, and Six," Ensign Souza told the captain. "What little I am getting sounds like a slaughter."

"Us or them?" Nathan wondered.

"Us, sir."

"Play back what you've got."

The overhead speakers crackled with broken, garbled transmissions, filled with bursts of static and the sound of energy weapons fire in the background. *"Four...check...heavy fire...I'm down to...and Lankin! We're...Six! We can't hold...back! Fall...copy? Fu... no way to get back to...hold at...over! ... too many of them! ... Six! Say ag... Six! ... read me? Six! ... Four... contact with Six! ... fall back to..."*

The playback ceased. Nathan looked at Ensign Souza. "Is that it?"

"Yes, sir."

"Sounds to me like they were being overrun," Jessica said.

"How long ago was that transmission?" Nathan asked.

"Two minutes, sir," the ensign replied. "Nothing else since."

Nathan sighed. "Let Telles know that we've lost all contact with the aft teams."

"Yes, sir."

"Captain, if they don't capture engineering and main power..." Jessica began to say.

"...It won't do any good to capture command and control," Nathan finished for her. "I know."

"Multiple contacts!" Mister Navashee reported. "They're launching more attack shuttles, Captain. Four of them, accelerating smartly."

"Comms, order Falcon Four to pursue and engage!"

"*Aurora, Falcon Four copies,*" Loki replied as he punched in a jump.

"Coming to two four seven, three down," Josh announced as he brought the interceptor into a hard left turn and pitched their nose down slightly.

"You read my mind." Loki finished entering the jump coordinates, and then locked in the jump. "Jumping in three......"

"On course and speed," Josh announced.

"Jumping."

The Falcon's canopy became opaque for a moment, protecting them from the brilliant flash of the jump, then cleared a moment later.

"Jump complete," Loki reported. "Four targets,

dead ahead, five hundred meters. Locking missiles on the closest two. Firing two!"

Josh peeked up over his forward console at the two glowing white nozzles on the tails of the missiles as they sped away and quickly disappeared.

"Their mass is changing," Loki added. "They're going to FTL. Remotely detonating lead missile."

"What? Why the hell would…"

A yellow flash of light appeared ahead of them.

"Yes! Impact in three……two……one……"

Another flash of yellow appeared in the distance directly ahead of their flight path, followed by an even bigger flash of yellow, orange, and then red, all of which disappeared a second later.

"What the hell just happened?" Josh asked.

"The EM pulse from the missile detonation fucked up the closest ship's FTL fields!" Loki explained with excitement. "That bought the second missile just enough time to catch him before he could rebuild his fields and slip away."

"Damn," Josh exclaimed. "That's some serious tactical warfare shit right there!"

"*Falcon Four, Aurora. Track and pursue remaining shuttles if possible. Captain wants to know where they're going,*" Ensign Souza ordered over the comms.

"Aurora, Falcon Four, Track and pursue the bad guys. We'll keep you updated," Loki replied. "Parallel their last course and speed, while I dial up a jump."

"Got it."

"At the speed they were going when they went to FTL, if we jump ahead in fifteen light second increments, we should be able to tail them without them ever detecting us."

"Like I said, some serious thinking going on back there."

Loki smiled. "Jumping in three..."

"Sir, Commander Telles indicates he cannot hold his current position for more than a few minutes without reinforcements," Ensign Souza reported. "They've lost team Five, and team One is down to four men. He's suggesting we target the section forward of midship and breach the hull to reduce their numbers."

"That's crazy!" Jessica exclaimed.

"Mister Delaveaga, can you pinpoint the commander's location?" Nathan asked.

"I can narrow it down to a particular section," Luis answered, "but that's as accurate as I can get."

"Do so, and then target the section just forward of it."

"Yes, sir."

"Captain," Jessica began to object.

"I'm not going to open up the section he's in," Nathan said, cutting her off, "that would be crazy. But if we can open up the next section forward, that might prevent more Jung combatants from joining the fight, or at least slow them down."

"Quads are locked on target, Captain," Luis announced.

"Comms, warn the commander we're going to fire on the section forward of them," Nathan ordered.

"Aye, sir."

"Lieutenant, wait thirty seconds, then..."

"Jump flashes! Three... Wait!" Mister Navashee paused a moment. "Make that nine jump flashes.

"Four troop jumpers, two Falcons, and three combat jumpers, sir."

"Hold your fire!" Nathan ordered.

"Holding fire," Luis acknowledged.

"Troop jumpers are carrying breach boxes on their backsides," Mister Navashee added.

"That must be what took them so long," Jessica commented.

"Ensign Souza, inform Commander Telles that his reinforcements are moving into position now."

"Yes, sir!"

Nathan smiled at Jessica and breathed a sigh of relief. "I was getting a bit worried."

"More contacts!" Mister Navashee warned. "Christ, there are dozens of them! They're launching fighters, Captain! A lot of them!"

"Lieutenant! Point-defenses! Target those fighters!"

"Aye, sir!" Luis replied.

"Comms! Order all friendlies to remain inside our defense perimeter, or jump clear and hold!"

"Captain!" Mister Navashee called, "half the fighters are leaving at top speed! They're departing on the same course as the attack shuttles!"

"Those fighters can't go to FTL, can they?"

"No, sir, not that we've ever seen, at least."

"Firing point-defenses," Luis announced.

"Captain! Incoming Mayday from Scout Two!" Ensign Souza reported. "They found Scout Three's wreckage, including two intact jump field generators. So did the Jung. They're trying to recover them. Scout Two engaged and destroyed one, possibly two fast attack shuttles, but they took heavy damage and had to abandon ship."

"Were there any survivors?" Jessica asked, urgency and desperation in her voice.

"Did they self-destruct?" Nathan asked in an equally worried tone.

"They didn't say."

"Falcon Four is headed for a hornet's nest," Jessica realized.

"Did Scout Two give a location?" Nathan demanded.

"Yes, sir," Ensign Souza replied.

"Feed it to those Falcons and tell them to back up Falcon Four," Nathan ordered. "Hell, send the combat jumpers as well. Tell them to make sure the Jung do not get away with any wreckage!"

"What about sending Scout One?" Jessica suggested. "She's got plasma cannons big enough to take those shuttles out with a single shot, right?"

"No good," Nathan shook his head. "Besides us, Scout One is the only other ship that can launch that last KKV, and if that battleship manages to restore main power and raise her shields, we're going to need it."

"Four more contacts!" Mister Navashee announced. "They're launching more attack shuttles!"

"Goddamn!" Nathan cursed. "For a ship without power, they sure are launching a lot of spacecraft!" Nathan turned aft. "Luis! Target their starboard launch tubes and close them up! Comms, tell the troop jumpers to jump to a safe distance and hold."

"Quads locked on their starboard launch tubes," Luis reported. "Firing!"

"What are you doing?" Jessica wondered.

"They're going to sacrifice their ship in order to keep us occupied so they can get a jump drive,"

Nathan explained as he turned forward. "Helm, move us under them and over to their port side, nice and smooth. Lieutenant, take out their shuttle bays next, then their port launch tubes."

"Moving under and to port," Mister Chiles acknowledged as he pushed the Aurora's flight control stick forward and began to nose the ship down.

"Starboard launch tubes destroyed," Luis said. "Preparing to target her ventral shuttle bays."

"Troop shuttles have jumped away," Mister Navashee reported.

"Moving under the target now," Mister Chiles announced.

"Firing quads," Luis reported.

"Keep our topside toward the target as we come around," Nathan instructed. "Don't stop until we're directly over her topside, and stand off inverted about fifty meters away."

Mister Chiles looked to his left, exchanging concerned glances with the navigator, Mister Riley. "Aye, sir."

"After you take out the port launch tubes, we'll move into position above them and create a shield for the troop jumpers. With us acting like an umbrella, those fighters will have no choice but to try and attack from the sides."

"And we'll nail them with our point-defenses," Luis realized, a grin forming on his face. "Nice."

"Comms, let those troop jumpers know what we're up to and tell them to be ready. They're going to have to jump into a very narrow space, very quickly."

"Port launch tubes destroyed," Luis announced.

"Captain, Commander Telles reports he is down to six men total!" Ensign Souza warned.

"Tell him to fall back to a safe position," Nathan replied. "In a few minutes, he'll have eighty men on his side."

"I'll have to coordinate defensive fire with their jumps," Luis explained, "so they don't jump through a field of fire."

"Comms, tie the lieutenant into the troop jumpers directly," Nathan ordered.

"Aye, sir."

"Two each, fore and aft of the breach," Nathan added.

"Yes, sir," Luis replied.

"We're in position directly over their midship, Captain," Mister Chiles called back over his shoulder. "Fifty meters above, topside to topside."

"Point-defenses are ready," Luis announced.

"Troop jumpers report ready," Ensign Souza added. "Patching you into their channel now," he informed Lieutenant Delaveaga. "Call signs are Packers One through Four."

"Laying down defensive fire now," the lieutenant announced as his fingers danced across his console. He paused and keyed his comm-set. "Aurora Tactical to all troop jumpers. You'll jump in pairs on my mark. Odds will jump forward of the breach, evens will jump aft. First group jump in as far fore and aft as possible while still staying between us and the target. Second group jump in close to the breach." Luis turned to call over his shoulder to Ensign Souza. "Souza, update the commander on the plan, tell him we execute in thirty seconds," he instructed as he waited for the four troop jumpers to acknowledge his message.

"You got it."

"Defensive fields of fire established," Luis announced.

"Comms, dispatch a comm-jumper and tell Scout One to set the last KKV for snap launch and then join us here, but at a safe range," Nathan ordered. He looked at Jessica, trying to interpret her facial expression, or lack thereof. He had never before seen her look this upset... Angry, yes, but never despondent and defeated like this. "Jess," he said under his breath, "he may have gotten out in time. There were still a couple pods left."

Jessica cast him a disapproving look. "Don't blow smoke up my ass, Nathan," she snapped quietly at him. "If he's dead, he's dead. Just make sure he didn't die in vain."

"It's working," Mister Navashee reported. "The fighters are attacking our ventral side to avoid our guns."

"Packers One and Two, Aurora Tactical," Luis called over the comms. "Jump in five......four......three..." he pressed a button on his tactical console to cease firing on all point-defenses. "...Ceasing fire...one......jump."

Nathan and Jessica watched the main view screen as a blue-white flash of light appeared between the Aurora and the upside-down battleship fifty meters above her.

"Resuming fire," Luis announced as he reactivated the Aurora's point-defense turrets. "Packers Three and Four, be ready to jump on my call."

Nathan continued to watch as the troop jumper quickly rolled over and maneuvered upward toward the hull of the enemy ship, expertly placing the breach box attached to his stern over a clear section of the ship's hull.

"*Packer One, contact. Breaching now.*"

"*Packer Two, ditto.*"

"Jesus, I'm having a hard time tracking all these fighters and still maintaining a good perimeter to protect the troop jumpers," Luis admitted.

"Jess, give him a hand," Nathan urged.

Jessica quickly moved back to the tactical console, relieved to have something to keep her busy. "You take port and I'll take starboard?" she suggested as she stepped in beside the lieutenant.

"Gladly," Luis replied as he moved over to make room for her. "Packers Three and Four, jump in five......four......three...holding fire..."

Jessica's hands went up off the console, demonstrating that she was not currently firing any weapons.

"...one......jump." He looked up at the view screen briefly as another troop jumper appeared from behind a blue-white flash, even closer to them than the previous one. "Resuming fire," he announced as both he and Jessica reactivated their respective weapons.

"*Packer One, deploying troops.*"

"Enemy fighter count is down to thirty-seven," Mister Navashee reported.

"Yes!" Jessica cheered. "Make that thirty-six!"

"How about thirty-five," Luis added.

"Nice."

"Jump flash," Mister Navashee reported. "Scout One, three hundred kilometers to our port side."

"*Packer Two, deploying troops.*"

"*Packer Three, contact. Breaching now.*"

"Scout One reports the last KKV is ready to snap launch," Ensign Souza reported.

"Very well," Nathan replied. "Tell them to jump out and launch the KKV without delay if that battleship gets main power back on line."

"Aye, sir."

"*Packer One, troops away, disengaging.*"

"*Packer Four, contact. Breaching now.*"

"Packer One, exit target aft, left of centerline, and jump clear," Luis ordered as he temporarily stopped firing with his forward turrets to starboard of the Aurora's centerline.

"*Packer One, exiting target aft, left of centerline. We'll reload and return.*"

"Comms, tell all Packers to jump in at a safe distance and do not approach unless cleared by site command," Nathan warned. "We may not be back by the time they return."

"Yes, sir."

"*Packer Two, we're empty. Disengaging.*"

"Two, exit target forward, right of centerline," Luis ordered. "Hold on your aft turrets," he told Jessica.

"I got it."

"*Packer One, jumping.*"

"*Packer Two, exiting target forward, right of center.*"

"*Packer Three deploying troops.*"

"Four fighters are grouping for a run at midship, target's port side," Mister Navashee warned.

"I've got them," Jessica assured them. "Cover my part of the bow with number seven so I can get extra guns on these fuckers," she told the lieutenant.

"Got it. Feel free to use the quads, if you'd like."

"*Packer Four, deploying troops.*"

"I like your thinking, Lieutenant," Jessica said as she brought the starboard quad rail gun online and swung it toward the target. "I'll just set it for a tight repetitive sweep...and...damn! That fucked them up, didn't it!"

"Packer Three is empty, disengaging."

"Three, exit direct target port," Luis instructed.

"Packer Three, exiting to target port."

"Dropping fire, starboard midship," Jessica announced.

"Three fighters coming over ventral from our port to starboard!" Mister Navashee warned urgently. "Midship line!"

"Packer Three! Nose down on exit!" Luis warned. "Three bandits coming over the top on your six!"

"They're going to get him!" Mister Navashee declared.

"Packer Three!" Luis yelled over the comms. "Jump, jump, jump!"

"He's jumping!" Mister Navashee exclaimed. "I think he made it. Yes, I've got him! Two hundred kilometers below and to starboard!"

"Packer Three is clear," the pilot reported from his new position clear of the danger. *"Y'all are too easily excited."*

Luis looked at Jessica. "Since when do Corinari pilots use *y'all*?"

"That's probably my fault," Jessica admitted as she continued firing.

* * *

Captain Nash continued to struggle within the confines of the maintenance crawler, straining to track the action occurring all around him. Falcons and combat jump shuttles jumped in and out of the area, both close in and further away, appearing and disappearing behind flashes of blue-white light. They hammered away at the enemy ships as they fought to keep them from picking through Scout Three's debris field at their leisure. Somewhere in that field there was at least one, possibly two, jump field generators, and the Jung wanted them badly.

As best he could tell, a combat jumper and a Falcon had already fallen victim to enemy fire, as had at least five Jung ships. But the chaos and explosions of enemy weapons fire had sent debris scattering in all directions, which all seemed to fly in the direction of Nash's fragile lifeboat. One of the crawler's legs had already been torn off by one of the impacts, as well as two of the mini-arms on the front of the unit. So far, he had been lucky, in that none of the debris had struck his windows, but he feared his luck would not hold out much longer. One inopportune strike...

He tried not to think about the danger he was in. In fact, he had already resigned himself to the fact that he would not survive. Instead, he tried to keep track of the activity around him, keeping score, so to speak, for what little good it would do him. He kept telling himself that he had to keep track of the two sections of wreckage that he believed still contained intact jump field generators, on the off chance that he *were* rescued.

A jump flash went off no more than ten meters away from him, above and to his right. Despite its silent entrance into his immediate area, the intensity of the flash at such close proximity startled him, causing him to duck instinctively. Had he been looking in the direction of the flash at the moment it had occurred, he would have an entirely new problem to deal with.

It was a Falcon, and it passed right over him at what seemed like incredible speed, although he was sure that to its pilot it was just the opposite. The interceptor fired weapons, both wing and nose turret plasma cannons. Two missiles dropped on rails protruding from the interceptor's open weapons bays, streaking away on fiery tails, a second after which the ship disappeared in another blinding flash of light.

Nash squinted his eyes tight as the interceptor jumped away, opening them just in time to see one of the departed Falcon's missiles destroy a Jung shuttle in a blaze of yellow light. The second missile turned sharply, following another shuttle that was attempting to evade attack, but they were unsuccessful. They too, disappeared behind the yellow flash of the missile's warhead.

"Damn!" the captain exclaimed, the excitement of what he had just witnessed causing him to forget the danger he was in. The entire scene was an almost ethereal spectacle to behold. Fighters and shuttles, dancing about in absolute silence, the only sound that of his own rapid, labored breathing. Examples of the ultimate in man's technology, flashing in and out of existence, as they tried to destroy one another. It was almost sad, in a way.

Another flash, much larger than anything he had yet seen, despite the fact that it was further away than the rest, interrupted his thoughts. "HELL YEAH!" he yelled at the top of his lungs, as he recognized the curved lines of the Aurora.

"Jump complete!" Mister Navashee announced from the Aurora's sensor station. "Multiple targets! I count six attack shuttles and twenty-three fighters!"

"Zoom in on Scout Three's wreckage," Nathan ordered. The view screen faded out briefly, then back in with a close-up view of the debris field and the Jung shuttles moving about within it. "Jesus," he muttered. "Mister Navashee, can you identify those sections? Can you tell which ones might have jump field generators in them?"

"Working on it now!"

"Tactical, target your fire on any enemy ships nosing around that wreckage, first," Nathan ordered. "How many Falcons do we have left?"

"I'm picking up two Falcons and two combat jumpers!" Luis replied.

"Comms, tell the combat jumpers to move to a safe distance and hold for now. Order the Falcons to concentrate on the outlying fighters so they don't get tangled up in our fields of fire."

"Aye, sir."

"Targeting bandits within the debris field!" Luis announced.

"I'll target fighters near us," Jessica told him.

Nathan continued to watch the view screen. "Helm, take us in close to that wreckage and pull us in underneath. I want to force them to come in from our dorsal side where we can keep the most guns on them."

"Taking us in close and under," Mister Chiles replied.

"I've got the port forward section," Mister Navashee reported. "Enough of it is intact that the port jump field generator is probably intact."

"Lieutenant, target that piece of debris and

take it out!" Nathan ordered urgently. "I don't want anything bigger than a pebble left out there! Hell, target everything that looks even remotely interesting!"

"Captain," Jessica objected, "what about survivors?"

"Mister Navashee, are you picking up any life signs, any escape pods?"

"Negative, sir, but between the residual static charges left over from Scout Three's last jump, and all the weapons fire around, someone could be standing on a piece of hull waving a flag and I could miss it."

"Are you sure about that port section?"

"Yes, sir," Mister Navashee assured him. "The silhouette matches, and there are no pressurized spaces within that section of a scout ship." He turned and looked at the captain. "There's no way anyone could be inside that piece of wreckage."

"Tactical, take it out," Nathan ordered.

"Targeting the wreckage with the port plasma cannon," Luis replied. "Locked on... Firing."

Bright, red-orange bolts of energy fired from the Aurora's midship plasma cannon, not more than a few hundred meters away from Captain Nash. The bolts slammed into the largest piece of wreckage left over from the propulsion section of Scout Three, blowing it apart. Debris spread out along an angle opposite the Aurora's plasma fire, slamming into pieces of wreckage further away, sending them ricocheting in different directions like an out-of-control cosmic billiard game. Like drops of rain tapping on a porch roof, tiny pieces of debris bounced off the hull of the captain's crawler-turned-lifeboat...turned coffin.

Something caught the captain's eye. A faint sparkle of light, repeating over and over... Something spinning, coming toward him...growing larger.

Captain Nash flinched as a spinning piece of debris the size of a man's head smacked into his left window, causing it to crack. "Oh, shit," he said out loud. The crack began to spread, little-by-little. "No, no, no!" He glanced at the backup mechanical pressure gauge and found it was dropping. He was leaking precious oxygen into space. "Fuck!" he exclaimed as he started fumbling around, looking for some way to signal the Aurora. "Jesus! She's right there!" he exclaimed in frustration. His salvation was not even a kilometer away, and yet he had no way to get their attention, no way to let them know that he was alive...at least for a few more minutes.

"Target destroyed," Luis reported.

"That's eight down," Jessica announced as she continued to target the attacking Jung fighters.

"Two Jung shuttles are leaving the debris field!" Mister Navashee warned.

"Target the fleeing shuttles and fire!" Nathan ordered.

"Targeting!" Luis replied. "Firing!"

"One down, one went to FTL!" Mister Navashee reported.

Nathan exchanged concerned glances with Jessica and Luis. "Comms, order one of the Falcons to pursue the fleeing shuttle and take it out."

"Yes, sir," Ensign Souza acknowledged.

"Keep scanning that debris field, Mister

Navashee," Nathan continued. "I need to know where that starboard jump field generator is."

"Yes, sir," Mister Navashee replied.

"That's twelve down," Jessica reported. "The remainder are breaking off," she added. "They're bugging out."

"To where?" Nathan wondered.

"Based on their course, I'd say they're headed for Kohara," Luis replied.

"Captain," Ensign Souza called from the communications station. "Combat One Five reports they've located Scout Two's debris field. They've also picked up transponders from four escape pods!"

"How much debris?" Nathan asked.

"A couple of larger sections," the ensign replied. "Nothing from the drive section, a few pieces from the forward section, including part of the forward cabin, with one survivor inside."

"Launch Bulldog Six to recover the escape pods, and send a SAR shuttle for that guy in the wreckage." He looked at Luis. "It's gotta be Roselle." His eyes shifted to Jessica. He could tell by her expression that she was trying not to get her hopes up from the news of the survivors.

"Captain!" Mister Navashee exclaimed. "Something strange in Scout Three's wreckage! Something moving!"

"Moving? Moving how?" Nathan asked.

The main view screen shifted, moving over and zooming in on a rather mangled looking object.

"Is that a crawler?" Luis wondered.

The screen zoomed in further.

"I think you're right," Nathan said.

"The arms are moving," Jessica realized.

The screen zoomed in even closer. The pair of arms

that the operator would use in order to manipulate objects outside of the crawler during exterior repairs were waving back and forth frantically. The screen zoomed in even closer still, revealing a man, animated and looking slightly panicked, with dried blood on his face and in his matted hair.

Jessica gasped. "It's Robert!"

"Is that a crack in his window?" Luis asked.

"He's losing pressure," Mister Navashee warned. "He's got maybe five minutes of air left in that thing."

"Ensign Souza, redirect Bulldog Six to recover that crawler and Captain Nash, ASAP."

"Yes, sir," Ensign Souza replied.

"Mister Riley," Nathan continued, "perhaps you can hit that crawler with one of our spotlights, and maybe flash our running lights, so Captain Nash knows we see him."

"Yes, sir!" Mister Riley acknowledged gladly.

Nathan watched as first one, then a second spotlight swung over to illuminate the mangled crawler. He could clearly see the expression on Captain Nash's face transform from desperation to joy, as he realized help was finally on its way.

Nathan turned around to face Jessica. "You're right, you Nash's *are* hard to kill."

Jessica smiled.

The cargo shuttle's crew chief and the two rescue technicians dragged the mangled crawler into the back of the shuttle's cargo bay, its mechanical arms scraping against the sides of the bay.

"*Closing cargo door,*" the copilot called out over the comms.

"*Bring the gravity up slowly!*" the crew chief called

over his helmet comms, *"and start the repress cycle, quick! He's almost out of air!"*

Three men in pressure suits guided the damaged crawler to the floor as the slowly increasing gravity pulled them all toward the deck. The hiss of pressurized air filled the cargo bay as the pressure slowly returned, now that the cargo door at the aft end of the shuttle was fully closed.

With the crawler now resting against the deck on its backside, the crew chief climbed up onto its face to access the front of the crawler's canopy. *"Pull that lever on your side down and twist to unlock the emergency canopy release!"* he ordered.

"We're not fully pressurized yet, Chief," the copilot warned over the comms.

"We've got more pressure than he does!" the chief argued. *"Do it!"* he ordered as he did the same on the other side. The canopy released its lock along all four sides, allowing the entire section surrounding the captain's head to fall backward onto the deck.

"Get the O2 on him!" the chief ordered.

One of the rescue technicians handed the other one, nearest the head of the crawler, an oxygen mask connected to a long feed line. The second rescue technician placed the mask onto the captain's face.

Captain Nash was pale, his lips blue from lack of oxygen. He looked like he'd been through hell, with dried blood all over his face and hair, his uniform soaked with sweat, lubricants, and whatever else he had come into contact with during his escape.

And he wasn't moving.

"We've got to get him out of there," one of the rescue technicians said.

"Grab the power wrench out of the tool cabinet on your side," the lead rescue technician instructed

the crew chief. *"Start removing the bolts along your side so we can remove the front arm assembly. That should give us enough room to get him out safely."*

"Can't we just pull him out the top?" the crew chief asked.

"No way. We don't know what injuries he has, yet."

"Pressure at seventy percent," the copilot announced.

Captain Nash's eyes started to flutter.

"He's coming around!" the second rescue technician shouted.

Both the crew chief and the lead rescue technician quickly removed their helmets, tossing them aside.

"Captain Nash!" the lead rescue technician yelled. "Sir, can you hear me? Are you all right?"

Nash opened his eyes, looking at the faces of his rescuers. "No, I'm pretty sure I'm not."

"Where do you hurt, sir?"

"Everywhere," Captain Nash replied. "Just get me out of this thing, will you?"

* * *

The sound of energy weapons fire, from both friend and foe, filled the corridor. Bolts of energy—reds, oranges, yellows, and ambers—ricocheted off the walls at oblique angles. Explosions echoed as every charge eventually struck something directly, blowing it apart. The walls were blood-stained, the decks littered with corpses—some in full battle armor, others in basic Jung uniforms.

Ghatazhak forces continued to advance down the main central corridor toward the battleship's command and control center. They fired as they sprinted forward, braving the incoming enemy fire that by now was mostly from small arms instead of the heavier, more powerful rifles used by their security forces.

As the commander had hoped, the influx of now more than one hundred and fifty Ghatazhak soldiers had caused the defenders to split their forces into multiple fronts, thus weakening them across the board. Now, with another eighty of his men about to join the battle, the tide was rapidly turning.

Familiar red-orange bolts of energy assaulted the force the commander faced from their rear. The enemy, mostly armed officers and technicians, was forced to defend in all directions as Ghatazhak troops advanced on them from all sides.

Commander Telles charged forward, followed closely by his trusted friend and right-hand man, Master Sergeant Jahal. He moved with effortless grace, leaping over the dead and the dying, firing his rifle with pinpoint accuracy as each target presented itself.

The eyes of the enemy widened as they realized their moment had come. Live or die, they would do so with honor. The senior of them met the challenge, his battle cry loud and confident as he charged headlong into the advancing Ghatazhak forces. His men followed, emboldened by their leader's confidence. The ones at the front of the charge were the first to fall, as were the ones at the rear, as more Ghatazhak forces attacked from the opposite end of the corridor. Those in the middle clashed with the commander and his men. Both sides fired at point blank range, then began swinging their weapons like clubs as the opposing forces collided.

With guns, the Jung officers and technicians

had a chance. In hand-to-hand combat, they had none. The Ghatazhak cut them down with ease, killing everyone they saw, even those dropping their weapons and throwing up their hands in defeat.

The Ghatazhak were not interested in surrender. They were in a killing frenzy, one that could only be brought on by the brutality of war, the death of comrades, and the taste of imminent victory. The commander and his men had suffered the humility of retreat earlier that day, and they had no intention of ever tasting it again. This battle would be theirs for the taking.

Commander Telles was the first through the entrance to the command and control center. He quickly fired seven shots, each of them striking an enemy that was making threatening movements. He continued forward toward the center of the room as his men followed behind him and spread out in all directions. More weapons fire was exchanged, as a few brave Jung officers attempted to mount one last defense of their ship, but the commander's men, their determination intensified by the rage of combat, were not about to allow it.

Commander Telles continued walking forward, dropping his rifle to let it dangle at his side. He pulled out his sidearm and pointed it at the cluster of Jung officers at the center of the room. "This ship is now the property of the Alliance!" the commander yelled, his tone that of absolute confidence and authority over the situation. "You are all my prisoners! Cooperate, and your lives shall be spared! Refuse, and you shall most assuredly die!"

A senior Jung officer at the center of the group, one who appeared to be the captain of the vessel, responded in vile fashion. His tone was seething with disdain, as he responded in Jung.

Commander Telles fired a single shot directly into the officer's forehead, blowing the entire top of his head away and sending the man's brains across the faces of the officers clustered around him. "I'll take that as a refusal, then."

"Commander," the master sergeant called. "We are still engaged on multiple decks."

Commander Telles pointed his weapon at the next officer. "Order your forces to surrender." The officer said nothing. He turned to the next man, giving the same order, but was met with the same stoic face. One by one, he gave each of them the opportunity to live, and each of them bravely refused.

"I am impressed," the commander said after killing the last officer in the group. He turned to Master Sergeant Jahal. "Have we captured main power and engineering?"

"Yes, moments ago."

"Good. Have all our men button up and go to suit air. Then find the damage control station and start venting every compartment where resistance is still in progress. Lock down everything else, and shut down all environmental systems. Those who do not surrender will suffocate."

"Sir?" the master sergeant replied. He was not questioning his commander's orders, rather, his tone was meant to verify that the commander was certain about his decision. It was a subtlety that only a friend could get away with.

"Enough Ghatazhak blood has been shed today," the commander replied. He turned and looked at his friend. "Not a drop more."

* * *

Naralena stared at the view screen in disbelief.

She had watched the entire invasion from the safety of her and Jessica's quarters at the Cetian Liberation Army's underground facility just outside of Kohara's capital city of Cetia.

The door burst open, and Gerard and two armed men entered the room in hurried fashion. "We must go," he told Naralena as he grabbed her jacket from the bed and handed it to her.

"Have you heard what's going on out there?" she exclaimed, pointing at the view screen.

"Yes, on the way in," Gerard replied. "Quickly..."

"Is it true?" Naralena asked. "Did the Ghatazhak really withdraw?"

"Yes, which is why we must leave, now," Gerard pleaded. "They will be searching for us...all of us."

"They left me behind?"

"They will come back for us," Gerard told her as he grabbed her arm and pulled her up from her chair. "The commander promised me as much."

"What commander?"

Gerard shook his head, "Tells? I think that was his name."

"Commander Telles...light brown hair, dark eyes, never smiles?"

"Yes, yes, yes. That was the one, quickly."

"Where are we going?" Naralena asked as she followed them out the door.

"As far from the city as possible," Gerard replied. "Into the wilderness. We have a place... Several of them, actually. We will disperse and hide for now, but we will need to change our appearance."

"How are we supposed to change our appearance?" Naralena wondered.

Gerard looked back, noting Naralena's long, dark hair. "How attached are you to all that hair?"

CHAPTER FOUR

"This can wait," Yanni whispered to Deliza as they continued down the corridor toward the conference room.

"You don't have to whisper," Deliza remarked. "These men are bodyguards, not spies."

"I'm just saying, a lot has happened in the last twenty-four hours. It might be better to wait a few days before making big decisions."

"I am not a child, Yanni."

"I was not implying such, and you know it."

"Mister Hiller does make a valid point, Princess," Captain Navarro chimed in from behind. "Good business decisions are never made while in an emotional state."

"I am not in an *emotional state*," she retorted, taking offense to his words. "As matter of fact, the two of you risk putting me into such a state with your chauvinistic attempts to placate."

"Forgive me, Princess..."

Deliza stopped dead in her tracks, turning to face him. "...And stop calling me 'Princess'," she demanded in hushed tones. She took a deep breath, pulling at the bottom of her tunic to smooth out its fit across the front of her torso. "The title no longer applies. Please, refer to me as 'Deliza', or 'Miss Ta'Akar'."

"As you wish," the captain agreed. Deliza turned away and continued on. Captain Navarro exchanged a knowing glance with Yanni, as they followed her down the corridor and entered the conference room at the end.

The room was well decorated, with the dark woods that were common in the halls of Corinairan business offices. An entire side of the room looked out over the city below, the glass so clear that one felt the overwhelming desire to reach out and touch it to confirm it was actually there.

"We've come a long way, haven't we?" Mister Lammond said as he entered the conference room from a side door. He walked up next to Deliza, joining her to look out at the city. "Hard to believe it's only been a year since your father and Captain Scott liberated us from the rule of Caius."

"It is a testament to Corinairan tenacity," Deliza replied as she stared out at the distant horizon.

"We were all deeply saddened by the news of your father's passing," Mister Lammond assured her in placating tones. "He was truly a great man. We have lobbied to make him a place among our Walk of Heroes. We expect no opposition from Parliament."

"Funny, since he was once considered an outlaw on your world." Deliza took a deep breath, pulling herself out of her brief melancholy and turning toward Mister Lammond. "If you truly wish to honor my father, you may do so by honoring your business arrangements with his house, through his heirs, of which I am the last."

"Of course, of course. Such has always been our intent." Mister Lammond turned and gestured toward the conference table as the other three partners, as well as their legal counsel, entered the room and took their seats. "I assume that you know the members of the partnership?"

"I have read the brief that you so generously prepared for me," Deliza replied. "Gentlemen," she added, nodding respectfully to the others in attendance. Deliza was born and raised on Haven, a world where men and women were equal in all ways. Then, she was thrust into the role of princess on a world where the power that women held was from behind the protection of the men in their family. Now, she was on a world where men and women were again equal, yet the women allowed the men to run the businesses and the government, while they pursued matters of science, technology, and art. All things said, she was more at home here than she had been on Takara. "May I introduce Captain Navarro, and Yanni Hiller."

"Gentlemen, a pleasure," Mister Lammond said in curt fashion as he sat down. "I am quite sure that I was not the only one among us to be surprised by your sudden appearance on our world," Mister Lammond explained, "let alone your request to meet."

"I felt it prudent to deal with matters at hand in timely fashion," Deliza explained.

"And what matters might those be?"

Deliza sensed Mister Lammond's apprehension and found it odd. "To ensure that revenue earned by my family's interest in this partnership continues to serve the interests of the Alliance. It *was* the primary reason my father formed this business arrangement, was it not?"

"Indeed it was," Mister Lammond agreed.

"So, naturally, it troubles me that his financial records show an indebtedness to all of you."

"A minor matter," Mister Lammond assured her. "The antimatter cores that your father purchased on behalf of the Alliance were quite expensive, as was their shipping and handling. Antimatter is rather finicky stuff..."

"I am aware of the safety precautions involved in the handling of antimatter, Mister Lammond," Deliza interrupted, irritated by his patronizing tone.

"Yes, of course."

"I trust that the antimatter *was* acquired and is en route to Sol?"

"Indeed. It should arrive within the week."

"According to my calculations, the balance sheet after the transactions, although lower than usual, was still positive *after* the purchase," Deliza stated.

"Yes. However, your father also requested that we procure as many Morquar BE729 engines as possible, as well the Conklin RT175B maneuvering thrusters."

"Both are rather antiquated and should be easy to find," Deliza surmised.

"Yes, but in the *volume* your father wished to purchase them, there were additional risks involved."

"Risks?"

"I believe your father was concerned that should he buy them in smaller batches, as funds became available, that someone *else* in the business of buying and selling such merchandise *might* take notice of the sudden demand and start buying it themselves, positioning themselves as a middleman in the hopes of driving up prices to make a profit," Mister Lammond explained. "The partnership agreed to cover the debt until such time as Casimir's portion of future propellant sales could repay that debt, with interest, of course. Unfortunately, no formal agreement had been reached."

"One moment," Deliza said. She leaned in toward Captain Navarro.

The captain pressed the privacy button built into the edge of the conference table in front of him, enveloping himself, Deliza, and Mister Hiller in a slightly opaque, soundproof field that separated them from the rest of the partners.

"Do you know anything about these purchases?" Deliza asked.

"I believe these items were to be used to drive jump-enabled fast-attack gunships," Captain Navarro explained. "They have been building an assembly line on Tanna for more than a month now, and they expect to start production soon. Admiral Dumar considers these gunships to be vital to the Alliance."

"I assume the items have already shipped."

"Indeed they have," Captain Navarro confirmed, "weeks ago. In fact, they have probably already been delivered."

"Then I suppose we shall have to pay for them," Deliza said, sitting up straight again.

Captain Navarro deactivated the sound suppression field, which dissolved from view.

Deliza looked directly at Mister Lammond. "What were the terms that you and my father discussed?"

"As you know, the profit split has always been fifty percent to your family, and fifty percent to be divided among the remaining partners. Your father offered to alter the profit split of the next four shipments of propellant to seventy-five twenty-five, thus giving up half of his profits over the next four shipments."

Deliza raised her eyebrow in doubt at the specifics of the deal. "Based on the sales reports of the most recent shipments, that appears to be a quite lucrative arrangement, for you and your partners, that is."

"Your father had always understood that the partnership takes considerable risk of retribution in other markets by the nobles for our support of Casimir's legal, yet somewhat clandestine business operations. Because of that, he has never begrudged us a profit."

"Perhaps," Deliza said. "However, I am not my father, and I do not consider the *risks* that you claim to be taking *worthy* of that level of compensation."

Mister Lammond and his partners appeared to be unfazed by Deliza's implied accusations. "I assume you have an offer you would like us to entertain?"

"Two shipments, at seventy-five twenty-five," Deliza replied firmly, her voice suggesting it was not open for negotiation. "That will still leave you plenty of profit in exchange for your so called *risks*."

"And if the market should change over the next few months, that margin may be insufficient. I see no reason why we should be expected to risk taking a loss simply because the Alliance's *needs* were greater than their benefactor's holdings." Mister Lammond waved his hand in dismissal. "I'm afraid we couldn't entertain anything less than three loads, unless of course you wanted to decrease your percentage, or float it on a market-based margin."

Deliza remained expressionless as she locked eyes with the elderly businessman. "Or, I could order Captain Navarro to jump the Avendahl to Sol, thus negating the need to build gunships, and allowing the Alliance to refuse delivery. I'm sure you can get your money back by selling those engines yourself.

It may take some time, but as you said, there are risks."

Mister Lammond laughed. "You would be in breach of contract."

"You had no formal agreement with my father regarding the repayment of this loan, and even if you did, how would you enforce it? By arresting me? By filing a civil action?" Deliza glanced at the four security guards from the Avendahl, standing outside the conference room as her protectors, as if to make a point.

"You and your Alliance *need* the revenue from the sales of propellant to fund your campaigns…"

"I'm sure I can find someone else to whom I can sell propellant. Perhaps the Paleans, or the Haven Syndicate?"

"Do you really think it wise to make idle threats, young lady?"

"I make no threats, Mister Lammond. I simply state facts."

"We have no need of the Avendahl's protection," Mister Lammond insisted, waving his hand in dismissal. "The nobles would never attack Corinair…"

"You're speaking of the very men who just hired Ybaran Legions to assassinate the leader of their world and start a civil war," Captain Navarro interjected. "Those are the men you trust not to attack you?"

Deliza politely motioned for the captain to be silent as she continued to speak. "The people of Corinair pledged their support for the Alliance. You are free to dictate the prices of the goods you export to Takara *because* of the Alliance."

"Surely you would not deny us a small profit," Mister Lammond protested.

"No, I would not. But you sir, think you can take advantage of a young woman in her time of mourning, which I find rather objectionable." Deliza rose to leave. "In fact, I see no reason to remain here and be insulted by a bunch of fat, pompous, old men."

Mister Lammond's eyes widened as Deliza headed for the door. He looked to his partners, their faces plastered with the same shocked facial expression. "Please, please..."

Captain Navarro looked at Yanni and rose to follow Deliza out of the conference room.

"Two and a half shipments," Mister Lammond offered. Deliza continued toward the exit with Captain Navarro and Yanni following. "Fine! Two shipments!" he exclaimed in frustration.

Deliza paused, then turned her head to look at Mister Lammond, this time with unveiled disdain in her eyes. "One shipment."

"One and a half? At eighty-twenty?"

Deliza paused for a moment, her stare unwavering. "Agreed. Write it up and send it to my local counsel for approval. If it passes his inspection, you will have my confirmation within the day."

Mister Lammond leaned forward in his chair, his arms on the table. "Your father would have been proud."

Deliza said nothing as she exited the room, fighting the smile of triumph that already threatened to form on her lips.

"Interesting negotiating style," Captain Navarro commented as they headed down the corridor toward the exit. "Although, I probably would have left out the 'fat' part, as only one of them fit the description. Might I inquire as to where you picked up such bargaining skills?"

"In the street markets on Haven," Deliza replied, finally allowing herself to smile.

* * *

"I apologize for the delay, Miss Mun," Admiral Dumar said as he led Jessica, Kata, and Karahl into a spare office at the Ghatazhak base on Porto Santo Island. "I could not get away any sooner, and we had to wait until the results of your blood tests were complete." The admiral gestured for them to take their seats in the office, choosing one himself. "I'm afraid that both of you have Jung nanites inside of you."

"We're well aware of that, Admiral," Kata said. "They help maintain our overall health."

"Did you always have them?" the admiral asked. "Even before the Jung came to Tau Ceti?"

"That was before I was born, but no, it's one of the many so-called 'gifts' that the Jung brought to our world."

"Your phrasing is unusual," Admiral Dumar observed. "I'm assuming you no longer see the things the Jung have done for Kohara as 'gifts'?"

"I did," Kata admitted. "At least, for most of my life, I did. To be honest, pretty much until yesterday I suppose."

"And you've changed your mind?"

"Quite frankly, Admiral, I don't know what to think," Kata confessed, shaking her head. "With all that has happened to us in the last twenty hours, I'm feeling a bit confused."

"How so?" the admiral wondered, leaning back in his chair.

"To start with, the nanites. I'm not sure why you're worried about them. Like I said, all they do is keep us healthy."

"They do a lot more than that," Jessica explained. "They turn you into spies for the Jung."

"And in extreme cases, saboteurs," Admiral Dumar added.

Jessica looked at the admiral in surprise. "What?"

"I guess you haven't spoken to your brother yet. I read his initial report, such as it was. He's still a bit out of it. He said his chief engineer, Lieutenant Scalotti, was the one who sabotaged the self-destruct system on their jump drive. He lost it... killed a couple people from what I gather. Your initial report also indicated contact with such an operative, did it not?"

"Nothing like that," Jessica insisted. "Ellyus Barton would just sit there like a zombie, staring at the wall for several minutes, and there was nothing you could do to get his attention. Gerard—the only other spec-ops left in the system—he told me they get that way when they're transmitting collected data."

"What are you talking about?" Karahl wondered.

"What's a 'zombie'?" Kata asked.

"Staring at the wall, eyes open, seeing and hearing nothing," Jessica explained. She stopped talking and stared unblinking at the wall for a few seconds to demonstrate. "Like that."

"I've seen that!" Kata realized, as she began snapping her fingers and looking at her porta-cam operator, trying to remember something. "What was her name? The field reporter from Annater precinct? Darah something?"

"Darah Koligene?" Karahl offered.

"Yes! I saw her do that in a cafe once, right after a news conference. I walked up and said hello to her, and she just stared at the wall in front of her. Didn't say a word. It was unnerving. I went and sat down and ordered some food, and then all of a sudden she's normal again and waving at me." She looked at Jessica, suddenly embarrassed. "Are you trying to tell me we all do that?"

"There's no way that's true," Karahl protested. "I'm pretty sure someone would have noticed."

"From what Gerard told me, it's only supposed to happen when the host is alone. And it doesn't happen to everyone. Usually only when the host is regularly privy to intelligence that the Jung would find useful. That's when the nanites start replicating in order to take control of the host. That's when they turn them into operatives. The hosts don't even know that they *are* operatives. Everyone else just uploads when they walk through what they think are just security checkpoint scanners."

"The Jung have them everywhere," Kata explained. "They're literally on every block. They can activate at any time, and when they do, you're required to go through them if you're walking by. If you don't, you'll get arrested. They believe that the randomness of such security screenings prevents people from carrying contraband items, like weapons and illegal substances."

"For all we know, they do scan the Koharans for such items," Jessica said. "They're just uploading any data the Koharans' nanites have obtained since their last scan at the same time. Jesus, it's hard to imagine a better intelligence gathering system, assuming they have really good algorithms to sort through all that intel."

Kata shook her head in astonishment. "This is exactly what I'm talking about. This is the kind of thing that has me confused. All this time, I thought the nanites were just keeping us healthy."

"Not to defend the Jung," the admiral said, "but they probably do just that. It's just not the only thing they do."

"There are people on my world who are convinced the Jung are trying to destroy us. Slowly, over time. They claim that birthrates are down and, despite improved general health, the average lifespan has become shorter. But people argue that we do more, take more risks, push the limits, and that more people are killed in accidents than ever before."

"And the Jung nanites don't help with that?" Dumar wondered.

"No, they don't."

"What else have the Jung supposedly done for your people?" the admiral asked.

"Well, for starters, they reconnected all three worlds in the Tau Ceti system."

"Then you were not back in space before the Jung arrived?"

"No, just like you, the plague set us back for centuries. We *knew* the other worlds were out there, even after the plague nearly wiped us out. At least, we assumed that if some of us had survived on Kohara, then it was likely that some had survived on Stennis and Sorenson, as well. Eventually, once the electricity was flowing again, we were able to send messages between our worlds, but that was about it. The Jung gave us back our technology.

They brought us forward several hundred years in only a few decades."

"But they didn't give you interstellar travel?" Jessica noticed.

"No," Kata admitted. "They told us there were many worlds still infected, and they would not allow anyone to travel between worlds without being carefully scrutinized to ensure the plague never spread in such a way ever again. And why would we argue that? The bio-digital plague died out on our worlds over eight hundred years ago. And with three worlds in our own system, we have little need to travel to the stars, as the population of all three worlds combined is still only a few billion."

"You say they *gave* you space travel..." Dumar began.

"They got us back into space, but they didn't *give* us space travel," Kata corrected. "Sure, they helped us build an orbital shipyard, and taught us how to build ships capable of interplanetary travel, so that all three of our worlds would be connected again. But the only space travel they gave us was what they allowed. Even within our own system, they still controlled every flight. Sure, we had plenty of Koharan pilots flying cargo and passengers between the Cetian worlds, but it was always under the supervision of the Jung. The thing is, no one really minded. Life was a lot better. The economies of all three worlds prospered like never before, and the standard of living improved."

"These dissidents," Jessica wondered, "the ones who raised concerns about the real motives of the Jung occupation, what happened to them?"

"Oh, they're still out there," Kata assured her. "They mostly spread their propaganda anonymously, through the nets, to avoid prosecution. The CLA loves them, as they help make young men ripe for recruitment."

"CLA?" Dumar echoed, unfamiliar with the term.

"Cetian Liberation Army," Jessica clarified.

"Hardly an army," Kata corrected her. "More like a bunch of loosely affiliated gangs. However, in retrospect, that may have been what the Jung wanted us to believe all along." Kata sighed. "You see what I mean about it being confusing?"

"And what did they tell you about the Earth?" Admiral Dumar asked.

Kata quickly turned to look at the admiral, hit by a realization. "You're not from here, are you?"

"No, I'm not."

"I guess that shouldn't surprise me," Kata said, shaking her head. "They told *us* that the Earth had been the source of the bio-digital plague, which of course was something we had always assumed to begin with. They said you found an ancient digital repository of knowledge, and used that repository to regain your technology, to get back out into space considerably sooner than you should have. They also claimed that the bio-digital virus was lurking within that repository, that it had re-infected the Earth, and that you were trying to get away from the source of the infection. They said they had managed to quarantine your world, but then you invented a new interstellar propulsion system using knowledge from this repository. They claim they were *forced* to attack the Earth in an attempt to sterilize it once and for all... for the benefit of *all* humans *throughout* the core, *and beyond*."

"How noble of them," Admiral Dumar muttered.

"I gather their claims are not accurate?" Kata guessed.

"Let's see," Jessica began, "the thing about us finding a repository of knowledge was true. After that, they pretty much threw the truth out the window."

* * *

"Ensign Hayes! Ensign Sheehan!" Jessica shouted above the din of the lift engines that filled the air of the busy Porto Santo airbase. Her smile nearly stretched from ear to ear as she approached the two young men.

Both men turned their heads in response.

"Jess!" Josh greeted her excitedly. He instinctively started to reach out as if to give her a hug, then stopped as he remembered he was no longer a civilian. "Sir," he replied smartly, coming to attention along with Loki. They both raised their hands to their brow in standard salute.

Jessica returned their salutes in lackadaisical fashion as she approached, her expression mocking their seriousness. "Ensigns." Her smile broadened again. "Come here," she added, extending her arms to hug them both. "Managed to get through another one, did you?" she said as she embraced her two favorite pilots. "And came out as ensigns, no less," she added as she pulled away and looked them over. "Not bad."

"Not bad?" Josh chided. "It was a bitch!"

"Hey, stop whining. It took the rest of us four years."

"It's great to see you back safe," Loki said. He

looked down for a moment, his voice lowering to a solemn tone. "We heard about Weatherly. Sucks."

"The sergeant died a hero," Jessica said firmly. "He stayed behind to make sure the Jung didn't get their hands on a jump drive."

"Where's Naralena?" Josh wondered.

"She's still down on the surface," Jessica said.

"Of Kohara?" Josh exclaimed. "That place is crawling with Jung..."

"I heard. She's safe though. I left her with an underground group run by an EDF spec-ops who's been undercover on Kohara for decades. I'm on my way to talk to Telles about getting her out."

"The sooner the better," Loki insisted.

"But first, I've got new orders for you two." Jessica turned back and gestured for Kata and Karahl, both of whom had been hanging back a few meters, to approach. "Boys, this is Kata Mun and Karahl Essa. Kata, Karahl, this is Ensign Josh Hayes, and this is Ensign Loki Sheehan, and they are, without a doubt, my two favorite pilots."

Josh and Loki exchanged greetings with Kata and Karahl as Jessica continued to speak.

"Kata is a journalist from Kohara, and Karahl is her videographer. Admiral Dumar has authorized them to conduct interviews and record video of pretty much anything they want."

"Anything?"

"Well, anything that isn't classified," Jessica corrected. "Don't worry, we'll be screening all their footage before releasing it."

"What are they going to do with these interviews?" Loki wondered.

"Well, the Jung have been spreading rumors among the Cetian people that we're all a bunch of whacked out, disease-infested killers trying to spread the bio-digital plague all over the galaxy, and that the Jung have just been trying to keep us quarantined to our own little world in order to protect all of humanity. Damn fine people, those Jung, aren't they?"

Both Josh and Loki looked confused.

"The admiral wants to show the Cetian people the truth," Jessica explained. "All of it, and as unfiltered as possible."

"I'm pretty sure the admiral wasn't talking about us," Josh insisted.

"Why not?" Kata asked. "You both look like fine young officers."

Josh snickered. "She got the young part correct."

"If she wants to interview the two of you, you will cooperate, understood?" Jessica cautioned.

"Yes, sir," they both replied.

Loki looked at Jessica. "Those are our orders?" he asked, one eyebrow raised. "To let Miss Mun interview us?"

"Not exactly," Jessica began.

Josh's eyes closed and his head drooped down. "Oh, no." He looked back up at Jessica, his face pleading. "Come on, Jess. Why do we always have to play chauffeurs?"

"Because you two are such wonderful guys," Jessica teased. "Besides, look around. It's not like we've got a lot of pilots to spare these days."

"But we're Falcon pilots, Jess," Josh argued. "We fly combat missions, remember?"

"Well, there's not going to be any combat for a few weeks now, is there? Would you rather be doing eighteen-hour recon cold-coasts? Because that's going to be what's filling the mission boards for the next few weeks."

Josh's eyes widened. "Oh, we'd love to fly Miss Mun and Mister Essa around, sir. I can't think of *anything* I'd rather do."

Loki looked off to the side, then at Kata and Karahl, feigning a smile.

"Look, check out a utility jump shuttle and find yourself a crew chief to go along. You'll also be taking a couple of Corinari along as security, just in case."

"Just in case of what?" Josh wondered.

"Then we're all set." Jessica ignored him and turned to Kata and Karahl. "If you two will follow Ensign Sheehan, he'll show you around a bit while they're waiting for a shuttle to be assigned to them."

"Thank you," Kata replied.

"If you'd both just follow me," Loki said, turning to lead them across the hangar bay.

Josh rolled his eyes. "I guess there's worse duty." He turned to follow Loki, but Jessica grabbed his arm to stop him.

"Hey, Josh, did they teach you how to use that sidearm, or did they just teach you how to zip up your jump suit and shine your boots?"

Josh looked at her, his brow furrowed. "Uh, yeah, they taught us how to fire a pistol. Why?"

"Good. Listen," she began, stepping in close so that no one else could hear. "If either one them suddenly go catatonic on you, just shoot them in the head, got it?"

"What? What the hell does catatonic mean?"

"You know, eyes roll back in their heads, staring at the wall. You know, like zombies."

"Zombies?"

"Zombies. If they do that, kill them." Jessica turned away, fighting back a smile.

Josh looked confused for a moment before it dawned on him. "Ah, you're joking, right? Sir? You *are* joking, aren't you? Jess?" Josh sighed, looking up at the ceiling. "Of course she's joking," he reassured himself as he turned to follow Loki. After a few steps, he turned around and continued walking backwards as he watched Jessica walk away without looking back. "She has to be joking," he muttered as he turned back around and continued walking.

* * *

Nathan entered the Karuzara's conference hall with Vladimir and Jessica, pausing inside the doorway to look around the room. The senior-most members of the Alliance's three remaining ships were present, each of them clustered in their own little groups. In addition, leaders from the different operating groups on Porto Santo were in attendance. In total, there were more than twenty people waiting patiently in a room designed to hold five times that number. The relatively low attendance was disheartening.

Nathan spotted plenty of empty seats to the right of Cameron and the Celestia's senior officers, all of whom appeared more comfortable in their surroundings than most of the others in attendance. They had been living and working on the Karuzara for more than a month, and today's meeting represented a welcome break from the never-ending grind of trying to repair and upgrade their battered ship.

Nathan and his group moved into the room,

making their way along the outside aisle and then in between rows. "Captain Taylor," Nathan greeted as he took a seat next to Cameron. "Commander," Nathan added, nodding at Cameron's XO, Commander Kovacic on her left.

"Good to see you all," Cameron replied. "How long have you been back?"

"A few hours," Nathan commented as he settled into his seat. "Had a long after-action debrief."

"I heard it was a rough battle. I heard you came out relatively unscathed, though."

"For once," Nathan said. "Unfortunately, others weren't so lucky."

"I heard about Tug," Cameron said, her tone becoming sympathetic. "I'm sorry, Nathan. I know how close you two were."

"Thanks."

Cameron leaned forward, looking past Nathan to Jessica. "Good to see you made it home, Jessica. How's Robert?"

"He's still out of it, but he'll recover. Probably killed a few thousand brain cells, so he'll be dumber than before..." Jessica stopped as Admiral Dumar entered the room and the murmurs began to fade.

The admiral walked up to the podium and paused to look out at the faces of his people. He had seen most of them less than an hour ago in the after-action debriefing. Others he either saw occasionally in passing, or on his frequent visits to the various facilities on Porto Santo Island. "First, I'd like to thank everyone who had to suffer through that rather agonizing debriefing. I know from experience that one of the hardest things to do, next to battle, is having to talk about it afterwards and listen to others critique your actions. But it is how we learn, from both our own mistakes and from the mistakes of others. My summaries and opinions of the Battle of Tau Ceti will be available for all command personnel by the end of the day. I strongly suggest that everyone, whether you participated in the action or not, read them."

The admiral took a moment to let his sink in before continuing. "As you all know, we lost a lot of good people yesterday, not only in the Sol sector, but in the Pentaurus sector, as well. We also lost a lot of ships. For those of you from the Pentaurus sector, you should know that yesterday, a rebellion occurred in the Takar system. A handful of noble houses, with the assistance of members of the Ybaran Legions, overthrew and unseated House Ta'Akar as the leading family of Takara. In the process, they executed Casimir Ta'Akar. His eldest daughter, Deliza Ta'Akar, along with Yanni Hiller and the original data cores from Earth, escaped with the help of Captain Suvan Navarro and the Avendahl. They are all currently in the Darvano system. The loss of civilian lives on Takara was minimal. However, the loss of military lives and equipment was substantial. Furthermore, the impact these events will have on Alliance efforts in the Sol sector have yet to be fully determined. However, it is safe to assume that the effects will be substantial. Going forward, we must assume that no further military assistance will come from the Pentaurus cluster, at least until such time as a new order has been established. Until that time, I suspect the Avendahl will be forced to remain in the Pentaurus sector in order to protect the Darvano and Savoy systems against potential expansion attempts by the noble houses of Takara."

"Have there been any indications of such intentions by the nobles?" Major Prechitt asked.

"As of yet, there have been none."

"How many ships do the nobles still have at their disposal?" Major McCullum wondered.

"The most recent report from the Avendahl was that Takara has two jump-capable battleships, one of which is heavily damaged, as well as at least one cruiser that has yet to be fitted with a jump drive."

"Can the Avendahl defend against two jump-capable battleships?" Nathan wondered.

"Technically, it is an even match in terms of firepower," the admiral explained. "However, I know Captain Navarro to be a gifted tactician. I am confident that, should the nobles press their attack with their current forces, the Avendahl will be victorious. The point, however, is that she will not be available to come to the Sol sector for some time. Therefore, it is best for us to plan our course ahead based on the assumption that she will *never* be able to come to the Sol sector."

Nathan glanced around the room at the faces of his fellow officers. Although none of them would say it, he could see the disappointment in their faces. A capital ship was exactly what they needed to stand up against the Jung battle platforms and, without the Avendahl, their only recourse was to conduct surprise attacks with KKVs, of which only a few remained.

"Unfortunately, the Avendahl is not the only resource we have lost. The conflict in the Takaran system has also cost us any hope of further Ghatazhak reinforcements." Admiral Dumar looked to Commander Telles. "Commander, what is your current force strength?"

"Four hundred and eighty-seven," Commander Telles replied. "Once the wounded have recovered, that number is expected to rise to approximately six hundred."

"Is that number sufficient to liberate a Jung-held world?"

"Possibly," the commander replied. "Depending on the enemy force strength, what close-air support we have available, and what level of collateral damage is deemed acceptable. However, no matter what those parameters may yield, there will always be friendly losses, and with each engagement, those losses become less affordable."

"Major Prechitt?" the admiral said, changing his focus.

"There are only two Falcons operating. Two more Falcons will be back online within the week, but the other four ships may not be repairable. We have five boxcars, six troop shuttles, twelve combat jumpers, and four cargo shuttles remaining. All of our Kalibris and heavy airships are still at full strength. And of course, the various shuttles assigned to both the Aurora and the Celestia are all still available. So that adds four utility, two personnel, two cargo, and two SAR shuttles from each ship to the count. Now that may sound like a lot of ships, but it is not. We barely have enough shuttles to deploy the entire Ghatazhak detachment on the ground at once, let alone give them any air cover. However, I do have some good news. It seems that the primary assembly facility used to produce the EDF Eagle fighters is not as badly damaged as we were led to believe. I inspected the site myself the other day, and we may be able to get it up and running in as little as two months, as opposed to the original estimate of three to four months."

"The Eagles are short-range interceptors," Luis pointed out. "You can't operate them from the surface against anything in space, and you'd need bases all over the world to provide any significant coverage, not to mention thousands of fighters and pilots."

"Could we put mini-jump drives in them?" Jessica suggested.

"No room," Nathan told her. "Plus you'd take a weight penalty, thus cutting into either her range or ordnance package."

"The Celestia's missile bays are being converted into a launch deck specifically for launching Eagles," Cameron explained. "Four side-facing launch tubes both port and starboard. Eight ready-birds in the tubes, and eight more on the deck on standby. We'll be able to launch sixteen fighters within five minutes and additional waves every fifteen minutes."

"Where are you storing all these 'waves'?" Jessica wondered.

"We converted both main cargo decks below the flight deck into hangars, maintenance areas, and weapons storage," Cameron answered.

"Where are you storing your consumables?" Commander Willard wondered.

"We turned the lower forward decks into consumables storage," Commander Kovacic explained. "You'd be surprised how much less cargo space you need when your average mission duration drops from years to weeks."

"How long will it take to get all these new fighters?" Nathan wondered. "It takes months to build each one, even with an efficient assembly line."

"By using Takaran fabricators and by purchasing used propulsion and maneuvering systems from the Corinairans, we have been able to get the production time per fighter down to two weeks," the admiral stated proudly. "That is also due largely to President Scott putting a number of infrastructure repair projects on hold in order to dedicate more of Earth's fabricators to reproducing themselves. In fact, we started fabricating structural components more than a month ago. We already have the components to build twenty airframes, and the engines should arrive in a few weeks."

"You're going to spit out a new Eagle fighter every two weeks?" Nathan asked, finding it difficult to believe.

"Yes. And we're giving work to people who need it," the admiral added. "Putting roofs over their families' heads, and food on their tables. A small production town has already sprung up around the plant."

"Where are all the resources for this project coming from?" Nathan wondered.

"The Earth has plenty of resources," Commander Kovacic explained. "Much of the raw materials have been sitting idle in warehouses since the Jung first invaded months ago. Industry was practically dormant during the initial Jung occupation. The most significant resource needed is labor, and people are lining up to work."

"How do we pay them?" Nathan asked.

"No one is asking for money," the commander continued. "Hell, the Earth's economy hasn't even been reestablished yet. The barter system still rules down there. People work for food, for housing, for medical care, for security. Hell, they work so that they have *something* to do...to have a *purpose*."

"With the profits from the sale of Tannan propellant to the Pentaurus markets," the admiral added, "we are able to purchase the food and resources necessary to not only build fighters, but also to feed and care for the workers building them, as well as their families. It gives them hope."

Admiral Dumar paused, taking a deep breath. "Based on Major Prechitt's assessment, I believe our days of liberating worlds are at an end. At the very least, we will have to take each case individually and decide if the rewards justify the risk. In the case of Tau Ceti, I believe it did. Thanks to the quick thinking of Captain Scott, and the heroic efforts of Commander Telles and his men, we now have another Jung battleship in our possession."

"How badly damaged is she?" Nathan wondered.

"We are still in the process of transferring prisoners to the surface," the admiral replied. "However, initial reports are promising. Since the Aurora sustained very little damage during the Tau Ceti engagement, and Lieutenant Commander Allison is busy finishing up the Celestia's refit, I would like Lieutenant Commander Kamenetskiy to take a team over, get the power restored, and conduct a thorough assessment of the Jar-Benakh's condition."

"Gladly," Vladimir replied. "May I ask, what are your plans for the Jar-Benakh?"

"It's an asset, Lieutenant Commander, and a sizable one at that. I plan to use it. Exactly how, I have yet to determine. At the very least, it would augment our defense of Earth."

"It will take seven months just to get her here," Vladimir said, "assuming her FTL systems are still functioning and she can make best speed."

"Not if we fit her with a jump drive," Admiral Dumar replied.

"The Jar-Benakh is more than five kilometers long," Vladimir reminded the admiral. "That's going to take well over one hundred emitters just to make a single array, and at least four jump field generators, maybe six."

"The Karuzara originally had nearly one thousand emitters, and thirty jump field generators. We've already started cannibalizing our jump systems in order to speed up the refit of the Celestia. I intend to continue to do so, making not only the Jar-Benakh jump capable, but also those two unfinished Jung frigates in the Cetian shipyards."

"But the Karuzara will no longer be jump capable?" Vladimir said, pointing out the obvious.

"We never intended for her to remain jump capable," Admiral Dumar explained. "We only needed to get her here, to the Sol system. That's why the entire system was installed over the surface, only routing the primary power and control feeds up to the surface at key points. It was a temporary installation from the start, as we fully anticipated using its components to outfit other ships in the Sol sector."

"We do not yet control the Cetian shipyards," Commander Telles reminded him.

"No, we do not," the admiral admitted, "and our failure to liberate Kohara has complicated the matter."

"It would not be difficult to take that facility by force," Commander Telles pointed out. "However, it would not be unlike the Jung to destroy the facility and the ships within it, rather than allow it to become an enemy's asset."

"I have considered that possibility as well," Admiral Dumar agreed. "After debriefing Kata Mun, the Koharan reporter who Lieutenant Commander Nash brought back from Kohara, I believe we may be able to convince the Cetian people to join the Alliance."

Nathan looked at Jessica, a quizzical look on his face.

"Oh, yeah," she whispered, "I knew there was something I forgot to tell you."

"It matters not what the Cetians wish to do," Commander Telles said, "not while there are still more than a thousand well-armed Jung on the surface of Kohara."

"Maybe we can coordinate something with Gerard and his people?" Jessica suggested. "Perhaps they can find a way to get the civilians clear of the Jung strongholds so we can take them out from orbit without too much collateral damage."

"While collateral damage to the civilian population *should* be considered, the securing of those assets should be of greater priority."

"So, we should just waste all the people unlucky enough to be in the neighborhood when we attack?" Jessica challenged, glaring at the commander.

"Civilian casualties are part of the horror of war," the commander stated coldly. "It is one of the reasons wars *are* avoided. However, it is insufficient as a reason to *not* take control of those resources."

"Please."

"The argument is immaterial," Admiral Dumar insisted, interrupting them. "Once the Jung realize they are losing whatever hold they have left on the Tau Ceti system, they will destroy whatever assets remain. We've already inflicted enough collateral damage to their world, when we struck to cover the withdrawal of forces from Kohara. I see no reason to inflict more, only to see the prize taken from us at the push of a button. Besides, we have a bigger problem to deal with…the fact that the Jung have a much better interstellar communications system than we had originally believed." Admiral Dumar looked at Jessica. "Lieutenant Commander?"

Jessica sat up as she prepared to speak. "While undercover on Kohara, we made contact with a deep-cover EDF spec-ops named Gerard Bowden. He's been there for at least twenty years. The Jung have a tiered communications system. The battle platforms act as central messaging hubs. Each of them knows where the others will be at any given time, as their movements are coordinated by Jung command, back on the Jung homeworld."

"I don't suppose he told you where their homeworld is located?" Nathan asked, knowing the answer.

"No. He confirmed that they go to great lengths to keep that information a secret. In fact, only clan leaders know how to find their way back to their homeworld."

"Clan leaders?"

"Yeah, I'll get to that," Jessica said. "Ships in the field exchange messages with the nearest battle platform, as do Jung-held worlds. At this level, most comm-drones travel at a top speed of twenty times light, so their communications between battle platforms never take more than a few months, tops. The leaders on the battle platforms make the decisions and give the orders to the ships and worlds within their sphere of authority, based on the governing protocols *they* receive from the Jung homeworld. The battle platforms have comm-drones that can travel at one hundred times light, at least that is the highest speed that Gerard could verify. It could be faster, we just don't know. That means that, even if a battle platform is on the opposite side of the sector, it's only going to take a year to get a message home. For most of them, considerably less, depending on their proximity to the homeworld."

"How do the battle platforms communicate with one another?" Nathan wondered.

"Directly, with high-speed comm-drones. They have thousands of the damn things on board, and they send them out on a weekly basis, to every other battle platform in the network, either relayed between platforms along their route, or direct."

"That would explain why we never found coordinates for their homeworld in the Jar-Keurog's navigational database," Vladimir commented.

"If only their clan leaders know the location of the homeworld, how do they get the comm-drones back to them?" Nathan inquired.

"Gerard said the drones used to communicate directly with the Jung homeworld are all automated. They *know* the way back."

"So all we have to do is catch one and get the location from it," Nathan concluded.

"That'll never happen. First, how are you going to catch a drone moving at one hundred times light?" Jessica asked. "Second, they're encrypted *and* protected. Everything will fry if you try to access it without the proper code, and the only people who *know* the codes are *on* the Jung homeworld."

"What if a drone is sent to a location but the battle platform isn't there?" Cameron asked.

"If a platform moves, it leaves a forwarding buoy to tell the comm-drone of its new destination and expected arrival date. If the drone arrives and finds no platform *or* forwarding buoy, it will either head for the next nearest battle platform or return to its last destination, whichever is closest."

"What does this all mean for us?" Commander Kovacic wondered.

"It means that by now, just about every Jung ship in this sector knows that Earth has been liberated, and that her forces represent a considerable threat," Jessica explained.

"It's worse than that, I'm afraid," Admiral Dumar added. "The nearer ships, the ones we were planning on taking out to complete our buffer zone around Sol, are also aware of our weapons and tactics. It means we've lost the element of surprise."

"But we've got superior firepower, and superior propulsion systems," Commander Kovacic pointed out.

"That's not going to be enough," Jessica warned, "not if they come in force. And I'm talking about real force. Thirty or forty ships, multiple battle platforms, waves of probing attacks to test and wear down our offenses."

"The lieutenant commander is correct," Commander Telles agreed. "Up until this point, the Jung have always come with the assumption that they held the advantage by a considerable margin. All of our intelligence indicates that the Jung prefer to engage with superior numbers. Once they realize that their previous numbers were woefully inadequate, they will come better prepared. They will come prepared to fight a war, not a battle."

"If that were the case, shouldn't they have set a better trap for us in Tau Ceti?" Commander Kovacic asked.

"Not really," Jessica replied. "Gerard said the Jung in the Tau Ceti system were aware that the Earth had been liberated. They were also aware that we had jump drives, but I don't think they had any idea that we had destroyed *two* of their battle platforms."

"That would make sense," Major Prechitt agreed. "The first platform only got one comm-drone off, and it was headed in the general direction of Alpha Centauri when it went FTL. So, whatever word they got was from the second battle platform, probably before they even left the Alpha Centauri system on their way to Earth."

"That's exactly what I thought," Jessica agreed.

"That would explain why their battle platforms weren't taking any evasive actions," Nathan added. "They weren't even trying to make themselves hard to hit."

"Because they didn't *expect* to be hit," Jessica surmised. "They probably thought that hiding two battleships to use for an ambush was more than enough."

"Regardless, this information changes our plans considerably. We had talked about adding more plasma cannon turrets to both the Aurora and the Celestia," Admiral Dumar said, "as well as broadside plasma cannons in the aft utility bays. However, the installation of shields had to take priority. We had planned on installing the additional weapons later, after we finished clearing the twenty light year sphere around Sol. Now that we've lost the element of surprise, we're going to accelerate that timetable and add them as soon as possible. We need the extra firepower."

"Can't we still just hit them with KKVs?" Vladimir wondered.

"They'll be making random course changes now," Nathan explained, "making it harder to target them."

"It's not that the KKVs will no longer work, it's that it will take more of them to score a successful hit," Admiral Dumar explained, "and we only have three KKVs left. Once you miss, the target will never hold a course long enough for you to take another shot, at least not for the rest of the engagement."

"Admiral, we're due to leave dry dock in eighteen days," Cameron reminded him. "You can't even fabricate a plasma cannon in that little time."

"We'll pull them from the Karuzara's defenses."

"And install them in eighteen days?"

"We can install the turret mounts and run the power feeds before you leave dry dock," the admiral explained. "Then we can install the turrets in port. A little more difficult, but doable. The broadside cannons can also be installed while you're operational. We can even do that while you're in standard orbit."

"If you keep pulling weapons and jump systems from this station, you're going to make yourself defenseless," Nathan told the admiral.

"We're a big hunk of rock, Captain," Admiral Dumar replied. "They can pound us all they want. We can rebuild. If they want to destroy us, they're going to have to hit us with their own KKVs, in which case all the guns in the universe aren't going to help. I'd rather we concentrate our efforts on hunting them down and taking them out *before* they get that close to Sol again."

"It doesn't matter how many plasma weapons you give us, Admiral," Nathan warned. "As long as their shields are up, we're not going to be able to touch those battle platforms. That's why we used the KKVs in the first place. Overwhelming amounts of kinetic energy is the only thing that can get through them. Jumping in and firing plasma cannons doesn't work, even with shields to protect us. The battle platforms have so much power available that their shields can recharge far faster than we can drain them."

"I don't want you to attack their battle platforms with plasma cannons while their shields are up, Captain. I've got something else in mind to deal with their shields." Admiral Dumar picked up a remote and activated the massive view screen on the wall behind him. Technical drawings of what looked like a Takaran FTL comm-drone appeared on the screen. "The advantage to the FTL KKVs was that they had their own propulsion systems that were able to get them up to near-relativistic speed rather quickly. This made them relatively easy to deploy, as you just had to park them somewhere, then jump out and send them targeting info and a launch order. However, their FTL systems added considerable complexity to their operation and maintenance. Surprisingly, jump systems are far less complex, from an engineering standpoint. Also, they needed large amounts of propellant to get up to speed in a short time. The FTL aspect added little to its destructive potential since, at the moment of impact, the drone's FTL fields would collapse, and the vehicle's kinetic energy would become the same as it was before the mass-canceling fields negated her mass. The FTL capabilities only allowed us to get the weapon to the target undetected, since you can't *see* the light of an object that is traveling faster than its own light before it hits you."

"Uh, Admiral?" Jessica asked, her hand raised. "What are we looking at?"

"It's a jump-enabled kinetic kill vehicle, or JKKV. It was Lieutenant Tillardi's idea, and we've been working on it for some time now. It's smaller than the previous KKVs, and its propulsion system only carries enough propellant to make small, last-minute course corrections."

"How are we going to get them up to speed so they can do some damage?" Vladimir asked.

"We're going to launch them from our fighter launch tubes," Cameron realized.

"Indeed we are," the admiral replied.

"Both our ships' fighter launch tubes were turned into plasma torpedo cannon bays," Vladimir reminded them.

"Not anymore," Cameron commented.

"The Celestia's fighter launch tubes have been restored, albeit in a different, more versatile configuration than before," the admiral explained.

"No super cannons?" Nathan asked Cameron under his breath.

"Moved them underside, coming out our bow, just forward of bulkhead two," Cameron replied in similarly hushed tones. "I'll show you the specs later."

"I don't see a reactor," Major Prechitt pointed out. "Where does the jump drive get its power?"

"From energy banks, pre-charged with just enough energy for a single jump. After getting up to a speed that will result in a sufficient level of kinetic energy, and after establishing an initial intercept trajectory, the devices will be launched. At the appropriate moment, they will jump to a point far enough away from the target to allow a last-minute course adjustment, but close enough that the target will have insufficient time to take evasive *or* defensive actions."

"The KKVs were traveling at eighty percent the speed of light," Nathan said. "It will take time, and a lot of propellant to get an Explorer-class ship up to that speed."

"Yes it will, but propellant is something we have in abundance, thanks to our Tannan allies. However, we were planning on launching them at forty to fifty percent light."

"Will that be enough to take out a battle platform?" Jessica wondered.

"Probably not," the admiral admitted. "At least not with one or two strikes. However, we calculate that it should be enough kinetic energy to bring down at least *some* of their shields. Hit them with three or four, and their shields will definitely be down, and they'll be hurting. Hit them with five or six and they'll be done for."

"If they're making random course changes, they're going to be hard to hit with even one or two, let alone five or six," Nathan said.

"Hence the need for greater firepower on your ships, as well as shields. Once you get her shields down with a few JKKV strikes, you may have to stand toe-to-toe with her and slug it out. *That's* why we're giving everyone shields, so that you *can* slug it out with them."

"Finally!" Vladimir exclaimed. "I was getting tired of patching holes in the hull."

"How soon will these be ready for use?" Nathan asked.

"The prototype will be ready for testing in a few days. We have an additional ten of them already built; we're just waiting for the prototype testing before finishing them up. If all goes well, we could have them ready for action in as little as three weeks, perhaps less."

Admiral Dumar looked around the room, noticing the less-than-enthusiastic expressions on their faces. These were the people who would be taking the new weapons into battle, and their very survival would depend on their effectiveness. "Look, this is the best weapon we've got right now. It's simple, quick and easy to build, and we can produce them in large numbers. And let's face it, we're going to have to take down a lot of Jung ships and battle platforms, in a relatively short amount of time. They may not have gotten hold of a jump drive this time, but they came frighteningly close. In fact, they may have captured a good scan of one. Next time, we might not be so lucky. And I don't need to remind you of what happens if the Jung get a working jump drive of their own. Now, I've been looking at the numbers on this, and everything else, for weeks now. The JKKVs, combined with the additional firepower on the Aurora and the Celestia, as well as shields, give us a fighting chance. Add in the Jar-Benakh and possibly a couple of frigates, not to mention the gunships that should start coming off the line on Tanna in a month or so, and we might be able to hold the Jung at bay long enough for the Earth to recover and build up adequate defenses, and for the Avendahl to finally come and help tip the balance of power." He looked out at his people one last time.

"We've got a lot of work ahead of us, people. Let's get to it."

Nathan sat for a moment, thinking, as the admiral left the podium and exited the conference hall.

"We meeting for dinner later?" Cameron asked.

"Sure," Nathan replied, snapping out of his thoughts. "Your mess or mine?"

"Mine isn't finished, yet," Cameron replied.

"I will make you a beet salad that will make you cry," Vladimir promised.

"I'm sure it will," Cameron retorted.

Nathan stood up, noticing that Jessica was two steps ahead of them and heading quickly toward the exit.

"Hey, Telles," Jessica called down the corridor outside the conference hall. "I need to talk to you."

Commander Telles stopped, turning back toward Jessica as she approached. "What can I do for you, Lieutenant Commander?"

Jessica looked about, glancing over her shoulder at the others in the hallway, making sure they weren't within earshot. "Over there," she said, pushing the commander toward the corner, away from the others.

Commander Telles raised his eyebrows momentarily. "Very well."

Jessica followed him a few steps down the hallway, then pulled on his shoulder to spin him back around to face her. She moved closer, standing nearly toe-to-toe, looking up at him with eyes narrowed but still piercing. "You told me you would make sure she got off Kohara safely, you son of a bitch," she accused, poking him in the chest with her index finger as she cursed. "So when the fuck were you planning on making that happen?"

Commander Telles looked down at Jessica, his gaze unwavering. "I assure you, *Lieutenant*... Commander, I had no choice in the..."

"Bullshit!" Jessica exclaimed, poking him in the chest again. "You get her the fuck off that rock, and you do it real damn soon, or I'm going to come looking for you. And when I do, I'm not going to be this fucking nice."

Commander Telles turned his head a bit to his right, cocking his head and squinting slightly as he continued to lock eyes with her. "You *do* realize that I outrank you."

"You *do* realize that I don't give a fuck." Jessica leaned even closer, rising up on her toes so that she was eye-to-eye with him. "Get her...*off...that...rock.*" Jessica lowered herself back down off her toes, turned and continued down the corridor, bumping shoulders with the commander on her way out.

Commander Telles turned his head and watched her walk away, one eyebrow raised in curiosity at the surprising confrontation.

Nathan and Vladimir walked up and stopped next to the commander. "What the hell just happened, Commander?" Nathan asked.

"I'm not exactly sure," Commander Telles admitted. "I believe Lieutenant Commander Nash just insinuated a threat of physical violence against me should I not fulfill a promise I made back on the surface of Kohara." He looked at Nathan and Vladimir. "Should she follow through on her threat, I do not wish to inadvertently harm her while defending myself."

"If I were you, I'd be more worried about Jessica harming you," Vladimir said.

"I'm quite sure that is not possible."

"I don't know," Nathan said, "I've seen her take out bigger guys than you, Commander. Especially when she's pissed." Nathan turned and continued down the corridor as he spoke. "If I were you, I'd fulfill that promise."

Commander Telles watched them walk away, a look of bewilderment on his face.

Commander Willard was next to approach the commander. "What's wrong, Commander? You look confused, which is odd for a Ghatazhak."

Commander Telles looked at Commander Willard for a moment. "Do you find Terran women to be... confusing?"

Commander Willard smiled, patting Commander Telles on the shoulder. "No more so than any others, Commander," he said as he continued on his way.

CHAPTER FIVE

"Then, you already knew each other before you joined the Alliance?" Kata asked from the foldout jump seat just behind the center pedestal in the jump shuttle.

"We flew together on Haven," Josh explained as he finished preparing the shuttle for departure. "For a couple years."

"What made you join the Alliance?"

"We didn't exactly join," Josh chuckled.

"Actually, the Alliance didn't even exist back then," Loki pointed out. "We flew a rescue mission to pick up Captain Scott and his people on Haven. They were under fire…"

"Oh! Remember how I took that sniper's head off with the front of the harvester? That was slick!"

Loki looked at Kata. "You might want to edit that part out."

"So, you rescued Captain Scott, and then what happened?" Kata asked, pressing forward with the interview.

"We all sort of got swept up. The Aurora jumped out of the Haven system to escape the Takarans, and a bunch of us from Haven were sort of stranded on board. A few got off on Corinair later, but most of us stayed on board and eventually ended up in the Alliance."

"I thought the Takarans were members of the Alliance?" Kata asked, a confused look on her face.

"They are now," Loki amended. "That was before the Alliance. It's a long story."

"You know, we used to fly the Aurora," Josh bragged. "Yeah, we were her primary flight crew."

"Why aren't you still flying her?" Kata wondered.

"'Cuz flying a Falcon is a lot more fun," Josh grinned.

Kata looked at Loki, expecting a different opinion.

"I don't know that I'd call it more fun," Loki argued. "We went where the captain needed us at the time. They tell us what to fly and where to fly it, and that's what we do."

"Sorry if flying us around is a bit on the boring side," Kata apologized.

"No, that's quite all right," Loki insisted. "I don't mind boring, really."

"I do," Josh disagreed. "You ready back there, Torwell?" He called over his comm-set.

"*We're ready,*" the sergeant replied, sounding bored.

"Karuzara Departure, Shuttle One Seven, bay four, ready for departure to Porto Santo," Loki announced over the comms.

"*Shuttle One Seven, Karuzara Departure, cleared for takeoff from bay four. Once clear the bay, climb to plus one hundred and head for tunnel one three. Contact Earth Control on exit.*"

"One Seven clear for takeoff, will climb to plus one hundred, exit one three, and switch to Earth Con," Loki confirmed over his comm-set.

Kata looked out the front windows of the shuttle as the big airlock door in front of them split vertically down its center and retracted, disappearing into slots in the rock walls on either side. Her eyes opened wide, and she gasped in awe at the view beyond the doors...a massive cavern, easily several kilometers in diameter.

Josh pushed the small joystick on the center console forward, causing the shuttle to roll forward out onto the apron.

Kata leaned forward, twisting her neck in order to take in the full view as the shuttle pulled out into the open. "Are you getting this?" she muttered to her porta-cam operator.

"You bet," Karahl replied, as he held the porta-cam with outstretched arms into the center of the cockpit, panning in all directions.

"Here, let me give you a better angle," Josh said as he fired his thrusters and lifted off the apron. He pitched their nose down as the shuttle floated upward, climbing slowly to their assigned transition altitude.

"Are those all bays like the ones we just came out of?" Karahl asked.

"Pretty much," Loki replied. "Some bigger, some smaller."

"And this is all in the center of an asteroid?" Kata confirmed in disbelief.

"Yup," Josh replied. "An asteroid from nine hundred-something light years away."

"Unbelievable," she mumbled.

"And it wasn't this big inside back then," Josh pointed out. "They've made the center at least fifty percent bigger since then."

"Are they going to make it even bigger?" she wondered.

"Doubtful," Loki said. "If they make the asteroid too hollow, it will lose too much of its integrity. It's down to a few kilometers thick in some places already."

"Is that…?"

"That's her," Josh replied. "That's the Aurora."

Kata stared through the front windows at the long, curved lines of the massive, gray-hulled ship. It filled their view, stretching from one end of the window to the other.

"It's huge."

"Not really," Loki shrugged. "Not compared to some of the Jung ships. It's not even half as long as a Jung battleship."

"How many ships can be held in here?" she wondered.

"Easily two about the size of the Aurora," Loki explained. "There are also a few dry docks. See, on the far side, that big door in the center, with the smaller ones on either side?"

"What's a dry dock?" Kata asked. "I mean, I know what it means to a boat, but I'm not sure what it means to a spaceship."

"It means that it's fully pressurized," Loki clarified. "It's still a zero-gravity environment, but the techs don't have to wear pressure suits. It makes it a lot easier for them to work, and they can get things done to the exterior of the ship a lot faster."

"And they have a 'dry dock' big enough to fit the Aurora?"

"Barely," Josh commented.

"The Celestia is in there now," Loki added. "She's been there for over a month now."

"What are they doing to her?"

"She was pretty badly damaged during the Jung's last attack on Sol. Took her a month just to limp halfway across the system to make port. They've been making repairs, fixing her hull, finishing her up inside, even making a few upgrades."

"Finishing her up?"

"She wasn't fully fitted out when the Jung first invaded," Loki explained. "No weapons...barely able to fly, really. They hid her on a tiny moon orbiting a gas giant further out in the system. We found her during the liberation of Earth."

"This is so much to take in," Kata said, shaking her head in disbelief. "It's overwhelming at times." She looked about the cockpit, feeling slightly disoriented as the shuttle's nose continued to pitch downward. "I feel like I should be falling forward into the windows," she observed, "yet I'm not."

"That's because our gravity fields are pulling you in a different direction than what you're perceiving as up and down, based on the bay deck that we just lifted off from," Loki explained. "It messes you up quite a bit at first, but you get used to it, eventually." He turned to look at her. "You guys didn't get to see any of this on the way in?"

"No, we were stuck in the back of a cargo shuttle. No windows at all." She continued staring at the Aurora. "That ship was built by people from Earth?"

"Yes, ma'am," Josh replied. "They used to have a big assembly facility in Earth orbit. They built all their ships there. First the Scouts, then the Defender-class ships, and finally the Aurora and the Celestia."

"They don't use it anymore?"

"Jung took it out during the original invasion of Earth," Loki replied.

"Sorry, but I gotta bring the nose back up," Josh said as he fired the shuttle's attitude thrusters, "unless you want me to fly backwards out of here."

"No, do what you... Wait, you can do that?"

"Sure!"

"He was joking, ma'am," Loki assured her. "We don't normally fly backwards out the transition tunnels."

The shuttle's nose swung briskly upward. Josh fired the thrusters again, bringing the change in pitch to a smooth stop as the shuttle slowed its ascent.

"Plus one hundred," Loki reported.

"Thrusting forward," Josh replied as he put the shuttle into forward motion.

Kata continued to look out the front windows as the shuttle accelerated toward one of the many tunnel openings on the walls of the great central cavern. "Those are the exits?"

"We call them 'transition tunnels'," Loki told her. "They can be used to enter or exit."

"How do you know which?"

"Generally, the even numbered tunnels are entrances, and the odds are for exiting. Besides, there are lights to remind you. See the border strips around the tunnel we're headed for? It's green, which means it's empty and since it's green around the inside entrance, it's an exit tunnel."

"And those red ones are for incoming ships?"

"Exactly. The tunnel we're entering now has a red-lit border around the outside entrance."

"How many tunnels are there?"

"Twenty-three in all, mostly the size we're entering now," Loki explained as the shuttle passed through the tunnel entrance threshold. "There are two big ones for ships the Aurora's size. Tunnels one and two."

"Aren't we going a little fast?" she wondered, tensing up at the sight of the rocky walls streaking past them on all sides at ever increasing rates.

"Not for him," Loki muttered as he checked their position. "Exit threshold in five seconds."

Kata kept her eyes on the fast-approaching tunnel exit ahead of them, afraid to look at the rock walls whizzing past. She held her breath as they breached the threshold and passed into open space. She could feel her pulse racing, and her breath quickening, as a blanket of distant stars loomed before her. "Oh, my God," she whispered in complete amazement.

"First time, huh?" Josh asked, smiling.

"Like I said, first time actually *seeing* it."

Josh laughed. "Oh, man, she has *got* to stand on the bridge of the Aurora someday."

"So where's the Earth?" she wondered. "I thought the Karuzara asteroid was orbiting it?"

"She's behind us," Josh replied.

"Departure, Shuttle One Seven, clearing Karuzara space, going to Earth Con," Loki announced over the comms.

Josh fired the shuttle's main engines and started a gentle turn to bring them around on a heading for Earth.

"*Shuttle One Seven, Departure, safe flight.*"

The Earth began to slide into view from the left. Josh rolled the shuttle over to put the planet above them for the moment, to give Kata and her porta-cam operator a better view.

"Earth Control, Shuttle One Seven, just off from Karuzara One Three, looking to transition down for Porto Santo."

"*Shuttle One Seven, Earth Control, you are clear to jump down at your discretion. Transition clearance good for seventeen minutes.*"

Loki looked at Kata and Karahl, their faces full of wide-eyed wonder as they gazed up at the planet above. "Uh, Earth Control, Shuttle One Seven, negative on the jump. We're going to take the scenic route and fly her all the way down."

"*Shuttle One Seven, Earth Control copies. You may start your descent.*"

Loki exchanged smiles with Josh as he prepared a course for him to fly all the way down through the atmosphere of Earth down to Porto Santo Island.

"So this is it?" Kata said in astonishment. "The birthplace of us all."

"Yes, ma'am," Loki replied.

"What did you mean by 'the scenic route'?" Kata wondered.

"We just thought we'd fly all the way down instead of jumping directly to Porto Santo Island."

"You don't normally fly it all the way down?"

"No, ma'am. Protocol says we jump. It's faster and it saves propellant."

"Won't you get in trouble?"

"Naw," Josh insisted. "We need to do it occasionally to keep our skills up."

"Besides, we thought you might like to take a good long look at the Earth," Loki added.

Kata smiled. "Yeah, I think we would."

* * *

Jessica peeked past the curtain around Robert's bed at the Porto Santo base hospital. Her oldest brother was lying there, eyes closed, with his head tilted left, sleeping. Intravenous containers hung from long metal hangers attached to a pole at the foot of his bed. Oxygen was being fed into his nose, and there was a tube leading somewhere under his gown between his legs that she didn't want to think about. She looked at the sensor panel mounted on the pole at the head of his bed. Although she didn't understand all of the readings and squiggly lines that flowed across the various colorful ribbon displays, she knew that green was good, and that was the predominant color on the screen at the moment. She moved inside, carefully pulling the curtain closed behind her, then moved along the right side of his bed as quietly as possible.

"Did you get it?" Robert whispered without opening his eyes.

Jessica looked disappointed. "How did you know?"

"Because every one of my siblings thus far has smuggled in a slice of pizza for me." He opened his eyes and turned to look at her.

"But did they bring you one with anchovies?" she asked with a grin.

"You didn't," he said in disbelief, scooting himself up in bed a bit.

She pulled the carefully wrapped contraband from her bag and handed it to him, unwrapping it as she passed it into his eager hands.

Robert was practically drooling. "Where the hell did you get anchovies?"

"I had to go all the way to Italy."

"You flew to Italy to get me anchovies? How on earth did you get permission to take a shuttle on an anchovy run?"

"Hey, I'm chief of security for the Aurora, remember? I can go anywhere I want."

Robert took a bite, savoring the tiny, fishy, slivers of salt.

"I can't promise they won't make you sick," she warned. "I got them at a street market in Naples."

"Worth the risk," Robert insisted as he took another bite.

"Then I win the sibling competition?"

"Hands down, sister."

Jessica smiled. "As usual." She looked at all the medical paraphernalia again. "What the hell are all these tubes and wires for? You'd think you were dying or something."

"They're just worried that I might develop DCS, like you did."

"Pray that they're wrong... Trust me. I thought you made it to the crawler before the ship came apart?"

"Not exactly. The ship broke apart right after we jumped. The compartment breached at the back end, and I got sucked aft. I made it into the access tube to the crawler as the ship was coming apart." He looked her in the eyes. "I saw fucking open space, Jess—stars and everything—under my feet at the open end of the tunnel. Scared the shit out of me. Quite frankly, I don't even remember getting into the crawler. Next thing I knew, I was in the crawler, floating in a field of debris, *from my own ship*, watching helplessly while Jung shuttles picked through the pieces looking for the jump field generators."

Jessica was silent for a moment, trying to imagine what it must have been like for him. "They pump you full of nanites?" she asked, trying to change the subject.

"Yeah. The fuckers feel like little needles poking me from the inside."

"Be glad that they do," she told him. "From what I've heard, that means you don't have any of the

Jung variety in you. That's how they got Scalotti, you know."

"Yeah, I heard." Robert tugged at his gown, pressing at his lower abdomen. "Why do they hurt mostly in the groin, though?"

Jessica snickered. "That's probably why they put a tube up your dick. What the hell were you doing in that crawler, Bobert?"

Robert looked at her crossly. "My dick is just fine, thank you." He adjusted himself in his bed and settled back down. "They have to monitor my fluid output, make sure my kidneys aren't damaged."

"So, anyway, I've got good news…and I've got bad news," she told him.

"Give me the bad news first," he said as he finished his last bite of pizza.

"I can't, it won't make sense."

"Then give me the good news."

"Because of that jump of yours, we managed to capture the Jar-Benakh intact."

"Seriously? You mean they boarded her?"

"Yeah. Telles took a handful of Ghatazhak in and kept the Jung busy until reinforcements arrived. It's ours. They're hauling prisoners down here as we speak. All because your little jump opened up a hole in her side."

"That's incredible," he exclaimed.

"Yeah, it is. Dumar wants to fix her up and put a jump drive on her."

"That's great!" he exclaimed. "Wait… What's the bad news?"

"They're giving command of her to Roselle."

"You're kidding me!"

"Sorry, no."

"That figures. I lose my ship, and he gets a new one... A bigger one at that."

"You're getting a new ship too," she told him.

"I am?"

"Actually, you're getting a whole fleet of ships, so to speak."

"What?"

"Remember the Tannan gunboat project? You're going to run the crew training program."

"I'm going to be a teacher?" Robert leaned back in bed and closed his eyes, sighing heavily. "*That* should have been the bad news."

"Only until the Tannans are up and running. Then they'll take over and teach their own. Hey, at least you're getting the first one as your own ship."

"So I'm going to be a test pilot as well?"

"I guess you could call it that. Someone's got to figure out how to fly the new ships, right? Figure out how to get the most out of them, develop attack strategies, discover their strengths and weaknesses?"

"Yeah, I guess so."

"And from what I've seen, the new gunboats are going to be pretty sweet."

"I don't know," Robert said, not quite convinced that his new assignment was as good as his little sister was trying to make it sound. "I think you're going to have go back to Italy and get me another slice of pizza."

"What," she said, reaching back into her bag, "you thought I went all the way to Italy and only bought one slice?"

* * *

"This is amazing," Cameron exclaimed as she

dished up another portion of the strange purple salad that Vladimir had made. "What did you call it again?"

A long string of Russian words poured out of Vladimir's mouth, which neither she nor Nathan could even begin to understand, let alone repeat. She stared at him for a moment, trying to form the words.

"Just call it beet salad," Nathan suggested.

"I had no idea you were so skilled in the galley," Cameron admitted.

"Russian winters…very cold," Vladimir explained as he shoveled a spoonful of the salad into his mouth. "I spent many evenings with my *babushka* in the kitchen, helping her cook."

"I'm actually becoming quite the connoisseur of Russian cuisine," Nathan boasted. "Not to mention I've put on a few extra pounds," he added, patting his belly.

"I wasn't going to say anything," Cameron teased. "But if you want to get some exercise, you're welcome to come lend a hand on the Celestia."

"Yeah, I heard you guys have been busting hump around the clock."

"You heard the admiral. He's kicking us out of dry dock in eighteen days, ready or not."

"That doesn't sound right," Nathan said, taking a bite of his dinner.

"It's not like we're not space-worthy," Cameron insisted. "Pretty much everything important that needs to be done to the exterior has been completed. We've just got to finish wiring up the secondary jump emitter array, install the second pair of jump field generators, and then connect the mounts for additional turrets. Like he said, the rest we can do in orbit."

"What about all your external doors?" Vladimir wondered. "They are all still off, no?"

"Yes, they are, but we're not putting them back on. As long as we're running shields, we don't need them."

"How about if you need to service one of your point-defense turrets, or your quads?" Vladimir asked.

"They installed collars around the turret bases, so that an external repair bay can be connected to the hull, completely covering the weapon in a pressurized maintenance bay. We're even going to carry one in our hangar deck that a utility shuttle can carry out and put into place."

"What about the quads?" Nathan wondered. "They're huge."

"Those will have to be serviced in port," she explained. "It's all about a change in mission profile, Nathan. The Explorer-class ships were designed to be out for years at a time, so we had to carry consumables, propellant, accommodations…hell, the Aurora even has a movie theater and a huge recreation facility."

"It *needs* an ice rink," Nathan muttered as he sipped his drink.

"The point is, we had a lot of wasted space and a lot of design features that, while logical for long-duration missions of exploration and diplomacy, made no sense for combat missions that don't even last a week."

"But what if they *do* last more than a week?" Nathan asked. "If our jump drive failed while we're away, we could be stranded for weeks just waiting for help."

"That's why we're getting *two* separate jump drive systems," Cameron reminded him. "That, and it doubles our jump range between charging cycles."

"Now *that* part I agree with," Nathan admitted.

"Wait until you see the new forward launch tubes," Cameron exclaimed. "Fifty percent wider, twenty-five percent taller, and twenty-five percent longer. They have three catapults built into the deck instead of the sides, just like the old aircraft carriers used to have. Two short, and one longer one down the center. We'll be able to launch pretty much anything that fits inside, plus they can be used as an entrance in a pinch."

"You were going to show me where they were putting the super cannons," Nathan reminded her.

"Oh, yeah," she replied, reaching for her data pad, "but they're not called super cannons anymore. They're called mark one, mark two, mark three, and mark four. Ones are the little guys, like on the Falcon and the combat jumpers. The mark one cannons were also used to replace all of our mini-rail guns, the ones we use for point-defense. Except now they're quads instead of twins, so they can lay down a lot more defensive fire. The original plasma cannon turret that you gave us used mark twos, and our fore and aft torpedo tubes use mark threes."

"So the old super cannons were mark fours then," Nathan surmised. "Is that what they're installing under your bow?"

Cameron leaned back in her chair and smiled as if her child had just brought home an award. "Mark fives."

"What are mark fives?" Nathan wondered.

"The big boys that the Karuzara uses to attack ships at a distance."

"*Bozhe moi,*" Vladimir exclaimed.

"Wait, it gets better," Cameron said, almost giggling. "The lateral track on all four cannons can be adjusted. They can fan out slightly, fire in parallel, or all focus on the same point, ten kilometers out. When we install the broadside cannons in the utility bays, the mark twos will be able to do the same thing."

"Jesus," Nathan exclaimed.

"That's brilliant!" Vladimir added. "Was that your idea?"

"I wish. It was your friend Tilly's idea."

Nathan sighed. "Maybe Dumar's right. Maybe we can stand toe-to-toe with a battle platform."

"Can you imagine how much firepower we could put on a single shield section, with two ships doing time-on-target attacks with those mark fives?" Cameron exclaimed.

"It might work on a battleship," Vladimir admitted, "but not on a platform. Weaken them noticeably? Yes. Maybe a fifty percent drop, if you can get enough shots in, but complete collapse? No."

"Can the mark fives fire triplets?" Nathan asked.

"No, singles only, and no more than one shot per cannon every fifteen seconds. Even *with* all the extra heat exchangers they put on the bottom of our hull."

"So a sustained fire rate of a shot every four seconds," Nathan nodded. "Not bad. Maybe they can add more heat exchangers and get us a quicker fire rate?"

"Doubtful," Vladimir said. "It's not the number of heat exchangers that is limiting. It is the amount of transfer area around the plasma generators themselves. The mark fives are very powerful, a lot of heat to get rid of, I'm afraid. I am surprised they can get it down to fifteen seconds."

"No matter how you look at it, both our ships are getting a lot more firepower."

"More importantly, we're getting shields," Vladimir reminded them both. "I cannot begin to make you understand how happy that makes me."

Nathan sighed, leaning back in his chair as he gazed at the design specs on Cameron's data pad. "We really could have used all of this yesterday."

"What happened yesterday wasn't your fault, Nathan," Cameron insisted. "You did what any of us would have done... You tried to give them a way to survive."

"But at what cost?"

"At no cost," Cameron argued.

"I nearly handed the Jung a jump drive, Cam."

"But you didn't."

"We still don't know that for sure."

"For all we know, they got one a long time ago. Maybe they had the plans for it all along and we just haven't seen it yet. Maybe they're working on it right now. That's a lot of maybes, Nathan. Besides, if you would've had that much firepower yesterday, we wouldn't have another Jung battleship to add to our fleet today," Cameron said.

"And I would not have a new and interesting project tomorrow," Vladimir added. "This, of course, means that I will not be cooking for you for a while, Nathan."

"I think I'll survive."

* * *

"What's with all the girls?" Jessica asked Master Sergeant Jahal as she walked across the tarmac toward him. "The Ghatazhak having a slumber party?"

"They are prisoners," the master sergeant stated, fighting back a smile, "from the Jar-Benakh."

Jessica stopped next to the master sergeant, turning to look at the group of women as they disembarked from the cargo shuttle. There were at least fifty of them, all dressed quite nicely in feminine attire of a fashion she had not seen before. "I thought the Jung didn't have women in their military."

"To my knowledge they do not."

"Captain's harem, then?"

"In a manner of speaking, I suppose," the master sergeant replied. "Most of them were found in a dormitory of sorts. However, others were found hiding in various officers' quarters throughout the ship, mostly those of higher rank."

"Mistresses, perhaps?"

"It would not be the first time I have heard of such arrangements. Many nobles, serving on board imperial ships, had similar personnel. They usually referred to them as 'housekeepers', or 'personal assistants'."

"Very personal, right?" Jessica commented, poking the master sergeant in the side with her elbow. When she got no response, she turned to look at him. "What's the deal, Master Sergeant, you're usually so jovial. Someone kick your dog?"

"No, my commander."

"Ah... Shook him up a bit, did I?"

"Do not flatter yourself, Lieutenant Commander. You are not capable of 'shaking up' Commander

Telles, or any other Ghatazhak, for that matter. However, you might want to review the commander's after-action reports before you attempt to—how do you Terrans put it—'get in his face' over his failure to rescue your associate."

"I see," Jessica replied, nodding her understanding. "Look, I know that the Ghatazhak don't have a problem leaving people behind, for the 'good of the mission' and all that, but us Terrans, we don't like leaving our people behind."

Master Sergeant Jahal turned and looked Jessica in the eyes. "You left Sergeant Weatherly behind—for the good of the mission—did you not? Or was it to save your own skin? Perhaps that is why you are so upset that the commander had to leave Miss Avakian behind?"

Jessica's expression became as cold as ice, as she stepped closer to the master sergeant. She stared up into his steadfast gaze, unflinching. "You're just begging for an ass-kicking, aren't you, Master Sergeant?"

"Please...... Sir."

Jessica stood there staring at him for several seconds. Finally, she stepped back. "Another time, perhaps. We're short enough of you boys as it is," she added as she stepped back further and turned to walk away. "There may be a woman named Kaya Allemahn among them," Jessica called back to the master sergeant. "Isolate her. I'll be back to question her later."

"Yes, sir."

* * *

Naralena followed Gerard and his two men as

they continued along the trail that followed the perimeter of the mountain lake. They had spent all night in the back of one of the CLA's smuggling vans in order to get as far away from the city as possible. After ditching the van in the river at dawn, they had spent the entire day hiking the river trail up into the mountains. After ascending at least a thousand meters, they had come to a lake, which they had spent the afternoon circumnavigating. There had been little discussion during their journey, partly because two of the men only spoke Koharan, and partly because they preferred to save their energy for the hike up the mountain.

Gerard stopped, kneeling down in the tall grass of the meadow that had just appeared beyond the forest. He signaled for his men to circle around, which they did so immediately.

"What is it?" Naralena whispered.

"Our destination."

"Great." Naralena looked around. "Then why aren't we going there?"

"We must be sure that it is unoccupied at the moment."

"I don't understand. Doesn't it belong to you?"

"Yes, but we cannot be too cautious."

"Okay. Cautious is good," Naralena agreed, kneeling down behind him. "I like cautious." She pulled out her last piece of rations. It was a chewy, overly sweet mixture of grains and dried berries, with a slightly bitter taste. It was not appetizing but, as far as she could tell, it was nutritious.

She gazed out across the meadow from her position behind Gerard. The grass was an unusual lime-green, unnaturally vibrant in its coloring. It was quite different than the grass she had seen on

The Frontiers Saga Episode #14: THE WEAK AND THE INNOCENT

Earth during her few visits to the surface, and it was even more different than the blue-gray vegetation that covered such areas on her homeworld of Volon. Still, it was better than Haven had been, where there was little growth other than the dead-looking tiga trees, dusty scrub brush and, of course, molo. She did not miss that place, and she thanked destiny that the Aurora pulled her from it.

She sat there, thinking about Jessica, the Alliance, and about Sergeant Weatherly who, despite her best efforts, kept creeping back into her mind to haunt her. She was sweaty, dirty, and thirsty, and she was tired. She knew the Alliance would come for her. She knew Jessica would not leave her behind. If there was a way, Jessica would find it.

If there was a way.

Naralena had almost fallen asleep, her head hanging low between her drawn up knees, when a gentle touch on her back startled her.

"I believe it is clear," Gerard said, rising to his feet.

"Finally," she sighed, taking his hand to steady herself as she stood. She followed him toward the cabin in the middle of the meadow, as the other two men approached from opposite sides. For a moment, she wondered how it might look if someone *were* already inside that cabin, looking out at such men, approaching cautiously from different directions. It was hardly inconspicuous, in spite of Gerard's insistence that they be as stealthy as possible.

The cabin itself was not much to look at. It appeared to be prefabricated and had been placed unceremoniously in the middle of the meadow. Beside it, a small creek stretched from the nearby hills on the left down to the lake not a hundred meters away on the opposite side. Now that they were deep into the meadow, she could see that the forest parted at the shore to reveal the lake beyond.

She followed Gerard up onto the front patio. He placed his hand on the control pad, and the door unlocked and swung slightly inward of its own accord. He pushed it open further with his foot, trying not to rush in while also trying not to look abnormally apprehensive. The interior of the cabin was dark, with the storm shutters blocking any light. He reached to the side, turned on the interior lighting, and looked about.

His two compatriots converged on the front patio at that moment and followed him in, moving quickly about the cabin as they checked every room. After a minute, Gerard gestured for her to enter as well.

Naralena entered the cabin and looked around. It was dusty, and somewhat spartan in its decor, but it appeared to have all the comforts of home. It had a small but functional kitchen and dining table in one side, with a living area centered around a large stone fireplace on the other. The ceilings were tall, and there were doors on either side of the fireplace. An open staircase along the far wall led up to a walkway above the fireplace and, beyond that, to two additional doors. "How long are we to stay?" she asked.

"Until your people come, or until it is no longer safe, whichever comes first," Gerard answered. "The master bedroom is to the right, and the only bathroom is to the left. We will occupy that room. The men will occupy the rooms upstairs."

"We?" she asked.

"If we are to appear as a normal couple who have brought two good friends to our cabin for a relaxing vacation of fishing, hiking, and hunting, we must play the part. Do not worry," he added with a smile, "I shall be sleeping on the couch."

"How will we contact the Alliance?" she asked.

"There is a hidden doorway, behind the towel cabinet in the bathroom. It leads to a small root cellar. Communications gear and weapons are stored there."

"Then we should begin listening for broadcasts as soon as possible," she said.

"It is too soon," he warned. "The communications gear does emit a detectable energy signal. Weak, but detectable. Should someone be monitoring the area, they might discover us. We should wait a day or two, maybe even three. We will explore the area, check out how many of our neighbors are in attendance, and look for any unusual activity. If we see no cause for alarm, then we will activate the communications gear."

"Very well. What do we do now, then?"

"My men will go out and canvas the area to be sure that no one is watching us. Meanwhile, I will begin making dinner. If you like, you may wash up."

"Is there running water?"

"Yes, from the creek that flows behind the cabin...and heat, from geothermal systems deep underground."

"Wonderful," she said, breathing a sigh of relief.

* * *

Deliza sat in the common area of their suite in one of Aitkenna's finest hotels, studying her data pad.

"What are you doing?" Yanni asked as he entered the room.

"I've been studying the technical drawings of the 402s, the ship my father used to have on Haven, the one they call a 'Falcon' now."

"What about them?" he asked as he sat down next to her.

"It occurred to me that the Alliance has not been using them effectively."

"How do you mean?"

"They have been using them as both interceptors and to attack surface targets, usually in support of surface actions."

"I was under the impression that the Falcons were quite effective in those roles."

"They are, but only because they are big and powerful ships. But much of their space is wasted on systems that are of little use to the Alliance."

Yanni moved closer to her on the couch, looking at the data pad that she held. "Such as?"

"Well, the lift systems, for one. It was designed and built for the Paleans. Palee is small and quite rocky, with very little flat land. Runways were difficult to build, and the atmosphere was rather thin, as well as having a much lower gravity than most human-inhabited worlds. The Falcons were designed to takeoff and land vertically, from surface bases. They have poor aerodynamic characteristics, which they made up for with brute force. But they were designed to be deep-space interceptors—to patrol the borders of the Palean system and engage any intruders. They were fast, with incredible acceleration, and were equipped with FTL systems."

"They sound like excellent ships to me."

"But the Earth has lots of flat, level land. Even

the airbase at Porto Santo has runways. There is no reason to waste all that space with powered lift systems."

"But if the Falcons have poor aerodynamic performance, don't they *need* those powered lift systems?"

"For sustained flight operations, yes, but that uses a considerable amount of propellant. And they fly well enough to takeoff and land from conventional runways if need be. The point is, they should not be using them for atmospheric operations. They should be using them strictly for space operations. Doing so would allow them to be reconfigured, giving them greater interior space and considerably more utility."

"Why do you think of such things?" he wondered.

"What do you mean? I'm always thinking of such things, you know that."

"I mean, why now. After all that's happened in the last twenty-four hours…"

"Twenty-eight," she interrupted in her usual, annoying way. She knew it irritated him, but she enjoyed watching his reaction.

"Twenty-eight hours. It just seems like you'd have other things on your mind, that's all."

"I'd rather *not* have other things on my mind, Yanni. I'd rather fill my mind with problems to solve, systems to analyze, equations to unravel…anything other than the events of the last twenty-eight hours."

"I guess I can understand that," he said as the chimes sounded, indicating a guest. Yanni got up and went to the door, checking the exterior camera display before opening it, as their security detail had instructed. It seemed a silly precaution to him, since there were two armed and well-trained guards at the door itself, and two more near the elevators.

"It's Navarro," he told Deliza as he opened the door. "Captain."

"Mister Hiller," the captain replied with a respectful nod. "I was summoned?"

"You were?"

"He was," Deliza called from the sofa.

"You were...she did..."

"I understood," the captain replied. "May I?"

"Of course," Yanni replied, opening the door further and stepping aside to let him enter the room.

"How may I be of service?" Captain Navarro inquired.

"I have decided that I would indeed like to go to Sol."

"Is there some urgency I am not aware of?"

"Not particularly. I just don't think it serves any purpose for me to sit around this hotel suite, wasting credits and accomplishing nothing of value. Besides, the data cores should be returned to Earth, now that it has been secured against the Jung."

"I am not certain that is the case," Captain Navarro warned her.

"They are certainly as safe on Earth as they are here, are they not?"

"I expect that is a matter of opinion."

"Well, my opinion is that it would be better for them to be in the hands of the Alliance, where they might be able to utilize some of the technologies contained within, rather than gathering dust in the Avendahl's cargo hold."

"I understand," Captain Navarro replied. "And how soon do you wish to depart?"

"Tomorrow morning would be fine," Deliza told him, "after I sign the papers granting you full legal authority over my family's business matters in my absence."

"Perhaps you could wait an additional day?"

"Whatever for?"

"My personal shuttle is being used to ferry the family of my first officer's wife to the safety of Corinair. It will be back tomorrow evening, after which it will need to be refueled and provisioned, as well as have the data cores loaded and secured for the voyage...a matter I expect Mister Hiller will wish to supervise, since the safety of the data cores is his responsibility."

"Why can't we just take a cargo shuttle?" Deliza wondered.

"The journey will take the better part of three days' time," the captain explained. "The accommodations on a standard cargo shuttle may not be to your liking, my lady."

"He's right," Yanni said. "Trust me on this."

"In addition, my shuttle is faster, better equipped, and has better defenses than a standard cargo shuttle. I would also like to send several fast-attack jump shuttles along as escorts, to ensure your safety. I believe that Admiral Dumar would welcome their addition to his forces, and I have more than enough for the immediate future."

"All reasonable arguments," Deliza conceded. "Very well, we shall wait until the day *after* tomorrow." Deliza cocked her head to one side and nodded respectfully. "Thank you, Captain. As always, your advice and concerns for my safety are greatly appreciated."

"The pleasure is mine," Captain Navarro replied, nodding in return. "Mister Hiller."

Yanni smiled at the captain, nodding politely as

well. He opened the door, let the captain depart, and then closed it again. He looked at Deliza. "For someone who insists she is no longer a princess, you sure do sound like one at times."

* * *

Naralena looked at herself in the mirror, unfamiliar with what she saw before her. Her face was unchanged, albeit without any subtle touches from the makeup she preferred to use, but her hair was...short. It had taken her more than an hour to get up the nerve to cut it off, and then another just to get it trimmed up into something presentable. She knew little of Koharan hairstyles, only what she had seen on their entertainment and news media. And she was not a hairstylist by any stretch of the imagination. She had kept the ends trimmed herself for several years now, both while living on Haven and during her time aboard the Aurora. But her hair had been well past the middle of her back for more than a decade, and now, it was just...short.

She had been staring at it for a quarter of an hour, making final adjustments, all of which accomplished nothing. She had carefully bagged up all the hair, just as Gerard suggested, so that it could be disposed of without a trace.

She was quite impressed at his level of expertise. It was evident in the way he moved, and in the way he considered every detail and every possibility, no matter how remote, in order to prepare for anything that might occur. It engendered trust in him, and it made her feel safe, or at least as *safe* as she could feel, considering the circumstances.

One last look in the mirror. "How did you get so

far away from home?" she asked her reflection. She took a deep breath, picked up the bag of hair, and finally left the bathroom.

Naralena walked confidently out into the living room, ready to face the rest of the group in her new persona. But the *group* was nowhere to be found. Only Gerard was there, standing in the kitchen.

"Finally," he said as he noticed her. "I was afraid something had happened to you in there." He turned to look at her as she approached. "Wow, you look great!"

"Really?" she asked, doubtful. "Wait, if you're lying, I don't want to know."

"No, really. You look much better. It was a good choice of cuts. It frames your face much better, makes you look half your age."

"You are well trained," she retorted, sitting down at the table.

"I'm sorry if it's cold. I've been holding breakfast for so long, I thought I was going to have to throw it out and start making lunch," Gerard said as he came over and sat down across the table from her. "It's not much, I'm afraid. Some fried potted meat and some rather stale biscuits."

"I'm sure it will be fine," she replied, picking up one of the biscuits.

"The others have gone hunting," Gerard explained as he took a biscuit himself. "With any luck, we will have fresh meat later today."

Naralena bit into the biscuit, tearing off a piece and chewing it.

"Is something wrong?" Gerard asked. "It's the biscuits, isn't it?"

"They are indeed stale," she said as politely as possible.

"They are supposed to have a very long shelf life, for storage in such remote cabins. I guess it has been some time since any of my people had a chance to rotate supplies."

"It's all right," Naralena assured him. "I've had much worse."

"I find that hard to believe."

"Why do you say that?" Naralena wondered.

"It's just that you have a rather stately, elegant manner about you. I am trained to notice such things, you know."

"I am surprised that recent experiences have not bred such mannerisms out of me," she said as she picked up a piece of the fried, potted meat.

"It is subtle, to be sure, but it is there nonetheless. I would guess that you came from a wealthy family, with a very proper upbringing and a good education."

"Guilty on all counts, I'm afraid." Naralena made a face as she chewed the meat.

"Too salty?"

"A bit."

"I tried to give it a bit of flavor. I guess I failed. To be honest, I never have been much for cooking."

"I never would have guessed."

"Hey, in all fairness, I didn't have much to work with," Gerard defended. "So, I know you're not from Earth," he continued. "So where *are* you from?"

"Volon."

A surprised look came across his face. "I would've guessed one of the core worlds, or maybe even the fringe. I've never heard of Volon."

"It's a very long way away from here," she told him.

"It's in the Pentaurus cluster isn't it? The one Jessica was talking about?"

"Not in it, but nearby."

"So how far away is it?"

"About a thousand light years."

Gerard looked even more surprised. Then he cocked his head to one side, squinting. "You're not kidding, are you?"

Naralena said nothing, only shaking her head.

"Jesus, how far can that jump drive take people?"

"It wasn't a quick journey," she assured him. "It takes more than a month for larger ships like the Aurora. But we have smaller ships that can make it in a few days. Jump-enabled comm-drones can make it in a few hours."

"Incredible," he muttered. After a moment of contemplation, he continued. "So, you're a well-to-do, well educated young lady from the planet Volon," he said as he choked down a piece of his biscuit. "What is your specialty?"

"My specialty?"

"What did you study in school? What career did you train for?"

"Languages. I was trained to speak many different languages."

"Really, I speak a few myself, I'm proud to say. English, Spanish, a little Russian, and obviously Jung, Cetian, and Koharan, which admittedly isn't that different from Cetian. How many languages do you speak?"

"At last count, thirty-seven."

Gerard's mouth hung open, a wad of half-chewed stale biscuit still visible on his tongue.

"You might want to close your mouth... You've still got a hunk of..."

Gerard closed his mouth and swallowed, nearly choking on the piece of biscuit. "Thirty-seven, huh?"

he said, trying not to appear to shocked. "That's impress... How the hell does anyone learn to speak thirty-seven languages?" he blurted out.

"I was genetically skewed in vitro," she told him.

"You mean, they gave you the ability to speak thirty-seven languages, genetically? They can do that?"

"On Volon, they can genetically enhance traits that an embryo already possesses," Naralena explained.

"How do they know?"

"There are tests that are conducted just after conception. But it just means that whatever natural linguistic abilities I had were increased. It's not like I was born speaking all those languages."

"Well, I figured that," Gerard said. "Do they do that with every embryo?"

"No, it's an elective procedure, and it's quite expensive. Very few can afford it."

"Then I was right, your parents were wealthy."

"They were not poor, but they were also not wealthy enough to afford the procedure outright. They had to take out loans to pay for it. They made payments on the loans for my entire life."

"If they couldn't afford it, why did they do it?"

"Only a select few get to attend institutions of higher learning," she explained. "Most go to trade schools, get decent jobs, then spend their lives working and living check to check. My parents wanted better for me. Skewing my genes insured that I would get into a university, and that I would have a chance for a better life."

"Then how did you end up in the Alliance, and a thousand light years from home?" Gerard wondered.

"My father was in an accident at work. After that,

they could no longer afford to make the payments. They were going to indenture my mother..."

"Indenture? You mean, like a slave or something?"

"On many of the worlds in and around the Pentaurus cluster, failure to pay a debt is punishable by indentured servitude. Once convicted, the creditor has the right to sell the debtor sentence to whomever they choose in order to recover the debt. They couldn't take my father, as he was disabled and could not fetch an adequate price to cover their bad debt. They were going to send my mother to work for the ring miners in the Haven system. I couldn't let that happen. I was young and healthy. She was not. She might not have survived."

"How long were you required to serve as a slave?"

"Five years. Early into my second year, the Aurora came to Haven. One thing led to another, and here I am, a thousand light years from home, hiding out in a lakeside cabin with three men I hardly know."

"So what happened with your debt?" Gerard wondered. He had long since stopped eating, enthralled by her tale. "I mean, if you left before they got their money's worth... They didn't go after your parents, did they?"

"They would have," Naralena admitted, "but after the Alliance formed and overthrew the Ta'Akar Empire, Tug... I mean, Casimir, he paid my parents' debt. He even got my father treatment. Last I heard from them, they were doing quite well."

"Damn," Gerard exclaimed. "That's quite a story." He watched her a moment as she suffered through another piece of over-salted meat. "It was all true, right? You weren't pulling my leg, were you?"

"Nope. It's all true."

"So, what do you do for the Alliance?"

"Since I spoke pretty much every language in the area, Captain Scott asked me to be his communications officer. I've been doing that for about a year and a half now."

"Then how did you end up on a covert mission on an enemy-held world?"

"Jessica wasn't getting the hang of Jung quickly enough. Her Koharan and Cetian were passable, but..."

"So they sent you to do the talking if any Jung asked you questions," Gerard surmised.

"That's about it."

"Man, and I thought *my* life was strange."

* * *

"We have confirmed Lieutenant Commander Nash's intelligence about the capabilities of the Jung nanites," Doctor Galloway told the admiral over the video comm-screen. "They appear to be simple sensory monitoring devices, designed to monitor and record visual and audio inputs from the host."

"How is that possible?" the admiral wondered from his office on the Karuzara. "Wouldn't they need an enormous amount of data storage capabilities?"

"One would think, yes. We're not quite sure, to be honest, but the prevailing theory is that only a small percentage of the nanites are used for sensory monitoring, while the rest are used for storage. Others are used to act as a sort of 'hive mind', a distributed intelligence capable of analyzing the data and deciding what should be kept for later transmission and what can be discarded."

"How did you figure all of this out, Doctor?" The

admiral leaned forward in his seat, curious about the doctor's findings.

"Well, a lot of it is still guesswork, I'm afraid. To be honest, without the descriptions from Lieutenant Commander Nash and the Koharan reporter, we'd probably still be rather clueless at this point."

"Can we do anything about them?" the admiral asked.

"Not yet. However, it should be relatively simple to create a method to screen everyone for the presence of Jung nanites."

"You can distinguish them from Corinairan nanites?"

"Oh, quite easily, yes," Doctor Galloway assured him. "Our nanites are made of synthetic materials, while the Jung nanites are made from materials found in the human body, or in the food that humans normally consume. That's why ours require booster dosages, or dosages based on the amount of treatment needed. The Jung nanites are able to replicate using raw materials found in situ. In fact, we believe that Mister Bowden's description of their function is likely quite accurate. Once the Jung have identified a host that is likely to be privy to desired intelligence, they can command the target host's nanites to start replicating in order to increase their capabilities as an unknowing operative."

"So you believe that the host has no idea they are acting as an agent for the Jung?" the admiral asked.

"That would have to be the case," she told him. "The human psyche is very powerful. If the host was aware that they were being forced to do things against their own ethics and beliefs, they would not make very effective operatives."

"Can we make use of these nanites, maybe somehow take control of them?" the admiral asked.

"Highly doubtful, sir. Their control codes are undoubtedly encrypted, and we don't even know yet how they communicate with their controllers. Maybe, in a few years..."

"Can you at least neutralize them?"

The doctor shook her head. "Not without harming the host... Not yet. But we should be able to come up with something without having to crack their control codes. At the very least, we could command our own nanites to go after and destroy the Jung nanites, but that would most likely only work on those individuals with low numbers of Jung nanites within them."

"Well, that's better than nothing," the admiral admitted. "Get me a way to detect them as soon as you can, Doctor. Something that is portable, easy to use, and that we can utilize everywhere."

"Yes, sir."

Admiral Dumar pressed the button to end the video communication link. He leaned back in his chair and sighed as he rubbed his temples. *Now I've got two battlefronts,* he thought. *Outer space* and *inner space.*

* * *

Deliza and Yanni peered out the window of the limousine as it rolled across the Aitkenna spaceport tarmac, heading for Captain Navarro's private shuttle.

"That's his private shuttle?" Yanni gasped in astonishment. "It's huge! It's more like a space yacht or something! How much money does a captain make around here?"

"Remember, the Avendahl *belongs* to House Navarro," Deliza explained, unfazed by the size of the ship. "Compared to the cost of the Avendahl, this ship is nothing."

"Come on, Deliza, it's a space yacht, for cryin' out loud."

Deliza smiled. "Okay, it's a space yacht. I admit it. It's huge, it's expensive, and it's probably incredibly ostentatious inside. But remember, these ships were all built during the reign of Caius. Such displays of wealth and power were encouraged among the nobles. It made them more dependent on the empire, and it spoiled them to no end, so that they would never want to return to their previous, less extravagant lifestyles."

"Oh, stop it," Yanni said. "Stop trying to be a princess and just admit that you're excited to go on a space yacht."

Deliza tried to maintain a dignified composure, but quickly failed as the car came to a stop. "Okay, it's a space yacht!" she exclaimed, no longer able to contain her excitement. She quickly regained her composure as a guard came and opened her door for her from the outside. She took his hand and stepped up out of the limousine. Yanni climbed out of the vehicle after her, trying unsuccessfully to hide the smile on his face as he took in the entire length of the ship.

"Miss Ta'Akar, Mister Hiller," Captain Navarro greeted them both as he approached. "Welcome to my personal pride and joy, the Mirai," he announced, sweeping his arm in grand fashion in a wide arc toward the ship.

"After your eldest?" Deliza asked.

"Indeed."

"A touching gesture by a father," she approved.

"I'd like to introduce your crew," Captain Navarro began. "First, we have Lieutenant Chandler, the pilot and ship's commanding officer."

"Pleasure, ma'am," the lieutenant said, nodding respectfully.

"This is the copilot, and engineer, Ensign Nambianno," Captain Navarro continued as he headed down the line. "Sergeant Isan, the ship's chief steward, Sergeant Liamo, the ship's cook, and finally Sergeant Annakeros, the assistant steward."

"It takes five people to operate this ship?" Yanni asked in disbelief.

"It can be flown by a single pilot," Captain Navarro explained, "but it takes a full crew to operate and care for her properly."

"It's a pleasure to meet all of you," Deliza told the crew. "We'll try not to be too much trouble during our long journey."

"I assure you, they will take good care of you, wherever you may choose to travel," Captain Navarro promised.

"Excuse me?" Yanni said.

"We're going to Sol," Deliza reminded the captain.

"Yes, I know," Captain Navarro replied. "However, to ensure your safety, I have instructed the crew of the Mirai to remain near you at all times, in case you need transportation in a hurry."

"Captain, that won't be necessary," Deliza argued.

"On the contrary, it is quite necessary. I made a promise to your father just before his death, a promise to see to your safety, and I intend to keep that promise to the best of my ability. As long as you are away from the Pentaurus cluster and out of my sphere of influence, this ship *is* the best of my ability."

Deliza took a deep breath and let it out in a long sigh. She turned to Captain Navarro. "I am humbled by your gracious offer, Captain. My father's instincts about you were correct. You are an honorable man," she added, placing her hand on his upper arm.

"My great-grandfather once told me that all anyone truly owns is their reputation, and that nothing speaks of one's reputation more than one's deeds." Captain Navarro looked at the Mirai fondly. "I shall miss her," he admitted. He looked back at Deliza. "But she now has a more worthy mission than hauling a spoiled captain and his family around on vacation."

"Would you like to show us around?" Deliza asked.

"Would that I could," the captain replied. "Unfortunately, I have pressing business to which I must attend." He bowed his head to them both before departing. "Until we meet again."

Deliza nodded respectfully as Captain Navarro turned and walked away, headed for one of the Avendahl's nearby combat jumpers. She turned and looked at the Mirai's crew. "I trust we can depart shortly?"

"Once Mister Hiller has inspected the cargo, yes," the lieutenant confirmed.

"If you will follow me, ma'am, I will help you both find your way aboard and show you around the ship," Sergeant Isan offered.

"Lead the way, Sergeant," Yanni replied, excited to see the ship up close.

The rest of the Mirai's crew turned and headed

toward the boarding ramp, taking care not to walk on the long, red carpet laid out for the guests. Sergeant Isan paused long enough for the crew to get a head start, and to make sure that the ground crew was taking care of their guests' modest luggage. He smiled at Deliza and Yanni, then turned and headed toward the ship as well, also walking alongside the carpet.

They followed the sergeant up the boarding ramp steps to the passenger hatch in the middle of the Mirai's port side. As they entered the ship, the sergeant took their coats, handing them to his assistant to carefully store for the journey. He gestured aft. "After you."

Deliza turned and headed down the short central corridor, past several storage lockers, as well as a steep staircase that led below decks. She stepped over the raised threshold of the next hatch and entered the ship's main salon. It was spacious and luxurious, with an abnormally high ceiling at the forward end that angled upward as it continued aft. There were large windows on all sides, as well as several more overhead. At the aft end was a balcony that overlooked the entire cabin, with a stairwell at each end. Through a set of double doors at the center of the balcony, Deliza could see into the spacious master suite.

The main salon was well furnished, but not overly done, which surprised Deliza. She had seen pictures of far more ornate ships used by the nobles of Takara, and the fact that this one was more understated reaffirmed her opinion of the leader of House Navarro.

"My God," Yanni said under his breath.

Deliza turned and flashed him an irritated look, followed by a controlled smile.

"Beats the hell out of a utility shuttle," he added.

"The main salon has everything you might need to relax during your time aboard," Sergeant Isan explained, as he pointed to the various amenities of the room. "There is a refreshment center and wet bar here, in the forward area, with a small dining area to starboard. A viewing screen drops down from the overhead, and we carry a vast library of entertainment videos from all of the industrialized worlds in the Pentaurus sector. The master suite is upstairs, and there are six more staterooms aft through the central corridor. All functions are operated via remotes conveniently placed throughout the main salon and in the master suite, as well as the staterooms. Should you need anything at all, there is a call button on each of the remotes. Are there any questions, ma'am?"

"No, thank you," Deliza replied. "I'm sure we will be quite comfortable."

"As soon as Mister Hiller has inspected the cargo, and I have checked that the ship is ready for departure, Sergeant Annakeros will be by to brief you on all the safety procedures for your journey."

"Very well," Deliza agreed.

"Mister Hiller, if you would please follow me aft, I will show you to the main cargo hold."

"Thank you, Sergeant." Yanni turned and smiled at Deliza as the sergeant headed aft. "I'll be right back."

CHAPTER SIX

Jessica entered the small office being used as an interrogation room at the Ghatazhak base on Porto Santo. The guard outside the door closed and locked it behind her as she approached the table in the middle of the room.

Jessica looked at the young woman sitting quietly on the other side of the table. She was about the same age as her, with long, wavy red hair that had been neatly tied back. She appeared fit and of average build, and had already been redressed in the standard orange jumpsuit given to all prisoners. The woman looked frightened, making only brief eye contact before looking away.

"Hello," she greeted as she pulled out a chair and sat down. "I'm Lieutenant Commander Nash."

"Nash? Are you related to Captain Nash?"

Jessica looked at her oddly, surprised by her question. "I am. He is my brother."

The women caught Jessica's use of the present tense, relief washing over her face. "Then he is alive?"

"Yes, he is," Jessica replied.

"We were speaking, and then there were explosions, and alarms, and... I was afraid he had done something terrible, that he..."

"Had blown himself up? Not exactly. I take it then, that you're Kaya Allemahn?"

"Yes."

"My brother spoke of you."

"I hope he does not think badly of me," she said. "I was only saying what I was told to say."

"I think he figured that much out," Jessica assured her. "That's why I'm talking to you, instead of a Ghatazhak interrogator."

"Ghatazhak?"

"The men who boarded your ship," Jessica explained.

"Oh my, yes. They were very frightening. Such eyes... Without emotion... Like machines."

"Yeah, they have their moments."

"May I ask a question?" Kaya wondered.

"Sure."

"Where am I?"

"You're on an Alliance military base, on an island, in the middle of an ocean," Jessica clarified.

"On what world?"

Jessica thought for a moment. "Well, you're going to find out sooner or later... You're on Earth."

A look of panic flashed across Kaya's face.

"Don't worry," Jessica told her, "there is no plague here. We're not a bunch of crazed wackos trying to infect the galaxy. Surprise... The Jung lied to you."

The panic turned to confusion as Kaya started to think things through. "But, this cannot be Earth. We were in that transport for only minutes. We could not have left the system..."

"Trust me, Kaya, you're on Earth."

"I do not believe you," Kaya said, shaking her head. "What you say cannot be true."

Jessica reached over and unlocked Kaya's restraints. "Come here," she said, motioning for Kaya to follow as she got up and headed for the window. She threw back the curtains, revealing a view of the Atlantic Ocean. "You have any oceans like that in the Tau Ceti system?"

Kaya rose and made her way cautiously to the window, unsure of what she'd find. Her eyes widened and her mouth fell agape as she looked out through the barred window at a vast ocean stretching out to the horizon. "This cannot be," she whispered in disbelief.

"You're just going to have to trust me on this one, Kaya," Jessica said as she returned to her seat. "I don't have any more evidence than that at the moment."

Kaya continued to stare out the window in wonder as Jessica sat back down. "As far as I know, the Jung don't allow women in their military. So what were you and your girlfriends doing aboard the Jar-Benakh? Civilian contractors? Tour group? Housekeeping? Am I getting any warmer?"

Kaya closed her eyes for a moment, overwhelmed by the realization that she had somehow been magically transported to another star system. But then she opened her eyes again, and that very reality was staring her in the face. "There are no such bodies of water on any of the Cetian worlds," she muttered, the truth finally settling in.

"So, how about it?" Jessica pressed. "What were you doing aboard the Jar-Benakh?"

Kaya looked down in shame. "It is not something that a woman can easily talk about."

"Yeah, that's what I thought." Jessica sighed. "Look, Kaya, nobody is judging you here. I'm just looking for answers. The Jung are bad, we all know that, so there's no reason for you to feel ashamed."

Kaya looked up again, her gaze returning to the

ocean outside. "I have been on the Jar-Benakh for three years now. I was attending the university at Collend when I was taken. I was in my final year."

"Taken by the Jung?"

"No, by Koharans. Men who sell young women to the Jung, as slaves."

"Okay, that's a different twist. These men, did they sell you to a Jung officer on the Jar-Benakh?"

"Technically, we belonged to the captain."

"All of you?"

"Yes. He would share us with his officers, as rewards for good performance. Each night, they would come and choose their companion for the evening. Sometimes, they would keep us for the night, sometimes for the day. If we were lucky, one would favor us and convince the captain to let us serve the one officer for an extended period." Kaya turned back to Jessica and started walking back to her seat. "It was often better than being ravaged by a different pig each night, especially if you were lucky enough to be selected by an officer who didn't enjoy beating his companion." Kaya sat down, holding her head up with some modicum of pride. "I was the favorite of Major Goya, and had been so for more than three weeks."

"And Major Goya didn't get off on beating women?"

"He was a pig, but he did not beat me."

"What was the major's job on the Jar-Benakh?" Jessica asked.

"He was chief of security. That is how I ended up speaking to your brother. The task of negotiating your brother's surrender fell upon Major Goya. He was quite fluent in the Cetian languages; however, his English was poor."

"How is it *you* speak such good English?" Jessica wondered.

"I studied classic human languages at the university. English is considered the language of scholars. It was the universal language throughout the sector, up until the great plague."

"Is that why the major chose you? Because you could speak English?"

"Partly. He hoped for a surface assignment on Earth, once the Jar-Benakh and the rest of the fleet were reassigned there." A wry smile formed on her lips. "He would not have gotten that assignment. His English was very bad."

"So, was this harem arrangement unique to the Jar-Benakh?"

"Before I was sold, I heard the men speaking of more than one ship. I heard them speaking about how to obtain more women, about making more money as more ships arrived. I believe they provided women to all the Jung ships."

"That's a lot of women to go 'missing' without explanation," Jessica observed. "How is it no one noticed?"

"I have spoken with the other women. Most are like myself, from less wealthy families, from small towns. Even if my parents were to ask, it is doubtful that anyone would do anything. The local authorities are not allowed to conduct criminal investigations, and most families cannot afford to hire private investigators. Many of us were forced to send messages to our families, telling them lies about how we found wonderful new lives working for the Jung on other worlds."

"To be honest, I'm a little surprised by all of this," Jessica admitted. "I always thought the Jung military was more disciplined, that their officers had a sense of duty and honor."

"It is different among each clan," Kaya explained. "One of the women had been traded from the Jar-Toritor. She spoke of much better treatment than on the Jar-Benakh."

"And that ship was run by a different clan?"

"Yes. The Mogan clan. The Jar-Benakh was of the Kirton clan."

"Yet both clans are okay with keeping sex slaves on board military ships?"

"They are men without women, and they are a long way from home," Kaya said, almost sympathetically. "It is expected of such men."

"They couldn't just have brothels on the surface, like everyone else?"

"Brothels?"

"Houses of prostitution," Jessica explained.

"The Jung serving aboard ships rarely travel to the surface," Kaya said. "At least not the officers."

"Hmm. That's interesting. The Jung do put a lot of boots on the ground, though."

"They are of different clans, I suspect."

"Interesting."

"May I ask another question?"

"Go ahead," Jessica replied.

"Will you be returning us to our homes?"

"Honestly, I don't know," Jessica admitted. She thought about all the Jung ships they had destroyed in recent months, wondering how many innocent young women had died, every time she had pressed a button to fire one of the Aurora's weapons. "I can promise you one thing, though. None of you are going back to the Jung, that's for sure."

* * *

"Lieutenant Commander," Commander Telles called after Jessica as she left the interrogation room.

Jessica turned back to face him. "What do you want, Telles?" she asked as she turned back and continued down the corridor to the exit.

"It's *Commander* Telles, Lieutenant Commander," he said as he followed her down the corridor, "and I would like a word with you, in private."

"I'm a little busy right now," Jessica said as she passed the guard station in the entry foyer and headed out the door.

"I can make it an order if you like?" the commander pressed as politely as possible.

"Don't push your luck," she remarked as she exited the building and descended the steps down to the walkway outside.

Commander Telles stopped at the top of the steps, standing fast, his hands behind his back as he spoke. "You will stop right there, Lieutenant Commander," he barked, "or I will have you arrested and brought up on charges. Am I making myself clear?"

Jessica turned back to face the commander, her head cocked to one side and contempt in her eyes.

"Stand at attention, Lieutenant Commander!" the commander demanded.

Jessica begrudgingly straightened her posture into something resembling full military attention.

"I believe a salute is in order when in the presence of a superior officer."

Jessica took a deep breath, stiffened up, and

slowly raised her hand to her brow in salute, holding it fast until returned, as per protocol.

Commander Telles slowly descended the steps, making her hold the salute for as long as possible to make his point. He walked up to her, stopping a meter away, then raised his hand and returned her salute. "At ease, Lieutenant Commander."

Jessica assumed a proper stance, her feet shoulder width apart and her hands clasped behind her back, again making an obvious effort to follow protocols. She stood there looking straight ahead, saying nothing.

"I would like a word with you... in private," he repeated slowly. He pointed to an open courtyard to his left. "If you please."

Jessica turned and walked over to the courtyard a few meters away, coming to a stop and resuming her original stance. "How may I help you, Commander?" she asked without emotion.

Commander Telles stood slightly less than a meter away from her. "What the hell is wrong with you, Lieutenant Commander? Making threats to a superior officer? Calling out my master sergeant? Insubordination, behavior unbecoming... Am I leaving anything out here?"

"Permission to speak freely, sir?" Jessica asked.

"Speak your mind, Lieutenant Commander."

Jessica maintained her posture as she looked directly at the commander. "You know damn well what this is about, Telles. You said you'd get her off of that rock. You said you'd take care of it yourself, didn't you?"

"I did."

"Then where the fuck is she, Commander?"

"She is with Gerard and the CLA. He gave me

his comm frequency and authentication algorithm before he left. When we were ordered to withdraw, I knew we did not have the resources to come for her and that doing so would likely endanger her further. So I sent Gerard a message, told him to take her and go into hiding, and that we would attempt contact later, when it was safe."

"That wasn't the plan," Jessica protested.

"Neither was withdrawing!" Telles argued, "and neither was losing half my men! In case you've forgotten, this is a fucking war we're fighting. Shit doesn't always go as planned. Now, when the opportunity presents itself, I *will* go in and get Naralena out, *myself*, or I *will* die in the attempt. Not because I made a promise to you, but because it is the right thing to do, and it will be the right time to do it. And just for the record, the Ghatazhak don't *like* leaving people behind. We're just smart enough and strong enough to know that, sometimes, the mission has to come first. And those who *do* get left behind know that as well."

Jessica stood there, saying nothing as the commander continued to stare at her. It was the most emotion she had ever seen him exhibit in all the months she had known him. She wanted to argue, but she had nothing to say. She knew he was right, and that she was wrong, and she wanted to apologize to him, but the words just wouldn't form. Instead, all she said was, "Is there anything else, Commander?"

"Negative," Commander Telles replied. "Actually, there is one more thing. I would recommend that you refrain from getting 'in the face' of any more of my men. They don't all like you as much as the master sergeant and I do."

A small grin threatened to peek out from the left side of Jessica's mouth. "Yes, sir."

Telles noticed the subtle change in her expression and decided that he had indeed accomplished this particular mission. "Dismissed."

Jessica turned smartly and headed for the airfield. As she turned the corner between the buildings, Kata Mun and her porta-cam operator came walking toward her.

"Lieutenant Commander Nash," Kata called out. "I was hoping we might see you. We heard you were on Porto Santo. Do you have time for an interview?"

"Now's not a good time for me," she said in all honesty. "However, there are a few dozen Cetian women being held over in the interrogation center that you might want to interview."

"Are we cleared for that?"

"I just cleared you. If they give you any guff, just ask to speak with Commander Telles, and tell him I said it was a good idea."

* * *

Naralena looked out across the lake, watching the sunlight dance off the ripples in the water. It was peaceful here, more peaceful than she could ever remember. It was hard to imagine that she was in any danger, and she had to remind herself not to let her guard down. The last time she had let herself relax on this world, Gerard's men had come bursting in the back door to rescue her and Jessica just as the Jung were breaking through the front door to arrest them.

She took in a full, deep breath, letting it out

slowly. "Not that I'm complaining, mind you, but why are we sitting here again?"

"It's what couples vacationing at a lake do, isn't it?" Gerard posed.

"I wouldn't know. We didn't have lakeside cabins on Volon. We didn't even have lakes on Haven."

"No lakes? Where did your water come from?"

"The ground. Haven has a long dark period while it goes behind its parent world. I don't even know how many Earth days it is. A few months, probably. It would rain constantly. Everything would get soaked. The ground would turn to mud, things would flood, it was awful. Then, the sun would return and the rain would stop. There would be a lot of ponds and such for weeks, but they would eventually dry up. The rest of the water would just seep into the ground."

"Where did the water for the rains come from?"

"There were some oceans on the far side, but no one lived over there. They were full of sulfur and they smelled horrible. You couldn't get within a few hundred kilometers of the coast."

"Doesn't sound like a place worth settling, if you ask me," Gerard commented.

"It was pretty much just a mining camp that eventually grew into a city. There's a huge ring of rock and ice, rich in all sorts of ores and minerals. The Haven Syndicate set up camp there centuries ago. Most of the worlds in the area go there to buy the ores that are unique to that system."

"What's the Haven Syndicate?"

"A couple of brothers who didn't want to work for the family business in some system. Nobody knows which one, actually. They got themselves a couple ships and struck out on their own. They found a mining camp where a handful of families were barely scraping out a living. They tried to buy in, but the families didn't want them. So they killed them and took it for themselves."

"Sounds kind of like the Jung Expansionist caste," Gerard said.

"Caste?" Naralena wondered. "I'm not familiar with that term."

"It's like a subgroup within a culture, one with certain common beliefs or goals that separate their group from other groups within the same culture. The Jung have four of them, at least at the top level. They used to refer to themselves as clans, but as the Jung Empire grew, the clans became more numerous and caste groupings started to form."

"What are the four castes?" Naralena asked.

"Ruling, Business, Military, and Labor," Gerard replied. "Ruling and Military can be further subdivided as well. The Ruling caste was originally composed of the founding clans from many centuries past. In recent centuries, they divided into two main branches. The founders became known as the Isolationists. They believe that the Jung should only be concerned with their own world. The Expansionists are the ones who are a threat, and there are two mindsets there as well; the ones who want to take over the entire sector, and the ones who want to rule everything. We call *them* the Conquerors."

"Shouldn't the military caste be the Conquerors?" Naralena questioned.

"You'd think so, yes. But the military caste doesn't concern themselves with politics. They only care about service. They, too, are divided into two sub-castes."

"This is getting complicated."

"The Honor caste is the original Military caste. They have always seen themselves as the protectors of the Jung Empire. The Warrior caste is far more aggressive, caring only about conquest. They see battle as the only path to honor. They'd rather die in battle than live a long, boring life just 'playing' soldier."

"It sounds like a very strange system," Naralena said, "and very confusing."

Gerard shrugged. "Not really. The more you study it, the more sense it makes. It's all about human nature. Every one of us has our motivations. That's the key to understanding such systems. You have to understand their motivations. What do they want? How can they get it? To what lengths are they prepared to go *to* get it? There's always a reason behind everything any person, or group of people, does. It doesn't always make sense to everyone else, but it must have made sense to those who chose to do it, or they wouldn't have done it to begin with."

"I don't know. My father used to say that some men are just evil. At the time, I think he was referring to Caius Ta'Akar."

"Who's that?"

"A prince who killed his own father, then tried to assassinate his older brother, all to start his own empire." Naralena explained.

"Others may judge him to be evil, and they may be correct, but I expect most of the conquerors throughout history, even the most ruthless ones, did not consider themselves to be evil. Most believed they were doing what was right for their people."

"My father also used to say that if you ask for too much, you might get nothing."

Gerard nodded. "*Za dvoomya zaitsamee pagonishsya, ni odnovo ne paimayesh.*"

Naralena smiled. "'If you run after two hares, you will catch neither.' I forgot, you mentioned you spoke Russian."

"On my father's side."

"So, who controls the Military caste?"

"For the most part they're controlled by the Ruling caste. Of course, since they are pretty much divided into, technically, three different camps, decisions are often unpopular with the masses."

"I don't see how the Jung can possibly exert any kind of control over such a vast area, even with comm-drones that can travel one hundred times the speed of light," Naralena argued.

"It's actually not as hard as you might think. Each region has a leader who is free to make decisions based on the Jung Empire's policies known to him at that time. The same is true of the commanding officers of each ship, be they gunships or battle platforms. If the next highest official cannot be consulted in a timely fashion, then the authority to make a decision falls on the highest authority in that area. In most cases, that ends up being either a system ruler or the admiral in command of a battle platform."

"What about their military? How do they coordinate on a strategic level? How do they plan for invasions and such?"

"That's where it becomes more difficult. Their comm-drones may be fast, but it takes a lot longer to move assets into place. Because of that, Jung forces are in a constant state of flux, moving about to be ready to respond when and where they are needed. That's why there were twice as many forces in this system as usual. They were building up their forces to reinvade Sol. I even heard rumors that there was another battle group expected in a few years."

"The Jung leaders are a patient bunch, I'll give them that," Naralena confessed.

"Some believe that the Jung, at least those living on the Jung homeworld, have much longer life spans than most humans, perhaps two to three hundred years. But I suspect they are indeed only rumors. Another rumor I've heard recently is that some of the Warrior caste ships are considering abandoning the Expansionist's plans to conquer Earth and rule the Sol sector. With the rise of the Alliance, and their ability to jump between stars at will, many are following other Warrior caste ships that left the sector decades ago in search of new human-inhabited systems to conquer. There are stories of hundreds, possibly even thousands of civilized worlds further out in space, in all directions, all inhabited by the descendants of refugees who fled the Sol sector to escape the bio-digital plague a thousand years ago."

"We've heard similar rumors," Naralena admitted. "Do you think they're true?"

"It's certainly possible. There is no shortage of Jung clan leaders who would love to start their own empire, free of the other castes. And one thing's for sure, the Jung do not like getting their asses kicked, so it makes sense that they would go someplace where they'd meet less resistance."

"Do you really think there are hundreds of human-inhabited worlds out there?" Naralena wondered.

Gerard looked over at her, surprised by her question. "That's an odd question, coming from you. How many inhabited worlds do you know of back in the Pentaurus sector?"

"There are at least thirty of them," she said. "Not all of them are fully industrialized, planet-wide civilizations, mind you; about half, maybe."

"How big is your sector?"

"About the same as Sol."

"There are at least fifty inhabited worlds here, and at least half of them are fully industrialized. So that's about eighty worlds right there. It only took three hundred years for those worlds to develop here, probably not much longer in your neck of the woods, not after you factor in the travel time getting out that far. So, imagine if one hundred ships left Sol a thousand years ago, all of them headed out in different directions. Each one of them settles a pretty little Earth-like world. They grow, they thrive, they overpopulate, like humans always do. Then they spread out as well, just like the people did in your sector. We probably *are* talking thousands."

Naralena thought about it for a moment, as Gerard leaned back onto his elbows and gazed up at the twilight sky. She looked up as well, noticing that a few stars had appeared.

"Man, what I wouldn't give for the life span of a Jung, and a ship with a jump drive. Can you imagine all the places you could go? All the people you could meet? All the things you could see?"

She looked at him, noticing a boyish look on his wrinkled, weather-beaten face. Despite all he had seen and done in his lifetime, he still looked up at the night sky in wonder.

"It's getting dark," he finally said. "We should probably head back. The boys should already have their kills cleaned and ready to cook."

"Just a few more minutes?" Naralena begged, looking up at the sky herself.

* * *

"Are you sure you want to do this?" Commander Telles said as they approached the door to the dormitory where the women from the Jar-Benakh were being detained.

"If these women are from the Tau Ceti system, then I think it's my duty to report their story to my viewers," Kata insisted. "Besides, Lieutenant Commander Nash said it would be a good idea."

"I know, that's why I asked," the commander replied, one eyebrow knowingly raised. "Sergeant," he said, nodding to the guard at the door.

The sergeant opened the door, allowing Kata and her porta-cam operator to enter.

"Just knock when you're ready to leave," the commander instructed, after which he nodded at the sergeant again to close the door.

Kata looked out across the large room. There were barred windows on either side, all with closed shutters on the outside, making it impossible for those inside to see out. There were metal bunk beds along either wall, none of which looked terribly comfortable. The women, which Kata guessed to be around thirty in number, were all attractive and young, none of them looking a day over twenty-five. They were all clad in orange, oversized jumpsuits and flip-flops, and every one of them had their hair unceremoniously tied back. The oddest thing was that, for women from worlds that were quite conscience about their appearance, not one of them wore any makeup.

At least half of the women were gathered around a woman with long, red hair, listening intently to her every word with looks of amazement and disbelief on their faces.

Several of the women nearest her saw the portacam and immediately withdrew, not wanting to be recorded on video. A few others looked curious.

The red-haired woman in the middle of the group was the first to speak to Kata, rising from the circle of women around her and walking toward her. "You're Kata Mun, aren't you?" she asked, almost in disbelief. "I've seen you on the news feeds." Her face suddenly became animated. "Then she was lying, we're not on Earth. We must still be in the Tau Ceti system!"

"No, no," Kata disagreed, "we're not in the Tau Ceti system. They weren't lying to you. We are on Earth. I've seen it, flown over it. I've even seen it from orbit."

Kaya Allemahn's face became crestfallen. "But..."

"I know, it's impossible, but it's true. We *are* on Earth. There is no denying it."

"Then the Jung *were* lying?" another women asked.

"Yes, they were...about everything," Kata replied.

"Then how... I mean, why are *you* here?" Kaya wondered. "Did the Jung take you as well?"

"How is a long story, why is simple... Wait... Did you just say *take*? As in 'against your will'?"

"Yes," Kaya replied. "We were all taken against our will, and sold to the Jung."

"How..." Kata stumbled, nearly speechless. "How long have you been...uh..."

"A slave?" Kaya looked down again. "Three years. Three very long years."

"Have all of these girls been slaves that long?"

"Some more, some less."

"My God," Kata muttered in disbelief. "We had no idea. Are you willing to talk about it on camera?" she asked Kaya. She looked out at the rest of them. "I can get messages to all your families. It may take some time, but I promise you, they will soon know that you are all alive and well, I swear it." She looked at Kaya again. "These people, the Alliance, the people of Earth... They are not our enemies. They will not hurt you. I am sure of it. Would you like to record a message for your family?"

Kaya's eyes began to tear up. "Yes, please," she replied in a squeaky, almost inaudible voice. She swallowed hard, wiping away her tears. "We all would."

Kata looked up, past Kaya Allemahn, at the rest of the women in the dormitory, as they all began to move toward her and her porta-cam operator.

* * *

Deliza and Yanni walked down the Mirai's boarding ramp. Deliza stopped a few steps from the bottom, scanning the various faces on the tarmac, hoping to see someone she knew.

The airbase they had landed on once belonged to the Jung. Now, its various hangars were connected by a series of large railroad tracks, winding their way in and out of each hangar along the flight line. Most of the hangars were open, as the weather was generally quite mild on Tanna this time of year.

An open-air shuttle with four rows of seats and a small cargo deck on the back pulled up. There were two people in the front... A driver and a passenger whose face Deliza *did* recognize.

She waved excitedly at the passenger. "Abby!"

she cried, still waving as she ran the last few steps to the woman she had so admired during her time on the Aurora.

Yanni also smiled, as it was the least 'princess-like' Deliza had been in weeks. It seemed the further away from the Pentaurus cluster they traveled, the less 'princess' remained in her. He hoped it was a good thing, as she had also become considerably stronger in the last few weeks. However, tragedy often required that of humans. It was something Yanni was quite familiar with.

Deliza threw her arms around Abby, wrapping her in a warm embrace. Abby reciprocated, a smile spread across her face. "I'm so happy to see you!"

Abby stepped back, looking the young woman over. The last time she had seen Deliza, she had been a skinny, seventeen year-old girl looking very uncomfortable adorned in noble Takaran fashions. Now, she looked every bit the mature young woman.

"Look at you, Deliza, you've become a stunning young woman, practically overnight."

"Thank you," Deliza replied, blushing. "To be honest, I can't wait to get to the Karuzara, put on some coveralls, and get my hands dirty again."

"I'll bet." Abby shook her head. "I can't believe how...well..." Abby suddenly looked uncomfortable.

"What is it?" Deliza wondered.

"Deliza, I'm so sorry about your family. I can't begin to tell you how sorry I am. I can't imagine what you must be going through."

"I'm fine, Abby. I mean..." She paused and took a deep breath. "Sometimes, it's like it never happened. Other times...well, sometimes it's all I can do to keep from crying."

"That I *do* understand," Abby said. "And you're

right, you do need to put on some coveralls and get dirty again. Having something to do helps, it really does."

"That's what I keep telling everyone," Deliza exclaimed. "It seems like they all want me to sit around depressed, like it's some kind of obligation, a way to show respect or something."

"Well, don't listen to them. You don't have to. You're a princess, remember?"

"That's the one thing I don't want to be," she insisted. "I'm half considering changing my last name back to Tugwell, to be honest."

"Don't you dare," Abby told her.

Deliza turned to introduce Yanni as he approached. "Abby, you remember Yanni, don't you?"

"Of course," Abby replied, reaching out to shake Yanni's hand. "A pleasure to see you again."

"A pleasure to be back," Yanni smiled, "almost back, I should say. We still have another forty-seven light years to go."

"Oh, that's less than an hour's journey." Abby looked around at all the Takaran security guards disembarking from the combat shuttles that had landed with them. "That's a lot of security."

"Captain Navarro insisted. We've got the data cores with us. Besides, he wants to give the shuttles to the Alliance."

"I'm sure the admiral will be happy about both, and about you."

"Is this where you're building the new gunships?" Deliza wondered.

"Yes, it is. Would you like to see it?"

"Are you joking?" Deliza turned to look at Yanni.

"Go ahead," Yanni told her. "I'm going to check

on the cores. I'm sure someone can help me catch up to you later."

"How long were you two planning on staying?" Abby asked.

"We hadn't really decided," Deliza admitted.

"If you can stay the night, we'd love to have you both for dinner."

Deliza looked at Yanni again.

"I'll arrange it with the crew," he told her. "I'm sure it won't be a problem."

"Will the cores be safe here?" Deliza asked Abby.

"This is probably the most heavily guarded place on all of Tanna, so, barring a Jung invasion, I'd say yes, they are quite safe. I can have additional guards brought in, if you'd like."

"I'll check with Lieutenant Chandler," Yanni told her. "I'll see you later." Yanni leaned over and gave Deliza a small kiss on her cheek, which Deliza leaned into with acceptance.

Deliza turned her attention back to Abby.

"Really?" Abby said, both eyebrows raised. "Is it serious?"

Deliza glanced back over her shoulder, checking that Yanni was out of earshot. "I don't know. How can one tell?"

"Trust me, you can tell," she said, putting her arm around Deliza's shoulder and leading her back toward the vehicle. "Come, let me show you what we're doing here. I have a feeling you're going to love it."

* * *

"Admiral?" Mister Bryant called from the doorway.

"Come," Admiral Dumar replied, his attention

still on the large view screen on the office wall. He picked up his remote and muted the sound.

Mister Bryant looked at the downtrodden faces of the young women on the view screen as he entered the admiral's office. "Are those the girls from the Jar-Benakh?"

"Some of them are no older than Deliza." The admiral sighed. "No woman, *especially* one so young, should have to experience the darker side of the human male."

"Speaking of Deliza, we received word from Tanna. Her shuttle has landed at the gunship plant. She plans to stay the night and will be here tomorrow around midday."

"Thank you."

"Also, flight ops contacted me not long ago. They said that Miss Mun has requested to travel to some of the core worlds we have liberated. I spoke with Ensign Sheehan about it. He said she wanted to see how the people we have already liberated feel about the Alliance."

Admiral Dumar leaned back in his chair, thinking. "Makes sense, I guess. Can you think of any way it might bite us in the ass if I give her permission?"

"I can think of at least a dozen, Admiral, the most obvious is the Weldonites. A lot of them are still unhappy with us shaking things up on their world."

"Yeah, I can't say that I blame them, really. I get the feeling a lot of those people didn't mind giving up some of their freedoms in exchange for security."

"I've heard that argument many times, sir."

"As have I," the admiral agreed. "Cases can be made either way, I suppose. She can go, but assign two combat shuttles full of Ghatazhak as escorts when they take her to Weldon. And have Commander

Telles remind Miss Mun that she is not to discuss anything she knows about Earth, the Alliance, or anything about the current state of affairs in the Tau Ceti system with anyone while she is traveling outside of the Sol system."

"Yes, sir."

"And I want her recordings transmitted back to me after visiting each world."

"Of course, sir."

"And make sure she visits Tanna a few days *after* gunship production begins. I'm sure she's going to want some footage of that, and it might inspire some confidence among the Cetians if they see us ramping up for defense."

"Understood, sir," Mister Bryant replied. "Is there anything else, Admiral?"

"I'm sure I'll think of something after you leave," the admiral jested.

"Oh, Lieutenant Commander Allison reported that the antimatter cores that arrived yesterday from Corinair checked out. They'll start installing them in the Celestia tomorrow."

"Wonderful," the admiral said. "I can't wait for that ship to be out of our dry docks. Her captain is driving me nuts, always requesting something else for her ship."

"Yes, sir," Mister Bryant replied.

* * *

Gerard switched on the light over the steep, narrow staircase leading down into the tiny cellar beneath the cabin. "Watch your step," he told Naralena as he led the way down. He got to the bottom and turned on the next switch, illuminating the cramped space.

Naralena joined him at the bottom of the stairs and looked around the room. There was a rack on the wall containing additional weapons, most of which appeared to be more recreational than military, and boxes of emergency rations. There were also lots of blankets, pillows, and several fold-up cots.

On the shelves along the far wall were several unmarked boxes, along with various pieces of camping and wilderness gear that one might find stored away in such a cabin. To her eyes, there was nothing stored in the cellar that looked suspicious or out of place for such a setting.

Gerard pulled a box from the bottom of one of the shelves, then one from the top shelf, placing them both on the ground. From the first box, he pulled out what appeared to be a very nice emergency radio. It looked very similar to the one Naralena's father had always kept at their home in case of a natural disaster. From the second box, he pulled out a large battery with a hand crank on one side.

He placed both items on the table and joined them together. "Please, if you could turn this crank for a few minutes, to build up a charge and get it going, it would be appreciated."

Naralena followed Gerard's instructions and began turning the crank on the battery. It offered quite a bit of resistance at first, but seemed to become easier once she got some momentum going.

As she continued to crank the device, Gerard opened up the back of the radio and pulled out two sets of wires. He stretched one across the room and plugged it into a power receptacle that looked like it had seen better days.

"If you have a power outlet down here, why do we need this battery?" Naralena wondered.

"It isn't a power outlet," Gerard explained. "It just looks like one. It connects to one of the solar panels on the roof, only it isn't a solar panel. It's a transceiver array. Its angle gives it a perfect line of site to a portable comm-unit we have hidden in a cave near the ridge. My men should have the unit deployed by now. This will allow us to relay to the comm-unit on the ridge line, and then up into space with a focused comm-beam in whatever direction we choose."

"How do we know which way to point it?" Naralena asked.

"You can stop cranking now," he told her as he plugged the second set of wires into the battery. "It's spinning on its own now." He plugged the wire into the transceiver and turned it on. "It's working. I've got the control signal from the comm-array on the ridge. Now all we have to do is point it to a standard orbital path and widen the beam enough so that a ship along that orbit will pick up our signal."

"So only the ship in orbit will detect the signal, and only if they pass through the beam?" Naralena asked, seeming skeptical.

"The Alliance knows you were in the general area of Cetia, so they will assume an orbit that puts them directly over the area. Of course, there may still be some Jung communications or surveillance satellites in orbit, ones the Alliance may not have taken out. So there is a small chance that our signal could be detected by the wrong people."

"Are you sure it's a good idea to do this, then?"

"If we do not, you may be stuck here for some time," Gerard explained. "Besides, our signal will be broadcast at random intervals, and on random sub-frequencies within the assigned spectrum that I gave Commander Telles last I saw him."

"If the Jung *do* detect the signal, surely they can determine the source?"

"Yes, but the signal will lead them to the comm-unit on the ridge. And the angle of the control dish could reach any of the cabins on this side of the lake. If the Jung go anywhere near that comm-unit, we'll know. That will give us a chance to depart before they determine from which cabin the comm-unit is being controlled."

Naralena shook her head. "How do you know all this? How do you remain so calm?"

"I was well trained," Gerard assured her. "And I have been at this for a long time."

"Why do you do it?"

"Someone has to."

"I know, but why would anyone choose to leave their home, probably never to return?"

"I was young. I wanted to serve. I wanted to make a difference, to do something important." He stopped fiddling with the transceiver, turning to look at Naralena. "It was all very exciting at the time...the idea of traveling to an alien world, blending into a completely foreign culture and society."

"It was very dangerous," she said. "And it's still very dangerous. What did your parents think?"

"My mother died when I was a teenager. My father and I never got along well after that. I signed up as soon as I was of legal age. The system is all set up. All we have to do is wait and remain vigilant."

"How long will it take?" Naralena wondered.

"To be honest, I don't know," Gerard admitted. "I was the last one to be inserted. This is the first time

I have ever tried to establish contact with a friendly ship overhead."

"But it *will* work?"

"Yes, it will work." His voice lacked confidence. He looked at her. "It *should* work... I hope it works."

* * *

Admiral Dumar, Nathan, and Vladimir stood to the side of bay eight as the Mirai rolled in from the transfer airlock.

"Wow," Nathan exclaimed. "That's what a Takaran captain gets as a private shuttle?" He turned to the admiral. "Sir, I think we need to talk about some upgrades to my personal shuttle."

"You don't have a personal shuttle," the admiral replied.

"That's what we need to talk about."

"Buy the Alliance a capital ship and we'll talk."

"I just want to get a peek at her propulsion systems," Vladimir said as the massive shuttle pulled up next them and stopped.

The midship hatch cracked open and swung outward from a point deep within the ship's hull and well below her main deck. It pivoted out as its built-in staircase extended outward, finally settling onto the deck and locking firmly into place. A young Takaran sergeant in crisp uniform came running down the stairs, immediately ducking underneath the ship and duck-walking aft as he inspected the underside of the ship.

At the top of the stairs, an older man wearing a well-fitted uniform waited patiently. A minute later, he turned and opened the inner hatch behind him and stepped aside, allowing the passenger waiting just inside to disembark.

Deliza appeared in the hatchway, pausing only long enough to spot her welcoming party of three and wave enthusiastically in their direction.

The three of them waved back.

"Are you sure that is her?" Vladimir wondered as he waved. "She looks older."

"She is older," Nathan replied.

"*Da*," Vladimir agreed lasciviously.

"Gentlemen—particularly you, Lieutenant Commander—as I am the child's godfather, as well as your commanding officer, it would behoove you to be on your best behavior."

"Yes, sir," Vladimir replied smartly, straightening his posture.

Deliza resisted the urge to run from the bottom of the boarding ramp, instead choosing an energetic stroll across the deck, grinning from ear to ear.

"Deliza," Admiral Dumar greeted, reaching out to embrace the young woman. "It is so good to see you once again. I only wish it were under more pleasant circumstances."

"Thank you, Admiral," Deliza replied. "Captain Scott," she said, turning to greet Nathan with a polite embrace.

"A pleasure to see you again, Deliza. I am so sorry about your family. If there is anything I can do for you, please, do not hesitate to ask."

Deliza smiled. "Thank you, Captain, but you may regret that offer someday." She turned to Vladimir next, wrapping her arms around him with even more affection than the others. "Vlad!" she exclaimed.

Vladimir hesitated for a moment, panic and confusion in his eyes, his hands flailing as he was unsure what to do. He glanced at the Admiral, who had one eyebrow raised, and flashed a look that begged the admiral's forgiveness as he resigned himself to her embrace. "It is wonderful to see you, Deliza," he said as they parted and she stepped back. "You look wonderful," he continued nervously. "This is just wonderful. What a wonderful ship you have…"

"I apologize that we cannot stay and visit," Nathan said, rescuing his fumbling chief engineer, "but we must catch a shuttle back to the Aurora as we have an enormous amount of work to do."

"Yes," Vladimir agreed readily. "An enormous amount of work."

"Admiral, Deliza," Nathan said, pushing Vladimir toward the exit.

"Gentlemen."

"Bye," Deliza said.

Admiral Dumar sighed. "He is right, you do look wonderful."

"Thank you."

"Where is Mister Hiller? I half expected him to be escorting you arm in arm."

"Abby sent word ahead, didn't she?" Deliza pouted.

"Not at all," Dumar insisted. "Your father noticed your affection for one another months ago."

"Really?" Deliza said, surprised. "Yanni is checking on the data cores. He does so quite often, actually. We were told that they would have to be loaded onto one of your shuttles. Apparently the Mirai is a bit too large for the landing pad at the Data Ark."

"Yes, I am aware."

"He insists on escorting the cores all the way back to the Ark."

"I can certainly understand his devotion to his task. It is an admirable quality. Would you like me to show you to your quarters?"

"Am I staying here on the Karuzara?" she asked.

"I just assumed so," the admiral replied. "Of course, you may stay wherever you wish."

"No, here will be fine, I'm sure. Besides, I was hoping to convince you to let me do a little experiment," she explained as she took his arm and they headed for the exit.

"What *kind* of experiment?"

"To put it bluntly, I'd like to fix your Falcons," Deliza told him as they walked across the deck and approached the main exit.

"You wish to work as a flight mechanic?"

"No, I want to *fix* them, as in *improve* them."

"I wasn't aware there was anything wrong with them," the admiral said as they entered the corridor.

"They are wonderful old spacecraft, to be sure, but they were ill-conceived to begin with, on top of which you're not using them effectively."

"I thought we *were* using them quite effectively," Dumar argued.

"Then why have you lost so many of them?" she asked.

"Deliza, this is a war, you know."

"Half your losses were in the atmosphere, Admiral. That's because the 402s were never meant for atmospheric combat. They're too big and they have terrible aerodynamic properties. Quite frankly, they're just not that maneuverable in the atmosphere."

"Ensign Hayes seems to have no trouble maneuvering his Falcon in the atmosphere."

"Only because he is using the brute force of her engines and her lift fans to compensate—at the cost of tremendous amounts of propellant, I might add. You see, Admiral, the 402s were built as deep-space interceptors. The only reason they even *have* atmospheric capabilities is because the Paleans couldn't afford to build spaceships big enough for the 402s to operate from. And the only reason they have lift fans is because Palee is rocky and has very little flat land, and their aerodynamics *are* terrible."

"Then what is it you propose, Deliza?"

"A major overhaul," she said, stopping in the middle of the corridor. "Pull out the lift fans and remove her atmospheric drives. She needs neither, *if* you stop using her in the atmosphere and keep her in space where she belongs."

"And what if the ship from which they operate is unavailable? Where will they land? You know, until recently, we *were* operating them from the airbase at Porto Santo."

"They would still be able to jump in near the airfield and land, but on conventional runways—preferably long ones, considering the amount of airspeed they need just to keep from falling out of the sky."

"Something tells me you've had this argument with someone before... Someone my age, perhaps?"

Deliza rolled her eyes. "He would never listen to me, either."

"I *am* listening, Deliza."

"Think of how much additional space you would have! You'd be dropping nearly half of her dry weight as well. Think of all the additional weapons she could carry. You could combine the weapons bays into one huge bay into which any number of specialized payload pods could be used. You'd have all that space where the atmospheric engines were. You could install more reactors, bigger plasma cannons... More plasma cannons. You could make additional room behind the flight deck for a cabin of sorts. My father used to complain about long patrols during which you'd both be stuck in your seats, urinating in relief tubes and eating meal bars. That cockpit is so wide, we could probably even change it to a traditional side-by-side configuration. Admiral, the possibilities are endless."

Her voice had turned to pleading, and personnel walking by were starting to stare as they passed.

"Deliza..."

"I spent years working on my father's 402. I know everything about that ship. I've even got preliminary designs and everything. If you'd just take a look at them..."

"I'll take a look at them."

"When?"

"I..."

"How about now? Over lunch? I'm hungry, are you?"

"Fine, we'll have lunch and I'll look over your designs," the admiral relented.

"Great!" She exclaimed, hugging him.

"Very well. We'll go to my quarters and I'll have the cook send something over," he promised as they started walking again.

"I have some ideas on how to improve the EDF Eagle fighters as well," Deliza told him.

"One ship at a time, young lady."

* * *

"This is unbelievable," Josh exclaimed as he peered out the window at the Swiss Alps below. "I thought we had seen most of what this planet had to offer as far as views were concerned, but...damn!"

"Awfully impressive, I have to admit," Loki agreed.

"And before the Jung invasion, you had never traveled outside of your home country?" Kata asked Yanni, as they both peered over the shoulders of Josh and Loki to see out the forward windows of the shuttle.

"No, never." Yanni leaned to his right, looking out the side window as they flew over the Mettelhorn.

"Must have been quite a shock for you," Kata commented.

"Yes. They did not even tell me where they were planning to take the cores. They just told me to stay with them, wherever they went, to take care of them." Yanni turned to face Kata, glancing at the camera in the center passageway. "So I did."

"What was it like, the first time you were in space? How did you feel when you first saw your planet from orbit?"

"I didn't," he replied as he turned to look out the window again. "I was in the back, with the cores. There were no windows. I could look forward and see the sky through the cockpit windows, and then space, and the orbital assembly platform, but that was all. I spent the next three and a half months in the back half of the Celestia, mostly cooped up in a separate, secured area, being guarded by several overzealous, EDF marines. No windows, not even a view screen to look outside."

"I thought all the view screens could connect to external cameras?"

"The Celestia was not completely built," Yanni explained. "She could fly, and she had life support, but not much more than that. The aft section didn't even have a pressurized connection to the front half of the ship at the time. Half the crew was stuck up front, and the other half in the back."

"And then the Aurora found you."

"Yes. Not long after, Captain Scott sent the cores and myself back to Takara, for safe keeping. That was ten months ago."

"Then I'll bet you're looking forward to getting home again?"

"Yes." Yanni looked down for a moment, smiling.

"What is it?" Kata asked, noticing the look of amusement on his face.

"It's silly, really." He looked at her. "I had a little dog, Inga, in my apartment in Grindelwald."

"That's a city?" Kata asked.

"More like a village," Yanni corrected. "Well, maybe a city, I suppose. There were a lot of people, but it still felt like a village to me. It was mostly people who worked at the Data Ark."

"And that was built inside a mountain?"

"Yes, the Mattenberg. It was a short ride to work, maybe fifteen, twenty, minutes by shuttle."

"You speak of it fondly," Kata observed.

Yanni smiled again. "It was a good job, a good life. I had friends. There was skiing. On the weekends, I could go to Interlaken, sometimes even Bern or Zurich, if I wanted to visit the big cities. In summer, we would visit the lakes and relax on the water." He looked out the window again. "Yes, I do miss it. I miss Inga."

Josh glanced at Loki, a concerned look on his face.

Loki turned half around in his seat, straining to look Yanni in the eye. "Uh, Mister Hiller, they did warn you... I mean, they told you that the Jung bombed the hell out of Earth on their way out, right?"

"Yes. It is obvious, even from this altitude. I can see the devastation myself. It is terrible."

"Yeah, but, they specifically targeted the Data Ark," Loki added.

"Surely they sealed it up after I left?" Yanni asked.

"Yes, they did. To make the Jung think that the cores were still inside. In fact, the Jung were never able to breach the facility. They even tried tunneling in from other directions."

"That would never work," Yanni insisted. "It took the original builders of the Ark years to dig into the mountain, and they were at least as advanced as the Jung are now, perhaps more so."

"Yeah, I know, but..."

"We're coming up on Mattenberg now," Josh warned.

"Just..." Loki sighed, realizing it was too late.

Yanni looked confused for a moment.

"Mattenberg passing to starboard," Josh reported. "Starting our final descent."

Yanni turned to his right to look out at the mountains below. "That's not Mattenberg..." His voice trailed off as his expression turned crestfallen. His face moved closer to the window, his hands touching the glass to steady himself. "Oh, my God," he whispered.

Below him was a scarred, misshapen mountain

range, its peaks no longer pointed and majestic. Instead, they were now smoothed over, their tips gone, rounded, as if someone had struck them with a gigantic hammer and smashed their tips away, then polished them clean.

The mountains passed under them and slid aft, out of Yanni's sightline.

"I'm gonna spiral us down," Josh muttered as he started a wide right turn on his way down to the Ark facility's landing pad.

Yanni continued staring out the window at the scorched landscape below. The entire northwest side of the mountain range, the one that had provided him with such spectacular views on his way to work each day, was now barren. The surface had been blasted clean, leaving nothing but dirt, rock, and the occasional blackened stump of trees that refused to let go of their roots. Gone were the farm houses, the fences, the barns. Gone were the ski lifts, trails, and forests. The only sign of civilization he could see was the road that led up to the entrance to the Data Ark, as it had recently been restored.

The shuttle continued its turning descent, bringing what had once been the town of Grindelwald into view. It too was desolate and barren. Cement slabs with the remnants of chimneys here and there. Rubble-strewn roads littered with the rusting shells of half destroyed vehicles, most of them on their sides or completely turned over. Everything was scorched as if a massive wave of fire had simply swept through the entire valley, destroying everything in its path.

"I don't understand," Yanni said in nearly inaudible tones. He turned to look at Kata, tears streaming down his face. "Why would they do this? If they knew they couldn't get in... Why?"

Kata felt herself tearing up as well as she exchanged glances with her porta-cam operator, Karahl, hunched down in the center passageway holding the porta-cam.

"They probably did it out of spite," Loki said in a sympathetic tone, "just like they did to the rest of Earth. No logic to their targeting, really. They just wanted to punish everyone for forcing them out."

Yanni could no longer look outside. Instead, he slid slowly down the side wall and sat on the deck behind Loki's seat, his arms wrapped around his drawn-up knees, face down in his arms, sobbing.

Josh and Loki said nothing, staring at their instruments as they continued their descent.

Kata Mun was also silent as she signaled to Karahl to turn off the camera.

They completed their descent in silence, with only the sounds of the shuttle's engines, Loki's voice speaking with Ark Control, and Yanni's muffled sobs.

CHAPTER SEVEN

Captain Roselle looked out the shuttle's cockpit windows as they approached the Jar-Benakh. "Holy shit," he muttered. "Scott really tore her up, didn't he? Where the fuck are we supposed to land?"

"We're still going in via one of the breach boxes near command and control, sir," the crew chief explained. "They're working on clearing the opening to one of the shuttle bays, but it's tough going. Their hulls don't have the grappling points for our crawlers, so they have to use mag-lock feet... Makes for slow going."

"Then we need to get some more fucking crawlers, don't we," Roselle complained. "You got that?" he asked his executive officer next to him.

"I got it, Captain," Commander Ellison replied. "A *lot* more fucking crawlers, by the looks of it."

"Damn straight. And remind me to exchange a few angry words with the Aurora's Tactical Officer... What's his name? Dela-v-a-hole, or something?"

"Yes, sir."

"Boy needs to work on his aim."

"We're turning to final now, sir," the copilot announced. "You and the commander should take your seats and buckle in. It's a bit of a pain to dock with a breach box, and it can get a bit bouncy. We don't want either of you bouncing around and hitting your heads on something."

"Very well," the captain agreed. He had just come

from a six-day stay in the hospital that had been five days more than he felt he needed, and six days longer than he'd liked. The last thing he wanted was to return to that disease-infested hellhole.

"We've got our work cut out for us, Gil," Commander Ellison said as they moved aft.

"Yeah, but at least we've got a ship," Roselle replied, "and a big bitch at that." He sat down and fastened his restraints. "Just imagine how much Jung ass we could whup once we get her working and get a jump drive in her. Makes the Aurora look like a fishing boat, doesn't it?" he added with a wink.

"Yes, sir, it sure as hell does."

Roselle nodded. "Exactly the way it should be. It was hard enough jumping around in that little peashooter of a scout ship, while Scott was in command of all that firepower. Christ, I would've had a stroke if I'd had to watch him play captain with no ship of my own to command."

"Come on, Gil, don't you think you're being a little hard on the kid?" Commander Ellison suggested.

"Someone's got to. Goddamn admiral loves that kid, thinks he walks on water."

"Dumar's a good leader, Gil. You know it."

"I got no qualms with his quals, Marty, but you gotta admit, he's a little blind when it comes to Scott's lack thereof."

"The kid has done well without much guidance at all, Gil."

"I'm not arguing that, Marty, but the stakes are higher now…much higher. He's not fighting spoiled rich boys in fancy uniforms who likely never took live fire before. He's taking on seasoned combat veterans. Ruthless sons of bitches who *enjoy* killing. Hell of a difference."

"Perhaps, but I still think he's doing okay, and will *continue* to do okay. I think *you* waste too much time worrying about it."

"Yeah, well, you're probably right about that one. Hell, we can't do anything about it anyway, right? But we *can* do something about this girl, and we *will*."

"Damn right we will," the commander agreed.

The cargo shuttle rocked abruptly as it made contact with the breach box, shaking its passengers despite the restraints.

"*Positive contact!*" the copilot's voice called over the loudspeakers in the aft cargo hold. "*Equalizing pressure. Stand by to disembark.*"

Captain Roselle released his restraints, then reached up and rubbed his shoulder after the rough docking. "First thing is that damned shuttle bay."

They rose from their seats and followed the Tannan volunteers who had come along with them, toward the aft hatch that had been fitted over the back of the cargo hold instead of the usual cargo ramp. The crewman opened the hatch, revealing a three-meter cubicle on the other side that was the interior of the Corinari breach box. The crewman looked forward at Captain Roselle and Commander Ellison. "Sirs?" he said, inviting them to lead the first group in the transfer process.

Roselle rose and headed aft, followed by his XO. "Sergeant," he said as he passed, stepping into the breach box.

"Next ten!" the crewman ordered.

Captain Roselle and Commander Ellison entered the breach box, floating as they stepped across the threshold and left the influence of the shuttle's artificial gravity. They pulled themselves along using the handrails that were located along every surface of the small compartment, until finally reaching the far side. Roselle rotated himself ninety degrees, bringing his feet to rest just above the hatch on the other side.

One by one, the first ten Tannan volunteers entered the breach box as well, floating into position, adjusting their physical attitudes in relation to the shuttle's deck in the same manner as the captain. Once they were all inside, the crewman on the shuttle began to close the hatch.

"Wait for the green light on this hatch, then the green light on the next hatch before you open it, sir."

Roselle put his thumb up to signal that he understood as the crewman slammed the shuttle's hatch. The inner hatch of the breach box slid closed and automatically sealed itself.

"Green light!" the Tannan next to the hatch announced, his pronunciation tinged by his thick Tannan accent.

Roselle waited for his light to turn green then squatted down and activated his hatch mechanism as well. The inner hatch slid away, revealing a long tunnel with a ladder directly below. "Alright, gents, the gravity's gonna grab you as you descend, so be prepared. It's one point three Gs in there, and we haven't figured out how to change that yet." He looked up at one of the Tannans nearby. "I forgot... What's the gravity on Tanna?"

"Normal," the Tannan said, smiling. "But I believe you refer to it as zero point seven."

"Then you boys are gonna get tuckered out rather quickly, so I suggest you pace yourselves," he advised as he put his hands on the edges of the hatch and lowered his feet into the tunnel, placing them on the ladder a few rungs down.

"We thought we would lower the gravity first thing," the Tannan replied. "We know where the controls are located."

"Even better," Roselle said as he headed down the ladder. As he descended, he heard the hatch at the bottom of the tunnel open. He glanced downward as he descended, noting the helmet of a Ghatazhak, along with the stern expression on the face of the soldier wearing it.

The captain exited the hatch, dropping the last meter to the deck. He landed a bit harder than expected. "Damn, that extra thirty percent packs more of a wallop than you'd expect, doesn't it," he said to the Ghatazhak soldier standing nearby.

"I wouldn't know, sir," the soldier replied.

"Think I can borrow one of your 'motion-assist undergarments'?" the captain asked.

"I don't believe we have them in your size, Captain," the soldier replied.

"Oh, yeah," the captain said as he moved aside. "I forgot all you boys are the same size. Must make life a lot easier for your quartermaster, huh?"

Commander Ellison was the next to drop down with a heavy thud. "Man, you weren't kidding."

"Yeah. You'd think we'd both be smart enough not to test it out that way, wouldn't you?" the captain chuckled as the first Tannan made his way down the ladder and stepped carefully onto the deck. "Well, at least those boys aren't as dumb as us. That's a good start."

"Welcome aboard, Captain," Vladimir greeted as he entered the compartment. "I'm Lieutenant

Commander Kamenetskiy. I am your temporary chief engineer."

"Lieutenant Commander," Captain Roselle greeted, returning Vladimir's salute and then reaching out to shake his hand. "Gil Roselle. This is my XO, Commander Ellison."

"Marty," the commander introduced himself, shaking Vladimir's hand.

"Vladimir, or Cheng... Whatever you wish, sirs. My team and I, with the help of the Tannan engineers you have brought with you, will be conducting a thorough inspection of the ship to help determine what needs to be repaired so that you may get her under way again."

"And into action, I hope," Roselle added.

"Of course, sir."

"That fella there had a good idea," Roselle said, pointing to the Tannan engineer who had spoken earlier. "Says he knows where the controls for the gravity are located. What say we get this thing dialed down a bit before these boys start complaining?"

"Yes," Vladimir acknowledged. "We have located the gravity controls. However, we did not want to make any adjustments until the Tannans had arrived, in case there were any significant differences between this ship's gravity systems and those of the Jar-Keurog. I would hate to adjust the gravity in the wrong direction and squash everyone like bugs."

"Yeah, that'd suck," the captain replied dryly. "Which way to command and control?"

"Down five decks and forward twenty-seven sections. The Ghatazhak soldier in the next compartment will guide you," Vladimir replied.

"How many Ghatazhak are on board?" Roselle asked.

"Three hundred and seven," Vladimir replied. "No one is allowed to move about the ship without an escort, for security reasons."

"Got no problem with that," the captain agreed as he headed for the exit. "Get those boys on that gravity, Lieutenant Commander. We'll be in command and control."

"Yes, Captain."

Captain Roselle stepped through the hatch and found a Ghatazhak soldier standing on the other side. "You my escort?"

"Yes, sir," the Ghatazhak soldier replied smartly. "Sergeant Ayers, Captain... Commander. If you'll follow me, I'll take you to command and control."

"He did say down five and *twenty-seven forward?*" the commander asked.

"Yup," the captain replied as he followed the sergeant down the corridor.

"I thought we entered at a point *near* C and C."

"Like I said, Marty, she's a big bitch," Roselle said. He looked back at his XO, a wry smile on his face. "Guess you're going to burn a few off that fat ass of yours, huh?"

* * *

"A lot better than five year-old potted meat," Gerard exclaimed as he cleared the table.

"That meat was five years old?" Naralena said, concern on her face.

"Give or take."

"Glad I didn't know that at the time." Naralena turned to the other two men at the table. "Thank you, gentlemen," she told them in Koharan. "I know it took you most of the day to stalk that animal. It was delicious."

"Your Koharan is very good," Gerard replied in the same language. "I'm amazed that you only studied it for…"

The kitchen lights began to flicker. Three times, a pause, then twice more followed by another pause, then they went out for a full two seconds before coming back on and remaining that way. Gerard immediately dropped the dishes on the table and headed toward the bathroom. The other two men got up as well, heading for the exit.

"What is it?" Naralena asked. "What's wrong?"

"We've got an incoming message," he replied as he made his way across the living room. "You coming?"

"Of course," Naralena declared as she quickly rose to follow him.

Gerard went into the bathroom, pausing long enough to let her enter as well before closing the door. He then lifted the center shelf in the towel cabinet behind the door, causing the latch to release, then pulled the cabinet away from the wall to reveal the steep, narrow, dimly lit staircase hidden behind it.

He moved quickly down the stairs, flipping on the cellar lights as he reached the bottom. He immediately headed for the transceiver and began making adjustments, entering numbers on the keypad. He wrote down the numbers that appeared on the display screen on a piece of paper, then started making calculations. Once he finished, he entered a new string of numbers into the keypad. The process repeated four times, until finally, a human voice was heard, but they were speaking a language that Gerard did not recognize. He looked at Naralena, confused.

"He's speaking Corinairan," she told him as she picked up the microphone and replied in the same language.

"Who is it?" Gerard asked. "What are they saying?"

Naralena gestured for him to be quiet while she communicated with the man on the comms. "It's one of our Falcons. They are in orbit. They want to know if we are in a good position for extraction."

"If they can do so immediately, yes," Gerard said. "Otherwise, we should wait at least twenty-four hours to make sure the Jung did not pick up the transmission and pinpoint the source."

Naralena continued talking over the comms in Corinairan.

"Keep it brief," Gerard warned.

"They cannot extract for at least two hours," she told him.

"Ask if they can extract tomorrow, same time."

Naralena repeated Gerard's request over the comms. "They can. They are leaving a comm-buoy in orbit, since the Jung have no way to take it out. If we need to send a message to them and no one is there, it will record the message. They can also leave messages for us, in case they call and we do not answer."

"That's great," Gerard replied.

There was another brief exchange, after which Naralena asked, "They would like to know what a safe comm interval would be, so as not to risk alerting the Jung to our location."

"Tell them staggered five one two, same as encrypt delta minus two," Gerard instructed.

"That will result in random comm windows varying between three and five hours. If the Jung have not come for us within that time, it's likely they have not intercepted the comm-beam and are not aware of our existence." Gerard looked at his watch, noting the time as Naralena relayed the information over the comms in Corinairan.

"Anything else?" she asked.

"Not that I can think of."

Naralena signed off and handed him the microphone, a look of relief washing over her face.

Gerard noticed the change in her demeanor. "You must be happy to be going home."

"No, I'm going back to the Aurora. I'm still a long way from home."

"That's true."

"You're the one who's finally going home," she told him.

Gerard leaned back, contemplating the possibility for the first time in decades. "It doesn't seem real."

"Well, it's not…not yet. But at least now it's a possibility."

Gerard sighed. "What am I to do there?" he wondered. "This world, these people, they are all I've known for more than twenty years. To be honest, this feels as much my home as Earth ever did. Perhaps even more so."

"Surely there is something you miss about Earth?"

Gerard thought for a moment. "Ice cream. They do not have ice cream here. They don't even have cows."

* * *

Captain Navarro sat in his office on board the Avendahl as they maintained their position in high orbit over Corinair. His family was safe, as were the families of everyone serving under him. He was fortunate that most of his enlisted were single and felt no loyalties to the nobles of Takara who had rebelled against House Ta'Akar. Many of them had, in fact, looked up to Casimir Ta'Akar as a symbol of the honor that Takara once, and should have always, represented. He was the man who had given up everything to try to remove the black stain from his world that had been placed on it by his brother, Caius.

Although Captain Navarro despised what the nobles had done to his homeworld, he anticipated liking this new assignment. His family was only a fifteen-minute shuttle ride away, and he and his senior officers had already worked out a rotation that would allow each of them to be home three nights out of each week, with a full two days off per month, not a small accomplishment for a ship that was technically understaffed.

Yet, as he scrolled through the latest reports from Admiral Dumar, he couldn't help but long for the glorious battles he could've fought if he was not stuck in the Darvano system for the foreseeable future. The Avendahl was a far superior ship to anything he had seen in any of the reports from the Sol sector, except for the battle platforms. He did feel confident that his ship could prevail against one, nevertheless.

His door chime sounded, breaking his daydreams of combat. He pressed a button on his desk to open the door.

The door split in half, the two pieces disappearing into the bulkhead.

"Ensign Permon," the captain greeted. "What messages have you for me on this morning?"

The young ensign smiled, mildly entertained by his captain's unusually cheery mood. "I thought you might like to know that Lieutenant Chandler of the Mirai reports they have arrived safely at Karuzara, and that Mister Hiller has successfully returned the data cores back to the Ark facility."

"That is good news, indeed."

"He also thought you might find the following information mildly entertaining. It seems Miss Ta'Akar has convinced the admiral to let her redesign and modify their last remaining 402s."

"Makes perfect sense," the captain said without hesitation, much to the surprise of the young ensign.

"Sir?"

"The 'Falcons', as they call them, were never designed for atmospheric flight. To be honest, they are an antiquated design that was flawed from conception. Their only real strength was their main propulsion system. And seeing as how they only have a few of them left, I don't see the harm in trying to utilize them as efficiently as possible. I had half considered making such recommendations to the admiral myself, but it wasn't really my place to do so then."

"But sir, she is just a child, and a female child at that."

"Do not underestimate that *female child*, Ensign," the captain warned him. "You'll likely regret it."

"Yes, sir."

"Was there anything else?" the captain asked.

"There was one other message," the ensign

replied. "It is encrypted and requires your bio-signature to decrypt. It is marked for your eyes only, sir." He reached out and handed a small data chip to the captain.

"Thank you, Ensign. That will be all."

"Yes, sir." The ensign turned and exited the captain's office, the door automatically closing behind him.

Captain Navarro stuck the data chip into a small slot on the comm-panel built into the top of his desk. He sat upright, looking straight ahead as a small beam of pale-blue light shot out of the comm-panel and spread out right and left, forming a triangle of light. The nearest side of the triangle extended outward until it enveloped the captain and then began to pan upward, across his chest, neck, and face. The light disappeared, and the comm-panel indicated the message was decrypted and ready for playback.

Captain Navarro pressed the button to play the message.

"Captain Navarro. Your presence is requested by several lords of noble houses of Takara, to discuss the future of the Takaran people and the Avendahl, as well as those of the Pentaurus cluster. Please respond with your preferred time and place for such a meeting to the coordinates contained herein. You are required to come alone, without military escort or weapons of any kind. These matters are most urgent, Captain. An immediate response is recommended."

The message ended, leaving only the return message coordinates displayed on the comm-panel's control screen. He knew that the coordinates would be in deep space, where a comm-drone no doubt currently waited for a reply, making it impossible to trace the origins of the message, or who had sent it.

The captain leaned back in his chair, staring at the painting on the far wall. *Where to meet?* he wondered. *Someplace the nobles of Takara would be unfamiliar with. Better yet, someplace they would loathe going.*

Captain Navarro smiled as he touched his intercom button. "Ensign Permon, please send Lieutenant Solomon to my office. Also, I'd like to send a message via jump comm-drone."

"*Yes, sir.*"

* * *

Kata Mun studied the Tannan technician sitting in the waiting room. "I was hoping for someone a little more presentable," she told Abby in hushed tones.

"We don't have a lot of Tannans who speak fluent English, I'm afraid," Abby explained. "Those who do are needed on the lines to interpret between Tannan and Terran technicians."

"What about your interpreter?" Kata asked. "He seems quite nice."

"Yes, he is, but he is not Tannan. He came over from Earth the same time I did. He married a Tannan woman rather early on and became fluent quite quickly. It seems he has a previously undiscovered knack for languages."

Kata sighed. "Oh, well. At least we might get some sympathy out of the viewers." She looked at Karahl. "Shall we?"

Kata Mun exited the office and walked across the

lobby, flashing the smile that had landed her the job as anchor years ago. "Mister Aronsana?"

"No. Aron is first name. Sanah is family name."

"Oh, of course. Mister Sanah. I'm Kata Mun. I'm here to interview you."

Mister Sanah looked confused, and a little frightened. "Did I do something not correct?"

"Oh, no. Nothing like that. I'm a reporter."

Mister Sanah still looked perplexed.

"I report the news." Kata pointed at the porta-cam Karahl was holding. "The news? I record what's going on in the world, talk to people such as yourself. Find out what you think about things, then broadcast it to millions of people on many different worlds."

"I am to be seen by people on other worlds?" he asked, his look of confusion momentarily turning into a smile.

"Yes, many worlds, and many people."

His frown returned, this time more worried than confused. "But not the Jung, yes?"

"No, not the Jung. We don't broadcast to the Jung."

Mister Sanah smiled again, shrugging his shoulders. "If you like?"

"Yes, I like. Thank you. Please, if you'll follow me into the next room where we won't be bothered."

Kata led Mister Sanah into a small conference room and pointed to a chair for him to sit in, then took a seat herself one chair over.

"Will my people see this as well?" Mister Sanah asked.

"I don't know," Kata replied. "Do your people have video broadcasts of news events, things happening that your people should know about?"

"Yes, of course. We call them *Tela boro intersnee.*"

"What does that mean in English?" Kata wondered.

"I think, 'Today's events of interest.'"

"That sounds about right." She looked at her porta-cam operator as he finished setting up. "We ready?"

"Yes, ma'am," Karahl answered. "Mister Sanah, if you could just turn a little more toward me, so we can see your face better?"

Mister Sanah turned a little, looking for confirmation from the porta-cam operator and smiling when he got it. He reached up and pushed his hair down in an attempt to look presentable, straightening his coveralls as well.

"We're recording," Karahl announced, the red light on the top of his porta-cam lighting up.

Kata paused a moment, getting herself ready and leaving a long pause to mark the interview starting point for later editing. She turned to the camera, her smile returning as she spoke. "I'm here at the gunship production facility on Tanna, in the 72 Herculis system approximately forty-seven light years from Earth, and just over fifty-five light years from Tau Ceti. The 72 Herculis system was one of the first systems to be liberated by Captain Scott and the Aurora more than ten months ago, long before the main forces of the Alliance arrived in the Sol sector. Since then, the Tannan people have welcomed nearly one million Terran refugees, and have provided abundant amounts of propellant to the Alliance. In exchange, the Alliance has provided the Tannans with the Takaran fabricator technology, which has greatly accelerated the Tannans' recovery since the Jung were driven from their world."

Kata turned to face Mister Sanah, as her porta-cam operator readjusted his focus and moved the camera slightly left to include the interviewee in the shot.

"With me today is Aron Sanah, an assembly technician here at the gunship production facility on Tanna. Mister Sanah, thank you for speaking with us today."

"The pleasure is all mine, Miss Mun," Mister Sanah replied politely.

"May I call you Aron?"

"Yes, of course."

"Aron, how has the Alliance treated the people of Tanna since they removed the Jung from your world?"

"Very well."

"Have they done anything positive for your people? Have they made your world better? Worse?"

"Oh, much better. The fabricators are wonderful pieces of technology. They allow us to build complex systems in a fraction of the time and cost than before. And the Corinairan nanites have helped many of my people. I have a friend, he works the line with me here, his mother was dying of liver disease. Our doctors knew of no cure for her ailment. The nanites healed her in less than one month. Now she is healthy and happy, and playing with her grandchildren."

"Do you feel the Alliance is treating the Tannan people as equal partners in their campaign against the Jung?"

"Our people go where they need us. Some of them fight and die alongside them. My cousin died serving on the Jar-Keurog. He died defending Earth against the Jung. They do not discuss their plans with us, no. But there is no need. We have no ships to give them. We have no military. But we soon will. What they did give us was our freedom. Everything else is merely extra. A bonus, as you say in English. Freedom was all we ever wanted, and we are willing to fight and die to keep it."

"The Alliance claims the Jung bombed Earth as punishment for fighting back. Do you believe their claims?"

"Yes, of course. The Jung came here many decades ago. They did not ask if we welcomed them or not. They simply started bombing us from orbit. For days they bombed. They destroyed nearly everything. They were worse than the great plague. At least the plague left everything intact and only killed the people."

"Why do you think the Jung bombed your world?"

"To make our world easier to control. There were too many of us, and they were but a few ships, and they were on their way out of the system. They wanted to create a resupply station for ships that would follow. They spared only what they needed. Less than a million people, some factories to make things their ships needed, and farmland to feed not only their crews, but also their new subjects. That very day, my people became slaves to the Jung. Nothing more."

"Has the Alliance shared their jump drive technology with your people as well?"

"Yes, but only on a few cargo ships, ones in which they installed the technology. But that is only because they are afraid. If such technology fell into the hands of the Jung, it would be catastrophic for us all."

"Does it concern you that Alliance ships are rarely present in your system? Are you worried that the Jung will return, and there will be no one here to protect you?"

"The Alliance has only two ships, and one was very badly damaged in battle. They cannot be every place at once. That is why we are building these gunships."

"But the gunships are small compared to the Jung ships, are they not?"

"Perhaps, but they are very fast, and they have very powerful weapons. More important, they have jump drives. And we can build *many* of them. Hundreds, perhaps. With these ships, we can patrol far out into space. We will know when the Jung are coming, long before they are to arrive. We will have time to send word to the Alliance, so that they can send ships to defend us."

"But what if they don't get here in time?"

"Then we will die, but we will die fighting as free people."

"Aron, other worlds that the Alliance has liberated have complained that many of their people died during the liberation, and that steps should have been taken to prevent such collateral damage. When Captain Scott and the Aurora liberated Tanna from Jung rule, how many of your people died that day?"

"Oh, very few. Less than one hundred, I think. They were very precise, very careful, and very swift in their attack. Captain Scott is a very good man. Very good indeed. It was very gratifying to see them defeat the Jung so easily. It inspired my people. It gave us hope. This is something that no one can live happily without. It is the fire that drives us. It is what makes us rise and face each day." Aron hung his head down in sadness. "It was something that we were without for many, many years. Now, thanks to the Alliance, we have hope again."

"Thank you, Mister Sanah, for speaking with us today."

"You are most welcome."

Kata paused, saying nothing further until the red light on Karahl's porta-cam turned off.

"We're out," Karahl announced.

"Well, you can't get an ending any better than that," Kata said as she let out a sigh of relief.

"Not very long, though," her porta-cam operator commented.

"We're going to have a ton of these interviews," she replied, "and we'll be lucky to get a full hour special back on Kohara. I'm pretty sure we'll have enough."

"Everything was good?" Aron asked.

"Yes, Aron, you did great," Kata assured him. "Thank you."

"Very well," Aron said as he stood to depart. "It was a pleasure to meet you both."

"You too, Aron, and thanks again," Kata replied as he left the room.

"You really think all the Tannans love the Alliance as much as that guy?"

"I don't know," Kata replied. "The people from Weldon sure didn't, and some of the people on Copora thought the Alliance had overstepped their bounds as well."

"The Kalitans sure didn't mind," Karahl said as he packed up his porta-cam and got ready to move.

"The Kalitans were being worked into extinction," Kata countered. "They really *were* slaves."

"Still, other than the Tannans and the Kalitans,

everyone else seems to be mixed. Some like them and some don't."

"Yeah, I'm starting to think this isn't going to be as easy a sell to our people back home as I thought it would be," Kata said. "Let's go get some shots of the production line, shall we?"

* * *

"I didn't think I'd be this nervous," Deliza confided in the admiral as they walked down the corridors of the Karuzara asteroid base.

"There's no reason to be nervous, Deliza," Admiral Dumar assured her. "Your ideas are well thought out, your designs are solid, and you know more about the aerodynamics and performance parameters than either your father or I ever did. You will do fine."

"What if they don't like me?"

"You don't need them to like you. You just need them to do what you tell them."

"What if they think I'm a spoiled little princess or something?"

"You were a princess for only a year, Deliza. For seventeen years, you lived on Haven. If anything, they'll think you're a dirty, uneducated molo farmer."

"I was not," Deliza objected. "Okay, I *was* a molo farmer...and I guess I was dirty a lot of the time, but I am most assuredly *not* uneducated."

"You're smarter than most of them will ever be."

"You think so?"

Admiral Dumar looked at her. "What happened? A couple days ago you were beaming with confidence as you walked down that boarding ramp."

"I had been pretending to be a princess for a

year, remember? I had a lot of practice. I've never *done* this before."

"I still say you'll do fine."

"I just hope they don't take pity on me," she said, looking down at the floor as they walked. "That's the last thing I need." She looked up again, an idea suddenly popping into her head. "I could use my old last name. I could be Deliza Tugwell... Or maybe Liza Tugwell?"

The admiral looked at her crossly.

"Deli Redmond?"

"You landed in what is probably the most luxurious ship this sector has ever seen. Everyone knows who you are, Deliza."

They turned the corner and headed down the final stretch to what was commonly referred to as 'the black lab'. It was a place no one talked about, yet everyone knew about it. It's where the guys in lab coats got together with the guys in coveralls and created new things. Unfortunately, not much had come out of the black lab since it had been started, just after the Karuzara arrived in the Sol system. Only one project had gone all the way to prototype, and that was the jump KKV, which they would be testing soon. Everything else had failed to match expectations. Admiral Dumar hoped Deliza's project would change that.

They came to a stop outside the door. Admiral Dumar turned to Deliza. "The men you are about to meet will not want to listen to you. Some of them are Takaran and were raised in that patriarchal mindset. The Corinairans will be a bit better, as their women are generally the better educated of the sexes. However, they won't want you to get in and tinker with anything, as they'll consider that their job."

"What about the Terrans?"

"They'll be a lot easier. Their society is pretty well integrated, so most of them don't really have any preconceived notions of male and female roles."

"Great."

"Unfortunately, you won't have any Terrans working for you. The only Terran in there is Lieutenant Tillardi, and he's running a different project."

"Poo."

"Try not to say 'poo'," the admiral told her.

"What's wrong with 'poo'?"

"It's too weak. They'll just laugh at you. Try to really swear once in a while."

"I don't think I know any swear words," Deliza admitted.

"All that time you spent with Lieutenant Commander Kamenetskiy and you didn't learn a single bad word?"

"He always swore in Russian."

"All I know is 'damn'," the admiral admitted, "and I suspect that's not much stronger than 'poo'. I'll ask Lieutenant Commander Nash next time I see her. Or maybe Ensign Hayes."

"Josh is an ensign now?"

"Yes."

"I didn't expect *that*," Deliza commented.

"No one did." Admiral Dumar took a deep breath and exhaled. "Are you ready?"

Deliza nodded.

Admiral Dumar looked at the guard at the door. "Sergeant." The sergeant placed his hand on the palm reader, then pushed a few buttons. The door slid open just enough to allow them to slip inside.

Deliza followed the admiral in and looked around as he signed in with the guard on the other side.

"Admiral on deck!" the guard barked.

Everyone in the cavernous hangar snapped to attention as the admiral and Deliza walked across the floor. Deliza studied the layout of the room as they walked. The hangar, like all the others, had been carved out by mining and boring machines, and was basically a massive cave. The walls were fused and ground smooth, same as the floor, but the ceiling was still rocky and uneven, with beams overhead and an array of lighting panels providing even lighting throughout the hangar.

As they walked toward the men, she noticed the hangar had been divided into three sections by sliding walls. Her team was in the middle section. The section to their right appeared empty, as the walls were slid back halfway, and the lighting in that section was off. The section to the left, however, was completely closed off, with its own guard at the entrance.

They came to a stop a few meters away from the line of technicians and engineers. She knew every one of their faces from their personnel records. She knew each of their strengths and weaknesses, along with their backgrounds, education, and experience.

The problem was that *they* did not know *her*. All they saw was a pretty young woman who thought she had all the answers. A princess whose father and sister had recently been murdered, and her palace had been taken away. Even worse, they would see her as a favorite of the admiral.

This was going to be a tough sell.

"Gentlemen," Admiral Dumar began. "Welcome to project 'Super Falcon'."

The men looked skeptical, more than one of them raising a single eyebrow.

"You're going to take a poorly designed spacecraft that has been inefficiently utilized, due in large part to my own short-sightedness, and turn it into a versatile space-borne weapons and utility platform that every mechanic will want to maintain and every pilot will want to fly."

"Sir, we've only got four Falcons still flying, and two of them are down for repairs," one of the technicians pointed out.

"But we've got at least four, maybe six, good airframes to work with as well," the admiral replied.

"The engines are shot on all of them," another technician said.

"Then we'll just have to fabricate new parts and fix those engines, won't we?" Dumar countered.

"Admiral, there's just not that much room left in those birds. Plus, if you add more weight to them, they won't be able to lift themselves off the surface," the first technician argued.

"That's why we're pulling the atmospheric drives and lift systems out of her," Deliza chimed in, using her overly confident 'princess voice', as Yanni often called her authoritative tone.

"What? You can't pull the lift fans out," the first technician objected, "she won't be able to fly."

"She'll be able to fly just fine in space," Deliza replied, defending her position.

"Sure, but she won't be able to take off and land on the surface."

"We don't plan on using them in the atmosphere any longer," Deliza explained. "And if, for some reason, they do need to land on the surface, they can do so conventionally."

The technician laughed. "402s fall out of the sky at slow speeds."

"Then they'll just have to land at higher speeds," Deliza responded in a condescending tone.

"Admiral," the technician complained, shaking his head. "Who's our team leader going to be on this anyway?"

"You're looking at her," Deliza replied firmly.

"Oh, come on."

"Don't like it?"

"No, I don't," the technician admitted.

"Well, I don't give a damn. The door's that way, asshole. I'm sure the admiral can find you a new job scrubbing carbon scorching off the inside of shuttle thrusters...you know, man's work?"

Admiral Dumar smiled, both eyebrows raised, looking at the technician, who immediately backed down.

"Gentlemen, my name is Deliza Ta'Akar," she began, pacing up and down the line of men as she spoke, "and I've been working on 402s since I was tall enough to climb her service ladders. I know every bolt, every wire, and every circuit in that bird, probably better than anyone in this whole damned sector. Now, the Falcon's a flying brick in the atmosphere. The only reason she can cut through the air is because of her overpowered engines and her damned lift fans. So I say stop using her in the atmosphere, and fit her out correctly...for space! Yank her atmospheric drives. She doesn't need them. Her space drive is more than powerful enough to keep her speed up for basic aerodynamic flight, and she's got a damned jump drive to get up into orbit and back down again if need be. Rip out her lift fans. This isn't Palee, gentlemen. The Super Falcon won't need to takeoff and land vertically, because she's a *spaceship*, not a jet plane. We'll have more room for reactors. More reactors means stronger shields, more powerful plasma cannons, *more* plasma cannons, and greater jump range. We can combine the weapons bays into one big bay, holding all kinds of fun stuff designed to blow the damned Jung to hell and back. We can elongate and widen the cockpit, and give her more crew space for longer duration missions, or for additional crewmen to operate more complex weapons and ECM systems. We're gonna make the Super Falcon the badass bitch of space she was always meant to be! When we're done with her, she'll be able to take a Jung frigate all by herself. Two or three of them will be able to take out a cruiser!"

"I think they get the point," Admiral Dumar muttered, ending her speech. "Gentlemen, this isn't an invitation, it's an order. You will follow Miss Ta'Akar's instructions to the letter. I expect this to happen and happen in short order. Any questions?" The admiral looked over his men. Although none of them looked genuinely enthused about the project, he knew they would all do as ordered. If not, he would find them another job, or simply send them back to the Pentaurus cluster, preferably on a nice, slow, propellant tanker. "Very well, as you were." Admiral Dumar turned to Deliza.

"Too much?" she asked.

"Maybe a bit," he replied. "Where did all that come from, anyway?"

"I tried to pretend I was Jessica."

"Good thinking. Now go and build me a Super Falcon."

Deliza smiled. "Yes, sir."

* * *

Suvan Navarro strolled casually through the crowded, dusty street market, feigning interest in the occasional items so as not to look out of place. He was wearing the traditional overcoat that men of this world generally wore, and carried a bag filled with various items he had purchased, to keep up appearances, over the last hour.

He paused momentarily to take in the alien sky. It was not often he got to set foot on such worlds. A pale-amber sky, with its distant orange-hued sun rising slowly on the horizon after its long absence. The massive gas giant, around which this moon orbited, filled the bottom half of the sky, its reflected light casting eerie secondary shadows opposite those cast by direct sunlight.

He wasn't looking at the sky to enjoy the view, however. He was scanning the rooftops for snipers. He was sure they were there, and he had spotted at least three men who looked suspicious to his trained eyes. But here on Haven, suspicious was normal, as many unsavory characters from every system in the sector seemed to flock to this dirty, strange little world.

He had arrived several hours ago, having come out of his jump just outside the system. He then used the Corinairan shuttle to finish the trip, using its old FTL drive, which had yet to be removed. He even had the gravity adjusted in his quarters, on board the Avendahl, to match the lesser gravity on Haven, so as not to appear awkward or overly 'bouncy' in his stride, a sure giveaway that he was not a local.

Satisfied there were no overt threats on any of the nearby rooftops, Captain Navarro wiped the sweat from his brow and made his way over to a nearby cafe. Business was good that day, just as he had expected after fifty days of darkness. More importantly, it meant that there were unlikely to be any empty tables, forcing him to share a table with another patron, which is exactly what he wished to do.

Captain Navarro spotted the person he was looking for. He had no description to go by, but the well-groomed hair and mustache, and properly fitted local attire, gave him away. He wondered for a moment if the man he was to contact had made such an obvious faux pas by intent, or by accident. He hoped for the latter, as it meant he was likely to make other errors as well.

He stepped up to the man's table and reached for the chair. "Mind if I sit a spell?" he asked, using his best Haven accent. "I won't be much bother to ya, I swear."

"Of course, my good man."

Good, it was an accident, the captain thought. If there was one thing about Takaran nobles that seemed truly universal, it was that they were all rather arrogant, himself included. "Thank you, kindly," he replied as he took his seat, purposefully not bothering to dust it off first, despite the fact that he desperately wished to do so.

"Glad you could join us," a third voice said as he came and sat down in the other empty chair.

Navarro looked at the other gentleman. "Ganna.

You're looking rather pale for a Havenite, aren't you?"

"Probably," Lord Ganna admitted. "You seem to fit in rather nicely, however. Perhaps there is a bit of commoner in your blood, from a few generations back, of course."

"Is that why you invited me here, Ganna, to make thinly veiled insults about my heritage?" Navarro looked unamused. "I'd suggest that such behavior is beneath you, but..."

"I feel it only fair to warn you that we have snipers ready to fire on your person should something go awry," Lord Ganna warned. "And of course, they are quite accurate."

"Probably not as accurate as the ones who just took yours down," Navarro replied with a wry smile.

Lord Ganna looked to the waiter standing in the shadows along the door to the cafe. The man held out four fingers. "Are you sure you got them all?" Lord Ganna asked.

"I don't need to. I just wanted to give my men some practice. Killing me would only bring the Avendahl's fury down upon all your houses, as my executive officer has standing orders to take out every noble house in the Takar system, should I meet an untimely demise during my little shopping trip. Now, would you like to tell me why you asked me here, or are we going to continue having our snipers kill each other?"

"We want to know what your intentions are, Lord Navarro."

"Well, I was planning on making a really nice molo stew for dinner tonight," he said gesturing to his shopping bag.

"About Takara," Lord Ganna added.

"That depends on what your intentions are, going forward," Navarro replied.

"We simply wish to run our system in peace, and continue with our current business relationships with others in the Pentaurus sector," Lord Ganna explained.

"And you have no dreams of expansion?" Navarro wondered, in obvious disbelief.

"I cannot speak for each and every lord's personal desires, but as a collective, we have no imperial designs, I assure you."

"You assure me?" The captain had to fight from laughing. "You brought me all the way to Haven to lie to me?"

"I am not lying to you, Lord Navarro, and it was your idea to meet on this desolate rock, not ours."

"That part *is* true."

"We were hoping you might pledge your loyalty to us," Lord Ganna stated. "It would put a great many noble hearts at ease, not to mention the Takaran people as a whole."

Captain Navarro leaned forward, his eyes narrowing as he looked into Lord Ganna's eyes. "I have pledged my ship to Deliza Ta'Akar. Fortunately for you, she has no interest in reclaiming her family's rightful title and holdings. Her only interest is in upholding her father's promise of support to the Alliance."

"I find that rather hard to believe."

A small laugh escaped the captain's lips. He leaned back and took a breath. "Believe me, Ganna, if Deliza Ta'Akar wanted you all dead, you would not be sitting here fouling the air and insulting my senses."

"Really, Navarro…"

Captain Navarro suddenly leaned forward, startling Lord Ganna, his second, and his bodyguard standing under the canopy pretending to be a waiter. Both the second and third men moved their gun hands toward their jackets but stopped short. Lord Ganna glanced at his body guard as the man's gun hand slowly lowered, this time flashing two fingers. He then turned to look at the captain once more.

Captain Navarro's eyes squinted again, taking on a sinister quality, one seething with controlled rage. "If you wish peaceful coexistence, so be it. However, be warned. The eyes of the Avendahl... my eyes...shall be forever upon you. Should even one of your warships leave the Takaran system, I will consider it an act of aggression, and I will act accordingly. Furthermore, should your own forces grow beyond that which is reasonably necessary to defend Takara, I shall also consider that an act of aggression... One that shall *also* be met with deadly force."

Lord Ganna did not budge and did not look away. He kept his eyes squarely focused on Lord Navarro's as he spoke. "Are you sure it's wise to make such overt threats, Lord Navarro?"

Suvan Navarro leaned back slowly, a confident smile forming at the corner of his mouth. "My dear Lord Ganna. I have the most powerful ship in the entire sector, with enough firepower to destroy your pitiful fleet several times over. The only thing that prevented me from doing so, nine days ago, was a promise I made to the most honorable man I have ever known. A man whose daughter the so-called nobles of Takara had murdered. A man who himself was murdered by the same nobles you choose to associate with." The captain paused a moment, as he received a transmission in his hidden earpiece. His smile broadened. "Those are the terms of Deliza Ta'Akar, and they are not negotiable. Now, I suggest you and your friends depart while you still can. It seems my men have run out of targets on which to practice."

Lord Ganna glanced over to his bodyguard. The man had a concerned look on his face and did not hold up any fingers. He looked at Suvan Navarro once more. "Good day to you, Lord Navarro," he said hurriedly as he rose from his seat and rushed out of the cafe.

Captain Navarro leaned back in his seat, feeling quite pleased with himself.

A man dressed in local attire, with mussed hair and many days' worth of whiskers on his cheeks strolled up to Captain Navarro. "You do have a way with words, Captain."

Navarro smiled. "I have to admit, that was far more satisfying than I had anticipated."

* * *

One of Gerard's men burst through the front door, panting. "They are coming, from the north and west."

"How long?" Gerard asked as he leapt from his seat at the table.

"Fifteen minutes at the most."

"You and Marten head south. We will go east. They know not our number and I will blow this cabin after we depart. With any luck, they will follow only one of us. Now go, and good luck to you."

"Good luck to you, as well," the man replied as he turned and headed back out the door.

Naralena slowly rose from her seat, fear evident on her face. "We have to send a message to the Alliance, let them know what has happened. They might be able to help."

"There is no time," Gerard told her. "Besides, they likely do not know which cabin the transmission was coming from. If we send a message now, they will be upon us even more rapidly."

"But you said you were going to blow up the cabin. Surely that will alert them as to which cabin the transmissions came from?"

"I meant that I will rig the cabin to blow when they enter," Gerard explained. "If we are lucky, ours will not be the first cabin they search. Now quickly, gather your things and follow me. We must cross the meadow before they are within scanning range. We have only minutes at best!"

"But where will we go?" Naralena asked as she grabbed her jacket and her bag.

"We have other hideouts, other cabins."

"Are they far?" Naralena asked as they headed for the exit.

"Yes, but they will get no closer until we start walking toward them." Gerard grabbed Naralena's hands, pulling them up to his heart as he looked into her eyes. "Do not be afraid, Naralena. I will protect you."

Naralena said nothing, only nodding and following him quickly out the door.

CHAPTER EIGHT

"We now have fifty Tannan technicians on board, as well as Kamenetskiy and his team," Commander Ellison reported, as he studied his data pad in the poorly lit ready room on the Jar-Benakh.

"So, not including all the Ghatazhak, that gives us what, sixty-two?" Captain Roselle concluded.

"Sixty-three."

"Hardly enough to run a five-kilometer-long battleship."

"About a tenth of what we really need, not including flight operations personnel."

"Yeah, well, I have a feeling about the only thing we're going to be flying off our decks are shuttles," the captain replied. "At least for the immediate future, that is."

"That's fine by me, sir," the commander agreed. "The last thing we need are a couple hundred more roles to fill."

"And fighter pilots, no less. Cocky fucking bunch."

The main lighting suddenly flickered, panels popping to life one by one.

"*Captain,*" Vladimir called over the intercom, "*I'm happy to report that main power has been restored.*"

"No shit," the captain muttered as he reached for his intercom control panel. "Nicely done, Lieutenant Commander. How are the engines looking?"

"*As best we can tell, propulsion was undamaged,*

sir. We should be able to get under way at any time. However, I would not advise using the FTL fields until we have had more time to evaluate those systems."

"How much time are we talking?"

"*Several days, at least,*" Vladimir warned.

"Very well. Get on it."

"*Aye, Captain.*"

Roselle looked at his XO. "Those Tannan boys figure out how to fly this thing yet?"

"They already knew," the commander replied. "Seems the Tannans who served on the Jar-Keurog kept pretty detailed records. Captain Scott insisted on keeping a copy on board the Aurora, just in case. Even had it updated several times a day."

"Guess he isn't as dumb as he looks," Roselle commented. "Where are we in relation to Sol right now?"

"We're on the opposite side of the Tau Ceti system from Sol, off to starboard a bit and a little low, relative."

"And Kohara? She on our way to Sol?"

"Yes, sir. More or less. What did you have in mind, Gil?"

"Well, I figure Dumar is going to send us one of two places. Either back to Sol, or to the Cetian orbital shipyards, assuming he finally decides to take them by force. Both are on about the same line, so why don't we turn this thing around and make way for Kohara for now."

"Beats the hell out of coasting in the wrong direction," the commander agreed.

"And make it nice and slow, Marty. No need to push the engines any harder than we have to. Not until the cheng sounds a little more confident in his assessments of all these Jung systems."

* * *

Captain Nash entered the hanger, making his way to the small stage along the wall. Once a bay that had housed several Jung fighters, it had recently been converted into a training facility for the Tannan gunship crews. It was a little small for their needs, but it was one of the last remaining buildings on the old Jung airbase that wasn't being used in support of gunship production.

He stepped up onto the stage and made his way to the podium, pausing to look out at the eighty faces staring back at him. These men and women were the most qualified volunteers that Tanna had to offer. Unfortunately, none of them had ever served in a military environment, and none of them had ever been in space. Even worse, none of them were pilots. Most of their qualifications were based on basic assessment scores, experience with technology, and the fact that they spoke English... barely.

"Good morning," Captain Nash began. "Welcome to your first day of training. I am Captain Robert Nash, and I will be in charge of your training. You will be learning to operate the new Cobra-class fast-attack gunships currently being assembled here on this base. You will also be learning how to behave in military service, how to follow the orders of your commanding officer, and how to work as a team. Most importantly, you will be learning how to *fight*, using your new gunships."

Captain Nash paused before continuing, scanning their faces for any signs of confusion. He knew that some of their English skills were subpar, thus it was important for him to speak clearly and deliberately. "Your training will be divided into four categories. Military procedures and protocols, flight operations, weapons and systems, and battle tactics. While each of you will specialize in certain tasks, all of you will receive the same basic instruction. Everyone will learn to fly the gunships, everyone will learn to operate their weapons and systems, and everyone will learn battle tactics. The reason for this is simple... Redundancy."

Captain Nash reached down and pressed a button on the control panel built into the podium. A massive view screen came to life behind and above him; on it, an exploded engineering plan of the Cobra gunship.

"This is the Cobra-class, fast-attack gunship," he began. "They are based on the old Scout-class ships built on Earth more than twenty years ago. We chose this design because it is rugged, easy to build, and has decades of performance experience behind it. More importantly, all the engineering has already been worked out and tested in battle, so there are no surprises awaiting us. All we needed to figure out was how to modify her to better suit her new mission profiles. Those profiles are to defend the Tannan system, to recon Jung controlled systems, to perform deep-space detection patrols, and to conduct wolf-pack style attacks against larger ships."

Captain Nash pressed the control button to change the image on the view screen. "The Cobra gunship will not be terribly fast, but she will be maneuverable. She will have a jump drive with a single-jump range of one light year, and will be able to jump repeatedly without recharging, giving her a theoretically unlimited jump range. In addition, her jump drive control systems will be more automated, allowing the use of preset jump distances, and automated series jumping, using a system of predetermined way points. This will allow you to utilize the jump system more rapidly, since the jump navigation computer will only need to calculate the jump parameters necessary to get you to the nearest waypoint."

Captain Nash paused for a moment, taking a drink of water to clear his throat. "The Cobra gunship will have advanced sensors of Takaran design, and will have an additional sensor module that can be swapped out according to mission profiles. She will be manned by a crew of six, whose positions shall be pilot, copilot, weapons systems, systems engineer, and two gunners. Her primary weapon will be four, independently powered, variable-output, forward-facing, mark three plasma torpedo cannons. At maximum output, these cannons can fire at a rate of once every ten seconds. At minimum output, they can fire once per second up to one hundred shots before reaching critical heat levels. The Cobra's secondary weapons will be two, quad-barreled, mark two plasma cannon turrets. They will be mounted on either side amidships, and will be manually operated. They will be mounted in tunnels that allow the weapon to extend outward several meters, giving them overlapping fields of fire. In other words, a target would have to be pretty damned close to *not* be in their field of fire. And lastly, there are four, double-barreled, mark one plasma cannon turrets mounted on the main drive section, fore and aft, and port and starboard, on both the top and the bottom, for a total of eight turrets. These turrets are operated by the weapons systems officer on the action deck, and can be assigned to operate in zones as point-defense weapons."

Captain Nash paused to take another breath before continuing. "In addition to all this firepower, the Cobra gunships are designed to use external hardpoints to carry any number of external weapons systems, such as intercept missiles, anti-ship missiles, and even kinetic kill vehicles. In short, there is little that the Cobra gunship will *not* be able to do. All *you* must do is learn how to operate her. Are there any questions?"

Captain Nash looked out across the room and sighed as a few dozen hands shot up.

* * *

After a quick dash across the meadow, Gerard and Naralena had been working their way up the rugged, steep terrain for several hours. The pace had been frantic, but steady, and it was wearing heavily on them both.

"I need to rest," Naralena begged.

"We are almost to the top," Gerard urged. "Just a few more minutes. Once we reach the summit, we will be better able to assess our situation. Perhaps then we can afford to slow our pace a bit."

Naralena groaned but continued up the trail behind him, nonetheless. The trees had begun to thin out twenty minutes ago and now they were becoming even more sparse as the ground became more rocky near the summit.

As promised, they stopped a few minutes later. Naralena immediately found the nearest large boulder on which to sit and rest, while Gerard scanned the valley behind them with a small pair of electronic binoculars that he carried in his pack.

"We may have been lucky," he said as he continued his scan. "It appears they have not yet reached our cabin. As I suspected, the Jung only knew the origin of the signal was somewhere around the lake."

"Maybe we should find somewhere to hide?" Naralena suggested. "The Alliance must know what area we are in. Perhaps they will come and search for us?"

"To do so would invite even more Jung patrols, as it would only verify what they already suspect," Gerard explained. "That is why your people did not simply send in an evac ship when contact was first made. They did not know the proximity of the Jung to our location. Based on the short amount of time it took for them to respond, we must assume that they have more men in this area than we anticipated."

"Couldn't they have just flown in recently?" Naralena wondered.

"The Alliance managed to clear the skies of Jung ships prior to their withdrawal. I do not believe they have any ships left, at least not in this area."

"What are we going to do, then?"

"We will make our way down the far side. There is a resort a few hours' walk from here. Many of their guests are people such as us."

"People running from the Jung?" Naralena wondered, finding it difficult to believe.

Gerard smiled. "Couples hiking the long trails between lakes. It is a common type of vacation this time of year, to hike from resort to resort. It is good exercise...cleanses the soul."

"I think I've had enough exercise for one day," she commented.

"We should be going," Gerard said. "It will be dark in a few hours."

"What about your men?" Naralena wondered as she reluctantly rose to her feet again.

"They know what to do. If we were able to get away, so should they... I hope."

* * *

"It doesn't look any different than a standard Falcon's console," Josh commented as he looked around the cockpit. He turned and looked at Deliza. "Are you sure it's a 'Super Falcon' and not just a regular old 'Falcon'? I heard they're easily confused."

"Are you going to take this seriously?" Deliza scolded, "or should I ask Loki to be my test pilot?"

"I'm just asking."

"It looks the same because we haven't changed anything...yet. We're waiting until after the prototype has flown and the admiral approves."

"Then, why am I here?"

"We've programmed the simulator with the Super Falcon's performance specifications. It should give us a good idea of how it handles."

"I've flown Falcons plenty," Josh argued, "I *know* how they fly."

"Super Falcons are different," Deliza insisted. "We don't want you to crash our only prototype, now do we?" she added as she stepped back down the access ladder and signaled the technician to close the simulator hood.

"Crash? Not a chance, princess," he scoffed as the sim hood came down over the Falcon's cockpit.

"Don't call me princess," she warned him through the crack as the hood closed and locked.

"Alright then," Josh said as he adjusted his comm-set. "I just love how roomy it is in here when you're not wearing a pressure suit. Hey, when you redesign the cockpit, can we make it a little roomier? That would be great."

"*You've already got the roomiest cockpit of any fighter,*" Deliza replied over his comm-set. "*In fact, you're going to have less space, as we're going to change it to a traditional cockpit instead of tandem.*"

"What? It's already cramped," Josh objected.

"*Don't worry, you won't be wearing a pressure suit.*"

"You mean I gotta rub elbows with Loki for twelve hours? You know how bad that guy smells by the end of a long mission?"

"*I heard that,*" Loki said.

"Loki! Hey! Glad you could make it!"

"*Uh-huh.*"

"Why aren't you in here with me, Lok?" Josh wondered.

"*They needed someone to run the sim. I'll do my tasks from here just like I was in the cockpit with you.*"

"But it feels so lonely in here without you," Josh joked. "Seriously, though. Tandem is better for long missions."

"*If we keep it tandem, then there won't be enough room for a cabin,*" Deliza told him.

"A cabin? We get a cabin?"

"*With standing head room, no less,*" Deliza added.

"What?" Josh pretended not to hear her, tapping his comm-set mic. "Did you say you want me to stand on my head?" he tapped the mic again. "I'm not sure this thing is working. Maybe we'd better abort?"

"*Powering up your systems,*" Loki announced as Josh's console came to life. "*We'll start you off already in space.*"

"I thought they weren't changing anything about the space systems?"

"*Your ship's center of gravity will be different without the atmospheric drives and the lift fans,*" Deliza explained.

"You're yanking our lift fans?" Josh exclaimed in disbelief. "How the hell are we supposed land?"

"*You've heard of runways?*" Loki asked, his tone dripping with sarcasm.

"You ever land on a runway?" Josh retorted.

"*Plenty of times.*"

"Recently?"

"*Well, not recently, but I made a few hundred of them in basic flight.*"

"Congratulations, you are the new Super Falcon test pilot," Josh announced.

"*I thought your nickname was Hotdog?*" Deliza said.

"Hot-*shot* is my handle, not my nickname...but, point taken."

"*You ready, Hotshot?*" Loki asked.

"Let her rip, Stretch," Josh said as he put his hands on the flight controls.

The simulator view screen that wrapped around the outside of the Falcon's cockpit came to life, displaying a wraparound view of space, complete with stars and the Earth below.

"*Alright, why don't you go ahead and put her through some basic maneuvers,*" Loki recommended over his comm-set.

Josh pushed his control stick to the left, initiating a longitudinal roll. "Nose spirals a bit on roll." He added more roll thrust, increasing the simulated roll rate. "Spiral increases with my roll rate. You want me to try and compensate?"

"*Negative,*" Loki replied. "*The thruster placements are designed for a different CG. They're reprogramming the thrust controllers now to adjust the strength of the thrust due to the offset center of gravity. Give them a minute.*"

"Copy that." Josh looked out his canopy, watching the simulated Earth circle around from left to right over and over again. "This is fun," he commented as he continued to watch the Earth circle around him. "Good thing I don't get motion sickness."

"*Okay, I think they've got it now. Resetting,*" Loki announced.

The wraparound view screen reset, and again he was in simulated flight in Earth orbit, with the planet off his port side.

"*Try that left roll again,*" Loki instructed.

"Sure." Josh touched his control stick, initiating another roll.

"*How's the spiral?*" Loki asked.

"Not seeing it."

"*Neither are we. Try increasing your roll rate again.*"

Josh added more thrust, causing the Earth to circle around him a bit faster. "Still not there."

"*A little more?*"

"Let's cut to the chase," Josh insisted as he pulled the control stick all the way left and held it for several seconds.

"*Josh!*"

The Earth began racing around his cockpit at incredible speed. "Damn! This is wild! Attempting to recover." Josh started applying counter thrust to slow his role. The speed of his rotation decreased slightly, but the spiraling effect returned, causing the Earth to appear lower, relative to his nose, with each revolution. "Spiral is back!" Josh exclaimed as he continued to fight with the controls. "Damn, this feels a lot more *different* than you might expect."

"*Josh, you're picking up some lateral rotation as well,*" Loki warned.

"Yeah, I noticed!" Josh exclaimed, frustration beginning to sneak in. The Earth outside started passing over him, at different locations each time, as his ship's lateral rotation increased. "I might have spoken too soon about not getting motion sickness! I think I'm gonna blow!"

"*You want me to reset?*" Loki asked.

"Not yet, I think I can get it... If I... can... just... Oh, shit!"

All rotation suddenly stopped, and his ship was again in level, simulated flight, in orbit above the Earth.

"What the hell?" Josh demanded. "I told you not to reset!"

"*You said you were going to blow!*" Loki defended.

"I was kidding, Lok!"

"*Sorry. I was just thinking of the poor guys who were going to have to clean up that cockpit.*"

"I never puke, you know that."

"Can we get back to work, gentlemen?" Deliza asked.

"What would you like me to do next, princess?" Josh asked.

"What did I tell you about calling me princess?" Deliza replied, her voice seething.

"Sorry, boss. Won't happen again. Promise."

"*Try pitching up and over,*" Loki suggested.

"Pitching up," Josh announced as he pulled back on the control stick, releasing it a split second later. He waited a moment, then added additional thrust to increase his rate of change. "Feels pretty much the same, no difference here."

"*Try the rotational thrusters,*" Loki instructed.

"You got it," Josh replied, twisting the control stick to the right for a moment.

"*I meant after you stopped your pitch-over.*"

"You didn't say that."

"*I didn't think I had to. Any normal pilot would have figured that out.*"

"Well, I'm not normal," Josh replied.

"*You got that right.*"

"I'm *better* than normal."

"*You realize what you just said doesn't make any sense?*"

"It wouldn't to a normal pilot," Josh teased.

"*Would you two stop!*" Deliza scolded. "*Honestly, you're like an old married couple.*"

"Listen, this would go a lot faster if you just let me wing-it for a few," Josh suggested. "You can look at the data later, right?"

"*Why not?*" Deliza agreed. "*I don't know what 'wing-it' means, but by all means, feel free.*"

Josh yanked his control stick over, gave it a twist, and then pushed it forward, bringing his space drive to full power at the same time. "Wing-it. To improvise, without plan or itinerary, usually by following one's instincts," he said as the Falcon came out of its turn and leveled off, diving toward the simulated Earth below.

"*What the... Josh, is that you?*" Loki wondered.

"I've been studying Earth expressions," Josh

explained, "trying to add some color to my witty banter."

"You've got more than enough color, Josh."

"What are you doing?" Deliza wondered.

"I'm going to jump her into the atmosphere and see how she flies without lift fans. You wanna dial me up a jump to Porto Santo's runway? About ten clicks out and a couple hundred meters up?"

"You're moving way too fast to jump in," Loki warned.

"Then make it a hundred kilometers out and a thousand meters up."

"Very well."

"Hey, boss? Did your aeronautical engineers calculate new stall speeds for this thing, now that she doesn't have lift fans and all?" Josh wondered.

"Yes, they did. Your velocity tape should indicate them correctly. They've only changed marginally from what they were for a fans-out emergency landing," Deliza told him.

"Never really practiced that one much," Josh admitted.

"Are you sure you don't want to slow down just a little?" Loki wondered.

"Fine." Josh twisted his stick hard to the left, pushing his nose around so that he was falling toward the planet tail first. He stopped his rotation and brought his main propulsion up to full power, waiting until his speed had reduced considerably. "Happy?"

"Well, you're still jumping in at about Mach twenty, but..."

"I'll be fine," Josh insisted as he brought his nose back around toward the planet. "It's a simulation, remember?"

"*The whole point of a 'simulation' is to 'simulate' real world scenarios that normal pilots would encounter...*"

"Oh, here we go with the 'normal' again..."

"*Enough!*" Deliza interrupted impatiently. "*Jump already.*"

"*Jumping,*" Loki announced.

The canopy turned opaque as usual, which struck Josh as funny since there wasn't actually a jump flash to block out. When it cleared a second later, his flight data display seemed all wrong. "What the hell?" Josh watched the displays as his ship descended through a simulated cloud. His attitude indicator was moving erratically, as if the ship couldn't decide which way it wanted to point. "Uh, I think I've got a problem," he announced as he fought to control his ship's attitude. "My nose is oscillating all over the place, guys, and I've got like no control authority here."

"*What do you mean?*" Loki asked.

"I mean my control inputs aren't doing much."

"*Are they doing anything?*"

"Yeah, just not much."

"*You came in too fast,*" Deliza admonished.

"It never used to be too fast."

"*The new control surfaces were made larger to give you more response in slow flight, so that you wouldn't have to come in so fast that you'd need a five-kilometer-long runway to stop.*"

"Then maybe you should've made the control servos bigger?" Josh suggested.

"*That would have required a redesign of the wing. We didn't want to take that kind of time.*"

"I don't know. I'm thinkin' it might've been worth it," Josh said as he continued to fight the controls.

"*Josh, you're dropping like a rock,*" Loki warned.

"Yeah, I noticed that. All this oscillating is probably fuckin' up the airflow over the... Jesus! Maybe you need to add some more area to the vertical stabilizers."

"*Maybe you should jump in with a little less speed?*" Deliza suggested.

"Yeah, I'll try to remember that next time."

"*You're busting one thousand meters, Josh,*" Loki warned him.

"I'm gonna try pulling the nose up a bit and see if I can get her to climb and lose some airspeed." Josh pulled back on the control stick, but got no response. "Nope."

"*Nine hundred meters,*" Loki warned. "*Eight hundred... Seven hundred...*"

"Oh, this is just stupid!" Josh complained. "You know, if I can't pitch up, I can't even jump back to orbit, people!"

"*Five hundred...*"

"Jesus! I'm still at Mach eight!"

"*Two hundred... one hundred...*"

The wraparound display screen went dark, and Josh's flight displays froze.

Josh threw his hand up in the air. "Guess that means we're resetting?"

"*I'm going to take you up to two thousand meters at three hundred meters per second,*" Loki announced. "*I'll put you about five hundred kilometers out from Porto Santo, on a really long final... Give you some time to get used to the controls.*"

"Thanks," Josh replied.

"*It's okay, Josh,*" Deliza assured him. "*That's what the simulator is for.*"

"I...don't...like...crashing," he replied emphatically. "Not even in a simulator."

"*See what I mean?*" Loki said. "*Not normal.*"

"*Guys...?*"

* * *

Captain Roselle walked into the Jar-Benakh's command and control center and made his way to the middle of the compartment. He looked around at all the unmanned stations. At least he had a helmsman, and a navigator, although he had no idea if they knew what they were doing. Thus far, all they had managed to do was turn the ship around and get her on course for Kohara, which wasn't difficult since they were still technically inside the Tau Ceti system. In addition, they were traveling slowly, which meant that they had plenty of time to react if something went wrong.

Luckily, so far, nothing had.

He also had a communications officer on loan from the Aurora, as well as a Tannan man who seemed pretty good at operating the Jung ship's sensors.

Still, there were an awful lot of empty chairs.

"Captain," Commander Ellison said as he stepped up to his commanding officer's side.

"Is it just me, or does this bridge seem unnecessarily large?"

"Well, technically it's not a 'bridge', sir. All of the ship's systems can be controlled from here, not just the usual things you'd find on a bridge. Apparently all the Jung warships are like this. They like to have one central point of control."

"Well, I suppose it made it easier for the Ghatazhak to seize control and all."

"It was hardly...*easy*," the Ghatazhak guard at the entrance corrected.

Captain Roselle and Commander Ellison both turned and looked at the guard.

"Didn't your DI tell you it's not polite to eavesdrop on a conversation?" Roselle wondered. He turned back around. "I suppose not."

"Lieutenant Commander Kamenetskiy reported a few minutes ago that both shields and weapons are back online."

"That was fast," Captain Roselle replied.

"As he explained it, when Nash jumped his ship, the section of the Jar-Benakh he took with him contained one of the main power relays. Apparently, their entire power distribution grid runs between the secondary and tertiary hulls, entering each section inward. The interruption caused a cascade failure that knocked all the reactors offline within seconds."

"Seems like a crappy design," Roselle commented.

"For normal conditions, probably not. The Lieutenant Commander believes the energy from Scout Three's jump fields somehow entered the Jar-Benakh's power grid when it sliced through her hull, causing the overload. He also believes it's what caused Scout Three to break up when she came out of the jump."

"Seems like knowledge someone could use, doesn't it?" Roselle observed. "Make sure that gets added to the next jump comm-drone run back to the Karuzara."

"Yes, sir."

"And tell Cheng good work."

"I did."

Captain Roselle looked around the room again. "From now on, let's just call this place 'command', shall we? Command and control center is a fucking mouthful, and C-C-C just sounds like you're stuttering."

"We could call it '3C'?"

Roselle looked at his XO in disapproval.

"Triple C?"

"I like 'command'."

"'Command' it is," the XO agreed.

* * *

Gerard came out of the small, rustic building at the front of the resort and headed across the clearing toward Naralena, his eyes darting about, looking for any signs of being watched.

"Did you get us a room?" Naralena asked as he approached.

"Yes. We were lucky. I was able to secure a small cabin on the edge of the resort. That should make it easy to slip away before daybreak without being noticed. Come."

She took his hand and stood, her feet and legs tired from their long, arduous hike over the pass. They strolled casually across the compound, holding hands to appear as just another couple on a typical, Koharan wilderness vacation. They made their way down the path and between the randomly placed cabins, each of them tucked away behind clumps of trees and flowering bushes. Although the grounds were obviously well maintained, they were done in such a way as to appear naturally occurring. The overall affect blended nicely with the wild surroundings just beyond the resort's unfenced perimeter.

"Should be the last one on the trail to the right, near the creek," Gerard said as he led the way.

A minute later, they entered the small cabin. It was tiny, with a large bed in the corner, a wood-burning stone fireplace, a table, and a small kitchenette. It was clean and modestly decorated in a way that spoke of the wilderness around them.

Gerard quickly checked the only other door. "Toilet and sink, no shower," he noted as he went across the room to check the kitchenette.

"No shower?"

"People on wilderness vacations usually bathe in lakes and rivers," he explained as he opened the small refrigerator. "Fridge is stocked as well," he said, pulling out a sealed package of sliced meats and vegetable sticks.

"All I want to do is take off my boots and pass out for a couple days," Naralena sighed as she sat down at the table.

"You can take them off for a while, if you like," Gerard said, "but do not go to sleep with them off, as we may need to leave in a hurry."

"Right," she said, deciding against removing them at all.

"I would suggest that you eat as much as you can. None of this food will last more than a few hours without refrigeration. They do that on purpose, so that frugal vacationers do not stay a single night and leave with several days' worth of supplies."

"You'd think they would at least have a shower. I mean, they have a toilet, so why not a shower?"

"It's not exactly a toilet," Gerard explained. "It's more like an indoor outhouse."

"A what?" Naralena asked, unfamiliar with the term.

"A box with a hole for your butt, over a deep hole in the ground."

"I don't understand. What happens with your bodily waste after you're done? Where does it go?"

"It just stays where it fell," Gerard told her.

"You're kidding, right?"

"Nope."

"Doesn't it smell?"

"They probably service it daily. Probably through a service hatch on the outside," he explained as he sat down at the table with her and unwrapped the tray of food. "They put a powder over it and then sprinkle some chemical on it. I forget the name of the chemical. It forms a solid layer, trapping the odor."

"What do they do when the hole gets full?" she wondered, unsure if she wanted to know the answer.

"Probably move the cabin and cover up the hole for good," he told her as he handed her a bottle of cold water.

"So, there's human waste buried all over this resort?" she said as she took a drink of water.

"Probably all over this valley. This resort has been here for more than a hundred years, and it is along one of the most popular routes in the area."

Naralena closed her eyes for a second. "Lovely." She took another drink of water. "We're only staying here for one night, right?"

* * *

"Thank you all for coming," Admiral Dumar said as he entered the briefing room on the Karuzara asteroid base in orbit over Earth. "I know you are all quite busy, as are we all." The admiral took his seat at the head of the conference table as he continued to speak. "Unfortunately, something of grave importance has come up that we need to discuss."

"What about Captains Nash, Poc, and Roselle?" Cameron wondered, noting their absence.

"Captain Nash is busy training the Tannans on how to operate their new gunships," Dumar explained. "Roselle is too busy getting the Jar-Benakh up and running, and Captain Poc is why we're here. Two days ago, we tasked Scout One with updating the state of all Jung assets, starting with those closest to Earth that we have not yet destroyed. The two closest were Delta Pavonis and 82 Eridani. As expected, all Jung assets within the Delta Pavonis system showed signs of increased alert status. Greater numbers of patrols, and her battle platform and battleship were both executing random course changes."

"Then they know we're coming," Nathan commented.

"It would seem so, yes," Dumar agreed. "This would be in line with Lieutenant Commander Nash's recent intelligence about the Jung's communications network. We have to assume that all Jung assets within thirty to thirty-five light years of Tau Ceti are, at the very least, aware of the new threat the Alliance represents. So the question is, what will they do about it?"

"If the Jung like to attack with overwhelming force, then they'll send everything they have in the area our way," Jessica said. "Perhaps to a prearranged staging point within easy striking distance of Sol?"

"Perhaps," the admiral agreed. "The question is,

do the Jung field commanders have protocols that automatically dictate such action, or do they have to wait for orders from higher up, like Jung command? If it's the latter, then we probably have plenty of time, but if it's the former..."

"There could already be ships on their way," Cameron finished for the admiral.

"That has always been a possibility," Commander Telles added. "The Jung move entire battle groups around like pieces in that board game of yours... *Chess*, I believe you call it... Positioning units in preparation for future actions. Considering the area of their empire and the limitations of their FTL systems, it is a necessity."

"The commander is correct," the admiral agreed, "and Captain Poc's discoveries confirm it. Two days ago, Scout One discovered that the Jung battle group once at 82 Eridani was no longer in that system." Admiral Dumar paused, noting the concerned looks of everyone in attendance. "That battle group was composed of a battle platform, a battleship, two cruisers, and four frigates. Knowing that the last recon of 82 Eridani was only a few weeks ago, Captain Poc realized that the battle group could not have gotten far. Since there were only two possible destinations of concern, he decided to search along the routes to both Sol and the Tau Ceti system."

"Gerard said there were rumors of a third battle group heading their way," Jessica reminded the admiral.

"Indeed, and Captain Poc was aware of that, which is why he chose to start by searching the route between 82 Eridani and Tau Ceti. Since the last recon of the system *was* so recent, he did not expect to have to search very far along that course.

Unfortunately, that was not the case. After searching more than halfway along that route, he had still not detected the missing battle group. However, since the distance between 82 Eridani and Tau Ceti is only twelve light years, versus the twenty light year separation between 82 Eridani and Sol, he decided to continue along the route to Tau Ceti, just to be safe. Captain Poc's thoroughness worked to our advantage, as he discovered a battle group only two week's travel from the Tau Ceti system."

"But, that's impossible," Cameron argued.

"Not if it was a different battle group," Nathan added.

"Precisely what Captain Poc concluded, which is why he went back and began searching the route from 82 Eridani to Sol, where he found another battle group, just over two weeks' travel from 82 Eridani at twenty times light."

"But they still won't reach Sol for nearly a year," Jessica pointed out.

"But they'll reach Tau Ceti in two weeks," the admiral said. "There are two nearly completed frigates in the Cetian orbital shipyards, and the Jar-Benakh... None of which we can outfit with jump systems and get them out before that battle group arrives."

"When the Jung arrive in the Tau Ceti system, they will destroy it," Commander Telles commented.

"Why?" Jessica wondered. "The Cetians didn't initiate the attacks. They had nothing to do with it."

"Neither did the people of Kent," Commander Telles replied. "The Jung drove a battleship full of antimatter into them, just to make a point. Most likely to us... Undoubtedly *not* the Kentarans."

"Potential assets or not, we have a responsibility to the people of Tau Ceti," Admiral Dumar insisted.

"Do we even have any antimatter warheads left?" Nathan asked.

"No, but we have a Jung battleship with twenty-two cores on her and, according to Lieutenant Commander Kamenetskiy, she can run on a quarter of that number, *if* she does not use her shields, or her FTL fields."

"That's going to take all the bang out of Roselle's new ship," Cameron stated.

"Frigates use antimatter reactors, don't they?" Jessica said. "Since they're building two of them in the Cetian shipyards, they probably have the ability to produce antimatter cores *in* the Tau Ceti system."

"Makes sense," Nathan agreed.

"It didn't work last time," Cameron reminded them.

"Because we didn't have KKVs," Jessica argued.

"But we've only got three of them left," Nathan added, "and so far, we've always needed at least two, and one time *three* KKVs to take down a battle platform. Now we have one headed for Earth, and one headed for Tau Ceti. Which one do we use them on? The one headed for a potential ally that *we* put in harm's way, or the one headed for our homeworld?"

The room fell silent.

"We may not have to," Admiral Dumar said, breaking the silence. "Lieutenant Tillardi is confident that his jump KKV prototype will work."

"We'd still have to manufacture a bunch of them," Nathan pointed out.

"Yes, but we would have nearly a year to do so," the admiral said, "enough time to build hundreds of them. We simply cannot, in good conscience, put the people of Tau Ceti at such risk. We must protect that system."

"Those ships are going to be clustered together, flying in formation instead of spread out all over a system," Nathan warned. "I'm not sure we can take them all on ourselves."

"The Celestia will be leaving dry dock in eight days," the admiral said. "We will wait until then."

"We may be *leaving* dry dock in eight days, but we won't have *all* our weapons systems by then," Cameron reminded him.

"But you *will* be as well-armed as the Aurora, perhaps even better with your mark five plasma cannons," the admiral pointed out, "*and* you'll have shields, which means you can go in close and fire repeatedly, while the Aurora must still fight using hit-and-run tactics. *You* can maneuver between them, push them apart, while Captain Nash attacks the ships on the outer perimeter."

Nathan looked at Cameron. "Looks like you're going to give your new shields a real workout, Captain."

* * *

"Thank you for agreeing to speak with us, Commander," Kata said.

Commander Telles stood at ease, feet shoulder-width apart, his hands clasped behind his back, looking at the camera.

Kata signaled for Karahl to pause recording for a moment. "Commander, are you sure you don't want to sit down? Maybe go inside?"

"I prefer to stand," the commander replied, "and I prefer to be outside."

"Right. Well, just try to relax."

"I am relaxed."

"Of course." Kata signaled Karahl to turn the porta-cam back on. She waited for him to lift the camera back up onto his shoulder and for the red light to appear before continuing. "How long have you been on Earth, Commander?"

"I arrived fourteen hours ago, at zero two thirty, Earth Mean Time."

"I meant how long ago did you *first* arrive on Earth?"

"Three hundred and eight days, twenty hours, forty-seven minutes, to be exact."

"Of course." Kata sighed. "Where are you from?"

"The city of Primetkin, on the planet Toradon, in the Takar system, in..."

"Yeah, the Pentaurus sector...we know," Kata finished for him, frustration in her voice. "How about this one? What is your job here?"

"I am the commander of all Ghatazhak forces attached to the Alliance in the Sol sector," the commander answered.

"And who are the Ghatazhak?"

"An elite fighting force."

"And how long have you been a Ghatazhak?"

"Seventeen Terran years."

"You don't look that old," Kata commented.

"I am approximately thirty-one Terran years in age. I believe that is approximately thirty-six Koharan years."

"Then you must have joined when you were quite young."

"I was accepted into Ghatazhak training at the usual age."

"And what age was that?"

Commander Telles looked at Kata Mun. "Is this line of questioning normal for such an interview?"

"I'm just trying to get you to open up a little, Commander."

"You are wasting your time. I do not...*open up*."

"I'm getting that impression."

"Perhaps if you were to inquire about my opinion of the Jung? That *is* the point of these interviews, is it not? To convince your people that the Jung are *not* who they pretend to be?"

"All right, Commander. Share with us your thoughts about the Jung."

Commander Telles looked at the camera again. "The Jung are a well-trained, well-armed, and well-disciplined military force, with hundreds of ships, and millions of men. They are ruthless and clever in battle, and they are quite unforgiving of those who refuse to bow down to them. As warriors, I respect them. As a civilization, I believe they are a disease that needs to be excised before it spreads into every corner of the galaxy and becomes impossible to remove. If your people are *not* willing to join the Alliance and *fight* the Jung, then your people *deserve* what befalls them."

Kata stood there, dumbfounded.

Commander Telles looked back at Kata Mun. "Do you have any further questions, Miss Mun?"

"Uh...no."

"Very well. Good day."

Kata stood there speechless as she watched him walk away.

"We're out," Karahl announced as he shut off the porta-cam.

Kata sighed heavily. "They were *not* kidding."

"Kidding about what?" Karahl wondered.

"They told me the commander would be a difficult interview."

"I don't know, I think you might have gotten a minute or two of usable footage out of him."

Kata looked at him, one eyebrow raised.

"Okay, maybe ten seconds."

* * *

After being cleared by the guard, Deliza stepped through the door leading into the next bay of the black lab. Ever since she had started working on the Super Falcon project, she had wanted to see what was happening on the other side of the wall. After days of begging, Admiral Dumar had finally granted her access.

The space was less than half of what her team occupied, but otherwise was identical in appearance. Polished rock walls and floor, an uneven rocky ceiling covered with arrays of lighting panels laid out in perfect rows. There were rolling tool carts and workstations everywhere, as well as several rolling cranes and powered carts. There were at least fifty men and women working in the bay, with most of the activity focused on one particular apparatus, despite the fact that there appeared to be eight more of the same lined up across the bay.

Deliza approached the long apparatus, around which everything was centered. It was at least twenty-five meters in length, and appeared to have an oval cross-section that was about seven meters wide and five meters in height. The apparatus was separated into five sections, with each section resting on powered lifting carts. Two of the sections had thick canards coming out of all four sides, with thruster ports on all its faces. Its mid-section seemed to be nothing more than simple propellant storage, while its forward-most section, whose cross-section was at least a meter larger than the rest of the vessel, appeared to be solid through and through.

It was the aft section that caught her interest.

"Can I help you?" a man asked as she walked toward the tail of the apparatus.

"No, I'm just..."

"You're Deliza Ta'Akar, aren't you?"

"Yes, I am," Deliza answered, her attention still focused on the tail section of the apparatus.

"Nathan told me about you. I'm Lieutenant Tillardi. Jonathon Tillardi," he said, holding his hand out in greeting.

Deliza shook his hand, still without looking at him. "That's a jump drive, isn't it?"

"Admiral Dumar told me you had been asking to visit our lab."

"Where's the reactor?" she asked, still ignoring his attempts at conversation.

"There isn't one."

Finally, Deliza turned her head. "Where is the power for the jump coming from?" Deliza suddenly looked embarrassed. "I'm sorry, what did you say your name was?"

"Jonathon Tillardi. I'm in charge of this project."

"Deliza Ta'Akar," she replied. "I run the project next door."

"Yeah, I heard. I can't wait to see what you're doing to those Falcons."

Deliza's attention returned to the apparatus. "You're building a kinetic kill vehicle...with a mini-jump drive, aren't you?"

"That's right," the lieutenant confirmed with

no small amount of pride. "Eight of them, in fact. Nine, including the prototype here," he explained, gesturing toward the apparatus she couldn't stop staring at. "We call them 'jump KKVs', or 'JKKVs' for short."

"Did you build all these from scratch?" she asked with amazement, as she moved closer to the tail of the prototype.

"Actually, they're built from unused missiles," Lieutenant Tillardi explained. "The Aurora still had a few left when her launcher was destroyed, and there are a few hundred of them stored in an underground bunker on Earth, still waiting for warheads. The Jung never even knew about them."

"You still never told me where your mini-jump drives are getting their power," Deliza reminded him.

"From energy banks, located all along the sides, from stem to stern. Eight of them, altogether. Each energy bank feeds directly to a single emitter, instead of all of them feeding into a distributive array."

"But energy banks are heavy," Deliza commented.

"Weight is good in a KKV," the lieutenant reminded her. "Granted, the presence of the energy banks doesn't really increase the destructive potential of the KKV all that much, but every little bit helps, right?"

"So, how does it work?" she asked.

"It's really just a big slug of mass. A ship will get the KKV up to speed along an intercept course, say, about fifty to seventy-five percent the speed of light, and then release it. The prototype's jump drive is only capable of making a single, fixed-distance jump of one light day, but the rest will be programmable with a range of as much as a light month. They just have to be fed their targeting parameters prior to launch."

"Why the maneuvering systems?" Deliza wondered. "They couldn't possibly create enough delta V to alter course at that speed."

"Actually, those tanks are empty. We just didn't bother removing the maneuvering systems. We probably will in the production models."

"I see," Deliza replied. "And the other eight? Are they different prototype variants?"

"No. The admiral wanted us to get a head start on getting some jump KKVs ready for use in actual attacks, since we're down to only three of the conventional FTL KKVs, and probably won't be getting..." The lieutenant stopped mid-sentence, realizing his blunder. "Oh...that was just...rude. I'm so sorry."

"It's quite all right," Deliza insisted. "Please, tell me more about jump systems, Lieutenant Tillardi."

"Please, call me Tilly."

* * *

Naralena woke with a start as a hand clamped down tightly over her mouth. Her eyes popped open in terror. It was dark, but she was able to make out Gerard's face not one hundred centimeters from hers.

Gerard put his index finger against his mouth, indicating she should remain silent. He then slowly removed his hand from her mouth and rolled silently out of bed, picking up his sidearm from the nightstand as he stood.

In a semi-crouch, he moved across the small cabin, heading for the nearest window.

Naralena fought back a scream as she saw shadows moving outside the window. Gerard sidestepped immediately, putting his back against the wall as he gestured for Naralena to get out of bed and follow him.

Naralena moved off the bed as quietly and carefully as possible, and moved to the wall behind Gerard.

The door burst open, and two shadowy figures, back-lit by only moonlight, rushed into the room. Gerard fired three shots, two of the red, needle-like bolts of energy striking the man on the right, dropping him instantly. The man on the left returned fire, his energy bolt slamming into the wood wall between Gerard and Naralena.

Gerard fired again as he crouched down and grabbed the edge of the bed frame and heaved it upward onto its side to provide some cover. Two more men rushed into the room, also firing.

"Alive!" someone yelled from outside. "I said, alive!"

The men stopped firing but continued rushing toward Gerard and Naralena as they crouched down behind the mattress. "The window," he instructed calmly and in a low voice. "Go!" He rose and fired at the charging men as Naralena moved quickly to the window, picking up the chair by the table and heaving it through the glass.

Gerard continued to fire as Naralena climbed out the window, but his shots seemed to bounce off his attackers.

"She's going out the window!" one of the charging men cried out.

Gerard rose to a fighting stance, taking one of the men diving toward him, and in a smooth twisting motion, guided him past and head first into the wall behind him. The second attacker threw his entire body into Gerard's chest, knocking him backward. As he fell, Gerard pushed the muzzle of his weapon into the attacker's side, feeling the give of his left flank and pulled the trigger.

The man screamed out in anguish as they both fell against the wall. Gerard, his weapon knocked from his hand, pushed the injured man off of him to his left, rolling right to retrieve his weapon. As he scrambled for his sidearm, he could hear the footfalls of others as they rushed into the room. His fingers touched the handle of his weapon, and he felt a sudden, tremendous pain in the back of his head.

Naralena fell to the ground, rolling several times down the small incline along the backside of the cabin. She could hear men yelling in Jung, "*She went out the window! Quickly!*"

She scrambled to her feet and began running down the dimly lit dirt path, not knowing where it led. She could hear men running after her...not far behind, and the voices, yelling in Jung.

"*She's getting away!*"

"*She's headed for the pond!*"

"*Two right, two left, we'll follow up the middle! Do not let her get away!*"

She stumbled, falling to her knees, tearing her trousers... Pain, in her knees and palms. She got back up, hardly missing a step, and continued running as fast as she could, struggling to see the trail in front of her in the darkness. The trees gave way to a beach. She was in the open.

"There she is!"

The dirt gave way to sand. *No, no, no...* The sound of a single energy weapon shot and a sudden burning sensation in her right leg. She fell, tumbling forward, her right leg no longer working. She lost her balance on her way down, spinning to her right and falling into the water.

Foul-smelling water filled her mouth as she tried to breathe. Her head broke the surface. She coughed, she gasped. She was underwater again. Hands grabbed her. Pain in her right leg. More hands reaching, pain in her upper back and head as she was struck repeatedly. Then...

CHAPTER NINE

"You sure this thing's not gonna blow up on me?" Josh wondered as the technicians finished strapping him into the Super Falcon prototype's cockpit. "This ain't a simulator, you know."

"It's not going to *blow up* on you," Deliza insisted from the top of the boarding ladder next to the Super Falcon's cockpit. "Just be gentle with her. Try to fly her like a..."

"If you say 'normal pilot', so help me... I got no problem punchin' a princess."

"Stop it," Deliza replied, taking him in jest as she turned to climb down. She paused a moment, looking back at him over her shoulder. "You were joking, weren't you?"

Josh smiled at her, saying nothing.

"Don't fuck up, kid!" Marcus called from the deck a few meters away.

Deliza climbed down the ladder as the Super Falcon's primary reactors began to spin up, their slow whine building with each passing second. The deck hands moved the boarding ladder away.

Josh watched his systems display as the power levels climbed. "If this thing ain't gonna blow up on me, then how come you're not coming with me, Loki?" he asked over his helmet comms.

"*Uh... Procedures?*"

"Yeah, that's what I thought." He glanced at his

power levels again. "Power's up, closing her up," he announced as he activated the canopy.

"*You're clear on deck, sir, good to roll,*" the ground crew chief announced over the comms.

"Thanks, Chief." Josh added another channel to his comms as his canopy came down and locked into place. "Karuzara Control, Soo-per Falcon, ready for departure, bay zero," he called as he released his parking brake and flipped the selector switch to change his control stick from flight to taxi mode.

"*Soo-per Falcon,*" the controller mimicked, mocking Josh's initial call-up, "*Karuzara Control. Clear for direct departure, bay zero. On departure, fly one seven zero, four up relative for Earth orbit intercept. Be advised your test area is clear of all traffic.*"

"Super Falcon, cleared for departure, bay zero, one seven zero and four up, and I copy the area is clear of all traffic." Josh pushed his control stick forward, sending power to the electric motors that drove all four pairs of wheels. The ship moved forward and turned to the right as Josh pushed the control stick to the side.

A minute later, he brought the Super Falcon to a stop inside the transfer airlock. He activated his parking brake again and set his control stick back to flight mode, as the big door behind his ship began to close.

Josh cycled through his screens one at a time as he powered up his engines and maneuvering systems. Without Loki in the seat behind him, he would have to keep an eye on a lot more than just his flight data displays, especially since he was flying a ship that had just had all its engines and internal systems completely reorganized. Although he knew the technicians in the black lab were there *because* they were the best, it only took one nut that wasn't tightened properly, or one valve not calibrated to spec... Josh had joked many times that he could easily operate the Falcon without Loki's help, but this was one time he wished he didn't have to, at least not this *Super Falcon*.

"*Telemetry looks good, Josh,*" Loki's voice called over Josh's helmet comms. "*Engines and maneuvering systems are online and at normal power.*"

Josh glanced through his canopy into the transfer airlock. The interior of the bay was bathed in red light, indicating it was depressurizing. Finally, the outer doors split down the center and began retracting into the walls. As they parted, they revealed a long, dark tunnel, lit only by four rows of dim lights, outlining the interior dimensions of the tunnel to guide the pilot during transition. Since bay zero was on the outboard side of the black lab complex, and did not open into the center spaceport cavern of the Karuzara asteroid, its exit tunnel to the outside was considerably shorter. It was also the only tunnel to the outside that was completely straight, and Josh could make out the stars at the far end.

"*Okay, nice and easy, Josh,*" Deliza reminded him as the outer doors reached their fully open position.

"Airlock gravity down to twenty-five percent," Loki announced.

Josh applied a tiny burst of upward thrust, lifting the Super Falcon from the deck. As the ship rose slowly, he applied a bit of forward thrust as well, imparting forward motion to get his ship out of the airlock and into the much wider transition tunnel.

Josh looked up as the outer door threshold slid

over him and aft. He looked down at his flight data display, watching as the dotted line that represented the threshold slid clear and behind him. "Here we go," he muttered as he eased the throttle forward.

The Super Falcon began to accelerate, slowly at first, picking up speed more rapidly as he advanced his throttle. "What the hell," he mumbled, a smile creeping onto his face. He pushed the throttle forward to nearly twenty-five percent. The rows of lights along the interior of the tunnel quickly turned into solid streaks as he blasted down the tunnel and out the far end.

"*JOSH!*" Loki yelled over the comms.

"Hey, you want this thing tested or not?" he said as he did a snap roll to the left, rolling one and a half revolutions before stopping his roll and initiating his departure turn. By now, his smile was ear to ear. "Guess I'm not gonna blow up after all," he added, chuckling to himself. "You know, it still doesn't have the acceleration that the old Falcon had."

"*It's not supposed to,*" Deliza explained.

"Hardly seems right to call it *super* then, doesn't it." Josh looked at his displays. "Orbital intercept in twenty seconds."

"*Go ahead and put yourself on a course for Porto Santo,*" Loki advised. "*It should be coming up on the horizon.*"

"Got it," he replied, calling up Porto Santo as his jump destination. "Hey, this interface is pretty slick, did I tell you that?"

"*It was your idea, remember?*" Deliza reminded him.

"That explains it." Josh could imagine her rolling her eyes and commenting about his character to Loki. "Yes, I am," he added.

"*You are what?*" Loki asked.

"Nothing. Got Porto Santo dialed in, coming to course now," he reported as he adjusted his course to meet the one specified by the jump navigation computer. He reduced his throttles to zero just before the course indicator turned green. "Green lines," he reported. A moment later the 'Jump Ready' indicator illuminated. "Jump is ready. Hey, this thing is faster than you, Lok," he declared as he activated the jump sequencer. "Jumping in three......two..."

The Super Falcon's canopy turned opaque.

"...one......jumping."

The ship began to shake violently as it came out of its jump. The canopy cleared, revealing a clear blue sky above him and a vast ocean below.

"Damn," he exclaimed. "Bumpy-ass ride!"

"*Is there a problem?*" Deliza wondered.

"Negative," Josh insisted. "I think the winds ain't what they were forecasted, that's all." He glanced down at his flight displays. "Airspeed is falling, Mach twenty and falling. Altitude is twelve thousand meters and falling. Pulling the nose up to slow her down a bit. Hey, next time, remind me to start from further out and come in more like Mach five or something. Any Mach in the single digits will do, I suspect."

"*I'm pretty sure that the flight parameters said something about Mach two as your jump-in speed.*" Loki reminded him.

"Flight parameters are for normal pilots," Josh teased. "Not gonna find out what she can do if we fly her by the numbers, now are we?"

The shaking began to smooth out, until it finally became just small bounces and shakes. "Mach ten, ten thousand meters. Mach eight, six, four, two......

subsonic," he finally announced, a wave of relief washing over him. "Hey, Deliza! You can tell your guys to rest easy. It appears they didn't forget to tighten anything. Hell, if she can take that much shakin' she can take anything."

"*That's good to hear,*" Deliza replied over the comms.

"Still doesn't qualify as *super* though," he mumbled. "Porto Santo is about one hundred out. Speed is down to eight hundred KPH, altitude four thousand meters. Looks like I'm on a really long final." Josh fiddled with the controls, rolling the Super Falcon left and right, checking her responsiveness to control inputs. "You know, your guys smoothed out her handling nicely. She feels pretty good at this speed. I'm still falling like a rock, but that's okay." He checked his displays again. "Four hundred, three thousand, and eighty out." He twisted the control stick slightly, first left and then right. "Rudders feel weak, though. I think you were right about it needing more surface area."

Josh looked around outside, enjoying the view as his ship continued to descend toward the main runway at Porto Santo airbase. "You know, we could have jumped in a lot closer."

"*Especially if you would've jumped in at Mach two, like we asked,*" Loki replied.

"I can see the runway now," Josh reported. "I'm a little high, though."

"*But I see you're making up for it by being a little fast, so...*"

"That's what air brakes and flaps are for," Josh insisted. "Dirtying her up," he said as he deployed them both. "Speed is coming down, and so is my altitude."

"*You might want to add some power so you don't slam into the runway, Josh,*" Loki suggested. "*Remember, you don't have lift fans on this one.*"

"I know that," Josh replied. His expression said something else entirely as he eased his throttle forward a bit. He strained to see over the forward console as the runway numbers disappeared under his nose. "We're gonna need some forward facing cameras under the nose," Josh said. "With my nose up this high, I can't see shit."

"*The new cockpit design will make up for that,*" Deliza assured him.

"Over the numbers," Josh reported as his ship began to buffet.

"*You're still a little fast, Josh,*" Loki warned.

"Any slower and I'll stall," Josh insisted. "I'm already picking up a lot of buffeting here." Josh braced himself as he watched his altitude above the ground indicator rapidly approach zero. "And...... Ugh!" he grunted, as the ship hit the runway rather hard. His nose quickly came down, and his forward gear hit hard as well. "Jesus!" he exclaimed. "Activating auto-braking." Josh could feel the ship slowing as the automated braking system tried to slow the Super Falcon. "Half my runway is gone," Josh warned. "I'm still pretty fast."

"*Did you land long?*" Loki wondered.

"Hell, no. Right on the marks. I don't think these brakes are..." A red warning light came on. "Uh, I think I may have broke something on that landing. My brakes are overheating, and I'm running out of fucking runway." Josh slammed his throttle all the way forward and deactivated his braking system, all in one motion. "Screw this, I'm taking off!" he announced as the Super Falcon began to accelerate down the runway. "I am *still* running out of runway," he warned, "and I do *not* have enough airspeed to rotate!"

"*Dial up an escape jump!*" Loki instructed. "*Select one hundred kilometers!*"

"Is that going to give me enough..."

"*Just do it!*" Loki ordered.

"Fuck, tell everyone to duck!" Josh exclaimed. He quickly rotated the distance selector wheel on his flight control stick so that one hundred kilometers showed as the selected distance to jump. "Snap jump!" he announced as he closed his eyes tight and pressed the button on his control stick.

The canopy became opaque only a split second before the flash. When he came out of the jump, Josh found his ship at three thousand meters above the ocean and falling, without enough airspeed to maintain straight and level flight. He immediately pushed his nose down, with his thrust levers already at maximum, allowing both his thrust and the pull of the Earth's gravity to accelerate him more quickly. The ocean came rushing up toward him, the ripples turning into waves, their crests clearly distinguishable as he dove toward them.

"*Pull up! Pull up!*" Loki ordered after finally reestablishing contact after the jump.

"Not yet," Josh replied, watching his airspeed tape climb. He started easing his nose up, little by little, so as not to over-stress the airframe that had just been torn apart and put back together in less than a week. His muscles tightened, and his eyes squinted as he leaned his head back into his flight seat, waiting for his ship's belly to impact with the waves below.

But it did not.

"Whoa, yeah!" Josh cheered as the Super Falcon leveled off only a few meters above the cresting waves. "Level flight and accelerating! Good call, Loki!" Josh quickly dialed up 'high orbit' as his jump destination and waited for both jump lines and jump-ready indicators to turn green before jumping.

A wave of relief washed over him as the canopy cleared to reveal the familiar sight of a star field in front of him. "All right, boys and girls. What's next?"

"Bring it home, Josh," Loki instructed.

"Already?"

"Yup. The engineers will make a few more modifications, and then install an upgraded weapons package on her for her next test flight."

"But we've barely flown her," Josh insisted.

"Doesn't matter," Deliza replied. *"The admiral wants a weapons test as soon as possible. I think that's how the admiral wants to make the Falcon 'Super'."*

"Works for me," Josh said, as he initiated a turn to head back to the Karuzara asteroid.

* * *

"Talk to me, Kamenetskiy," Captain Roselle said as he entered the Jar-Benakh's briefing room.

"FTL systems have been thoroughly inspected, Captain. I believe it is now safe to use them, should you so desire."

"You *believe*?" Roselle said as he took his seat at the table with everyone else.

"I am sure?"

"You don't sound sure," the captain replied.

"I *am* certain, sir. The FTL systems are safe to use."

"Great. So we can fly, we can shoot, we've got shields, *and* we can travel faster-than-light. Now, if we just had enough crew to do them all at once, we'd be set."

"Not exactly," Commander Ellison corrected. "A comm-drone from command jumped in a few minutes ago. There's a Jung battle group on their way here from 82 Eridani and they're only two weeks out."

"Then we'd better get ready to fight," the captain said. "I'd love to see the look on their faces when one of their own ships opens up on them."

"Not going to happen, I'm afraid," the commander commented, handing his data pad to the captain.

Roselle read the message. "Are they fucking joking?"

Vladimir looked expectantly from the commander to the captain, and to the others at the table, wondering what the message was.

"They want to pull half our cores and turn them into antimatter mines to knock the Jung out of FTL so they can take them down before they arrive," the captain announced to the rest of them.

"It does make sense, Captain," Commander Ellison admitted.

"Yeah, I know it does," Captain Roselle reluctantly agreed. "It doesn't mean I have to like it, though."

"Captain, with only half our cores, we will not be able to run shields, weapons, and FTL systems at the same time," Vladimir warned.

"Not your problem," the captain told him.

"What?"

"The communiqué included orders for you as well," Commander Ellison told Vladimir. "You are to pull the eleven cores and bring them back to

The Frontiers Saga Episode #14: THE WEAK AND THE INNOCENT

Karuzara as soon as possible. Several cargo shuttles will be arriving in a few hours."

"But, there is still so much to do, so much to learn," Vladimir argued.

"Look, Lieutenant Commander, you got us up and running and on our way. You did well, son," Captain Roselle assured him. "Captain Nash managed to scrape up another fifty Tannans to come and help us out. They're not all as qualified as we'd like, but they're warm bodies and they want to help. We'll be fine," he assured them. "We'll be without half our damned cores, but we'll be fine. Just make sure our cores don't go to waste. Make sure those mines work."

* * *

"I thought this room might be more appropriate for the interview," Admiral Dumar said as he led Kata Mun and her porta-cam operator, Karahl, into the massive chamber.

"Whoa," Kata exclaimed, her eyes wide and her mouth falling open. One whole wall was transparent, looking directly out into space. The Earth could be seen along the lower left corner, with her moon in the upper right corner in the distance. Beyond them both was Sol, shining ever brightly.

Karahl kept his porta-cam aimed at Admiral Dumar, as the admiral extended his right arm, waving it in a graceful arc from front to back as he spoke. "It's the only actual 'window to space' in the entire facility. We call it, 'the gallery'."

Kata strolled out into the center of the room, turning around slowly as she walked to get a full view of the room. There were ten rows of seats opposite the window, each of them raised two steps higher than the one before, giving every seat in the room a clear view of the outside. "It's perfect," she agreed. "What's it for?"

"In every ship on which humans serve for long periods of time, there is always an area such as this. Some have a window, others use a large view screen linked to external cameras. People need to *see* outside every so often. They need to be reminded that their existence is not confined to the windowless corridors and compartments within."

"Where did you get such a large window in the first place?"

"Actually, the materials used to create it came from the excavation of the kilometer-long corridor leading to this chamber, which, originally, was a small cave on the outside of this asteroid."

"I noticed there are several large caverns with simulated outdoor spaces within this base as well," Kata commented. "Were those built for the same reason as this chamber?"

"Yes and no. Both are meant to expose the staff to something beyond the interior spaces, but *this* room does something unique. It shows us the vastness and the majesty of the environment that we work in. More importantly, the view of Earth reminds us of what we are here to protect."

"But that is just one planet," Kata pointed out. "Isn't the Alliance made up of many worlds?"

"Yes, but the Earth is unique. It is the birthplace of us all. It is the center of the entire, human-inhabited portion of our galaxy. It is a symbol that reminds us that we are all linked. Regardless of where we were born or raised, or where we currently reside. As long as *it* survives," he explained, pointing to the planet below, "there is still hope that we can all coexist, peacefully."

Kata nodded in understanding.

"Shall we sit?" the admiral suggested, gesturing to the two chairs that had been perfectly placed in front of the window facing back inward.

"Thank you," Kata replied as they took their seats.

Karahl moved around to the middle of the front row of seats, taking his porta-cam off his shoulder, while keeping it trained on both Kata and the admiral. He pressed a button on the side of the porta-cam, and the bottom opened up, allowing a stand to unfold into a tripod. He lowered the porta-cam onto the floor, made a few adjustments, then nodded to Kata that he was ready to continue recording.

"Admiral, this probably is unimportant in the grand scheme of everything, but I just have to ask... Why spend months jumping an asteroid a thousand light years, when a ship, or even several ships, would have been easier?"

"Logistics and opportunity," Admiral Dumar replied. "We already had this base within the asteroid, although it was considerably less complex at the time. In addition, the people of Earth *needed* a base of operations, one where they could service their ships, or even build new ones. The asteroid was already ours to use as we saw fit, and there was plenty of its interior that we could mine for the raw materials needed for not only its construction, but also for the fabrication of equipment, weapons, parts...all manner of things. Then, when Prince Casimir noticed that an opportune alignment was approaching, it just seemed predestined."

"Interesting that you should bring that up," Kata

said. "I was reviewing the history of events since the Aurora was originally flung out into space. It almost seems like a string of fortunate events and circumstances."

"Some call it destiny, some call it fate, others call it 'dumb luck'."

"What do you call them?"

"Opportunities."

"What about the legend of Na-Tan?"

"Myths and legends," he said dismissively.

"You don't think it is an amazing coincidence?" Kata wondered. "That the man who suddenly appeared, against what most would agree are astronomical odds, bears the same name as the legend predicts?"

"He could've had any other name, and those who wanted to believe him to be the *Na-Tan* of legend would have done so," Dumar argued.

"Yet, Captain Scott not only *allowed* them to believe he was the *Na-Tan* of legend, but in some ways he even helped perpetuate their belief."

"It was a tactical decision on his part. However, in his defense, I must point out that a woman named Jalea was the one responsible for feeding the fires of their beliefs, and without the foreknowledge *or* the consent of Captain Scott."

"Of course. I'm just curious as to *why* he allowed it to happen."

"Perhaps *that* would be a question better asked of Captain Scott?"

"Of course." Kata paused, glancing down at the list of discussion topics on her data pad. She took a deep breath, and then looked back up at him. "Admiral, many of the inhabitants of the very worlds the Alliance has liberated feel that the Alliance had no right to interfere with the running of their worlds. They feel their worlds have been attacked without justification, and that innocent people have been killed. Many consider these attacks to be acts of war against their people, and not ones of liberation. How would you respond to these accusations?"

Admiral Dumar took a deep breath and sighed. "It is always difficult to justify acts of aggression, especially when such acts result in the loss of life, be they innocent or not. However, the Jung occupation of worlds within twenty light years of Sol represents a significant threat to the security of Earth. Steps had to be taken to mitigate that threat, especially in the wake of the Jung's repeated attempts to not only capture and control the Earth and its people, but also to destroy it once they realized they could *not* control it."

"But why attack the ground forces?" Kata wondered. "Surely *they* presented no threat to the people of Earth?"

"Of that we cannot be sure. There may have been comm-drones hidden within each system that could have been used by those forces on the ground to communicate with the nearest Jung forces, or the Jung homeworld itself. Such calls for help could result in renewed attacks against Earth."

"But *innocent* people died during those attacks. *Civilians*, in addition to military."

"How is it that a civilian population of a world that hosts, and possibly even *supports* the Jung Empire's actions, holds no responsibility *for* those actions?" the admiral countered. "If you tell me you are planning to murder your cameraman, and I do nothing to stop you—perhaps warn the authorities, or the potential victim himself—am I not considered culpable in the eyes of the law?"

"What if those people were unaware of the Jung's actions outside of their system?"

"Is it not their responsibility to *know* what those they allow to reside upon their worlds are really doing, *especially* if they are helping them by providing resources?"

"Some of those worlds were taken by force, were they not?" Kata answered. "How are they 'culpable', as you put it?"

"They are not. However, those worlds have welcomed their liberation, haven't they?"

"Couldn't you have warned the populations of those worlds prior to invasion in order to reduce or eliminate the deaths of innocent people?" Kata asked.

"We are outnumbered, and outgunned, by a substantial margin. Our two greatest weapons thus far have been our ability to instantaneously jump between the stars, and surprise. Had we alerted the worlds we intended to attack prior to doing so, we would have lost the element of surprise, and quite possibly might have lost the battle as well."

"But you could have conducted a surprise attack against the ships in space, and *then* issued a warning to the civilians on the surface that you intended to attack the Jung forces on the surface as well. *That* would have given them time to get out of harm's way."

"Had we done so, the Jung forces on the surface would have either taken the civilian population as hostages, using them as a shield against attack, or simply executed them to punish *us* for daring to attack them."

"Admiral, I find it hard to believe that the Jung would murder the entire population of a world just to send a message to the Alliance..."

"I must remind you of the Kentarans," the admiral interrupted. "They had no foreknowledge of our attack against those forces, and we did not even *attempt* to attack the Jung forces on the surface, for exactly the reasons that you seemed to be so concerned about. Yet, the Jung had no problem driving a battleship loaded with more than twenty antimatter cores on board, *with* their containment fields in the process of collapse, *into* that world, utterly destroying it, just to send us a message. The Kentarans did not rebel or revolt against the Jung, despite the fact that their world had only recently been occupied... *by force.*"

"But..."

"Miss Mun," the admiral continued, not allowing her to get a word in just yet, "are you aware that the Jung have been rounding up anyone on Kohara they suspect of being an Alliance collaborator, and executing them on the spot? No investigation, no evidence, no trial..."

Kata Mun glanced at Karahl behind the porta-cam, wondering if he had heard anything about the executions on their homeworld, but he only shrugged his shoulders.

"...And why might they do that," the admiral continued, "if not to send a message to either your people, mine, or perhaps both? Are those the actions of a just and benevolent ruler, or are they the actions of a totalitarian regime bent on galactic conquest, regardless of the human cost?"

Kata took a moment to regain her composure before continuing, obviously affected by the admiral's revelation about the continued suffering on her homeworld at the hands of the Jung. "If the Alliance is outnumbered and outgunned, how do you expect worlds with no space-borne military to resist Jung occupation? You yourself said the Jung are willing to destroy entire worlds just to send a message. How can Kohara, who has never had *any* military forces, let alone ones in space, fight such a force?"

"They cannot," Dumar replied. "And I do not expect them to. That is *why* the Alliance takes the actions it does... To protect the weak and the innocent from those who would prey upon them."

Again Kata had to stop and think, as none of her remaining questions seemed relevant. After a heartfelt sigh, she finally continued. "Admiral, why now? Why not years from now, when the Alliance is stronger, the Earth is stronger..."

"The Earth did not start this war," Admiral Dumar replied, "and neither did the Alliance." Dumar paused a moment. "Earlier we spoke of destiny...of events falling into place, a string of opportunities that, when seized, led to bigger things. This *is* such a string of opportunities...or, if you prefer...destiny. Could it have been avoided? Yes. In fact, the unified government of Earth was building the Aurora for the very purpose of reaching out diplomatically to the Jung in order to explore ways to coexist in peace. Unfortunately, the Jung were not interested, and chose to attack the first ship that attempted to leave the Sol system. Did they do so *because* of its jump drive, or because they wanted to destroy it *before* it could be put into use, for they *knew* it would lead to their downfall? We will never know. However, I do know this. We must *all* deal with the Jung now, while it is still possible to do so. For if we chose to turn our backs, eventually we will have no choice, and by then it will be too late."

* * *

"Launch speed in three minutes, Captain," Mister Chiles reported from the Aurora's helm.

"Very well," Nathan replied. He slowly rotated to his left, coming around to check on the utility station in the aft port corner of the bridge. "How's it looking, Lieutenant Tillardi?"

"Jump KKV prototype systems all show green, sir," the lieutenant replied. "We're ready to raise the device into launch position."

"Mister Delaveaga, if you please?" Nathan requested.

"Raising starboard main elevator pad to launch position," Luis replied.

"Shuttle Four has just jumped into the launch area," Mister Navashee reported.

"Receiving message from Shuttle Four," Ensign Souza announced. "The target area and all areas downrange are clear."

"Very well." Nathan turned back to Lieutenant Tillardi. "There's no chance we're going to send some chunk spiraling toward Earth, is there?"

"Not a chance," the lieutenant assured him. "If the weapon even glances that chunk of ice, there won't be anything bigger than a snowflake left of it."

"Just checking," Nathan replied.

"One minute," Mister Chiles said.

"Starboard pad is in position," Lieutenant Delaveaga reported.

"Running final checks now," Lieutenant Tillardi added.

"Coming up on launch point," Mister Chiles announced. "Speed is fifty percent light."

"Kill your mains," Nathan ordered.

"Mains coming down," the helmsman replied.

"Release the device," Nathan instructed Lieutenant Tillardi.

"Release the device, aye," the lieutenant responded. "Device is away."

"Translate downward, Mister Chiles... Nice and easy," Nathan directed. "Put up the pad cameras."

The image on the main view screen changed suddenly, showing the jump KKV as it slowly rose from its launch cradle sitting in the middle of the starboard elevator pad at the top of the Aurora's forward section.

"Three meters separation, and increasing," Lieutenant Delaveaga reported.

"Bring up the deceleration drive, Mister Chiles," Nathan ordered. "One percent only."

"Opening outer doors," Mister Chiles replied. "Decel drive is hot. One percent, firing."

The image of the jump KKV rising from the top of the ship appeared to drift forward as well, as the Aurora's forward speed began to fall in relation to the device.

"Increase separation rate by fifty percent," Nathan ordered.

"Increasing separation rate, aye," Mister Chiles responded.

"Device jump point in two minutes," Mister Riley reported. "Our jump point in ninety seconds."

"Running final systems check now," Lieutenant Tillardi announced.

"The device is on course and speed," Mister Navashee confirmed from the sensor station.

"Decel up smartly, slow us down," Nathan ordered.

"Deceleration drive to full power," the helmsman replied.

Nathan watched as the jump KKV rapidly shrank, disappearing from view seconds later as the Aurora fell further and further behind it with each passing second.

"I don't suppose you're planning on putting engines in these things?" Nathan wondered.

"Not at the moment, no," the lieutenant replied.

"Seems like a lot of propellant to burn, bringing the whole ship up to half light just to launch a KKV."

"It would take a hell of an engine to get them up to speed on their own," Lieutenant Tillardi explained, "but we *are* working on a variant of the Scout-class, with beefed up engines and greater propellant storage, that should be able to launch them instead."

"Thirty seconds to jump," Mister Chiles reported. "I have the final jump algorithms for the device ready, sir."

"Transmit the updated jump algorithms," Nathan ordered.

"Transmitting," Ensign Souza replied.

Lieutenant Tillardi watched his telemetry screen for a moment. "Algorithms updated," he finally announced. "We're good to go."

"Clear to jump, Mister Riley," Nathan ordered.

"Aye, sir. Jumping in ten seconds."

"Forward cameras."

The view screen switched back to the main forward-facing cameras again.

"Jumping in three……two……one……"

The jump flash briefly illuminated the interior

of the Aurora's bridge with its familiar blue-white light.

"Jump complete."

"Target in sight," Lieutenant Delaveaga reported. "Twenty seconds to impact."

Lieutenant Tillardi turned to face forward. There was nothing left for him to do but wait, and hope.

"Verify range is clear," Nathan ordered.

"Range is clear, Captain," Mister Navashee replied.

"Ten sec..."

"...Jump flash!" Mister Navashee shouted, cutting the lieutenant off.

"Weapon inbound, impact in five..."

"Full magnification," Nathan ordered.

"...three..."

Lieutenant Tillardi stood, moving slowly forward as if drawn toward the tumbling chunk of ice on the main view screen.

"...one......imp..."

A flash of light appeared on the main view screen where the chunk of ice had once been. The light immediately faded, revealing a spreading sea of tiny particles of ice, reflecting the faint light from the distant star like a glimmering mist.

"Target is destroyed," Mister Navashee reported, disappointment evident in his voice.

Nathan looked at Lieutenant Tillardi, who looked crestfallen. "Something wrong?"

"It was early, wasn't it?" he replied, turning toward Luis at the tactical station.

"Only half a second, Til," Luis replied sympathetically.

"But it did work," Nathan reminded them. "The target was obliterated."

"Yeah, but it was a head-on shot," Lieutenant Tillardi replied. "If it had been a side shot at a fast-moving target, it would've missed."

"Mister Chiles," Nathan said as he rose from his command chair, "continue deceleration and jump us back to Earth as soon as we get down to something resembling orbital velocity again."

"It's got to be something in the jump sequencer," Luis suggested. "A few lines of unnecessary code, or something?"

"We went over that code a hundred times," the lieutenant said.

"Don't worry, Tilly, you'll fix it," Nathan assured him as he turned to head aft.

Lieutenant Tillardi looked at Nathan. "How can you be so sure?"

"Because billions of Cetian lives depend on it," Nathan replied with an impish grin as he patted him on the shoulder in passing.

Tilly sneered at him. "Oh, thanks. Thanks a lot... really."

* * *

Naralena felt weak. She had eaten only a single piece of flat bread per day for the past three days, and had been given precious little water to wash it down with.

The last thing she remembered before her prison cell was the burning sensation in her leg, and then falling in the water...

Then hands. Lots of them.

There had been voices speaking Jung during her attempt to escape. She remembered that. Odd, though, that she had heard no one speaking around her since her capture.

She had been locked in a small room, barely large enough for her to lie down. There had been a couple of ratty blankets, a very old pillow, and a large bucket for her bodily waste, of which luckily there had been little.

There was also a small window—more of a vent, really—that was so high up she could not reach it to see outside. It was her only source of light, as well as her only method to track the passing of time. She had found it oddly amusing that she couldn't find anything in her cell with which to scratch markings on the wall to count the days of her imprisonment. Then again, it had only been three days.

Or was it four?

She had tried to pass the time as best she could. She even tried singing, but by the end of the second day, her spirits had declined so much that she couldn't bring herself to utter a note. The nights were the worst. In the daytime, she could fold up the blankets and make herself a nice pad to sit upon. Night was different. Night was cold. Not the bitter, frigid cold that eventually knocks you out, but the lingering chill that just keeps you awake.

The cement floors did not help.

Her only contact with the outside world was the man who would slide open a small hatch at the bottom of the door and slip the flat bread and a cup of water through to her. She called to him each time, all three of them... *Or was it four?* She begged him to tell her where she was, who they were, and what they wanted from her. Had they asked, she would have gladly told them anything.

Shameful, really. Without any real torture, she

was willing to tell them everything she knew. Then again, it wasn't like she really *knew* anything of value. Not like Jessica. Jessica would have been a gold mine of information, if captured by the Jung.

Of course, Jessica would never have allowed herself to fall into the hands of the enemy.

Even worse, the isolation made it impossible for her to not think about things that only served to depress her even more. Sergeant Weatherly, Gerard, Major Willard. The millions who had died on Earth, as well as all the other worlds the Jung had conquered...or punished for not *allowing* themselves to be conquered.

Of course, such thoughts only served to boost her defiance. She would *not* tell them anything, no matter how much they tortured her. Then again, she didn't really *know* anything. So why were they keeping her locked up for days on end, without so much as a single question? They had not even asked for her name. But they would, of that she was sure.

And she was right.

She had no warning, no footfalls in the corridor outside her door, if there was a corridor. The door just suddenly swung open, bright sunlight spilling inside, silhouetting a burly man with a bag in one hand and a rope in the other. She cried and pleaded as he approached her with menacing intent. She thought about trying to get around him, to make a break for the door, but with her wounded leg and her weakened condition she had not the strength to resist.

So she did not.

The bag came down over her head, she was pushed to the ground, and the rope was tied painfully tight around her wrists. She was then picked up from the floor and led out of her cell. Where was he taking her? What was going to happen to her?

All she could do was sob.

She felt the warmth of the Cetian sun on her shoulders as she was marched, limping, across bare open ground. She could smell the dust, taste it as the breeze whipped it around them. Her foot struck a step and she tumbled forward, her brutish escort roughly grabbing her arm to keep her upright as they entered another building. He shoved her to the left and they walked down another corridor. Another left, and then he pushed her down, into a chair.

An actual chair, she thought with relief. A silly thing to be thankful for. She heard more footsteps, but still no talking. The man pulled at her hands, but not to untie them. Instead, he bound them to the chair in which she sat.

Then the door slammed shut.

She sat there for perhaps a full minute, fighting back the tears, and listening. Listening for the sound of movement. Listening for the sound of someone breathing. Was she alone?

"Hello?" she asked in Jung. "Is anybody there?"

There was a rustling of fabric nearby, then the hood covering her head was pulled away. Bright sunlight shone through the open window, blinding her. She had barely seen any light at all, over the last few days, save for that tiny stream coming through the vent in her cell.

She tried to look at the man standing before her, but her eyes were not yet accustomed to the light. "Who are you?" she asked, still in Jung. "What do you want from me?"

"The very questions I wish to ask you," the man replied, but not in Jung.

The man was speaking Koharan.

"Who are *you*?" the man asked.

"I am Naralena Avakian," she replied, still speaking in Jung.

"That is not a Koharan name," the man replied, sticking with the Koharan language.

"Avakian is my father's family name," she told him. "He is not from Kohara." Naralena surprised herself that she had not lied, yet had not offered him any information either. It was a small victory for her, but an important one nonetheless.

"Why did your people attack my world?" the man asked in Koharan.

"My father?" she asked, still speaking in Jung.

"You obviously speak Koharan, so do so. I am not in the mood to speak Jung at the moment."

"I don't understand," Naralena told him, switching to Koharan.

"Why did your people attack my world?"

"What people?" Naralena wondered.

"You can drop the pretense, Miss Avakian. We saw the reports. The Jung are looking for you and your friends, the Earth woman and the Koharan man."

Jessica and Gerard, she realized.

"They are offering a substantial reward for your capture," the man said. "Why is that? Are you one of the infected ones from Earth? Have you been sent here to spread the bio-digital plague to my people?"

"Are you insane?" Naralena said. "My name is Naralena Avakian. I live *in* Cetia. I do not know that woman."

"How do you know you do not know her? I have yet to tell you anything about her."

"You said she was from Earth. I don't know anyone from Earth."

"If you live in Cetia, what were you doing so far from home, and in the middle of an invasion, no less?"

"We were on a nature hike," she told him, "for nearly a week..."

"We who?"

"My husband and I."

"Your husband? Odd then, that it took you this long to ask about him."

"I am weak with hunger, and I have not slept in days..."

"...You can stop the pretense," the man told her. "Our doctors sampled your blood. You have no nanites within you, therefore, you are either a member of the CLA, or you are not of this world. Given that I can find no government records matching your description or biometric signature, I must conclude the latter." The man paused to take another breath. "So I ask you again... Who are you, and why did your people attack my world?"

Naralena stared at him defiantly.

"I can put you back into your cell until you cooperate," he warned, "giving you just barely enough sustenance to keep you alive, and in misery, until you are willing to tell me the truth."

Naralena continued to stare at him. "I already did," she stated. "You simply choose not to believe me."

"Then back to your cell it is," the man said, rising from his chair to depart. He stopped suddenly, turning back to her. "Of course, there is another way. Unpleasant, but effective." He turned toward one of the inside walls and pulled back the long curtain. Behind that curtain was a window. On the other side of that window was another room, and in that room was Gerard, sitting in a chair just as she was, bound and gagged, his hands behind his back.

Gerard's eyes suddenly opened wide, silently pleading with her, as if he knew something terrible was about to happen.

And so did she. She could feel it with every fiber of her being.

"Interestingly enough, although there is no record of your existence on this world, *that* man's record is quite extensive...dating back more than twenty years, I believe. In fact, he is suspected of involvement with the Cetian Liberation Army, no less." He paused a moment, then turned back to look at Naralena. "Odd that it goes back no further than that, though." He sighed. "Anyway, you can see how this all starts to piece together? Something about each of you is not as you say it is."

A man entered the next room...the same burly man who had taken her from her cell. He pulled a Jung energy pistol and pointed it at the side of Gerard's head, then looked at the window, waiting for a signal from the man interrogating Naralena.

"So tell me, Naralena Avakian... Who are you, and why did you attack my world?"

"We are from Earth," she admitted without hesitation. She felt as if the gates had been opened, and there was no turning back.

"Why is it that he has records and you do not?" the man began, sensing the opportunity and running with it before she changed her mind.

"I only arrived a month ago."

"And he has been here for twenty years?" he asked in disbelief.

"Yes."

"How many more like him are there among us? Spies from Earth?"

"He is the only one left alive," she told him. "You killed the others."

"And the other woman, the one spouting lies while holding Kata Mun and her coworkers hostage."

"She is from Earth as well. We came together. However, she was not lying, and you know it. The Earth is no longer infected, and has not been for nearly a thousand years. You have been lying to these people for decades."

"It is you who are lying!" the man shouted. "Admit it now, or I will have him killed!"

"I am telling you the truth, damn you!"

"I will kill him!"

"Then do it, you bastard!" she cursed back defiantly. "Do it!"

Her interrogator spun around and nodded at the man in the next room who immediately fired his weapon. There was a flash of red-orange light and a spray of blood and tissue that splattered across the window, as Gerard's body was pushed to the side by the force of the energy charge impact against the side of his skull.

Naralena collapsed forward, nearly falling out of her chair, held up only by her restraints, as she sobbed uncontrollably, cursing them in a language that none of them understood.

She hung there, dangling to one side from her restraints, sobbing for what seemed an eternity before she noticed the boots of the man who had been her interrogator were gone, replaced by dress shoes of a much nicer quality. She raised her head, slightly at first. It was someone new. An older man she realized as she sat upright. In her grief, she had never even noticed the change of interrogators. "What do *you* want?" she asked, her voice seething with anger and contempt.

"First, I would like to apologize for your treatment, Miss Avakian...assuming that is your real name."

The man was also speaking Koharan, but his syntax was more polished and formal.

"Does it matter?"

"I suppose not. All that matters is that we find out the truth about Earth, and about the Jung."

Naralena suddenly found herself confused.

"It has been a difficult couple of weeks. Many of my people have died. I simply want to know why."

"And you had to kill Gerard to find out?" Naralena asked in accusatory tone.

"We have killed no one," the older gentleman replied. He reached out and tapped on the door. It opened, and Gerard was led in, still tied but no longer gagged...and very much alive.

Again, Naralena wept, this time with relief.

The guard pulled up a chair and sat Gerard down next to her. Naralena leaned into him, her head against his shoulder, still sobbing. He tilted his head toward her, kissing her affectionately on the head and whispering, "I am so sorry." He repeated the words over and over, almost crying as he begged her forgiveness.

"Again, I regret that we had to put you both through all of this..." The man sighed. "This, unpleasantness. But again, these are very difficult times."

"Who are you?" Gerard asked.

"I am Titus Kanor."

Gerard shook his head. "Wait, I know that name..."

"I am the leader of the Koharan parliament, fourth in the line of succession. The Jung have executed all the leaders before me, and many of those who followed. I am therefore the de facto leader of the Koharan government."

"What do you want from us?" Gerard wondered.

"As I said, I only wish to learn the truth about the Earth, and the Jung."

"How did you find us?"

"Your images are everywhere," he told them. "Since several days *before* the invasion. The clerk at the resort notified my people. Lucky for you, I might add. Had he notified the Jung, you would both be dead and they would know all that you know."

"And that's it?" Gerard asked, not quite convinced.

"Not exactly. We have detected an unusual series of tones. They are being broadcast at random times, and on random frequencies. I assume they are hailing tones of some kind. A way for you to make contact with the people of Earth?"

"Yes," Gerard replied.

"Then I would like you to do so."

"Why?"

"I wish to speak to them."

"Why?" Gerard pressed.

"They managed to destroy all the Jung ships in our system, yet they were not able to destroy all of their forces on the surface of Kohara, despite having easily eliminated them on both Stennis and Sorenson. Why is that? What is their intent? Are they planning on returning to finish the job?" President Kanor shook his head. "I have so many questions. Is it so much to ask to simply *speak* with your leaders?"

"And if we cooperate, what will happen to us?" Gerard asked.

"We will see to your safe passage to wherever it is you wish to go."

"Even if it's back to Earth?"

"Even if it's back to Earth," he affirmed.

Gerard looked at Naralena for her opinion, but her eyes offered no advice. He looked back at President Kanor. "The last time we spoke with them, the Jung came looking for us within hours."

"We have ways of masking our signal against triangulation by Jung ground forces," the president promised.

"Very well," Gerard agreed. "But first, untie us."

"As you wish," the president replied, signaling the burly man.

The man stood to one side of Gerard, reaching around to untie his hands. His hands freed, Gerard brought them around in front and rubbed his wrists while the man untied Naralena's hands as well. The man stepped back, moving back in front of Gerard on his way back to the door. Gerard lashed out, driving his knee into the burly man's gut, causing him to double over as Gerard drove his left fist into his nose with all his might.

The man fell to the ground, his nose broken and bloodied. A moment later, the room was full of armed men, their weapons all trained on Gerard.

"That was for pretending to shoot me in the head, asshole," he said in English.

* * *

Gerard fiddled with the controls of the communications equipment in the room, attempting to isolate the frequency that, by his calculations, should be the one currently used by the communications buoy in orbit over Kohara. Despite the president's reluctance, Gerard had convinced him that only he could successfully initiate the link to the comm-buoy. Hence, he and Naralena had been moved out of the makeshift interrogation block to an equally makeshift communications room in the next building. During their transfer between buildings, it became obvious to Gerard that the acting president had little in the way of manpower and resources, and that he too was attempting to operate covertly, without the Jung's knowledge.

"I have established contact with the comm-buoy," Gerard told President Kanor.

"Comm-buoy?"

"It is not the correct time for direct contact. The buoy will allow us to leave a message for them when they return at the correct contact window."

"Then perhaps we should wait until the next window?" the president suggested. "I would prefer to speak with them directly."

"The next comm window is not for sixteen hours," Gerard told him. "Besides, my leaders will not be present at that time. The ship making contact is only a messenger, meant to exchange messages and retrieve any missed messages from the comm-buoy and relay them back to command. If you wish to speak with them, you will have to let them know, so they can be present, *in orbit*, at the time."

President Kanor looked at Gerard with suspicion. "And your people can really travel nearly twelve light years so quickly?"

"Yes, they can."

The president shook his head in disbelief. "Amazing. I can see now *why* the Jung are so concerned." He thought for a moment, looking first at Naralena, then at Gerard, then at one of his men. After a sigh of resignation, he spoke. "Very well. Send the following message. Tell them I wish to speak with someone of authority. Your president, or at the very least, the commander of your armed forces... The ones who attacked our world." He looked at the clock on the wall of the communications room. "Tell them they have twelve Koharan hours to respond... or we shall turn you *and* Miss Avakian over to the Jung."

Gerard began to rise from his seat to attack, only to find four weapons aimed at him, fully charged, ready to fire.

"*Exactly* twelve hours. No more, no less. As I said, these are difficult times, hence, they require difficult decisions be made."

* * *

"Captain," the guard called from the hatch to the captain's ready room. "Miss Mun and Mister Essa are here to see you."

"Send them in," Nathan instructed.

The guard stepped back, allowing the captain's guests to enter the ready room.

Nathan rose from his desk to properly greet them.

Kata and Karahl entered the ready room, both of them looking surprised.

"I'm sorry," Kata said, "I was told we were meeting Captain Scott?"

"I am Nathan Scott," Nathan replied.

"*Captain* Nathan Scott?"

"The one and only."

"I'm sorry," Kata apologized, "I didn't expect you to be so young."

"I'm a quick study," Nathan joked as he stepped out to shake her hand.

"Ah, yes. I forgot you were a lieutenant when your captain died and command of this ship was passed to you."

"For only a few weeks, I believe," Nathan replied.

"Excuse me?"

"I had only been a lieutenant for a few weeks when the incident occurred," Nathan explained, gesturing for her to sit.

"Of course. Captain, this is my porta-cam operator, Karahl Essa."

"Mister Essa," Nathan replied, shaking his hand as well. "Shall I sit here, or behind my desk?"

"How about on the couch?" Kata suggested. "We only have the one porta-cam, so..."

"Of course," Nathan agreed. He waited for Kata to take her seat before joining her. "So, how does this work?"

"I'll just ask you some questions, and you answer them however you like," she explained.

"Very well."

Kata looked at Karahl, who had already extended his tripod and had the porta-cam up and running.

"I know you're pressed for time, and something could come up that would pull you away from the interview, so I'll begin with what I think are the most important questions for my people, given what I already know about the previous chain of events."

"Sounds like a good idea to me," Nathan agreed, trying to hide his nervousness.

"Captain, why did you choose to play the role of Na-Tan back on Corinair? Didn't it feel like you were deceiving the Corinairans in order to achieve your goals?"

Nathan paused a moment, considering his answer. It was not a question he had anticipated. "I suppose it would seem that way, but to be honest, it wasn't really a conscious decision on my part. It was sort of thrust upon me. Long afterward, we learned that one of the Karuzari rebels had, in fact, fed information to key people on Corinair, leaders of the Followers of Origin, in order to create a wave of support that would help the rebels achieve their goals."

"But you knew what was going on. You could have denounced the legend and told them you were not the Na-Tan of legend. Yet you did not."

"How do I know I wasn't?"

This time, it was Kata who appeared surprised. "Pardon me?"

"Seriously. There was nothing in the legend that identified exactly who this *Na-Tan* was. I showed up as if from nowhere, at the very time they felt they needed *Na-Tan* the most."

"But Captain..."

"Don't misunderstand, I don't seriously believe I'm some kind of legendary savior. I have no doubt this legend was a story made up centuries earlier in order to give those who suffered at the hands of the Ta'Akar Empire hope... Hope that someday someone *would* come and save them, or lead them to freedom. For quite some time, many believed that the leader of the Karuzari rebels was Na-Tan, but then he disappeared, and that belief died away. It was merely a coincidence...our sudden arrival at a dire moment, or defeat of the enemy, my name being Nathan..."

"You cannot *be* the Na-Tan of legend if you don't believe the legend to be true," Kata argued.

"I don't know that it *isn't* true. Anyone who led them to victory over the empire could have been seen as Na-Tan. Had we failed, many might have simply decided that I was not the true Na-Tan. You see, the prophecy is written in such a way that it really cannot fail. If you succeed, you're Na-Tan. If you fail, you're an impostor. That's how most prophecies are written."

"Seems you've given this a lot of thought," Kata commented.

"More than you might imagine," Nathan admitted. "To be honest, at the time, I didn't like playing the role of Na-Tan one bit. But I didn't really have a choice. My ship was damaged, half my crew and *all* my commanding officers were dead, and we were stranded a thousand light years from home. To make matters worse, we knew we needed to get our ship home to help defend Earth against a pending Jung invasion. We desperately needed the help of the Corinairan people."

"Is that why you stayed, to defend the Corinairans against the Yamaro?" Kata asked.

"I made that decision because it was the right thing to do. The captain of the Yamaro was trying to force me into giving up the jump drive. The Ta'Akar Empire was no better than the Jung, they just had fancier uniforms and titles. They were still just as ruthless."

"But you could have left and jumped your way back to Earth."

"Perhaps," Nathan replied. "We might have made it back, then again, we might not have."

"And because you *did* stay and fight, and eventually led the people of Corinair in an attack against the Ta'Akar Empire that successfully deposed their ruler, you were able to return to Earth with additional advanced technologies to help you with your fight against the Jung. Is that correct?"

"Yes," Nathan nodded, "but more importantly, we created an Alliance. One to not only stand against the Jung, but against any force that tries to impose rule upon the unwilling by force or intimidation."

Kata took a deep breath, pausing to contemplate her next question. "Captain, the people of Kohara have never had a military. Not even before the great plague. They have never needed one. We have always been peaceful people who believe in settling our differences diplomatically. The Jung had never raised a gun at us, until your Alliance came along and attacked them. Many would point out that the Jung have greatly improved the lives of not only Kohara, but of all the Cetian worlds. Now, your Alliance comes along, perhaps with truly noble intent, but you attack with force, killing thousands of Jung as well as thousands of innocent Koharans. How would you respond to that?"

"I'm not sure you'll like my answer," Nathan warned.

"I'll like it if it's the truth, Captain," Kata insisted.

"Very well." Nathan took a breath. "Although I regret having to take innocent lives, I shall not apologize for doing so. The Jung have killed *trillions* of lives, for no reason other than those people refused to be subjugated. Your people can choose to live under the rule of any power you choose. That is your right. However, we have a right to defend ourselves as well. The Jung attacked our world, multiple times. When we took innocent lives, it was because the situation forced us to do so. I hated every minute of it, believe me. But where is the line to be drawn? At what point do we say, we cannot defend ourselves because we might harm others by doing so? I understand that your people prefer non-violent solutions, and I applaud your resolve. The problem is, humanity *is* a violent, predatory species, and our favorite prey is one another. It is sickening to think of, but it is true nonetheless. Perhaps it is *that very reason* that humanity continues to survive, *and* thrive, against overwhelming odds, time and time again."

The intercom beeped, interrupting Nathan's response.

"*Captain, urgent message from Admiral Dumar. He is on his way over and needs to meet with you and Commander Telles, ASAP.*"

"Did he say what it was about?" Nathan asked the comm officer.

"*No, sir, just that it was urgent. He should be arriving in ten minutes.*"

"Very well." Nathan sighed, looking at Kata. "I'm sorry, Miss Mun, but duty calls."

"Quite alright, Captain," she assured him, standing. "Perhaps we can continue later?"

"Of course," Nathan promised, showing her to the exit.

CHAPTER TEN

"Can we determine their precise location from their transmission?" Commander Telles asked.

"They are likely masking their source," Admiral Dumar replied.

"We destroyed the Jung satellites in orbit over all three of the Cetian worlds during the initial attack," Nathan reminded them. "If this guy *is* the Koharan president, wouldn't he be trying to hide his signal from ground-based detection, the kind the Jung on the surface would be using?"

Admiral Dumar nodded. "I see your point."

"If so, Mister Navashee can probably pinpoint their location to within a meter," Nathan insisted. "We could send a team in and rescue them both."

"They will undoubtedly be well guarded," Commander Telles pointed out.

"How do we know that?" Nathan wondered. "Maybe they're just a handful of guys with guns?"

"Mister Bowden is a trained operative. Were they *not* well guarded, they would have escape on their own."

"But Naralena is not. He may be waiting for the right moment," Nathan argued, "and this may be that moment."

"Do not misunderstand, Captain," Commander Telles replied. "Even if they were being guarded by all of the Jung on Kohara, I would still be willing to attempt a rescue. I am simply weighing the odds and trying to determine the best plan."

"We will need a way to communicate our intent to Miss Avakian and Mister Bowden," Admiral Dumar commented.

"Naralena speaks many languages, which her captors do not," Commander Telles said.

"Perhaps Corinairan?" Admiral Dumar suggested. "I speak it as well."

"It would be better if it were a language that both of them spoke," Commander Telles pointed out. "Are not all EDF special operatives required to speak at least a few languages?"

"We are," Jessica said as she entered the command briefing room. "Sorry it took so long, sir. I had to dig pretty far back to find Lieutenant Bowden's original graduation records. Primary Earth languages are English and Spanish, off-world are, of course, Koharan and Cetian, both of which are very similar. He also speaks passable Russian, due to a grandparent."

"Naralena speaks Russian as well," Nathan pointed out. "You should have seen how excited Vlad got when she spoke Russian to him in the mess hall, once."

"Then Lieutenant Commander Kamenetskiy will pretend to be the comm officer," the admiral decided, "just long enough to warn her and the lieutenant that the Ghatazhak are about to attack."

"I will need more information about the area in which they are being held before I can determine a plan of action," the commander warned.

"Once we determine the location of the transmission, Mister Navashee can give you all the site data you need," Nathan explained. "Right down to the color of their underwear."

Commander Telles cast a sidelong look at the captain. "That level of detail will not be necessary, Captain."

Admiral Dumar took a deep breath, exhaling slowly as he contemplated the situation. "If we go in, I want the man claiming to be the Koharan president as well."

Commander Telles exchanged glances with Jessica and Nathan.

"If he wants to talk, then we will talk," the admiral continued, "but we will do so here, on board the Aurora."

* * *

Jessica walked quickly across the Aurora's main hangar deck, trying to catch up to Commander Telles and his men as they headed toward one of the four combat jump shuttles idling at the aft end of the bay. "Telles!" she called out, breaking into a jog.

Commander Telles looked back, taking note of the fact that the lieutenant commander was dressed in EDF spec-ops battle gear. "I will catch up to you in a moment," he told Master Sergeant Jahal, who was walking in front of him.

The master sergeant looked back as well, also noticing the lieutenant commander's attire. "Oh, not a chance..."

"...I will take care of this," Telles assured him. He stopped and turned to face Jessica as she approached. "Lieutenant Commander?"

"I'm going with you," Jessica, determination in her tone.

"No, you are not," the commander replied with unwavering confidence.

"The hell I'm not," Jessica insisted, looking him straight in the eyes.

"Lieutenant Commander..."

"Out of my way, Telles," Jessica demanded.

Commander Telles stepped directly in Jessica's path, forcing her to stop. He looked down at her, standing toe-to-toe. "You will follow my orders, or I will forcibly subdue you, and it will not be a pleasant experience for you...I promise."

"Telles..." Jessica began, as if giving him a final warning.

"...You are neither trained nor qualified for operations with the Ghatazhak," he explained. His voice was calm and even, but full of confidence and conviction. "In addition, you are in an emotional state. These factors create additional risk to the well-being of my men, as well as to the people we are attempting to extricate. I cannot allow this."

Jessica said nothing, just standing there staring at him, seething with frustration and anger. Her anger was not at the lieutenant, rather at the situation, and the fact that she felt helpless to do *anything* to help her friend. She had felt the same way when she had stood on the bridge, wondering if her brother was still alive.

"Are we clear?" Commander Telles asked calmly.

Jessica stared at him a few seconds longer before speaking. "I can take you, you know."

Commander Telles almost smiled. "No, you cannot." His expression suddenly turned into one of fierce determination, the likes of which Jessica had never seen. "Are...we...clear?"

Jessica's eyes narrowed, as if she were sizing up the commander's resolve.

"You have five seconds to respond, Lieutenant Commander, or I will drop you where you stand."

"Yeah," she finally replied. "We're clear."

"We're clear, sir," Commander Telles insisted.

"Perfectly...clear...sir," Jessica replied, having to force the words past her lips.

Commander Telles did not back away as she would have expected. Instead, he turned his back on her and continued toward the waiting jump shuttles. She thought for a moment, wondering if he was honestly that confident that she could not harm him, or if he was just stupid.

As much as she hated to admit it, she decided he wasn't stupid.

* * *

"We are in comm position over Kohara," Mister Riley reported.

"Very well," Nathan replied as he rotated his chair aft. "Ensign Souza, you may initiate contact."

"Yes, sir," the ensign replied as he went to work. "You can start your hail, sir," he said to Vladimir, who was standing next to him wearing a comm-set.

"One Four Romeo Sierra, One Four Alpha Alpha," Vladimir began in English.

"It is them," Gerard announced, reaching for the comm-unit controls. The guard next to Naralena raised his weapon to her head in response. Gerard looked up at the president. "I have to respond..."

"Not you," the president said. "Her."

"But…"

"You have been operating on our world covertly for twenty years, without being caught," the president explained. "She, on the other hand, was captured within weeks of her arrival. She will answer."

Gerard got up and exchanged seats with Naralena. She picked up the microphone and replied. "One Four Alpha Alpha, One Four Romeo Sierra."

"*Tui v poryadke?*" Vladimir asked over the comms.

"*Da.*"

President Kanor eyed her suspiciously, unfamiliar with the language they were speaking.

"*Tui mozhesh gavareet?*"

The president looked at Gerard. "What are they saying?" he demanded.

"*Da,*" Naralena replied again.

The president's concern increased with each unfamiliar word that was spoken. He glanced at the nearest guard, who responded by putting the muzzle of his weapon against Naralena's head to quiet her.

"*Mui seichas tam bydyem. Byd'gotova,*" Vladimir said over the comms.

"It's an authentication handshake!" Gerard explained.

The other three guards in the room also advanced in response to Gerard's shouting.

"To prove her identity!" Gerard continued.

The president eyed Gerard suspiciously, as his guard pushed Naralena's head to one side with the muzzle of his weapon in a threatening manner meant to prevent her from speaking further.

"They always do it in a language the enemy is not likely to understand," Gerard explained, lowering his tone in an attempt to get everyone to calm down. "If you don't let her finish the authentication, they will assume that she is not who she claims to be, and that neither are you. You will get to speak with no one!"

The president looked at Gerard, then back at Naralena. Finally, he tilted his head briefly to the side, gesturing for his guards to back off. "Finish," he instructed Naralena.

"*Ponyala*," she answered hesitantly. She glanced sidelong toward the guard, making sure that he was no longer pointing a gun at her head before continuing. "*Ne zastreli prezidenta. Eto tot starik s blestyashei golovoi.*"

"*Stand by*," Vladimir replied, switching to English.

"Authentication has been accepted," Naralena announced. "They are now convinced of our identities."

"*This is Admiral Travon Dumar, commander of all Alliance forces within the Sol sector.*"

"The Aurora reports they've located the source of the transmission," the copilot reported over the commander's helmet comms. "*Mister Navashee is linking his live ground surveillance sensor data to your tactical systems now, Commander.*"

"Very well," Commander Telles replied.

"Center building, in the room to the south," Master Sergeant Jahal said, also watching the feed on his tactical display. "Those are our subjects, the two sitting down."

"Five in the room with them, four with guns," the commander said as he watched the infrared sensor readings being displayed on the inside of his helmet visor, as if looking down at oddly colored people, going about their business in a building without

377

a roof. "Good bet the one without the gun is the president... Old and bald."

"Two more at each end of the corridor, also armed," the master sergeant added. "More men in adjacent buildings. Some armed, some not."

"Lieutenant," the commander called to the combat jump shuttle's pilot. "Instruct all ships to prepare to jump in around the central building. One ship on each side. Three meters off the deck, three out from the building. One minute."

"Those are awfully close parameters, Commander," the pilot warned.

"I thought you Corinari were good?"

"Damn good, sir."

"We were not attacking Kohara, per se," the admiral explained over the comms, *"but rather the Jung forces on the surface."*

"Yet your attacks killed thousands of my people," President Kanor accused him. "Thousands of innocent people, I would add."

"We regret the collateral damage that our attacks have caused, Mister President, but you must understand..."

Naralena and Gerard exchanged knowing glances.

"Had we simply destroyed the Jung forces in space and left those on the surface alone, those Jung on the surface would be even more convinced that your people were collaborating with the Alliance. Even more executions would be taking place in your street than already are."

"Which is why you never should have attacked any..."

There was a brilliant blue-white flash of light

and a tremendous explosion outside that shook the entire building and blew out the windows in the communications room. Naralena and Gerard both fell to the floor instantly. Naralena covered her head with her hands and Gerard scrambled across the floor to her, covering her with his body. There was a deafening roar of multiple rocket engines outside. Sections of the wall blew inward as energy weapons fire blasted rows of holes at chest height, spraying the still-stunned guards with debris. The president fell backward from the shockwave, as several of his guards took energy weapons fire directly in the chest.

Another explosion rocked the room, as the sound of heavy energy weapons outside screeched repeatedly. A portion of the roof collapsed, and four Ghatazhak dropped into the room from above.

Two of the Ghatazhak soldiers moved between Naralena and Gerard and the exit, dropping to one knee to act as physical barriers against incoming fire. The other two moved to the doorway and opened fire on the guards rushing toward them from the two opposite ends of the corridor.

"Corridor is clear!" Master Sergeant Jahal called from the doorway.

Commander Telles stepped back from the doorway, leaving his master sergeant to cover the corridor. The two Ghatazhak soldiers acting as shields for Gerard and Naralena rose and moved into covering positions; one at the window, the other at the door with the master sergeant.

"*Building one is secure,*" a voice called over the comms.

"*Building two; secure.*"

"*Building three; secure.*"

The President rose to one knee, coughing and sputtering from the dust still swirling about the room.

"Are you President Kanor?" Commander Telles yelled.

"Yes...yes... Please, do not hurt me!" he begged, shouting to be heard above the cacophony of shuttle engines.

"You are to come with us!" Commander Telles ordered.

"But..."

"You may remain, and explain to the Jung what happened here, if you prefer!"

"No...no! I will come with you!"

"*Perimeter secure!*"

"Jahal!" the commander barked. "Time to go!"

Master Sergeant Jahal grabbed the president by the arm and pulled him to his feet, shoving him through the door and down the corridor.

Commander Telles turned toward Naralena, reaching down to help her up. "Miss Avakian, are you ready to return to the Aurora?"

Naralena said nothing, only nodding.

"Lieutenant?" Commander Telles said, addressing Gerard as he pulled Naralena to her feet. "I assume you are coming as well?"

Gerard stumbled to his feet, still in shock as he glanced about at the precision and devastation he had just witnessed. "Hell yes!"

* * *

President Kanor sat at the conference table, attempting to look as dignified as tattered clothing would allow. His business jacket was torn and covered with dust, as were his pants and his shoes. Try as he might to maintain his composure, it was obvious he had just been through an ordeal.

Admiral Dumar walked into the room and sat down in the chair next to him. "Mister President. I am Admiral Dumar. I apologize for all that has happened, and I truly wish that our meeting could have been under…more pleasant circumstances. But you, sir, threatened the well-being of my operatives, people who risked their very lives in their attempts to reduce the number of innocent lives lost during our attacks. I cannot abide such treatment. Not even by the leader of an entire world."

"Of course," President Kanor replied, his voice still a bit unsteady.

Admiral Dumar leaned back in his seat. "You wanted to talk, Mister President? What is it you wish to know?"

The president looked around the room, unsure of what to say. Finally, one word came out. "Why?"

"I assume by 'why' you mean, why did the Alliance attack the Jung forces in the Tau Ceti system?"

President Kanor nodded.

"The Earth has suffered incredible devastation over the last year at the hands of the Jung. Millions upon millions of innocent people, just like the ones who died needlessly on your world, were slaughtered simply because it is Jung policy to punish a world that they cannot control. The Earth *needs* at least a year, preferably many more, to get back on her feet and survive, let alone be prepared to defend herself. We are attempting to give her the time she needs by getting rid of *all* Jung forces within a twenty light year radius of Sol. Once successful, we intend to push further outward, extending that perimeter to thirty light years, then forty... Well, you get my meaning. In the process, we had planned to liberate each world from Jung rule."

"And what do you do with such worlds," the president asked, "after you have *liberated* them? Subjugate them as your own, just as you claim the Jung would do?"

"Not at all. The Alliance has no interest in being conquerors. Each world is left to govern themselves as they see fit. However, they *are* invited to join the Alliance in our fight against the Jung, just as your worlds will be invited."

"But the Jung have done so much for our worlds," the president told him. "I doubt the people will be so willing to forsake them."

"Even once they know the truth about them?" the admiral wondered.

President Kanor sighed heavily. "The truth can be quite subjective, Admiral. It is altered by the filters of personal opinion and prejudices. Through such filters, the truth can be difficult to see with clarity."

"Very true, Mister President," the admiral agreed. "That is why we must shine a light...the light of truth...in order to show them the way."

President Kanor looked confused. "What is this light?"

Admiral Dumar picked up the remote from the table and turned on one of the many large view screens on the wall. Unedited footage, shot by Kata Mun and her porta-cam operator during their interviews, began to play. "See for yourself," the admiral told him. "We will speak further when you are ready."

* * *

"Kata Mun," President Kanor greeted. He picked up the remote as she walked toward him, pressing the mute button to silence the video still playing on the view screen. "You were the last person I expected to see. Everyone on Kohara believes you were killed by your captors."

"Anything but, Mister President," she replied, taking a seat next to him.

"Is all of this true?" he asked.

"Every bit of it."

"And they did not control where you went, who you spoke with, what they said?"

"To the best of my knowledge, no. I was allowed to go wherever I wished, speak with whomever I wished. Yes, there were places I was not allowed to go, either because of the extreme danger, or because they were top-secret areas, but I was basically given complete freedom."

"Did they censor *anything*...anything at all?"

"Of course they did, but only when necessary to maintain security. We were not allowed to reveal which worlds had been liberated, or where any of their facilities were located. But they allowed all opinions to be shared, all things to be shown. They even allowed the dissenting opinions of those from worlds they have liberated. I have hours and hours of this, sir."

"Then it is true," the president said, his head hanging down in defeat. "Not only have we been lied to all these years, but we have been duped into *helping* the Jung destroy other worlds, other peoples. We helped them nearly destroy the Earth."

"We did not know," Kata reminded him, trying to ease his guilt. "I believed them as much as anyone."

The president shook his head. "What are we to do, Kata? What are we to do?"

"We must convince our people to renounce the Jung and join the Alliance. We can right our wrongs by joining the fight."

"But we are not warriors. We are a peaceful people," the president pleaded.

"There are more warriors among us than you might realize," Kata said. "Many of these images have made me want to pick up a weapon and join the fight myself. At the very least, we must show the Cetian people the truth and *let them decide.*"

"Yes, yes. Of course." The president looked at Kata. "Do you think they will forgive us?"

"Yes, I do. They did not allow me to document everything without reason. I believe they need our help. I believe they need *everyone's* help."

President Kanor pulled himself together. The last two hours had been difficult ones. "I would like to speak with the admiral again."

"One moment," Kata told him. She rose and left the room, returning a few minutes later with Admiral Dumar.

President Kanor stood, wanting to demonstrate respect for the admiral, something he had failed to do when they had first met. "Admiral Dumar. It seems that you are correct, that we have been misled by the Jung. For that, I would like to offer an apology on behalf of the Cetian people. Still, as much as I think my people would like to do something to help, I'm not sure what *help* you think we can be."

"No one is asking your people to march into battle, Mister President. However, there is still much that you can do to help. The Earth needs sources of basic consumables, at least until she can get her industry up and running once again."

"The farms and ranches on Sorenson have been producing massive amounts of grains, meats, and produce to feed the Jung for decades," Kata said. "More than half of it is shipped out every few months to Jung ships elsewhere."

"Your people also have an orbital shipyard, with *four* assembly bays. We have only a *single bay* large enough to service this ship if badly damaged. In fact, she has had to fight without shields and other improvements for quite some time, while her sister ship has undergone repairs and upgrades. That shipyard of yours *alone* could turn the tide of this war, not to mention the two Jung frigates currently under construction within her. I assume your people are the primary source of technical labor for their construction?"

"Indeed they are. I'm ashamed to admit that my people have built at least a dozen ships in that very shipyard. All of them for the Jung."

"And the propellant that fuels them?"

"From refineries on Stennis."

"You see, Mister President, there is much that the people of Tau Ceti can do to help the Alliance stop the Jung. And in return, there is much the Alliance can do for the Cetian people."

"Such as?" the president wondered, sounding very much the politician again.

"Protection *against* the Jung for one," the admiral told him. "There is a Jung battle group not two weeks away, en route from 82 Eridani to Tau Ceti at this very moment. We intend to intercept that battle group and destroy it *before* it reaches your system."

"*If* we agree to join your Alliance?"

"Regardless of whether or not your people decide to join the Alliance. Your protection became our responsibility the moment we destroyed the Jung forces in your system. However, your people can *help* us protect you. We can also provide you with advanced technology..."

"...From that Data Ark?" the president realized. "The one that was nearly destroyed from orbit?"

"From the Data Ark, as well as from the other members of the Alliance, several of whom are far more advanced than the Jung."

"Really?"

"Yes. My own people, for example."

The president looked surprised. "You are not from Earth?"

"No, I am not. I am from the Pentaurus cluster."

"The one a thousand light years away?"

"Indeed."

"And you came all the way to Sol to fight the Jung?"

"We came all the way to Sol to help those who helped us escape a similar fate."

The president shook his head. "Incredible. However, I am afraid I cannot speak for all the Cetian people. I am only the de facto president, and only of Kohara. There are still two other worlds in our system. If the entire Tau Ceti system is to join your Alliance, they must *choose* to do so...by election."

"Of course," the admiral agreed.

"But how do we conduct such an election, when there are still nearly eight hundred Jung soldiers on Kohara? They are executing people in the streets based only on suspicion. How can *any* Koharan vote to join the Alliance with such a threat looming over them?"

Admiral Dumar sighed. "Unfortunately, we suffered heavy losses during our initial attempt to remove the Jung from your world, and we cannot afford to lose many more."

"Can you not destroy them from orbit?" the president wondered.

"The remaining Jung facility is embedded in the middle of one of Kohara's most heavily populated cities," the admiral explained. "In addition, it extends deep underground. It may even connect to other bunkers not yet detected. I fear destroying them all from orbit would result in thousands more Koharan deaths. Possibly hundreds of thousands."

"Then what are we to do?" the president wondered.

"I do have an idea. It is risky, but it might work, with *your* help."

* * *

Gerard entered the recovery ward in the Aurora's medical department. He spotted Jessica talking to one of the medical staff at the desk and headed toward her.

"Lieutenant," Jessica greeted.

"Sir," Gerard replied, offering a salute after noticing she outranked him. "Sorry, it took me a moment to realize. The uniforms are a bit different."

"Don't worry about it. It is *I* who should be saluting *you*. Thanks for taking care of her."

"I did the best I could," he replied. "I only wish I could have done better."

"Well, you got her back alive. That's all that matters," Jessica insisted.

"She got herself back," Gerard said. "She's one tough lady."

"That she is."

The lieutenant looked around. "It's really strange. Everything on board this ship... It feels familiar. I mean, we didn't have ships like this when I left, but still..."

"I think I understand." Jessica looked over at one of the curtained-off beds in the far corner of the ward. "I think she's still awake, if you want to talk to her."

"I don't want to disturb her, or anything. But... well, I'm going back down soon, and I wanted to say goodbye."

Jessica looked for approval from the doctor sitting at the desk, who nodded. "Sure, Lieutenant, sure."

"Thank you." Gerard nodded politely at the doctor and headed over to Naralena's bed. He carefully pulled back the curtain to peek inside.

Naralena was lying in a semi-sitting position, her leg propped up and bandages wrapped around it. Her eyes were closed and her head was turned away from him. She looked so different. Peaceful, happy, safe... So much so that he decided he didn't want to disturb her. News that he was returning to the surface might upset her, and he couldn't have that, not after seeing her so relaxed. He would have to see her when he returned.

If he returned.

He let the curtain slowly close and turned to leave.

"Gerard?" Naralena called out in a faint voice. "Is that you?"

He froze for a moment, unsure of what to do.

"Gerard?" she called again.

Jesus, Gerard, you're a grown man, he thought.

He turned back around and pulled back the curtain just enough to slip inside. "Hello. I thought you were sleeping. I didn't want to disturb you."

"It's all right. I'll have plenty of time to sleep while my leg heals," she replied.

"How bad is it?" he asked.

"Doctor says it will be all healed in a few days."

"But, I thought it was much deeper... I mean..."

"Nanites. We've got them too."

"Ah, yes. I forgot."

"How are you doing?"

"Fine, fine. I just finished my debrief. Told them everything I could think of that might help. I could probably tell them a lot more, but, there's no time."

"What do you mean?"

"They need me," he told her. "They need me to go back down...to Kohara."

"What? Why?"

"They think I can help them get rid of the Jung without anyone else dying."

Naralena's head fell back against the pillow, her eyes looking up at the ceiling in frustration and disappointment.

"It's okay, Naralena, really..."

"No, it's not," she disagreed, raising her head to look at him again. "You gave them more than twenty years of your life, Gerard. Isn't that enough?"

"I have to see this through to the end, Naralena."

"But why?"

Gerard looked around, confused. "I don't really know. Those people down there. They're more *my* people than these people are. I mean, I was only twenty-five when I left Earth. Seems like I've lived on Kohara longer than I did on Earth, if that makes any sense."

Naralena sighed. "Actually, it does."

"It shouldn't take more than a week...maybe less." He looked down at the floor. "If everything goes well."

She knew what he meant. "And then you'll come back?"

He stepped closer and took her hand, avoiding eye contact. "I can't promise that." He raised his eyes to meet hers. "I can only promise that if I am ever in a position to find you again...that I *will* find you. That much I promise."

Naralena said nothing, just staring sadly into his eyes.

Gerard reached out and wiped away her tears, then leaned in to kiss her forehead ever so gently.

"I'm going to hold you to that promise," she whispered.

* * *

President Kanor walked briskly across the Aurora's hangar deck, a man filled with new purpose. Ahead of him were Kata Mun and her porta-cam operator, Karahl, recording the president's departure from the Aurora.

"It is a bold plan, Admiral," the president told Admiral Dumar as he escorted him to the jump shuttle that would take Gerard and the president back to Kohara. "Do you really think it will work?"

"The advantage to *bold* plans, Mister President, is that the enemy rarely expects them."

"Those young women, they will be returned as well?"

"Of course," the admiral promised. "But it is best to wait until after the Jung have been removed."

The president stopped for a moment, turning toward the admiral. "If we time their return to the day of the broadcast, the night *before* the election, I believe it will have the greatest impact."

"Spoken like a true politician," the admiral replied, smiling. "And I actually mean that as a compliment."

"Interesting," the president commented, an inquisitive look on his face. "So politicians are disliked on *all* worlds?"

"Not *all* worlds," the admiral clarified, "and certainly not *all* politicians."

President Kanor smiled back at him. "You'd make a good one yourself, Admiral." The president shook the admiral's hand.

"Good luck to you, Mister President."

"To us all, Admiral. To us all," he replied as he turned and headed for the shuttle.

"Admiral," Gerard greeted as he approached.

"You know what to do, Lieutenant."

"Yes, sir. I will not let him near any Jung scanners, and I will not let him be captured alive."

"You have three days to gather your men and be ready for evac."

"We will be ready," Gerard promised. "And I will make sure the president is secured until after the operation is over, sir."

"Very well. Good luck, Lieutenant."

"Thank you, sir," Gerard replied, saluting the admiral.

Admiral Dumar stood and watched as the president and Gerard boarded the shuttle, followed by Kata Mun and Karahl Essa, and finally the shuttle's crew chief, who retracted the boarding ramp and secured the hatch. They had one chance to pull off a miracle, and it all hinged on a forty-eight year-old spec-ops lieutenant, and his band of ex-Jung soldiers turned rebels.

* * *

Nathan stood on the lowest platform of the Karuzara's primary dry dock, gazing up at the Celestia floating before him. He had not been here since she had originally docked almost two months earlier. At the time, she had been a mess. Her entire front end had been mangled, with sections of her hull torn away to the point that one could scarcely make out the line of her bow. She had been scorched and battered, and had hundreds of holes punched into her outer hull from heavy rail gun fire from that last Jung battle platform. She had given her all in defense of Earth. It was only fitting that she was now being given a new lease on life.

And now, she was a completely finished ship.

Not only was she finished, but she was better. Better even than her original designs. Although they still had additional weapons to add, she now had four mark five plasma torpedo cannons peeking out from a slit across the underside of her new bow, and rows of heat exchangers under her midship dedicated to keeping the massive plasma generators that powered those cannons cool during battle. Even more noticeable were the numerous emitters all over her hull. Primary and secondary arrays of jump field emitters, each of them tied into separate field generators and energy banks, giving her twice the usual jump range between charges. More important were the equally numerous shield emitters, an entirely different system, designed to protect the ship from rail gun fire by robbing them of their kinetic energy as they passed through the shields so that they would bounce harmlessly off her outer hull.

"Come to wish us a *tor tuyasya mayeeth*?" Master Chief Montrose asked as he approached the captain.

"Excuse me?" Nathan said.

"I believe the translation would be 'good voyage'," the master chief replied.

"Something like that, I suppose." Nathan looked back up at the Celestia. "Actually, I just wanted to take one last look at her while she was still in dry dock. It's still pretty amazing to look at her this way."

"Indeed, she is an impressive sight," the master chief agreed, his heavy brogue tainting every syllable.

"Especially just hovering there, like magic."

"Aye. It has been something to work on her in this fashion. You know, I have actually walked across her topside, stem to stern. Let me tell you, the climb up her drive section is not an easy one, even in zero gravity and mag boots."

"Really?"

"Indeed. My legs were sore for a week."

"Stem to stern, huh. You realize that's almost fifteen hundred meters, Master Chief? In mag boots, no less?"

"I won't be doing that again, Captain. Trust me. Just figured I'd do it once, while I had the chance. It gives you an entirely different perspective on her, I'll tell you that."

"Then why didn't you walk her bottom side as well?" Nathan wondered. "Stem to stern."

"I'm not crazy, Captain," Master Chief Montrose

replied. "Besides, after walking her topside, I'd had enough."

"Of course," Nathan agreed. "Pretty nice looking cannons you got there."

"You noticed, did you?" the master chief replied. "We'll be firing them tomorrow, after we pull out of here, that is."

"When do they start the depress cycle?" Nathan asked.

"In a few hours."

"Then she passed her final exterior checks?"

"Mostly, yes. But it takes fourteen hours to depressurize this bay, so they'll finish up in suits while they're sucking the air out of this place."

"I see."

"You'll be pulling the Aurora in here in another week."

"Indeed we shall," Nathan confirmed.

"It's about time she got a good overhaul," the master chief said.

"I'm sure Lieutenant Commander Kamenetskiy would agree with you, Master Chief."

"She deserves it. She's done a lot, and so have you. You both deserve some time off." The master chief looked at Nathan. "Are you taking a vacation, Captain, while your ship's in repairs?"

"I was thinking about it," Nathan admitted. "Although it will probably feel odd to be away from her for more than a few hours."

"It'll do you right, sir. Bring you back fresh, and ready to fight."

"Let's hope, Master Chief," Nathan replied. "I suspect there's still a lot of fighting left to do."

* * *

The Frontiers Saga Episode #14: THE WEAK AND THE INNOCENT

Gerard and his men squatted in the bushes along the clearing, deep in the mountains along the northernmost tip of Kohara's main continent. It had taken them nearly a full day's travel, using various vehicles, to reach this valley. It was as far from Cetia as they could get in only a day. The ranges were tall, and this particular valley was quite deep, requiring a three-hour journey along narrow, winding roads that had been carved into vertical rock faces. It was a place only the most dedicated wilderness enthusiasts ventured, and even then, not during the more frigid months.

Gerard took his hands from his pockets and rubbed them together vigorously to warm them, blowing on them repeatedly afterward. He could see the breath of all his men as they waited in the darkness.

"You are sure about your friend, Doran?" Gerard asked the man next to him.

"You worry too much, Gerard."

"I do when it is this important, Tomas."

"The president is unconscious, and will be for days," Tomas reminded him, "locked away far from any Jung scanners."

"He is old," Gerard said. "I hope he will survive the procedure."

"He chose to undergo the procedure willingly," Tomas said.

"But he did not know that he would not be allowed to awaken if the procedure was unsuccessful."

"Better he is unconscious anyway," Tomas pointed out. "If I remember correctly, it was most unpleasant."

The cry of an animal sounded from the far side of the meadow. It repeated a second later.

"That is the signal," Tomas said. "Nyle has completed the perimeter check, and all is clear."

Gerard looked at his watch. "With very little time to spare. We have but thirty seconds."

"They are so precise?" Tomas wondered, finding it difficult to believe.

"If you had seen them in action, you would not ask that question." Gerard looked at his watch again. "Everyone, eyes tightly closed, heads down."

Gerard's men closed their eyes tightly, then curled down into balls on their knees. Gerard made the same animal call as they had heard a moment ago, making it three times, each of them evenly spaced. He then closed his eyes and assumed the same balled-up position as his men.

A brilliant flash of light illuminated the valley, lighting up the steep walls of the mountains on all sides. There was a thunderous clap and a roar of rocket turbines, followed by a wave of displaced air that washed over them as the light quickly subsided.

Gerard looked up, peering through the bushes as the cargo jump shuttle hovered only two meters above the flowing grass of the meadow.

"Oh, my God," Tomas exclaimed in Jung. "How is this possible?"

"Exactly," Gerard agreed in the same language.

The shuttle hovered above the ground, rotating a full three hundred and sixty degrees, its cargo ramp opened to a level position, as Ghatazhak soldiers jumped to the ground in pairs. As they landed, they ran outward, establishing a perimeter. The shuttle stopped its rotation and waited, its engines roaring to maintain position.

Gerard pulled out a small signal laser and activated it. He pointed it at the nearest soldier, tracing it up to the man's visor as he had been instructed. The soldier immediately turned toward Gerard and his men, and gestured for them to advance. "Let's go," he ordered his men, again in Jung.

Gerard was the first out of the bushes, staying low in a crouch as he ran across the open meadow toward the shuttle. The ship descended and touched down, its engines immediately spinning down to idle.

Gerard ran up to the now-standing Ghatazhak soldier.

"Sergeant Targus?" the soldier asked.

"Targus is the name of a poorly made car on Earth. My name is Bowden, and I am a lieutenant."

"Pleasure to meet you, Lieutenant. I'm Sergeant Lazo. I have orders to take you and your men to the Jar-Benakh."

"Lead the way, Sergeant," Gerard replied.

Tomas grabbed Gerard's arm, a look of panic and confusion on his face. "The Jar-Benakh?" he asked, his eyes wide. "You did not say anything about a Jung battleship."

"Trust me, Tomas," Gerard replied as he led the way to the waiting shuttle.

CHAPTER ELEVEN

"New contact," Mister Navashee reported, "just out of FTL. It's the Jar-Benakh, Captain. She's twenty kilometers to port. Her shields are up and her weapons are hot."

"Sound general quarters," Nathan ordered calmly. "Helm, full power. Climb to higher orbit and give us some maneuvering room."

"Climb to higher orbit, aye," Mister Chiles answered smartly as he brought the Aurora's engines up to full power in order to accelerate and climb.

"General quarters, aye," Jessica replied from the tactical station. "Powering up point-defenses."

"More contacts," Mister Navashee reported. "Eight missiles inbound. Impact in thirty seconds. They're not exactly pulling punches, are they?"

"Well, I told him to make it look good," Nathan replied.

"Tracking all eight," Jessica announced. "Firing point-defenses."

"Jar-Benakh is firing her main rail guns, sir!" Mister Navashee looked over his shoulder at the captain. "Low velocity."

"Two down," Jessica reported, "three...four..."

"Missile impacts in fifteen seconds," Mister Navashee added.

"Recommend rolling forty-five to port to put more guns into action!" Jessica urged.

"Forty-five roll to port!" Nathan ordered.

"Forty-five to port, aye," the helmsman acknowledged.

The planet Kohara, below, began to rotate and slide up the left side of the Aurora's spherical main view screen as the ship rolled onto its port side.

"Ten seconds," Mister Navashee warned, "still four inbound!"

"I'm working on it," Jessica muttered as she brought additional weapons from the Aurora's starboard side onto the incoming missiles.

"All hands report general quarters!" Ensign Waara reported from the communications console.

"Five down!" Jessica reported, "six..."

"All hands brace for impacts!" Nathan ordered. "Helm! Kill your mains, full decel burn and barrel roll us down and to port!"

"Two detonations!" Ensign Marka reported from the Jar-Benakh's sensor station. "She's decelerating and in a descending barrel roll. I'm picking up debris, as well... A lot of it!"

"That close enough for you, Scott?" Captain Roselle muttered with satisfaction. "Ventral guns, keep firing, low velocity."

"Uh...right," Sergeant Shugart replied. He leaned toward Sergeant Garza, who was operating the Jar-Benakh's ventral weapons. "How do you adjust the velocity, again?"

"Sugar?" Roselle inquired.

Sergeant Garza reached over and made the adjustments for Sergeant Shugart. "Got it?"

"I got it, I got it," Sergeant Shugart replied. "Firing ventral guns, low velocity," he told his captain.

"Target is killing their decel burn and pitching

around... She's trying to bring her main plasma cannons on us, sir."

"Shields at full strength?" Roselle checked.

"Yes, sir!" Commander Ellison replied from the main tactical station.

"Then let'em," Captain Roselle said. "Queue up another round of missiles, Commander. We need to slap them around a bit."

"Forward tubes in ten seconds!" Jessica reported from the Aurora's tactical station.

"More contacts!" Mister Navashee announced. "Eight more inbound!"

"Point-defenses are firing again! Need to put our topside toward the incoming missiles again!"

"Do it!" Nathan ordered his helmsman. "Fire all forward tubes when ready!" Nathan instructed Jessica. "Mister Riley, stand ready on the fake escape jump."

"Yes, sir," the navigator reported.

"Mister Lawrence, be ready to release another batch of debris," Nathan added.

"Both lifts have been reloaded and will be topside in ten seconds," Mister Lawrence reported from the port auxiliary station.

"Missile impacts in twenty seconds."

"One down!" Jessica announced. "Firing all forward tubes!"

Nathan glanced at the main view screen as eight red-orange balls of plasma streaked away from either side toward the Jar-Benakh.

"Four down! Five! Six!"

"Detonations!" Mister Navashee reported. "Two nukes, two kilometers above us!"

"Release debris!" Nathan ordered. "Stand by to detonate charges!"

"Debris away, both lifts!" Mister Lawrence replied.

"Detonate charges!" Nathan ordered.

"Detonating charges!" Mister Lawrence replied.

"Execute fake escape jump," Nathan instructed his navigator.

"Executing!" Mister Riley replied.

Nathan watched the main view screen as the blue-white light spilled out in all directions from the field emitters on the Aurora's forward section, but failed to spread out and establish a stable jump field.

"More missiles launched!" Mister Navashee reported. "Sixteen of them! Two separate tracks! He's targeting both our ventral and dorsal sides!"

"Jesus," Nathan muttered. "I'm glad he's on our side."

"And he's holding back," Jessica reminded him.

"Missile impacts in thirty seconds!" Mister Navashee warned.

"This is it, people," Nathan announced, shifting in his command chair. "Let's make it look good."

"Keep our topside to the targets," Jessica reminded the helmsman. "Firing all point-defenses, firing all quads."

"Remember," Nathan warned, "You need to let half of them get through."

"I'm trying," Jessica promised. "It's a lot harder to purposefully *miss* an incoming target than you might imagine."

"Impacts in twenty seconds!"

"Four down!" Jessica reported.

"Keep our nose on them as well," Nathan instructed, "and keep firing those torpedoes."

"Firing forward tubes," Jessica replied.

"Final loads of debris are ready," Mister Lawrence announced. "Both lifts, *and* we've got the flight apron packed as well. Charges are all armed and ready."

"Stand by on the *real* snap jump, Mister Riley," Nathan instructed.

"Ready to snap jump, sir."

"Ten seconds!" Mister Navashee warned.

"Six down!" Jessica reported. "Firing all forward tubes, triplets and singles!"

"Five seconds! Three..."

"Seven down!" Jessica reported.

"...two..."

"Nine still inbound!"

"...detonation!"

"Eight down!"

The entire interior of the Aurora's bridge was filled with brilliant white light, as eight nuclear warheads detonated both above and below her, only two kilometers away.

"Release all debris!" Nathan ordered. "Dump the forward propellant tanks!"

"Releasing debris," Mister Lawrence replied. "Dumping forward propellant tanks!"

"Detonate all charges! Snap jump!"

"Detonating all charges!"

"Snap jump, aye!" Mister Riley replied.

The jump flash washed over the Aurora, this time in proper fashion.

"Snap jump complete," Mister Riley reported, audible relief on his voice.

"Position?" Nathan asked, not yet ready to feel safe.

"Two light years outside the Tau Ceti system," Mister Navashee replied.

Nathan's entire posture changed as he practically melted into his chair, an enormous wave of relief finally coming over him. He turned aft, toward Jessica. "Good thing they weren't firing antimatter warheads at us," he told her. "Who knows where we'd end up?"

Jessica smiled. "Let's just hope the Jung on the surface of Kohara don't have very good sensors."

Nathan took a deep breath and sighed, straightening up into a normal posture once again. "Stand down from general quarters," he ordered. "Mister Riley, set course for our rendezvous with the Celestia. It's time to do it for real."

* * *

Ten Jung troop shuttles approached what was left of the Jung airbase just outside of Cetia. The first ship came in quickly—almost too quickly—touching down with a slight bounce not more than fifty meters from the formation of Jung troops on the tarmac. The rough landing drew a look of concern on one of the Jung officers' faces. However, when the troop shuttles that landed after them also made such imprecise approaches and landings, he attributed it to the urgency of their mission.

Josh and Loki both bounced in their seats as the troop shuttle touched down rather abruptly.

"Jesus, Josh," Loki exclaimed. "You might want to wait until you get a gear contact light before you kill your landing thrusters."

"Which one is the damned contact light?" Josh wondered. "I can't read any of this shit!"

"I told you, those four lights over there, just above the range controls."

"Well why the hell aren't they above the gear status lights, like every other fucking ship in the galaxy?" he exclaimed in frustration.

"You want me to fly this thing?" Loki asked.

"You just look out the window and look like an adult for the crowd of Jung out there, Lok. You're the only one of us that can."

Loki looked out the starboard window, peering down at the group of Jung soldiers lined up in perfect formations on the battered tarmac. "Damn, there sure are a lot of them out there."

"Please, don't talk about it," Josh begged. "I just want to get this crappy fucking assignment over with, and get back to flying Deliza's psychotic engineering experiments."

"That makes two of us," Loki agreed. "Just be glad that our passengers won't be able to speak to us."

Boarding hatches on both the forward and aft sections of the first massive troop shuttle to touch down, immediately lowered to their loading position. Gerard appeared in the hatch, dressed as a Jung commander. He started down the boarding ramp in a hurry, his sergeant, Tomas, close behind. Upon reaching the bottom, he marched smartly toward the assembled men waiting to board.

"Lieutenant Commander," Gerard began speaking in Jung, as he approached the young officer.

"Sir!" the lieutenant commander replied smartly, snapping to attention and offering a crisp salute.

"Is this it?" Gerard inquired. "I was under the

impression that there were several thousand of you?"

"Three thousand, four hundred, and twenty-eight, sir," the lieutenant commander replied.

"Then where are they?" Gerard asked impatiently.

"We were told that only one thousand men could be evacuated at a time, sir. I thought it best to assemble only those about to be evacuated, so as not to expose all of our remaining forces to a concentrated attack."

"Attack?" Gerard wondered, almost laughing. "By whom? The Koharans are pacifists, are they not?"

"Pacifists *can* grow teeth, if provoked, sir," the lieutenant commander explained. "Word of our withdrawal will spread rapidly, and it will take time to conduct four rounds of evacuation, sir."

"Yes, yes," Gerard nodded. "Good thinking, Lieutenant Commander. I take it you have arranged a method to cover the evacuations?"

"Yes, sir," the lieutenant commander replied. "The last group is maintaining the perimeter. They have wired it with mines and automated defenses. We have also shut down all public transit. Very few will be able to make it to this base, if so inclined."

"Excellent," Gerard congratulated. "Well done."

"Sir, if I may?" the lieutenant commander asked, leaning closer to Gerard.

"What is it, Lieutenant Commander?" Gerard wondered, turning his ear to the Jung officer.

The lieutenant commander glanced right and left, as if verifying that no one other than the commander could hear his words. "Commander, we can hold this world. I know we are few, but as you said, the Koharans are mostly pacifists. Now that the Jar-Benakh has defeated the enemy ship that has so plagued us these past weeks, we can…"

"Captain Tahn has given the order to sterilize all three of the Cetian worlds," Gerard explained. He was careful to appear unaffected by the nature of such an action.

"But, sir…"

"Haven't you been killing suspected collaborators in the streets?" Gerard asked. "Were you not telling the people of Kohara that the enemy who destroyed our ships could not have done so without help from those collaborators?"

"Yes, sir, but…"

"So, you can see how the sterilization protocol *is* warranted in this case?"

"Yes, of course, Commander…but all three worlds?"

"If we sterilize only the one, then we will be seeding even greater rebellions on the other two," Gerard explained, becoming impatient. He cast a suspicious look on the lieutenant commander. "You are not *questioning* Captain Tahn's orders, are you?"

"Of course not, sir," the lieutenant commander replied vehemently. "I…"

"What is it?" Gerard wondered, appearing even more irritated.

"It's just that…some of the men…they have taken girlfriends, wives. Some of them even have children."

"So?" Gerard wondered, appearing indifferent.

"Some of the men may *not* want to leave."

Gerard looked at the lieutenant commander, one eyebrow raised in discontent at his remarks. "Then let them remain. They can perish along with their garbage wives and their half-breed children," Gerard declared with obvious disgust.

"Yes, sir."

"On second thought," Gerard said, "Assign anyone you believe does *not* wish to be evacuated to the last group, and have them provide security. Tell them... Tell them that Captain Tahn will *allow* them ample time to gather their families and seek shelter. Then, when the last group of *loyal* Jung soldiers are about to leave, have them shoot those who wanted to remain with their little rodents, rather than serve the empire." Gerard pretended to look pleased with his impromptu decision. "It will send quite a strong message to the rest of your men, don't you think?"

The lieutenant commander said nothing, instead just stood there, staring at Gerard with his mouth open, in shock.

"Lieutenant Commander, don't tell me that *you* have a little Koharan whore yourself?" Gerard asked as he removed his gloves.

"No, sir," the lieutenant commander insisted without hesitation. "Of course not, Commander. I live to serve the empire!"

"That's what I thought," Gerard replied indignantly. "Now, will you please get the first group of men aboard my ships so we can get on with this? I am so looking forward to finally getting out of this godforsaken system."

"May I inquire as to our new destination, Commander?" the lieutenant commander asked.

Gerard smiled. "We are going home, Lieutenant Commander. We have captured one of the enemy's new propulsion systems, and we are going to deliver it, *personally*, to our caste leaders."

The lieutenant commander looked as if he would burst with excitement.

"That's right, we're all going to be hugely rewarded

for our contribution to the empire," he said, tapping the lieutenant commander on the chest with his gloves as he strolled past on his way to watch the embarkation.

* * *

Captain Roselle and Commander Ellison stood on the catwalk overlooking the Jar-Benakh's main hangar bay, as several hundred Ghatazhak soldiers escorted the unarmed Jung troops as they disembarked from their shuttles, to detainment areas that had been set up in several adjacent hangars. The looks on the faces of the Jung men were a mixture of confusion, frustration, and disappointment. In some cases, the captain thought he saw looks of embarrassment as well.

The captain watched the activity below, shaking his head in disbelief. "You know, I was sure that wasn't going to work worth a *damn*. I guess that's why I'm not an admiral…yet."

"We've still got three more loads to go," the commander reminded him, "not to mention another couple hundred men still at the orbital shipyards."

"I suppose fear of getting nuked from orbit will make a man quick to do as he's told," the captain said with a wink as he turned to exit. "Make sure they don't dally, Commander. I want to make sure we're ready to bug out fast, in case the next part of this plan goes to shit. We could have a whole battle group dropping in outta FTL at any moment wondering what the hell we're doing."

"Yes, sir."

* * *

"Half light, sir," Mister Chiles reported from the Aurora's helm. "Killing the mains."

"Very well," Nathan replied. "Open the doors and stand by for deceleration burn."

"Opening decel doors," the helmsman replied.

"Lieutenant Tillardi, you may deploy the jump KKVs," Nathan instructed.

"Aye, sir," the lieutenant replied.

"Topside camera," Nathan added.

The Aurora's spherical main view screen switched to the forward-facing camera on the front of the main drive section.

"Magnify," Nathan instructed.

The image on the view screen cross-faded, revealing a magnified image of the two JKKV deployment racks, each of them sitting on one of the topside launch and recovery platforms. Nathan squinted, straining to see the clamps that held each weapon in place on the rack as they all opened at once, releasing their hold on the weapons.

"Weapons are free-floating," Lieutenant Tillardi reported.

"Downward translation, Mister Chiles," Nathan ordered.

"Translating downward, aye," the helmsman reported.

All eyes on the bridge, except for those of her helmsman, were locked on the main view screen as the two pairs of jump KKVs rose slowly upward out of their cradles. The weapons had to remain on their precise course and speed in order for them to successfully intercept their targets more than a light hour away.

"Separation is ten meters and rising," Mister Riley reported.

"One percent on the deceleration engines, Mister Chiles," Nathan ordered.

"One percent decel burn, aye."

Nathan continued to watch the main view screen as the Aurora began to gradually decelerate, making it appear as if the four JKKVs were pulling ahead of them when, in fact, the Aurora was falling behind them. The devices continued to rise upward on the view screen, as the Aurora fell further behind them and continued to drift downward from them as well.

"Safe maneuvering distance in ten seconds," Mister Riley announced.

"Stand by for full deceleration burn," Nathan instructed.

"Full decel burn, standing by," the helmsman replied.

"Celestia is approaching safe maneuvering distance as well, sir," Mister Navashee reported.

"On Mister Riley's count, Mister Chiles," Nathan added.

"Decel burn in three......two......one......burn."

"Deceleration engines at full power," Mister Chiles reported.

"Speed is decreasing," Mister Riley reported. "Estimate combat maneuvering speed in fifteen minutes, thirty seconds."

"Very well," Nathan replied.

"Celestia reports their JKKVs are away, and the Celestia is at full deceleration," Ensign Waara reported from the comms station.

"Mission clock shows eighteen minutes to first attack jump," Jessica reported from the tactical station.

Nathan turned to his left and rose from his chair. "Now let's just hope that those antimatter mines do the trick," he said as he headed toward his ready room, "or we're going to be chasing down those jump KKVs for hours."

"Not to mention having to fight this battle *in* the Tau Ceti system," Jessica added as the captain walked past her.

Nathan looked at her as he passed, a look of uncertainty on his face. "Fingers crossed. You have the conn."

* * *

Captain Poc walked through Scout One's EVA bay, between the rows of spacesuits on either side, making his way forward. They had been following the Jung battle group on its way to the Tau Ceti system from the 82 Eridani system for several hours, ever since they left the Karuzara with ten antimatter mines on a makeshift deployment rack attached to their underside.

"How are things looking, Mister Todson?" the captain asked as he stepped through the hatch into the operations compartment.

"No change, sir. The target is still on the same course and speed."

"Then we're good for deployment?"

"Yes, sir, it looks that way," the ensign replied.

"Excellent," the captain said, glancing up at the mission clock to the right of the cockpit ladder. "Racks looking good as well, Lieutenant?" he asked his chief engineer monitoring the console just forward of the sensor officer.

"I wouldn't call them *good-looking*," the lieutenant replied. "More like a mess, really. They slapped that thing together in one hell of a hurry, if you ask me.

To be honest, I'm just praying none of those mines snag on release. Last thing we need is an antimatter mine dangling from our belly when we jump away."

"Have a little faith, Lieutenant," Captain Poc said as he ducked his head under the bulkhead up into the hatchway and started up the angled ladder that led up a meter and a half to the scout ship's cockpit.

The captain climbed up the ladder through the angled hatchway and stepped onto the deck of the cockpit just behind the flight seats. "Commander," the captain greeted as he stepped over the center console and climbed into the pilot's seat.

"Coming up on the deployment jump," Commander Jento reported.

"Very well."

"Jump point in ten seconds," the commander added.

Captain Poc settled into his seat as his executive officer and copilot counted down to the jump point. Everything about the deployment of the antimatter mines had been calculated down to the millisecond, and the entire sequence was being handled by the scout ship's flight control computers. All they had to do was keep the ship on the assigned heading and speed which, once established, required no effort at all.

"Jumping," the commander reported.

Captain Poc glanced at the displays, which were the only way they had of knowing they had jumped. He hated the few-second lag that always followed the jump, while the ship's navigation system recalculated their location, course, and speed, after instantly transitioning between distant points in space.

"Jump complete," the commander reported.

"Deploy the mines," the captain ordered over his comm-set.

On the underside of Scout One, ten ungainly looking devices were released and began floating away. Tiny maneuvering jets began to fire, first on the outermost mines, then inward, one pair at a time. The mines began to spread out evenly as they continued on the forward trajectory that their host ship had imparted onto them.

"*We have a good deployment,*" the lieutenant reported over the comms. "Mines are spreading out, nice and even."

"Arm the mines," the captain ordered.

"*Mines are armed.*"

"Begin deceleration burn," Captain Poc ordered.

"Beginning decel burn," the commander replied. "Two minutes to detonation."

"*Two minutes ten seconds until the battle group can detect them,*" Ensign Todson added.

Captain Poc studied the deployment display as the icons representing each mine continued to maneuver into position, spreading out evenly in both height and width to cross the flight path of the approaching battle group.

"*Deployment pattern looks right on the money, Captain,*" Ensign Todson reported.

"That's it," Captain Poc said. "We've done our part, let's clear the area. I don't want to be anywhere near those mines when they detonate."

* * *

"Captain on the bridge!" the guard announced as Nathan came out of his ready room.

"One minute to mine detonation, Captain," Jessica reported from the tactical station.

"Set general quarters," Nathan ordered as he headed to his command chair. "How are the jump KKVs doing?"

"Still running true and sending back good telemetry," Lieutenant Tillardi reported. "They're currently about three million kilometers ahead of us."

"Thirty seconds to detonation," Jessica updated.

"All hands report general quarters, Captain," Ensign Waara reported from the comm station. "The XO is in combat, and the chief of the boat is in damage control."

"Very well."

"Twenty seconds to detonation."

Nathan sat in his command chair, reviewing their carefully orchestrated battle plan in his head as he waited for the last few seconds to pass until the mines detonated and started the ball rolling. Once that happened, the element of surprise, if they had it at all, would be lost. He looked over his shoulder at his old academy friend, Jonathon Tillardi, carefully studying the telemetry from the eight jump KKVs he had spent the last two months building. The lieutenant's eyes were dancing back and forth, and he was biting his upper lip. The poor guy was nervous. Nathan remembered how nervous he had been the first few times he had taken the Aurora on the offensive. It was different than when you were attacked. You were taking an action, the result of which would be the deaths of hundreds if not thousands of human beings, quite possibly the ones on your very ship. He knew that his friend was feeling that kind of pressure at the moment, as lives were depending on his devices working properly.

"Detonation in five seconds," Jessica reported. "Three......two......one......detonation."

Nothing happened on the bridge, not even an electronic beep. The scheduled detonations were occurring more than one billion kilometers ahead of them. If their calculations were correct, it occurred right in the path of the approaching battle group, only a hundred kilometers ahead of them.

The seconds continued to tick by as they waited. Five, then ten, then twenty seconds passed.

"Contact!" Mister Navashee reported. "Jump flash! It's Falcon One!"

"Incoming transmission from Falcon One," Ensign Waara announced. "Detonation confirmed. Battle group is out of FTL."

"Transmit the launch codes," Nathan ordered.

"Transmitting launch codes, aye," Lieutenant Tillardi replied.

"Mister Riley, stand by to execute first attack jump," he added.

"Ready for jump one," Mister Riley replied.

"Current speed?" Nathan asked, realizing he forgot to inquire when he had first returned to the bridge.

"We're at standard combat maneuvering speed, sir," Mister Chiles replied.

"Eight good jump flashes," Mister Navashee reported.

"Execute jump one in ten seconds," Nathan ordered.

"Jump one, coming up in...five..."

Nathan glanced up at the mission clock. They were right on the money.

"...four..."

"All weapons show ready for action," Jessica reported.

"...three..."

Lieutenant Tillardi was facing forward, but his eyes were closed. Nathan wondered if his friend was praying. He had always worn a cross around his neck, but Nathan had never asked him about it.

"...two..."

An odd thought suddenly crossed Nathan's mind...

"...one..."

Who do the Jung pray to?

"...jumping..."

Nathan closed his eyes momentarily as the jump flash washed over the Aurora's bridge.

"Jump complete," Mister Riley reported.

Nathan opened his eyes. The main view screen was littered with secondary explosions across its right side...

"Multiple contacts!" Mister Navashee reported with earnest.

Sections of the Jung battle platform, many of them larger than the Aurora herself, were spiraling away from the main cluster of explosions...

"Eight contacts, varying class and size!" Mister Navashee continued.

...Nathan could make out the two Jung cruisers on the far side of the battle platform as it came apart. Both were maneuvering to...

Did he say eight? Nathan thought.

"Is that including the Celestia and the Falcon?" Nathan asked urgently.

"Yes and no," Mister Navashee replied. "One of the eight *is* the Celestia. She jumped in on the opposite side of the platform, but the Falcon is not on my sensors!"

"ID those seven contacts!" Nathan barked.

"The battleship is undamaged!" Jessica warned. "I've got her dead ahead and turning into us! Helm! Two to port and four down! Fast!"

"Two to port and four down!" Mister Chiles replied as he pushed the Aurora's nose down and left as instructed.

"That can't be?" Lieutenant Tillardi declared in disbelief.

"Tillardi! Transmit the self-destruct orders to all surviving jump KKVs!" Nathan ordered.

"She's firing!" Mister Navashee warned.

"Firing all forward torpedoes!" Jessica announced. "Triplets across the board!"

Nathan spun around to look at the lieutenant, having not heard an acknowledgment from him. "Tilly!" he yelled as the red-orange light of the Aurora's plasma torpedoes streaking away from her lit up the inside of the bridge. "The self-destruct!"

"Yes, sir," the lieutenant finally acknowledged, coming out of his stupor and returning his attention to his console.

"She's taking us head-on!" Jessica declared. "All eighteen guns!"

"Helm! Up ten and go to full power!"

The bridge shook as rail gun fire slammed into their bow. Nathan watched the main view screen as chunks of their forward section were blown in all directions as the massive rail gun slugs from the Jung battleship tore into the Aurora's hull.

"As soon as you get a clear jump line, get us out of here!" Nathan added.

"Ten seconds!" Mister Riley replied.

"Damage control reports multiple hull breaches in the forward section!" Ensign Waara reported.

Nathan felt the shaking lessen slightly as the Aurora's nose came up and the enemy battleship's incoming fire began to strike their heavily armored undersides.

"They're firing missiles!" Mister Navashee added. "Four inbound! Twenty seconds to impact!"

"Tilly! Did they detonate?" Nathan demanded.

"Unknown..."

"Five seconds," Mister Riley reported.

Nathan glanced out the main view screen as the looming image of the approaching battleship fell down below the Aurora's bow.

"Executing escape jump!" Mister Riley reported as the blue-white light of the building jump fields began to spill out rapidly across the hull.

But the jump flash didn't occur.

"Jung frigate! Directly to port and twelve degrees down," Loki reported as the Super Falcon's jump flash subsided. "She's eight kilometers out and turning away."

"Turning into her to pursue," Josh replied as he rolled the Super Falcon onto her left side and pulled his nose back to initiate the turn. "We can still out accelerate her in this thing, right?"

"Hell yes," Loki replied.

"Just checking," Josh said as he pushed his throttle to maximum.

"Seven kilometers," Loki reported. "She's painting us. Attempting to jam."

Josh kept his eye on the target reticle on his flight data display, adjusting his turn to keep it just in front of the fleeing frigate.

"Six kilometers. She's firing missiles! Four inbound. Impact in ten!"

"Take them out!" Josh declared.

"I'm working on it," Loki replied as he tapped the icons representing the incoming missiles on his targeting screen. "Firing nose turret."

Josh glanced up over his forward console as thin bolts of red plasma energy leapt from beneath his nose in four, short blasts, walking from left to right with each volley. Four small explosions went off a few kilometers ahead of them as the bursts of plasma energy found their targets.

"Incoming missiles destroyed," Loki reported. "Range to target is three kilometers! Torpedo cannons are at full yield, single shots. Fire when ready!"

Josh checked his targeting reticle again and then pressed the firing trigger on his flight control stick. Four bright, red-orange balls of plasma, each of them the size of the Super Falcon's entire cockpit, streaked forward, slamming into the Jung frigate now only two kilometers away.

"Direct hit!" Loki exclaimed. "Multiple secondaries! Hit her again!"

Josh pressed the trigger again, figuring enough time had elapsed to allow the plasma generators to dissipate their heat from the last firing. Four more red-orange balls of plasma energy leapt forth from beneath either wing, immediately slamming into the frigate and breaking her apart.

"DAMN!" Josh exclaimed with glee. "You wanna talk about SUPER!" he added as he rolled to starboard and turned away from the doomed frigate as she was consumed by multiple explosions from within her own hull. "Find me another fucking target, Lok!"

"Negative jump!" Mister Riley announced.

"Missile impact in five seconds!" Mister Navashee warned.

"All hands! Brace for impact!" Nathan ordered as he grabbed the arms of his command chair and held on tight.

The bridge rocked, its aft end heaving upward. Nathan felt three distinct thuds reverberate through the structure of the ship. Alarms began to sound from any number of consoles around him.

"Hull breaches!" Ensign Waara declared as the calls from damage control began to flow into the communications center at the back of the bridge. "Multiple breaches along our bottom side."

"We took three direct hits!" Mister Navashee reported.

"What about the fourth missile?" Nathan demanded.

"I got one of them at the last second!" Jessica announced.

"Helm! You still have maneuvering?"

"Aye, sir," Mister Chiles replied.

"Bring our nose up and over and bring all tubes onto that battleship," Nathan ordered. "Jess! Pound her as soon as you can get guns on her, then hit her with another round of triplets!"

"Contact!" Mister Navashee reported. "Jump flash! The Celestia is engaging the battleship!"

"Keep firing as long as you have the angle, Lieutenant," Cameron ordered. "Mister Lange, how are our shields holding?"

"Forward shields at ninety percent and falling," Mister Lange reported from the Celestia's systems console. "All other shields at full power."

"Keep a close eye on all of them," Cameron ordered. "Let me know if any of them drop below fifty percent."

"Firing another round with the mark fives," Luis reported from the tactical station.

The Celestia's main view screen dimmed slightly to attenuate the brilliant light from the massive balls of red-orange plasma that shot forth from their four new, mark five plasma cannons under her bow. The four triplets of energy streaked out, one after the other, slamming into the Jung battleship's shields, causing them to turn an opaque yellow in the area of each impact.

"More direct hits," Ensign Kono reported from the sensor station. "Ten percent drop in their number four port shields."

"That's a hell of a lot better than the one percent we used to get with the mark fours," Cameron said. "Comms, raise the Aurora. Find out why she hasn't jumped clear."

"Aye, sir," Ensign Souza replied.

"Keep firing, Mister Delaveaga. Throw in our mark threes as well."

"Aye, sir," Luis replied. "Firing mark fours and fives."

"Captain, Aurora reports she's lost half of her

forward emitter array!" Ensign Souza reported. "She can't jump!"

"She took eighteen rail guns in her nose and several missiles in her belly," Cameron commented. "She's lucky she can still maneuver, let alone jump."

"Falcon One has just taken out another frigate!"

"Score another kill for Deliza Ta'Akar," Cameron muttered. "Kono, is the Aurora still in the fight?"

"Yes, sir," the ensign replied. "She's firing her quads at the battleship now, as she pitches over. I believe she's trying to bring her mark fours to bear."

"Which shields?" Cameron asked.

"Looks like their dorsal side, aft."

"Helm, slip us under and bring our nose to bear on the same shield panels," Cameron ordered.

"Aye, sir," Ensign Hunt replied.

"Ensign Kono, where's that last cruiser?"

"Fourteen kilometers to the battleship's starboard side, sir," the ensign replied as she double-checked her readings. "It looks like they're turning toward an intercept course for the Aurora, Captain."

"As soon as we take the next shot along with the Aurora, swing our nose around and turn us into that cruiser," Cameron ordered her helmsman. "Prepare a ten-kilometer jump to execute on my call."

"Aurora is firing!" Ensign Kono announced.

"Firing all forward torpedo cannons, fours and fives," Luis added.

Falcon One slid over the top of the third Jung frigate at a range of only three hundred kilometers, passing from her port to starboard. The Super Falcon's nose continued to alter its pitch as it passed, firing its four, under-wing-mounted mark two plasma cannons in rapid succession as it passed. Its rounds slammed into the enemy frigate's unshielded hull, cutting it in half and setting off numerous secondary explosions. No more than twenty seconds after the Super Falcon had appeared from behind a blue-white flash of light, it disappeared behind another.

"I'm telling ya, Lok, these frigates are nothing!" Josh declared as he brought the Falcon's nose back in line with her flight path.

"Don't get cocky," Loki replied.

"Where'd that other cruiser go?" Josh wondered. "I wanna take a crack at her as well!"

"Sorry, the Celestia just finished her off. Maybe you want to attack the battleship instead?"

"Why not?"

"I was kidding, Josh," Loki replied. "Besides, there's still one more frigate left."

"Bring it on!"

"We'll take her from her stern, translating down her length toward her bow."

"Why her stern?" Josh wondered. "Why not just cut her in half like we did the last one?"

"She's got fewer guns near her stern," Loki explained. "The last one didn't know we were coming because she was on the far side of that battle platform coming apart when we attacked the first two frigates. She no doubt saw us take out that last one, so she's going to be expecting us."

"Right," Josh agreed as he brought the Super Falcon on to its new jump course. "How's the Aurora doing?"

"Not good," Loki replied solemnly.

"What the hell are they doing?" Jessica wondered aloud. "They're moving into my firing line."

"They're moving in to protect us," Nathan realized.

"Captain! Incoming from Celestia Actual," Ensign Waara reported. "They're requesting we move off to a safe distance while they cover our retreat with their shields."

"But we just started fighting," Jessica declared.

"And we already got our asses kicked," Nathan reminded her. "Mister Chiles. Move us away, best speed."

"It's not going to be much, sir," the helmsman warned. "We lost eighty percent of our propellant in that last round of missiles. If I fire up the mains at anything over one percent, we'll suck through what's left in minutes."

"Then start with best speed with maneuvering thrusters only," Nathan decided. "We'll hold off on the mains until we have no choice." Nathan turned to his sensor operator. "How about the other ships in the battle group?"

"The battleship is the only one left, sir," Mister Navashee replied. "The Celestia took out both cruisers, and the Falcon took care of all four frigates."

"The Falcon took out four frigates?" Jessica said in disbelief. "Way to go, Deliza."

"Our dorsal shields are down to sixty percent," Mister Lange reported from the Celestia's systems console.

"Which ones?" Cameron asked.

"All of them, sir!"

"What about the target's shields?" the captain asked her sensor officer.

"They've climbed back up to ninety-five percent, sir," Ensign Kono reported. "We just can't make a dent without the mark fives."

"Damn it," Cameron cursed. "We can't bring our nose to bear until the Aurora gets farther away, or they'll fire *past* us and hit *them*."

"Captain, Falcon One is requesting permission to attempt to jump between the battleship's shield layers and collapse a portion of her shields from close range."

"Negative," Cameron ordered firmly. "Tell them to hold a safe distance and stand by."

"Captain, the target is accelerating toward us."

"Match speed and maintain distance," Cameron ordered.

"Aye, sir," Ensign Hunt acknowledged.

"Captain, if they continue accelerating, in a few minutes they will be traveling faster than the Aurora is capable of, in her current condition," Ensign Kono warned.

"How long?"

"Five minutes, maximum."

Cameron thought for a moment. The situation was surreal, as if in a simulation. Before, the entire ship would be shaking violently as rail gun rounds slammed into them. Now, with fully operational shields, even when down to sixty percent strength, they felt nothing.

But such would not be the case on the Aurora's bridge, and Cameron knew it. "Comms, warn the Aurora about the target's speed increase, and tell them to keep tight within our shadow...which is about to get a lot more narrow. Mister Hunt, bring our tubes to bear, and do your best to keep us between the Aurora and the damned battleship."

"Yes, sir," the helmsman replied.

"Be ready to blast away with all forward cannons as soon as you have a firing line, Lieutenant," Cameron instructed Lieutenant Delaveaga. "Pick one shield section, and keep pounding it. Our only chance is if we can collapse one of their shields before they collapse one of ours."

"Got it," Luis replied. "A good, old-fashioned slugfest."

"Exactly."

"Sir, the target is accelerating," Mister Navashee reported. "The Celestia is matching her speed. They'll overtake us in four minutes...maybe five."

"Captain," Ensign Waara interrupted, "the Celestia is warning us that they have to pitch over to get their forward tubes on the target. We might take some fire that gets around them."

"She's going to try and slug it out with them," Nathan realized. "Mister Navashee, how long can..."

"Not long, sir," Mister Navashee replied.

"Who's going to win?"

"No way to tell, sir," Mister Navashee said. "Two different kinds of energy, Captain, and two different kinds of shielding."

"Best guess, Mister Navashee," Nathan urged. "I need your best guess."

Mister Navashee shook his head in frustration. "The Jung, sir. By sheer firepower alone. That battleship can concentrate massive amounts of firepower on multiple points at the same time. In this situation, the Celestia can only concentrate on one shield section. Even *if* they manage to get one of the battleship's shields to fail, they *still* have to take her out. And don't forget, the Jung can extend their shields—not just outward, but in different directions. They can practically cover a downed shield section with neighboring sections."

Nathan sighed. "Then that's it."

"I'm sorry, sir," Mister Navashee apologized, feeling as if he'd failed his captain.

Nathan turned to face aft, looking Jessica directly in the eyes as he gave the order to his communications officer. "Ensign Waara. Call to all sections..." Nathan swallowed hard. "...Abandon ship. All non-essential personnel to the jump shuttles. The rest will use the escape pods."

Jessica looked crest-fallen. "Nathan..."

"We'll fire our mains and ram them, detonating our antimatter reactors as we impact," he explained. "There will be nothing left of either of us."

"But..."

"It's a good trade, Jess," Nathan insisted. "One ship for several billion lives...*innocent* lives, and we'll get two more ships to replace this one."

"Two measly frigates," Jessica argued, half-heartedly.

"Two frigates that the admiral will fit with jump drives, shields, and mark fours and fives. They'll be every bit as tough as any ship out there."

"Not as tough as this one," Jessica insisted.

Nathan took a deep breath. "Comms, get me the Celestia."

"Nathan, there has got to be another way," Cameron pleaded over the comms.

"There isn't, Cam, and you know it," Nathan insisted.

"Maybe we can alternate sides...show them our port side, then starboard..."

"You don't have enough guns," Nathan reminded her. *"Your only effective weapons are your plasma torpedoes, and you've got to be facing forward to use them. It's only a matter of time before they collapse your shields and blast through you to get to us. The only chance you've got to defeat that bastard is hit-and-run, and even then it's a long shot...and we'd still be destroyed. At least this way, the Aurora will die for a reason...for a victory."*

Cameron sighed. "I'll buy you as much time as I can, Nathan. Get your people out."

"The shuttles are leaving in two minutes. The rest are going in escape pods. Bridge staff will be the last to eject...but..."

"I know." Cameron looked down at the deck. "Good luck, Nathan."

"The blast range," Luis said, "...they won't have enough time to get clear."

"Not the last pod, no," Cameron said.

"The last of the shuttles have jumped away," Mister Navashee reported from the Aurora's sensor station.

"Remaining crew are ejecting now," Ensign Waara reported.

"How many pods are left?" Nathan asked.

"Two pods, sir," Mister Lange reported.

"Everyone, get to the escape pod," Nathan said. "I'll get to the last pod before impact."

No one left their station.

Nathan looked around. "That was an order, people."

"Sorry, Skipper, but we're not leaving," Jessica insisted.

Nathan turned around to look at her. "Jess..."

"You need us, Nathan," Jessica insisted. "You *need* me. I'm a Nash, remember? Nash's are hard to kill."

Nathan laughed. "Damned near impossible, I'd say." He looked around the bridge at his crew. "If you don't leave now, it's highly unlikely you'll make it to a safe distance before the antimatter reactors detonate."

"Beg your pardon, sir," Mister Navashee interrupted, "but it's likely we won't make it to a safe distance, even if we *do* leave now. I've done the math."

Nathan looked at his sensor operator. "I'm sure you have."

Vladimir entered the bridge and took a seat at the auxiliary station.

"Vlad..."

"And if the detonators do not work, like on Scout Three? Do you know how to override the containment field controls and force them to collapse on command?"

Nathan took a deep breath and sighed heavily. "No, I suppose I don't." He sat back down in his command chair. "Very well. How long do we have, Mister Navashee?"

"Two minutes."

"Vlad, make sure those escape pods are warmed up and ready to launch," Nathan said, mostly in jest.

"They are escape pods, Captain. They are always ready to launch."

"Comms, patch me through to the Celestia."

"Aye, sir," Ensign Waara replied.

"*Go for Celestia Actual,*" Cameron replied over the loudspeakers.

"Captain," Nathan began. "In just over a minute, you're going to jump away, and we're going to fire our mains and plow into that ship."

"*That is not leaving you much time to get to your escape pods, Captain,*" Cameron argued, "*let alone to get clear of the blast radius.*"

"No time for bullshitting each other, Cam. That's the plan. You can either get out of the way or go out with us."

"*Yes, sir.*"

"Time?" Nathan asked Mister Navashee.

"One minute."

"We go in fifty seconds, Cam. I'll call your jump," Nathan told her.

"*Understood.*"

Nathan took a deep breath, letting it out slowly. It had been a long couple of years. He had left Earth in order to escape his family, to escape responsibility, yet all he had done over the last two years had been to *be* responsible, to do what had to be done, no matter how terrible the consequences might be.

"Thirty seconds," Mister Navashee updated.

Nathan kept his gaze straight ahead on the main view screen, the image of the Celestia growing ever larger in his screen, already stretching halfway across at zero magnification.

Another deep breath. "It's been an honor to lead you all," he told them. "No captain could dare ask for a better crew."

"Self-destruct is armed," Vladimir announced. "Enter your code, Captain."

"Twenty seconds," Mister Navashee added.

Nathan pulled out his data pad to enter his authorization code.

"New contact," Mister Navashee announced. "Oh, my God, it's another Jung battle... It's the Jar-Benakh!"

"We're being hailed!" Ensign Waara reported as he piped the call through to the overhead loudspeakers.

"*Aurora! Peel to starboard! Celestia to port, and fire on me!*" Captain Roselle called over the comms.

"Hard to starboard!" Nathan ordered. "Full power!"

Nathan watched the main view screen as the Celestia pulled off to the left and the Aurora started her turn to the right. "Stand down the self-destruct!" he ordered. "Jess! Target the Jar-Benakh and open fire!"

"Jar-Sino! Jar-Sino!" Gerard called over the comms in Jung. "This is Captain Tahn of the Jar-Benakh! We have come to join the fight, but our shields are down!"

"*Jar-Benakh! Where did you come from?*"

"We were also attacked," Gerard explained in Jung. "We were nearby, on our way back after destroying a recon ship. We will maneuver alongside you so that you can extend your shields to protect us while we combine our firepower and destroy the enemy. We can capture their crippled ship and take their propulsion technology back to the homeworld, together!"

There was no immediate answer.

"What's going on?" Captain Roselle asked.

"I don't know," Gerard admitted. "Maybe he's not buying it?"

"Can we go toe-to-toe with that ship?" Commander Ellison wondered.

"Not without shields, we can't, not unless we get lucky."

"*Jar-Benakh, pull along our starboard side, one hundred meters distance, and we will extend our shields to include you.*"

"Jar-Sino, understood. We shall comply." Gerard turned to Captain Roselle. "They bought it, sir. They told us to move in close, one hundred meters, and they'll extend their shields around us."

"Hot damn!" Roselle exclaimed. "Looks like we just got lucky!" he added, patting his XO on the shoulder. "Weapons, keep firing on the Celestia as she passes, and don't pull any punches. We've gotta make this look good."

"Do you have any idea what the hell is going on?" Luis wondered from the Celestia's tactical station.

"Not a clue, Lieutenant," Cameron admitted. "Just keep firing at both ships equally."

"Yes, sir," he replied as he continued firing.

"The Jar-Benakh is moving in alongside the enemy battleship, sir," Ensign Kono reported.

"Our shields are dropping fast, now that there are *two* battleships firing on us, Captain," Mister Lange reported. "Dorsal shields are at thirty percent, port and ventral are at twenty-five."

"Just need another minute," Cameron replied, "I think I know what Roselle is up to."

The bridge shook violently as rail gun slugs again pounded their battered hull.

"I hope Roselle is pulling his punches!" Nathan exclaimed.

"No, sir, he's not!" Mister Navashee replied.

"Be sure to return the favor, Jess!" Nathan ordered.

"They don't have any shields, Captain!" Jessica reminded him.

"Neither do we!"

"The Jar-Benakh has pulled in tight to the enemy target, along her starboard side," Mister Navashee reported. "The target is extending her starboard shields around the Jar-Benakh!"

"The Jar-Sino is extending her shields around us," Ensign Marka reported.

"Hold on, everyone, wait for my call," Captain Roselle warned. He stepped up behind Ensign Garza, who was running the Jar-Benakh's port guns. "Okay, Flash. It's going to be you. On my mark, sweep all your guns over to port and blast that Jung bastard all the way back to Eridani, understood?"

"Yes, sir," Ensign Garza replied, nervously.

"Wait," Roselle told him. "Wait..."

"Jar-Benakh's shields have fully formed," Ensign Marka reported.

"Now, Flash," Roselle ordered. "Let'em have it."

The Jar-Benakh's port guns swung to the side, still firing. Their massive rail gun rounds tore through the Jar-Sino's hull, destroying everything in their path. Debris shot out in all directions. Secondary explosions went off inside her hull, sending sections of her spewing into space, some of it slamming into the side of the Jar-Benakh.

The loudspeakers blared as the communications officer yelled something vile over the comms at the Jar-Benakh.

"What the hell did he say?" Roselle asked.

"Something about our scrotums rotting painfully for all eternity, and something about our mothers being whores," Gerard said. "I didn't quite catch it all, to be honest."

"Jar-Sino is trying to get some distance between us!" Ensign Marka reported. "All her starboard shields are down, sir."

"Helm, move us off, quick as you can," Roselle ordered. "She's going to try to put missiles on us since she's got no turrets left on her starboard side."

"Aye, sir," the helmsman replied.

"Mas, tell our ships to pound that fucker's starboard side, quick!"

"Jar-Benakh is ordering everyone to target the Jung battleship's starboard side!" Ensign Waara reported.

"You don't have to tell me twice!" Jessica declared as she brought the Aurora's quads onto the target. "Firing quads!"

"Celestia is firing her mark fives," Mister Navashee reported. "Target is coming apart!"

"Back us away, best speed," Nathan ordered.

"Last thing we need is to take a large chunk of debris in the face."

"Backing away, best speed," Mister Chiles replied.

"Target has broken up into three pieces," Mister Navashee added. "Multiple secondaries. Her cores are ejecting. She's done, sir!"

Nathan fell back in his command chair, a wave of relief washing over him.

"Looks like Roselle just saved our ass," Jessica said as she powered down the Aurora's weapons.

A small laugh escaped Nathan's lips. "It had to be Roselle, didn't it?"

CHAPTER TWELVE

Nathan once again stood on the lower platform of the Karuzara asteroid's massive, pressurized dry dock, staring upward at a massive ship. This time, however, he was looking at his *own* ship.

The Aurora looked nearly as bad as the Celestia had over two months ago, although her bow was pretty much intact. Her underside, of course, was a different story. The massive Jung rail guns had taken their toll on his ship, nearly costing her life... *All* their lives.

"Looks a lot worse than it is, Captain."

Nathan turned toward the gruff, familiar voice to see Master Chief Taggart coming toward him. He looked back upward, as he continued to survey the damage. "A captain doesn't often get to look at his own ship in this way. She's usually just technical drawings and plans, specs, reports... Sometimes, you forget that she's this massive, mechanical resemblance of a living entity."

"She's not a resemblance, sir, she *is* a living thing," Marcus replied.

Nathan cast a skeptical look the master chief's way.

"Maybe not in the way we normally think of life," the master chief explained. "I mean, it's not like she thinks and all. But she's got fluids coursing through her, and air, and all sorts of electrical impulses and such. More importantly, if she gets too tore up, she dies." Marcus sighed. "If that ain't life, well..."

Nathan was suddenly seeing the gruff old ring miner he had practically kidnapped nearly two years ago in an entirely different light. "A rather profound statement, Marcus."

"Yeah, well, I have my moments, I suppose." Marcus smiled. "Just don't tell anyone. You'll ruin my reputation as a hard-ass."

Nathan smiled back. "Your secret is safe with me, Master Chief." Nathan looked back up at his ship one last time before leaving. "I never did thank you and your men for doing such a good job on damage control. We never would've gotten her back if it weren't for your efforts."

"Just doing our jobs, Captain."

"Guess I was right making you a chief to begin with," Nathan said, a satisfied smile on his face.

"Maybe you can remind the lieutenant commander about that once in a while," Marcus suggested. "She still rides my ass on a daily basis."

"She's just doing her job, same as the rest of us," Nathan replied as he started walking toward the exit.

"Suppose you're right," Marcus admitted, following the captain. "Did you get a chance to watch that Koharan lady's broadcast?"

"I've got it on my data pad. I'm going to give it a look on the way down."

"I think I came off rather proper and respectable," Marcus boasted. "I even managed not to swear... much."

"I'll be sure to pay attention to that part," Nathan replied, smiling.

"Have a good trip, Captain. I'll keep an eye on her while you're away."

"Thank you, Master Chief."

Nathan left the dry dock and made his way to the elevators, riding up to the main concourse level, where he caught one of the many automated transit cars that constantly circled the core of the asteroid base. He was amazed at how complex the interior had become since they had first set eyes on her. What was once a small mining base inside a half-hollowed-out asteroid was now a thriving facility boasting a staff of nearly a thousand technicians, engineers, scientists, and a host of other disciplines. What had once been a rather compact facility stuck into the side of the central cavern had grown to encircle an even *larger* central cavern. What once took minutes to explore by foot would now take days, if not for the automated transportation systems that the admiral and his staff had wisely installed.

Another elevator ride, followed by a ride on a mechanic's cart, and Nathan found himself in yet another hangar bay, staring at yet another ship.

The Mirai was an odd ship. She was a bit larger than a scout ship, somewhat triangular in shape, and had an extension added to her back end. She had two massive engines perched on the port and starboard points that rotated downward to provide lift for takeoff and landing, along with a third, smaller engine pointing downward hidden just behind her flight deck. Upon closer inspection, he wondered if her designers had intended for her to be able to glide to landing during total engine failure. He suspected, however, that such a landing, although possibly survivable, would not be pleasant.

Like all Takaran ships, she sat on four pairs of

massive, steerable, self-powered wheels that allowed her to move about within the hangar with ease.

Despite her unusual appearance, Nathan decided that he rather liked the Mirai. He made his way to her boarding ramp and headed up.

Deliza appeared at the hatch. "Welcome, Captain."

"Thank you," Nathan replied. "Permission to come aboard?"

"Of course," she replied. She turned to lead him aft. "I know it's rather large, but it is quite a nice ship."

Nathan followed her into the main salon, where he paused, looking up at the balcony at the aft end of the cabin. "I'll say."

"Yanni calls it a 'space yacht'."

"An apt description," Nathan agreed as he moved into the cabin.

"Sit anywhere you like," she told him. "We'll be departing momentarily."

"Why are you going to the surface?" Nathan wondered as he took a seat on one of the overstuffed chairs.

"We're going to spend a couple days helping redesign some of the Eagle production lines," she explained. "We're going to turn them into 'Super Eagles'."

"Well, if they're anything like your Super Falcons, they'll definitely be an asset. Any word on when they'll be starting production?"

"In about six weeks, assuming we can get a prototype up and working within four."

"Think you can do it?"

"I believe so, yes," she replied as she took a seat on the sofa.

"Even with the stuff you're doing on the Super Falcons?" Nathan asked, as the ship began to roll.

"We've already got the Super Falcon prototype fitted with a new cockpit. We're just running instrumentation and control lines. The rest is all creating different modules for both the weapons bay and the cabin area, depending on the mission. They don't really need me for any of that."

"Where's Yanni?" Nathan asked.

"Oh, he's already on the surface, at the Data Ark. They've been getting the cores back on line. He's going to meet up with me later."

"I see."

"So, you're finally going to take a vacation," Deliza commented.

"Nothing special. Just taking care of some business, then visiting family in Winnipeg." Nathan looked out the large windows as the Mirai lifted off the deck and slid out into the main cavern at the center of the Karuzara asteroid.

"Surely you're going to do more than just visit family?" she wondered. "The Aurora is going to be in dry dock for at least a month, possibly two."

"I was thinking of visiting Abby on Tanna, checking out the gunship production facility. I might even go to Tau Ceti and check out those two Jung frigates in her shipyards."

"I was thinking someplace nice... and *relaxing*," she told him. "Not a bunch of military bases."

"Most of the 'nice and relaxing' places *I* know of have been blown to hell," Nathan reminded her.

"At the very least, you could spend a few days on the beach at Porto Santo. I'm told it's quite nice."

"Maybe," Nathan replied.

The big windows around the main salon turned

opaque momentarily as the Mirai jumped to final approach into Porto Santo. Nathan rose and walked over to the window on the starboard side of the cabin and looked down at the island, the lights of the base and the city that surrounded it glowing in the darkness below. "I miss flying," he muttered.

"Pardon?"

Nathan turned back to Deliza. "I miss actual flying," he told her as he returned to his seat. "We jump everywhere now."

"Saves time and propellant, doesn't it?"

"I suppose. It doesn't mean I can't miss it, though."

Nathan felt the Mirai's engines rumbling as the ship lowered itself to the landing pad and set down.

"Are you sure you wouldn't like us to wait, and take you to Winnipeg when you're ready?" Deliza wondered.

"No, thank you," Nathan replied. "I really don't know how long I'll be. Besides, I'm sure Commander Telles can arrange transportation to Winnipeg for me."

"As you wish, Captain."

"Thank you again for the ride," he told her as he rose and headed for the exit.

"Oh, Captain?" Deliza called. "I forgot to ask if you've heard anything about the Cetian vote?"

"Yes," Nathan replied, "yes I have." He smiled. "It was an overwhelming yes. They'll be signing the charter in a few days."

"That's wonderful news," she replied. "Goodnight, Captain."

"Goodnight."

Nathan made his way forward and down the boarding ramp, climbing into the open-top utility vehicle waiting below. Without a word, the driver pulled away, heading across the tarmac for the main gates.

It was a clear night on Porto Santo, with a sky full of stars. They exited the base and drove through the town that had cropped up around it, heading for the residential districts.

"If you don't mind my saying, sir, I think it's a very good thing you're doing," the driver said.

Nathan looked at the young man. He was obviously a fresh recruit, barely out of basic training. "Thank you, Private."

"It means a lot to everyone serving," the young man continued. "Knowing that a captain of a ship would go out of his way to do something like this for a member of his crew."

Nathan said nothing, only watched the rows of houses pass by. The task he was about to perform was quite possibly the hardest one he would ever face. He dreaded its execution, yet, he had never wanted to do something so much in his entire life.

The vehicle pulled to a stop in front of a modest little house with a picket fence around its front yard. Nathan stared at that house for what felt like an eternity, before finally getting out of the vehicle.

"I'll be waiting here to take you back, sir," the driver promised.

"It could be a while," Nathan warned.

"I don't mind, sir," the driver insisted. "Really."

Nathan forced a smile for the nice, young private behind the wheel, then turned and walked up the path to the front door. He looked at the sign on the door that said 'Weatherly'. He paused, remembering the sergeant's face, and then knocked.

Thank you for reading this story.
(*A review would be greatly appreciated!*)

COMING SOON

"WHICH OTHER MEN CANNOT DO"

**The Conclusion
of
Part I
of
The Frontiers Saga**

Visit us online at
www.frontierssaga.com
or on Facebook

Want to be notified when
new episodes are published?
Join our mailing list!
http://www.frontierssaga.com/mailinglist/

Made in the USA
Columbia, SC
13 August 2018